Forged Lines

Book Four in Red-Line: The Fletcher Family Saga
J. T. Bishop

Eudoran Press LLC

Eudoran Press LLC

6009 W. Parker Rd. Su. 149, #205

Dallas, TX 75093

www.jtbishopauthor.com

Publisher's Note: This is a work of fiction. Names, characters, places, and incidents are a product of the author's imagination. Locales and public names are sometimes used for atmospheric purposes. Any resemblance to actual people, living or dead, or to businesses, companies, events, institutions, or locales is completely coincidental.

Updated Cover by J.T. Bishop

Author Photos by Mayza Clark Photography

Book Editing by Amie McCracken

Forged Lines/ J.T. Bishop -- 1st ed.

ISBN 978-1-7325531-1-8

To Taylor, Alex and Sydney,

You're all grown up now, but you'll always be little to me. I wish I'd had your extraordinary intelligence, wit, and confidence when I was your age. I can't wait to see where your talent will take you. May passion guide you and laughter and love always accompany you on your journey.

Love you tons.

Other Books by J. T. Bishop

<u>Detectives Daniels and Remalla standalones/novellas</u>
The Girl and the Gunshot (subscribers only)
A Hamburger Christmas
The Magic of Murder (subscribers only)
Murder Unveiled—a prequel to Haunted River

<u>Detectives Daniels and Remalla</u>
Haunted River
Of Breath and Blood
Of Body and Bone
Of Mind and Madness
Of Power and Pain
Of Love and Loss
Dominion
Illusions
Vendetta

<u>The Redstone Chronicles</u>
Lost Souls
Lost Dreams
Lost Chances
Lost Hope
Lost Lives
Lost Time
Lost Love

Chapter One

VERONICA CHAPPELL FOCUSED ON the glimmering object in the night sky through her binoculars. It blinked several times and appeared to be descending.

"Look at that." She pointed. "Southwest quadrant."

Larry raised his own binoculars. "Where?"

"There," she said.

"That's a plane."

"No, it's not. Planes don't descend like that, and not at that rate of speed."

Larry huffed. "Vee? How long do you want to keep doing this?"

Veronica continued to watch the unidentified object. The blinking lights went from white to multicolored and it turned in circles. "Are you seeing this? This is a bona fide sighting. I told you it was a great night to look for UFOs." She glanced at Larry, who sat on a nearby log. "Why aren't you watching?" She peered through the glasses.

"Vee. This is our third night this week. By virtue of the fact that it is dark, anything we see, if it isn't a plane, would be considered unidentified. That's a pretty broad scope."

"On the contrary. Planes, shooting stars, satellites are easily seen, and that's most of what we find." The object suddenly stopped its descent in mid-air but continued to turn. "Get my camera. Take pictures of this thing."

"Pictures? You're not going to be able to see it. Your camera sucks."

"Take some pictures, Larry. Now."

Larry grunted, but she heard him rifle through her bag. After a few seconds, she heard the shutter clicking. "I don't see squat. I'm probably taking pictures of a bored airliner crew."

"It's not that," said Vee. The craft dropped, and Vee briefly lost sight of it but picked it up again just as it descended behind a tree line in the distance. For a split second, Vee thought she saw smoke. She lowered her binoculars. "Did you get that?"

Larry was wiping the lens with his shirt.

"What are you doing?" She walked over and took the camera from him.

"I got a few shots. It had some pretty colors."

"Get your stuff. We're going after it." She stuffed her camera and binoculars into a bag and grabbed her water bottle.

Larry's jaw dropped. "We're what?"

"I think it crashed. In the trees. On the outskirts of town."

Larry pulled his jacket tighter around him. "It's midnight, and it's cold out here."

"It's fifty degrees. It's not cold."

Larry gaped at her as she picked up her bag. "How long are you going to keep doing this?"

She stopped. "Doing what?"

"You joined this MUFO group—"

"It's MUFON."

"Whatever. You come out here every night looking for little green men. You never find anything. Why are you wasting your time? You have a good job with the local police department. People respect you. You're smart and pretty. You should be out on a date tonight, dancing and making out with that local cowboy. He likes you."

"You're my brother, Larry. Not my mother. And Jed is not a cowboy. He owns a dairy farm."

"He has cows, right?"

She rolled her eyes. "I don't like Jed. I'd rather date a little green man."

"How long is it going to take before you're laughed off the force?"

"I don't have any secrets from my peers. They know what I do in my free time."

"Yes. I've heard your nickname. VT. I assume that has something to do with the movie *E.T.*"

"I don't care about that. I like what I do. I'm convinced that life exists outside of our own. And if I can find a shred of proof, then people like you might start to take this seriously." She turned and headed toward her car. "You coming?"

He followed her. "If you want to go off on a wild goose chase, then have at it. But drop me off on the way. I'm tired of this foolishness."

"You've only been out here for three days."

"It feels like three years."

Vee got behind the wheel, and Larry joined her in the front seat. "Fine. I'll check out the site on my own."

"You're never going to find anything tonight. You go into those woods, you're more likely to run into a bear."

She grinned at him. "Or even better, a Sasquatch. Just think of those photos. I could become a Bigfoot hunter. Would you like that better?" She turned the ignition, and the engine roared to life.

Larry rubbed his face and groaned. "Just take me home."

Chapter Two

JOHN RAMSEY FLIPPED A burger on the grill and was rewarded with a satisfying sizzle. He flipped the remaining burgers and looked over his backyard, which was rapidly filling with people. He and his wife Sarah had arranged a dinner and invited almost everyone they knew. Declan, his half-brother, and Hannah were busy setting the table outside. Grayson Steele, the wealthy entrepreneur, and Gillian carried plates and silverware. Considering the sunny weather and the number of people arriving, they'd decided to eat on the patio.

He heard the doorbell and shook his head, wondering who it was. The sliding glass door opened and Eve Fletcher, Gillian's sister, and her boyfriend, Adam stepped out. "Need any help out here?" asked Eve.

"Grab the water glasses," said Gillian. "Sarah has them in the kitchen."

Eve turned just as Ethan and Rosie, John and Sarah's three-year-old twins, squealed, ran outside, and headed for the swing set.

"Push me, Uncle Declan," yelled Rosie as she sat in a swing.

"Me too!" said Ethan.

Declan smiled. "All right, you two." He walked over and helped Ethan into a swing. "Hold on." He pushed Rosie, and she giggled in delight.

"Higher," said Ethan.

Charlotte Ramsey, Ramsey's mother, poked her head out the back door. "You watching them, Declan?"

"Sure am," said Declan. "They're fine."

Charlotte nodded and went back inside just as Morgana and Drake stepped outside. Ramsey turned a few more patties and lowered the grill cover.

Morgana and Drake approached him. "Ramsey," said Drake, using John's last name which most did, other than his best friend Leroy, who insisted on calling him by his middle name, Sherlock.

"Drake. Morgana," said Ramsey. "Welcome. Glad you were able to make it."

Morgana, her silver hair pulled back in its usual chignon style, wore a navy-blue pantsuit with a cream top and matching silk scarf. "Ramsey."

"Glad you dressed down for the occasion," said Ramsey.

"I find my attire to be quite satisfactory," she sniffed the air. "Burgers?"

"Yes. I'm making yours extra greasy," he said.

She wrinkled her nose. "I don't suppose you will have any lighter fare?"

"Oh, for God's sake, woman. It's a burger. It won't kill you," said Drake.

"Sarah's got a whole slew of side dishes. I'm sure you can find something to eat," said Ramsey.

"Ah, yes. I have no doubt of that. You're so lucky she married you," said Morgana.

"We agree on that," said Ramsey.

On cue, Sarah stepped outside. "Drake. Morgana. I didn't see you come in." She wiped her hands on her blue apron speckled with sunflowers. "Glad you could make it." She gave them both a brief hug. "Morgana, I've made a lovely salad for you."

"Thank you, my dear." Morgana eyed Ramsey. "Very lucky indeed."

"Royce here yet?" asked Drake.

"He just came in. He's talking to Leroy and Olivia inside," said Sarah. She glanced at the table that was almost set. "Looks great. Thanks."

"It was a great idea to eat out here," said Eve. "It's a beautiful evening."

"Thank your sister," said Sarah. "It was her idea."

Gillian picked up a flowered plant and put it on the table as a centerpiece. "It felt like the right thing to do."

Drake eyed the backyard and house. "Looks like you and Declan finally got the extra room finished."

Ramsey nodded. "We had a little extra help from Royce and Adam. But yes, it turned out pretty well. Now we have a guest bedroom for anyone who needs it."

"Gillian and Grayson are staying tonight," said Sarah. "They'll head home tomorrow."

Royce stepped outside. "There you two are."

Gillian and Eve waved and gave their brother a hug. Royce narrowed his eyes. "Adam. Steele." He shook hands with his sister's significant others and greeted Ramsey as well.

"Glad you could make it," said Ramsey. "Morgana says it was an interesting Council meeting."

"Council meetings," said Royce. "I'd rather cut my toenails."

"You and me both," said Ramsey.

Morgana tipped her head. "While you gentlemen cannot appreciate the benefit the Council provides, Drake and I find that a gathering of intelligent people to discuss important issues is quite valuable, especially considering what we're facing."

"Intelligent?" asked Drake.

"For the most part," said Morgana.

"It's been almost eight months," said Royce. "I'm thinking we've been forgotten. Perhaps Roma and her cronies realized we're not a threat so long as we stay here and they stay there."

"That would be a logical conclusion," said Ramsey.

"Let's talk shop once we all have a drink," said Sarah. "How are the burgers doing?"

Ramsey turned. "I'm on it." He went back to the grill.

Leroy popped his head out the door. "I'm making drinks. Who wants one?"

Twenty minutes later, everyone had a drink in hand and a burger on their plate. The vegetables and side salads were passed around and quickly disappearing. Everyone helped themselves to the food, and the group went silent as they ate.

"Must be hungry. We're never this quiet," said Ramsey as he reached for more green beans.

Adam took a large bite of his hamburger and helped himself to some chips. "It's delicious, Sarah."

"John made the burgers, so he gets the credit," said Sarah.

"My salad is delicious," said Morgana as she bit into a carrot.

"This potato salad is very good," said Gillian. "I'd love the recipe."

"Olivia brought that," said Sarah. "She's a great cook."

"I'd be happy to share it with you," said Olivia.

"My wife is talented in the kitchen," said Leroy. He winked at her. "Among other places." Olivia elbowed him in the ribs, and Leroy grunted and smiled.

Drake took a sip from his almost empty glass. Looking across the table, he whispered. "That's Grayson Steele?" he asked Ramsey, eyeing the man sitting beside Gillian. "He's from Stone and Steele Enterprises, right? The head honcho?"

"More or less," said Ramsey.

Drake paused. "He's married to Gillian?"

Morgana raised a brow. "Have you suddenly gone daft? You know who he is."

They watched Grayson pass the potatoes to Eve.

Drake glowered. "I know who he is, but the obvious question is, does he know who we are? We can't exactly sit here and discuss our issues if he doesn't."

"He knows," said Sarah.

"What issues?" asked Ramsey. "We have issues?"

Grayson looked up. "Don't worry. I know everything."

Drake lifted a brow. "Everything?"

"Everything," said Royce. Lifting his hand, he paused, and the ketchup bottle lifted and drifted into his palm.

"Yup," said Grayson, shaking his head. "Everything."

Gillian smiled at her brother. "Show off."

Royce grunted. "You're just jealous."

The table went quiet again as everyone continued to eat. Ramsey glanced at Morgana. "So, you want to start this conversation, or should I?"

Morgana dabbed at her lips with her napkin. "Be my guest."

Ramsey took a swig of his beer before standing. "Everyone. Can I get your attention?" The murmuring of talk at the table quieted. "Thanks. First, thank you to my lovely wife Sarah for pulling this shindig together." He raised his glass and drank from it, as did everyone else.

"Here, here," said Declan.

"To Sarah," said Grayson. "A lovely meal, as always."

"Thank you," said Sarah. She wiped Rosie's face, which was smeared with mustard.

"Now, you all know what we came to discuss. Morgana and Drake have just come from the latest Council meeting and thought it best that we get together."

"Has something happened?" asked Leroy. "Any new developments?"

"Nothing," said Royce. He looked at Gillian and Eve. "Any activity with you two?"

"None," said Eve.

"No," said Gillian. "But Grayson's got so much security at home right now, I doubt the president could visit."

"Only if he calls ahead," said Grayson. He took Gillian's hand. "I'm not taking any chances."

"I haven't sensed any threat," said Declan. He spoke to Adam. "Have you?"

"Nothing," said Adam. "It doesn't mean anything though. They can cloak their presence, so we may not discern anything until they're already here."

Morgana put down her fork. "Which is exactly why we need to take precautions and not become reticent. I realize it's been several months, but we cannot let our guard down. We must be vigilant."

"Vigilant of what?" asked Ramsey. He sat and offered a bite of potato salad to Ethan, who ate it with relish. "We've been looking behind us since this started. Maybe at some point, we need to get back to our normal lives and assume they're not coming back. Maybe Burke never made it home. And your friend," he regarded Adam, "Tez. Maybe he didn't throw us under the bus like you suspect."

"Do you think that's possible?" Eve asked Adam.

Adam shook his head. "Burke will bide his time. He won't make the same mistakes twice. He'll do whatever it takes to get back into Roma's good graces. And Roma will use that. He'll be patient, but if he made it back to Eudora, then he'll return at some point. And Tez, well, I hate to say it, but if they offer him enough money, he'll likely lead the search party."

"No need to search. We aren't exactly hiding," said Royce. He played with the rim of his glass.

"How do you feel about all of this, Royce?" asked Gillian. "Knowing that Sarna and your daughter Greta are alive on Eudora. I know you'd like to find your way back to her."

"Get me on one of those ships and I'm the first one out," said Royce.

"If we could find a way to get you there, we would do it," said Morgana.

"Money is no object," said Grayson. "Whatever you need, you'll get."

"What about the ship that Varalika came in on?" asked Declan. "You have it in hiding."

"Too damaged and now in a decrepit state of disrepair," said Drake. "Even if we could use it, we don't have any idea how to fly it or where to go."

"That ship is not the answer," said Morgana. "Our answer is their return. When they do, we have to be prepared. It is our hope that we can find a way to get Royce back to Sarna and his rightful place as High Child once they do."

"How do we prepare?" asked Hannah. She gave a strawberry to Ethan, who sat next to her. When Rosie bellowed, she handed a strawberry to her, too. "It's not like we have a secret weapon to defeat them. We are only Grays, except for Sarah and the Fletchers. There is no way we can overpower them."

"That's not exactly true," said Leroy. He picked up the other half of Olivia's uneaten burger and took a bite of it. Olivia brushed a leaf off of his hair.

"Get me in front of them again and we'll see who wins," said Royce.

"You do that, and you'll only get yourself killed," said Eve.

"The three of you together are very powerful," said Sarah, giving Rosie a drink of water. "Don't discount that."

"I don't want Eve and Gilli anywhere around if they return," said Royce. "You two understand that?" He pointed at Grayson and Adam.

"I'll have Gillian on the first plane out," said Grayson.

"I'm not leaving you to fend for yourself, Royce." said Eve.

"Me either," said Gillian.

"He's right," said Adam. "You both need to disappear."

"What about you?" asked Eve. "It's just as dangerous for you if you stay. You're considered a traitor."

"I know Tez, and I know Burke," said Adam. "I know their tricks. I can help Royce."

"I don't need anyone's help," said Royce. "Your only job is to make sure Eve is safe."

"You can't slay all the demons by yourself," said Ramsey. He wiped Ethan's greasy fingers with a napkin and his son dropped down off his seat to chase a ball in the yard. Rosie jumped off her chair and joined him.

Ramsey's mom stood. "Ethan. Rosie. Time for a bath."

"Sit, Charlotte," said Sarah. "I can get it."

"No, that's fine. I like to do it while I'm here. You stay and talk with your friends." She walked over and took Ethan and Rosie by the hand, and led them inside.

"Thanks, Mom," said Ramsey. He watched his kids walk with his mother and looked back at Morgana. "What's your big plan? How can we be ready and be safe at the same time? How can we prevent these people from coming and taking what they want?"

Royce shoved his plate back. "There is no way to prepare."

Morgana took the last swig of her scotch and put the glass down. "I disagree. We have numbers on our side. There's more of us than them."

"Not if you start sending Gillian and Eve away," said Leroy. "They are two of the most powerful among us," said Leroy.

"They go," said Royce. "No questions asked."

"We can decide that for ourselves," said Eve.

Olivia stood from the table. "While you all talk, I'm going to clear the table."

"Leave it, Olivia," said Sarah. "John and I can clean later."

"She's right, Olivia," said Ramsey. "I'll make Leroy do the dirty work."

"All this preparation talk makes me nervous," said Olivia. "I'd rather keep busy." She picked up the potato salad and a jar of mayo. "I can at least bring some stuff inside."

Leroy stood as well. "I'll help you." He picked up the remains of a salad and the uneaten hamburger buns. "You all let me know what you decide." He followed his wife into the house.

Grayson's phone rang, and he glanced at the display. "Sorry. I have to take this. Be right back." He stood and went into the house.

"Decide?" asked Declan. "We've been talking about this for eight months and we still haven't decided anything. At this point, it looks like Royce is going to take down everyone with his bare hands."

"Sounds like a plan to me," said Royce.

"That's silly and you know it," said Gillian. "We defeated Galen. We could do it again."

"And you almost died because of it," said Royce.

"So, we're back to square one," said Drake. "We don't know what we're doing."

Eve stood. "I'm going to use the facilities." She kissed Adam on the cheek. "Hold my spot."

"You know I will," said Adam.

Royce rolled his eyes.

Ramsey shook his head and sat back. "The answer is not necessarily to all disappear. I'd love to keep Sarah and the kids safe by sending them away. But if we don't know when the bad guys are coming, that's hard to do unless we just up and move."

Sarah reached over and took his hand. "We are not leaving our home. We've dealt with difficulty before and survived. We can do it again."

He squeezed her fingers and recalled sliding his hand down her thigh that morning. He shivered at the thought of anyone hurting her. "That was before Ethan and Rosie came along. We have more at stake now."

She nodded, but didn't say anything.

"We have a few options on the table. All is not lost," said Morgana.

"You've said that a few times now, but I have yet to hear what you and the Council have got up your sleeve," said Ramsey.

Morgana sat back. "All will be revealed when the time is right."

"You act as if we can't be trusted," said Royce. "You think by telling us we'll spoil the surprise?"

Morgana eyed Drake, who nodded back. "Very well. We have something in our possession which could turn the tables to our side, provided we use it appropriately."

Sarah leaned over and spoke in Ramsey's ear. "I'm going to see if Charlotte needs help. The twins can be a handful at bath time."

Ramsey played with the rest of his salad with a fork. He'd never been a big fan of lettuce. "My mother handled me. The twins are a cinch after that."

"Your mother was younger and tougher then. These are her grandchildren. They'll be running around the house in their birthday suits the moment she turns her back, and she probably wouldn't stop them either."

"She's tougher than she looks," said Declan.

"I'll just check in," said Sarah. "I'll be right back." She stood and patted Ramsey on the back before returning to the house.

"You know something we don't, which you seem to think can improve our chances, is that right?" asked Royce.

"Between your cloaking abilities, our secret weapon, your sisters and Sarah, we make a formidable team," said Morgana.

Royce banged on the table, and Hannah jumped. "I told you I don't want my sisters involved."

Morgana raised a brow. "Don't think I'm easily intimidated. I know how you feel about your family. We all care about our loved ones. I don't wish to see anyone harmed, either. But let's get something straight. If we're going to defeat them, the only way to win is to do it together. Once we scatter, we are easy targets, and we won't last long."

"I agree," said Gillian.

Royce groaned and ran a hand through his hair. "I don't even know why we're talking about this. For all we know, it could be another eight months, or eight years, before we even hear another word from them." He rested his forehead in his hand.

Ramsey could only imagine what Royce was going through, wondering when or if, he would ever see or touch the woman he loved again. He thought back to a time when he and Sarah had been separated and a chill moved through him. It was not something he remembered fondly.

"I think that's my cue for another drink," said Drake, standing. "Anybody else want one?"

Grayson and Adam asked for another beer.

"I'll be right back," said Drake, heading inside.

Ramsey started to speak, but noticed Declan, eyes squinting, turn toward the back gate. Ramsey also turned. "What is it, Declan?"

Declan studied the woods. "Someone's at the back gate."

Royce frowned. "Who?"

"I don't know. I sense urgency, fear." Declan's face clenched. "Pain."

"I feel it too," said Gillian.

"It's a man," said Adam. He paused and frowned toward the sound. "Someone we know."

The back gate banged. Ramsey stood along with Declan. Royce ran around the table and off the patio.

"Royce, wait," said Declan, but he jumped up and followed Royce across the yard, as did Ramsey and Adam. Morgana, Gillian, and Hannah stayed back.

When they neared the back fence, Adam ran in front of them. "Hold on. Stop."

Royce stepped to the back gate. "Who's there?"

"Royce," said Adam. "The energy ..."

Royce tensed. "What? Who is it?" The fence banged again and this time the gate jiggled as if someone were trying to open it. Royce reached out and yanked it open. A man fell inside the yard face down, and they stared in shock. His hair was askew, what they could see of his face was dirty, he wore tattered clothes and blood speckled his shirt.

"Who are you and what do you want?" Royce grabbed the man by the shoulder.

"Royce, no," said Adam. He kneeled beside the figure, who was wheezing from exertion. "Oh my God. It's Jasper."

Royce froze. Ramsey had learned enough to know that Jasper was Royce's half-brother and was supposed to be back on Eudora. He made eye contact with Declan.

Royce relaxed his grip and dropped beside him. Carefully, he rolled the man over. The man groaned, but once Ramsey saw his face, he could see the resemblance between the brothers. Jasper was not as big as Royce, but they had the same eyes, although one of Jasper's was bruised and swollen.

"Jasper?" asked Royce. "Is that you?"

The man seemed to catch his breath. He nodded and finally spoke. "Help me up."

Royce and Adam took Jasper's hands and helped him stand. Jasper shook with the effort, but held himself upright on his own, although he looked pale.

"Jasper," said Royce, looking around. "How are you here? Are you alone?"

Jasper shook his head and grabbed Royce by the shoulders. "Listen. We don't have time. They're coming." His breathing picked up again.

"Who?" asked Ramsey, his heart picking up speed. "Who's coming?"

Jasper's eyes widened, as if finally noticing there were others there. "You. Your family." He studied Adam. "Adam?"

"Yes. It's me."

Jasper clenched Royce's arm. "You got Sarna's letter?"

"Yes. I got the letter," said Royce, looking almost as pale as Jasper. "Where is Sarna? Is she okay?"

Jasper winced and held his ribs. "We can talk about Sarna later. We have to get you out of here. Where are your–our–sisters?" His eyes darted around. "Some place safe. We have to find some place safe to go."

"Gilli and Eve are here, in the house," said Royce. "Jasper. You're rambling. Tell me what's going on. Did you come alone?"

Jasper tried to speak, but he coughed instead.

"Come inside," said Declan. "You need some water, food, rest."

"No," said Jasper. "Now. We have to leave now. Burke is here."

Ramsey's blood went cold. "Where?"

Royce clenched a hand into a fist. "How do you know he's here?"

"I intercepted a transmission. He was on his way. And he's not alone. I came as fast as I could, but he was ahead of me."

Royce looked at Ramsey. Their gaze traveled back toward the house as if they sensed the same thing at once. Feeling a jolt move through him, Ramsey knew something wasn't right.

Jasper coughed again and leaned over, holding his chest. "He's going to do something. He wants to hit hard. When you're all together."

Ramsey's blood turned to ice. He stared at his home, realizing they were all vulnerable.

"No," said Royce, as if sensing the same fear.

Terror racing through him, Ramsey sprinted forward, as did Royce. "Get out of the house!" he yelled, but within two steps, a bright light blinded him, just as an explosion ripped the air and earth, and Ramsey caught a brief glimpse of wood and debris flying upward before he was thrown backward into the dirt.

Chapter Three

Vee walked through the heavy brush, pushing back tree branches and scanning the dense forest. She'd attempted to explore the area the previous night, but Larry had been right. It was too dark, and a flashlight was not adequate.

It was a warm evening, and she unzipped her jacket. Having gone to work that morning, she still wore her police officer's uniform. If she'd taken the time to go home and change, she'd have lost valuable light.

Remembering the previous night, Vee felt confident she was in the correct area. The ship, or whatever it was, had gone down somewhere near here. It was an area thickly populated with trees, but not people, making it an ideal area to hide something big.

Continuing to walk, she scanned the brush, looking for anything out of the ordinary. Her mind briefly wandered back to her workday, and she wondered if her coworkers and Larry were right. Was she crazy? She could live with being called "VT." She knew it came with the territory when you revealed to people that you were a lifelong MUFON member, and your dream one day was to find proof that alien life existed. She'd dreamed about it since she was young and she and her dad would sit out on the porch, watching the night sky. They used to compete to see who could count the most shooting stars until one night when they'd seen much more.

It had been chilly, and she'd been wrapped in a blanket, holding a hot chocolate, when something very bright appeared in the sky. It was too slow to be a meteor and too fast and bright to be a satellite and as she and her dad continued to stare, the object moved closer and became brighter. It almost seemed to be scanning the area. She hadn't spoken, and neither had her dad, but they continued to watch as the object slowed, hovered, and then moved at a right angle over the trees, before it suddenly ascended, shot up and away, and was gone. Mouths open, she and her dad had sat in shocked silence.

Ever since that night, Vee couldn't learn enough about UFOs. She'd searched with her father the area where the ship had hovered, but had found nothing. They'd continued to watch the night sky in hopes it would return, but it never had. Veronica had not stopped looking, though. One day, she knew she would find the answers she sought.

She pushed back a bushy shrub and stepped into a small clearing. The golden-brown dried grass was uniform except for two small patches of dark circles. Vee walked over to them and studied the ground. From her view, it looked as if the stalks were burned. She kneeled and touched the area, then smelled the ground. It definitely smelled as if someone had lit the grass on fire. She looked up and surveyed. Standing, she saw an area of trampled foliage and disturbed dirt. Looking closer, she realized it was human footprints. Someone had been walking through here. A drop of rusty brown liquid dotted a leaf, and she touched it. Rubbing her fingers together, she realized it was blood. They'd been injured. She followed the footprints back into the brush and was about to step into another clearing when the radio on her shoulder squawked to life. She was off duty now, and she reached to turn it off when she heard the call.

"All units, respond. We have ten-eighty on 5967 Maple. People trapped inside. Fire department is responding. All units respond. Over."

Vee heard the address. She stepped away and jogged through the clearing and back out beyond the trees. In the distance, she saw the thick, black smoke drifting out of a wooded neighborhood a few miles away. Judging by the amount, there would likely be casualties.

She would have to save this hike for later and reached for the radio. "Ten-four, control. Officer Chappell responding. Over." It was going to take her at least twenty minutes to get to her car, but if she ran, she could try to get there faster. Jogging and dodging loose rocks, she flew down the trail.

Chapter Four

RAMSEY BLINKED HIS BURNING eyes. The sky and clouds swirled together into what resembled Olivia's mashed potatoes. Everything was eerily quiet until his ears began to ring. Then it came rushing back. The house. An explosion. Sarah and the kids. His mother. Terror seized him, and he sat up, shaking off his dizziness. Smoke poured from his home, or what remained of it. His body wouldn't respond until he saw Declan stand and Royce jump up. Adam was attempting to get to his feet, but he held his arm and blood trickled through his fingers. Jasper appeared dazed as he struggled to get to his knees.

"Eve. Gillian." Royce yelled as Ramsey sprung up.

Ramsey finally shook off his paralysis. Once he moved, his feet wouldn't run fast enough. He sprinted toward the house, with Declan and Royce beside him. He heard Eve's name called and suspected Adam was right behind them.

They reached the patio, and Morgana was lying beside the overturned table. She was conscious but wide-eyed. Plates, silverware, and uneaten food were strewn all over the yard. Gillian was beneath the table, and Royce ran to her. Hannah was slowly getting up, but she held her head and blood poured down the side of her face. Declan reached her and kneeled beside her.

"Grayson? Where's Grayson?" Gillian yelled as Royce pushed the table off of her.

Ramsey ran for the house. Smoke billowed from what remained of the roof, which sported a large, jagged hole. The main part of the structure had taken the brunt of the blast. The back door and wall were blown out and glass littered the ground and crunched beneath his feet. He ran into what was left of his living area and kitchen, which was mainly charred and broken debris. His furniture was in ruins and flames licked the wrecked kitchen walls.

"Sarah!" he screamed. Fear curdled his stomach, and he fought the urge to be sick. "Ethan? Rosie? Mom?" He was frantic when he didn't see them. He ran for the kid's room, which was next to the living area that no longer existed. The only thing left of the wall between them was blackened chunks of drywall. He stepped over what looked like the remains of his sofa and moved into the ruins of his children's bedroom. He saw no one, and he screamed their names again. A moan caught his attention. Ethan's car bed was destroyed and Rosie's princess bed was flipped up and against the wall. John ran over and pushed the bed back and saw Sarah's crumpled form on the floor.

The smoke was getting thicker, and Ramsey coughed, but he barely noticed and kneeled beside Sarah. "Honey? Sarah? It's me, John." She was lying on her side facing the wall and he could see no outward signs of damage, but she was not conscious.

"Eve? Where are you?" He heard Royce's voice.

Declan ran into the kid's room. "John? You okay?"

John nodded. "I found Sarah." His panic was so intense he could barely speak. Declan started toward him. "No," said John. "The kids. Mom. We have to find them. Hurry." He shivered. "My God. Leroy and Olivia."

Declan nodded, looking pale despite the soot on his face. The smoke was getting thicker and Declan disappeared into it.

John reached for his wife. In the distance, he could hear sirens approach, but his brain couldn't focus. He touched her shoulder and gently rolled her over. She moaned, but her eyes stayed closed. Ramsey stared in horror at the jagged piece of metal that protruded from her belly. Blood flowed from the wound. "Oh God. No." He leaned close to her. "Sarah, sweetheart. It's me. I'm going to move you." He slid his arms beneath her and lifted her. She moaned again, and her head rolled onto his shoulder. His fear almost froze him to the spot, but he pushed it back, stood, and carried her through the rubble. The front door was gone, but burning beams hung from the ceiling and he stepped below them and brought her out and laid her down in the grass. He was coherent enough to see Royce carrying Eve, who also appeared to be unconscious. Blood dripped from her arm, and she had a large bleeding gash in her leg. Gillian ran over to her when Royce put her down. He saw Grayson, shirt red with blood, holding his arm with a stunned look on his face. Blood streamed from his forehead. Morgana, hair spilling from her chignon, had managed to get to the front yard, and she sat in shocked silence.

Hannah, face still bloody, ran over to Sarah. "How is she?" Seeing the jagged piece of metal, she stilled.

"Hannah ..." Ramsey didn't know what to say. "I–I have to look for the kids."

Hannah nodded. "Go. I'll watch out for her."

Ramsey stood slowly, watching Sarah, but then turned and ran for the house. Royce joined him. "How's Eve?" asked Ramsey.

"Not good," said Royce. He looked just as stunned as Ramsey felt.

"My kids. I have to find my kids."

"We will."

They ran back inside. Declan met them at the entrance to what would have been the kitchen. He held an unconscious Drake in his arms. It took only a glance to see the burns on Drake's right side. "John." He paused, looking terrified. "Leroy and Olivia ..." He swallowed.

"Where?" asked Royce.

Ramsey heard a cry from the back of the house. The new guest room seemed to have suffered the least amount of damage. He turned toward the sound. "Ethan? Rosie?" He listened again and heard his name. "Mom?"

"Go," said Declan. "Royce can help me."

Ramsey raced to the back room. The door was blown off and part of the ceiling was damaged, but the rest of the room looked intact. The bathroom door opened, and Ramsey's mother poked her head out. Tears streaked her face, and he heard his children crying. Relief poured through him and he choked back his own tears. Rushing toward the door, he let out a sob when he saw Ethan and Rosie, safe and sound, attached to his mother's legs. He dropped down and pulled them into his chest, crying tears of relief. His mother crouched next to them. "My God. What happened?"

Ramsey sputtered, thinking of what was left of his kid's bedroom. "You took a bath in here?"

Charlotte nodded. "It's so drafty in the other bathroom. I thought it would be warmer in here."

"Thank God," said Ramsey, pulling his children closer. "Thank God."

Rosie whimpered. "Daddy. You're squishing."

Ethan continued to cry. "I'm scared."

A nearby beam crashed from inside the house, and Ramsey heard the sirens screeching from outside. Smoke billowed into the room, and he picked up his kids in his arms. "Follow me, Mom." He coughed from the smoke but left the room and stepped back into the rubble. Firefighters met him at the front, and he rushed past them and returned to Sarah's side. He put the kids down, and his mother kneeled beside them.

"Mommy," said Rosie, who ran over and flung herself on Sarah's chest before Hannah could gently ease her away. Ethan held onto Ramsey. "It's okay," said Ramsey, knowing it wasn't. "Mommy's going to be okay."

Hannah took Rosie in her arms. "That's right, honey. Mommy's hurt, but she'll be okay."

Paramedics arrived and dropped beside Sarah. A firefighter approached Ramsey. "Is everyone out of the house?"

Ramsey surveyed the scene. Everything was chaos. Eve lay unconscious as paramedics treated her. A stunned Gillian sat beside her husband, Grayson, who held his arm as blood streaked down his face. Royce, looking pale, kneeled beside Eve. Morgana, her hair askew and her blouse dirty and torn, watched as paramedics loaded Drake onto a stretcher.

Declan ran over, his relief evident. He spoke to the firefighter. "Everyone's out." The firefighter nodded and jogged off. Declan squatted. "Thank God. You found them. Ethan. Rosie. You okay?"

Ramsey rubbed his face, trying to understand. He kept a worried eye on Sarah as paramedics put an oxygen mask on her.

"How is she?" he asked.

asked his mother, shaking her head.

He found it hard to speak. Fire engines and police cars lined the street and fire hoses were being pulled from the trucks. Smoke curled into the air from what remained of his home. On the far side of the front yard near the street, a firefighter carried an inert form and laid it next to another on his lawn. For a moment, he couldn't compute who they were. He stood, staring, wondering who else was hurt, and why weren't they being treated? He moved to walk closer.

Declan stepped in front of him. "John, wait. Don't go over there."

Another firefighter carried a blanket, which he opened and used to cover the forms. Ramsey kept walking. Declan tried again, and Ramsey saw the tears in his eyes. "Please, John."

Ramsey pushed his brother out of the way. Approaching the two unmoving, covered forms, an icy dread froze his heart, and he felt the blood drain from his face. He reviewed in his mind the people he'd seen on his lawn. He knew who was not accounted for. "No."

Royce came up beside him. "There was nothing we could do."

Ramsey approached the covered bodies. He fell to his knees. "No. Please, no." He stared, unable to think, knowing it was his best friend Leroy and Olivia. A bloody hand poked out from the covering, and Ramsey recognized Leroy's wedding ring. Barely able to breathe, he crawled over and pulled back the tarp to reveal his friend's lifeless face and blank eyes. He touched his friend's arm. "Leroy?"

"They were in the kitchen," said Royce. "It took the brunt of the force."

"The dining area was destroyed," said Declan, his voice shaky. "If we'd been eating inside ..."

"It would have been much worse," said Royce. He took a stuttering breath. "I'm so sorry."

Declan kneeled beside Ramsey but didn't say anything. Ramsey couldn't move as every fiber in his being screamed in protest. Leroy. He'd lost Leroy. He shook his head and moaned. Leaning forward, he dropped his head to the ground. He heard a low mewling sound, but couldn't determine its source. Gripping the grass in his fingers, he rocked back and forth. The whimpering grew, and after a moment, he realized it was coming from him. He pounded at the ground with his fists. Declan's arm went around him and pulled him close. Ramsey tried to resist, but Declan wouldn't let go. Relinquishing the effort, he dropped his head into Declan's neck as Declan held him tighter.

"I got you," said Declan, and that's all it took for Ramsey to dissolve into agonizing tears.

Chapter Five

VEE PULLED UP ON the scene and parked behind another police car. Firefighters were hosing the house down, but the blaze appeared to be contained. Heavy smoke billowed into the air. She jumped out of the car and approached a fellow officer named Nathan Huxton, who appeared to be overseeing the scene.

"Huxton," she said. "What happened?"

A stretcher carrying an unconscious woman covered up to her neck and an oxygen mask on her face was loaded onto a nearby ambulance. A man with a dazed look, his face bandaged and shirt drenched in blood with his arm wrapped in a brace, was also assisted onto the ambulance. A woman with wavy brown hair stood with him.

Huxton yelled at another officer. "Johnson, make sure we get an accurate count of who was here." He glanced at Vee. "It's a mess. Looks like a gas explosion. Multiple injuries. Two dead on the scene. Three critical. They're lucky though. Could have been worse."

"What can I do?"

"There's a lot of casualties. I want to be sure everyone's accounted for. Johnson, as usual, has got his head up his ass. We believe everyone's out of the house, but do me a favor and look around. I don't want any surprises."

Vee nodded. Viewing the area, she saw what Huxton meant. There were several people in various states of shock and injury and two covered forms on the far side of the yard. Assuming the people she could see were all accounted for, she walked toward the back of the charred remains of the home. There were a couple of firefighters in the backyard directing water into what was left of the structure. Seeing the damage, it was obvious the explosion came from inside and appeared to have blown out most of the rear of the home. Plates, food, and broken glass littered the grass. Bits of furniture, pictures, and other belongings, charred and soaked from the water, lay tattered in the yard. Seeing nothing unexpected, she was about to return to the front of the house when she saw movement toward the far end of the wooded lot. It was a man, struggling to stand. He had lighter hair and a lean, muscular frame. Running over to him, she saw him fall on his back into the grass, coughing. She spoke into the microphone on her shoulder. "This is Chappell. I've got another victim in the back of the property. Male. Request paramedics."

The radio squawked back a confirmation, and she kneeled beside the man. "Stay still. Help is coming."

He was pale, despite his bruised face, and he was shaking and continued to cough. "I have to help them. Please. Help me get up." He grabbed at her arm and pulled her close. "I have to stop him."

Vee held his hand. "It's okay. Police and paramedics are here."

"No. That won't help. It won't stop him."

"Stop who?"

He grabbed his chest and moaned. "Burke. He's here. He did this."

Vee tried to calm him, assuming he had a possible head injury. "Nobody's here. You're safe. We'll get you to the hospital."

"No hospital," he spoke roughly. "I need my pills."

"Pills?" She looked around but didn't see any pills. "Are you sick? What pills?"

He struggled to sit up, but she pushed him down. "My ship," he said. "They're on the ship."

She figured her assumption about the head injury was accurate. "You need to relax. Take it easy. The doctors will get you your pills."

He pulled on her arm. "No. Please. Listen. You have to tell them. Burke's here. He's coming." He coughed again. "My ship. The pills are on my ship."

Paramedics ran up. "We got him," said one of them.

Vee hesitated. Something about this man had her attention. "What ship? Where is this ship?"

The man blinked several times, as if trying to stay conscious. He tried to push the paramedics away but was too weak to be effective. Managing to keep his eyes open, they darted around until he found hers again. His voice was low. "In the woods. Not far." He winced as the paramedics examined him. "Hidden." The paramedics put a mask on his face, but he pulled it off. "Landed ... last night."

"He's hallucinating," said a paramedic. "Let's get him in."

Vee stepped back to give them room to work, but the man's words reverberated in her ears. He'd landed last night? On a ship? She thought back to what she'd seen the previous evening. Lights hovering in the sky and then disappearing behind the tree line, not far from where she was investigating before this call came in. Her mind wandered. Could this man have some connection to that?

A stretcher arrived, and the paramedics lifted him onto it and wheeled him off. Huxton walked up beside her. "And idea who he is?" he asked. "You get a name?"

A chill ran through her. "No. No idea."

Huxton wrote in a notebook. "Okay. We need statements. They're taking everyone here to the hospital. I want you to go there and talk to the victims. Find out what happened."

She nodded.

"See if you can find out who the mystery man is."

"Will do." She stared off into the woods, calculating how far away this property would be from where she'd seen the blinking ship descend the previous night.

"Earth to VT," said Huxton. "You there?"

She ignored the nickname. "I'm on my way."

Chapter Six

ROYCE PACED THE WAITING area. After the chaotic energy of the emergency room, this room was more peaceful, although no less worrisome. They waited to hear about Sarah and Eve, who'd both been wheeled into surgery. The nurse's station hummed with activity as one nurse talked with an older woman and her apparent husband, and another nurse typed into a laptop while talking into a phone.

John Ramsey sat in a chair with his head in his hands, and Declan and Hannah sat with him. Hannah sported a large bandage over her left eye and still wore her bloody shirt. Despite Declan's attempts, she'd refused to go home until she knew Eve and Sarah's condition. Adam stared out the window into the parking lot. He'd received stitches in his shoulder and wore a green scrub shirt since his other shirt had been cut off in the ER. Gillian was downstairs with Grayson who'd been admitted for observation with a severe concussion, broken ribs, and lacerations to his head and abdomen. Considering he'd been inside the home at the time of the explosion, he'd been lucky it wasn't worse. Jasper had been wheeled in not long after Sarah and Eve, and Royce checked periodically on his condition, but he'd heard nothing. Drake, having suffered critical injuries, had died soon after arriving at the hospital. Morgana, rattled but stoic, had delivered the news, and once handling the required paperwork and notifying relatives, had left the hospital to convene an emergency Council meeting, although Royce doubted much would come of that. He kicked a chair in frustration.

Declan walked up beside him. "You okay?"

Royce's anger bubbled up. "No, I'm not."

"Me either."

Royce thought back. "What the hell happened?" He rubbed his eyes and his mind tried to focus. "Did we miss something? How did we not see this coming?"

"How would we have known? It's not like Burke's going to walk in and put a bomb under the coffee table while we're eating lunch."

Royce threw out his hands. "Why didn't we feel something? With all of us and our capabilities, we should have realized something was off."

"That's a big assumption. Burke's abilities put us at a disadvantage. He knows what we're capable of and he worked around it."

Royce punched the wall. The nurse and the couple looked over. Royce ignored them. "I don't accept that. We should have been better prepared."

Declan sighed. "Maybe. That's probably why he waited so long. He wanted us to relax. Let our guard down."

"I should have insisted Gillian and Eve leave."

"What were you going to do? Force them? They're as headstrong as you."

"I gave in too easily. And now Eve's fighting for her life and Gillian almost lost her husband." He bobbed his head at Ramsey, who hadn't looked up, "and Ramsey's lost his best friends and almost his entire family." He groaned and curled his fingers into fists. "Son of a bitch, I'm pissed."

Declan nodded. "I know. I wouldn't mind knocking over some furniture and venting my fury. But blaming ourselves and destroying a few chairs is not going to fix anything. The question is what do we do now?"

"We find Burke, and we kill him."

"I think we're all on board with that, but first we have to figure out where he is. And don't forget what Jasper said. Burke didn't come alone."

"Whoever came with him will die too."

"How do you plan to do that? We're not dealing with your random human psychopath. Burke comes with considerable skills. The last thing we need is for someone else to die."

Royce heard a grunt and saw Ramsey rub his head before standing and walking over. His eyes were puffy and bloodshot, and he looked like he'd picked a fight with the devil and lost. "I don't care what it takes. If I have to wrap my hands around Burke's throat and watch him writhe and take his last gasping breath while I squeeze the life out of him, then I'm going to do it."

"John," Declan held up a hand.

"Don't tell me otherwise," said Ramsey, glaring at Declan. "I want to see him suffer."

"You're not the only one," said Royce.

Ramsey closed his eyes and let go of a ragged breath. The man looked like he was barely holding on. "What's taking so long?" He looked toward the nurse's station. "Why haven't we heard anything?"

"They said it would be a few hours."

Hannah joined them. "We should know something soon." She rubbed Ramsey's arm. "Why don't you come back and sit down?"

Ramsey pulled away. "I don't want to sit anymore." He walked away and rubbed his neck.

Royce took a deep breath and spoke to Ramsey. "I'm sorry about Leroy and Olivia. And Drake. This should have never happened to you and Sarah. They were after me. I should have stayed away."

"Don't do that," said Hannah.

Adam turned away from the window. "It's not your fault. I'm to blame. I led them to the Ramsey's."

"Both of you stop it," said Declan. "If we had a crystal ball, then I'd let you take the responsibility. But we don't. We're all in this together, and we have been from the start. So, let's not begin this game of who did what when. It will only tear us apart, which will only make Burke's job easier."

Royce heard their words, but still felt the guilt. He knew how he'd feel if their situations were reversed. "It doesn't change the fact that they want me," Royce said. Ramsey didn't move. "And three people are dead because of that and two others are fighting for their lives. I'll have to live with that."

Ramsey's only response was to clasp his shaky hands together. Royce was about to say more when a doctor in green sweaty scrubs walked into the room.

"Eve Fletcher?"

Adam walked over, and Royce turned. "Yes? That's us. How is she?"

The doctor took off his cap. "She's stable. We've repaired the damage to the artery in her leg. She lost a lot of blood, but we got to her in time. She's received transfusions and as long as there are no other issues and we can keep her away from infection, she should be fine."

Adam's shoulders dropped. "She's going to be okay?"

The doctor nodded. "Yes. I think so."

The deep constriction in Royce's chest eased. An unexpected well of emotion bubbled up, and he swallowed it back. "When can we see her?"

"She'll be in recovery for a couple of hours. As soon as she's out and we get her settled, we'll let you know."

Declan stepped closer. "There was another woman in surgery. Sarah Ramsey. How is she?"

Ramsey looked up, his eyes like a child who's afraid to ask an angry parent for a favor.

"I'm sorry. I'm not her doctor. But I'm sure the nurses can inquire. If you haven't heard anything, though, she's likely still in surgery."

Declan nodded and Ramsey deflated.

"Thank you, doctor," said Hannah as the doctor walked away.

Declan turned and put a hand on Ramsey's back. "Hang in there. It shouldn't be much longer."

Ramsey walked away and took Adam's place by the window.

Royce picked up his phone. "I'm going to tell Gillian and see what I can find out about Jasper."

The elevator dinged, and a woman in a police uniform stepped out. He recognized her from the ER a couple of hours before. She'd walked in and sat along with Royce and the others, watching but never approaching them. She had a small physique and short black, wavy hair which framed her large almond eyes. Royce thought briefly of Sarna and paused as the woman walked toward them, holding a small notepad in her hand.

"Hello. I'm Officer Chappell." She pulled a badge and showed it to Royce and Declan. Royce studied it and saw her first name was Veronica. "I'm investigating what happened at the Ramsey home." Her eyes found each of them. "I know this is a difficult time, but I'd like to ask some questions." She glanced at Ramsey, who didn't move.

"You're right Officer Chappell," said Royce. "This isn't a good time." He started to push past her when Declan responded.

"How can we help, officer?" he asked.

Royce frowned, but Declan ignored him.

"We're a little ragged," said Hannah, "but we can try to answer your questions." She took Declan's hand.

"Thank you." Officer Chappell flipped her notepad open. "Can you tell me what happened?"

"What happened?" asked Royce. "How about we got our asses blown up? I think that's pretty obvious."

Officer Chappell nodded, but appeared unfazed by Royce's outburst.

"We were having dinner in the backyard," said Declan.

"It was a lovely night, so we ate outside," said Hannah.

"Then all hell broke loose," said Adam. "The house exploded."

"Killing three of our friends," said Royce. "And putting two others in surgery."

She wrote in her notepad. "Preliminary indications are that this is a gas explosion. Did anyone smell gas prior to the incident?"

Royce wanted to grab her notepad and rip it to shreds. "Incident? Is that what you call it? And you think this was a gas explosion?"

She frowned. "You think this was deliberate?"

Royce stammered, and Declan put a hand on his arm. "We actually don't know what happened. We're as in the dark about this as you are. But no, I didn't smell any gas."

"Me either," said Hannah.

"I didn't smell any gas," said Adam.

Royce gritted his teeth. "Nor did I," he answered.

She tapped her pen on the paper and spoke to Royce. "Any reason you think this would be deliberate?"

Royce wanted to yell at her and tell her to pull her head out of a dark place, but he felt the wave from Declan and willed himself to stay cool. "Mainly because I want someone to blame. Someone who I can wrap my—" he curled his fingers.

"Royce," warned Declan.

Royce put his hands down and gritted his teeth. "No. I don't know why anyone would want to do this."

She paused and Royce got the distinct impression she didn't believe a word he was saying.

"There was a man on the scene," she said. "In the backyard. Tall with light hair."

"Jasper," said Royce. "Yes. They're treating him downstairs."

"Jasper," she repeated, writing in her pad. "Last name?"

Royce was about to yell at her when Declan answered. "Fiss."

She wrote some more. "When I found him, he said something about a man named 'Burke.' Said he had to stop him. You know what he's talking about?"

Royce went still, as did everyone else. Officer Chappell waited.

"No," said Declan.

"No idea," said Hannah.

"Is Jasper a friend of the family?" asked Chappell.

"He's my half-brother," said Royce.

She wrote some more. "Is he sick?"

"Excuse me?" asked Royce.

"His injuries did not look like the result of the explosion. He was coughing and pale. Said he needed his pills." She watched them as she spoke, as if gauging their reactions. "He said the pills were on his ship, which he'd landed nearby." She paused, but no one responded. "You know anything about that?"

Royce just stared, openmouthed.

"His ship?" said Adam.

"Yes."

"It sounds like he was hit on the head. You sure he didn't get injured by flying debris?" asked Declan.

"It didn't appear that way," she said.

"Well, when you've got your medical degree, I'm sure your diagnosis will mean something, but until then, please stop taking the ramblings of a sick man seriously," said Royce.

"So, he is sick?"

Royce held eye contact with her. It was rare for most people not to look away from his penetrating gaze, but she didn't budge.

"I guess we'll find out when the real doctors evaluate him." He narrowed his eyes, and she narrowed hers and pointed toward Ramsey. "Is that Mr. Ramsey?"

"It is," said Declan. "But now is not the time to talk with him."

"His wife is one of the victims in surgery?"

"She is," said Hannah. "We're still waiting to hear from the doctor."

Chappell nodded. "Okay. But I will need to talk to him at some point."

"We understand," said Declan.

"Anything else?" asked Royce.

She cocked her head. "You sure you don't know who this Burke is? Your half-brother seemed very concerned about him. You seemed to think this was intentional. Should we be looking for this man?"

Royce set his jaw. "I wish I had someone to blame for this. But I can't help you. I'm sure my half-brother will explain everything when he's well. You can ask him all about it then," said Royce.

"What's the next step?" asked Declan. "How will they determine the cause of the explosion?"

"The fire department will do an investigation. They'll verify if it was accidental." She looked at Royce. "Or deliberate."

Royce crossed his arms.

"How long will that take?" asked Adam.

She studied her notes. "Not sure. Maybe a week? Possibly longer. Depends on what they find."

"You need anything else from us?" asked Declan.

"Just your names and contact information, in case I have more questions."

"I can get you all of that. Just contact me if you need to reach anyone," said Declan. He gave her his phone number and email.

She closed her pad. "That should do for now. I'll be in touch, though. We'll likely have more questions when we learn more about what happened. And I'd like to talk to Jasper again, when he's better."

"I'm sure that can be arranged," said Royce, arms still crossed. He wasn't sure if he admired the woman or hated her.

She bobbed her head toward Ramsey. "Please offer my condolences. I understand he lost close friends."

"We all lost close friends," said Declan. "It is devastating."

"Of course," she said. "My condolences to all of you." She put her pad in her pocket. "Thank you for your time." She turned and walked toward the elevator.

Once she was gone, they huddled together. Adam grimaced. "Shit."

"That's a fair assessment," said Declan.

Royce squinted. "What's the problem? She knows nothing."

"Burke? She knows about Burke." said Adam. "And Jasper's ship."

"From the ravings of a sick man. She'll be laughed off the force if she takes it seriously," said Royce.

"And they'll learn soon enough it wasn't a gas explosion," said Hannah.

"Maybe. Maybe not. We don't know how this happened," said Declan. "For all we know, it was a gas explosion, or Burke made it look like one."

"You and I both know this wasn't because of any gas, and Burke's not going to care how it looks," said Royce.

"What does it matter?" asked Hannah. "Even if they learn it was deliberate, they'll never find Burke. Our bigger concern is keeping him from finishing the job."

"There's another concern," said Adam. "Did you hear what she said about Jasper?"

"Yes," said Royce. "His pills. He needs his pills." He recalled Jasper's last visit with Sarna. As Red-Lines from Eudora, they require pills in order to survive the harsh frequencies of Earth.

"He said they were on his ship," said Adam.

"Hell," said Royce. "Any idea how we're going to find that?"

"Especially if he cloaked it," said Adam.

"Well, we better figure it out," said Royce. "Or we're going to have a fourth victim on our hands."

Another doctor appeared, taller and heavier than the first. "Sarah Ramsey?"

Ramsey turned and hurried over, his face pale. "Yes. She's my wife. How is she?"

"She's doing well. We removed the shard from her abdomen, as well as some other shrapnel. She's very lucky. The shard missed her vital organs. She's lost blood, and we'll have to keep an eye out for infection, but I'd say her prognosis is good."

The energy in the room lifted tenfold, and Royce let out a relieved breath. Ramsey bent over and put his hands on his knees. "Thank God," Royce heard him say.

Declan put a hand on his brother's shoulder. "That's great news, doctor."

"She's a tough lady. I'd swear she's got some supernatural powers. She soared through the surgery with flying colors."

Ramsey managed to stand upright. Some color had returned to his face. "That's my wife."

"As soon as she's out of recovery, we'll let you see her. Shouldn't be long."

Ramsey rubbed his face and moaned. "Thanks, doc. I appreciate it."

The doctor reached out and shook Ramsey's hand. "You're very welcome. I'm glad I could deliver good news."

Ramsey's eyes turned watery. "Me too. Me too."

The doctor dropped his hand, nodded, and walked back into the surgical area. Royce surveyed the group, happy to know that Sarah and Eve would pull through.

"They're going to be okay," said Adam. "Thank God." He sat and hung his head.

Ramsey stared off, as if not sure what to do next. After a few seconds, he wiped his eyes and composed himself. "Declan?" he said.

"Yes?"

"Morgana is holding that Council meeting?"

Declan scrunched his face. He glanced at Royce. "Yes."

"When?"

"I don't know." He looked at his watch. "It's probably going on right now."

"Come on. Let's go," said Ramsey.

"Go where?" asked Declan.

"To the meeting." Ramsey straightened, looking more clear-headed and determined, and headed toward the elevator. "We need to talk to them."

"I'm going with you," said Royce, following Ramsey.

"What about me?" asked Adam.

Royce turned. "You keep an eye on Eve and Jasper. See if you can find out where Jasper landed that ship. I'll call Gillian and tell her what's going on."

"Hannah," said Ramsey. "You let me know when I can see Sarah?"

Hannah nodded. "As soon as I hear something, so will you."

Declan kissed his wife. "I'll be back soon." He pointed at her. "Take it easy."

"I will."

Royce got on the elevator with Ramsey and Declan. "What happens when we get there?"

Ramsey aimed a hard stare at the elevator doors. "We figure out how to find Burke, and we kill him."

Royce couldn't help but smile.

Chapter Seven

"SIT DOWN, DAPHNE. THIS is not the time for histrionics. We have enough to deal with as it is." Morgana sat forward in her seat and gripped the armrests on her chair. Usually known for her steely gaze, brutal honesty, and unflappable composure, she felt the latter begin to slip. She made a sizeable effort to take a slow breath and regain control. It had been a long day, and it didn't look to be ending anytime soon.

She'd debated calling this meeting so late, but considering the circumstances, she knew she wouldn't be sleeping and she doubted anyone else would either. This attack upon her people had been shocking and brutal, and taking the time to sleep seemed ill-advised. They had to determine a course of action. The sooner, the better.

She thought briefly of Drake, and the heaviness in her chest threatened to overtake her. It was times like these that she'd relied on him as a sounding board. As the head of the Council, it was not always wise to say what she truly thought, but she could with Drake, trusting him to keep her secrets. Drake, who'd served on the Council almost as long as Morgana, had the reputation of being a hothead and acting first before thinking, but she'd known him to be the opposite. His wisdom and forethought had prevented her from making a few rash decisions. If anything, she was the hothead, she was only better at hiding it.

She studied the ebony tabletop and wished he was there. Despite his reputation, Drake's ability to sense the energy of the Council members and somehow speak the words that brought them back to the point were needed right now. Plus, he was a great friend and good man. A lump welled in her throat.

"Morgana? You all right?"

She glanced up to see Randolph studying her with worried eyes. His thinning silver hair glimmered in the light, and he wore a dress shirt and pants despite the lateness of the hour. She straightened her shoulders and took a deep breath. "I've been better, but now is not the time for emotion."

"How can it not be?" asked Estelle, dressed less formally in a sweatshirt and jeans and her graying hair pulled back in a bun. "We've lost Drake. And Sampson Leroy and his wife. How can we not be emotional about that?"

"I, for one, think this meeting should be ended and reconvened at a later time. It's close to midnight, for heaven's sake," said Daphne, checking her watch. Her dyed black hair and heavy make-up and jewelry appeared garish compared to the others, but Daphne was never seen without them. "I find it hard to believe we all agreed to this. Out of respect for the dead, we should be mourning them, not conducting business."

Morgana placed her hands on the table and stood, leaning over. Her composure was crumbling fast. God, she missed Drake. "It is exactly because of their deaths that we are meeting. If you'd like to go home and mourn for them, please do, but we cannot sit here and twiddle our thumbs and hope there isn't another attack. We waste precious time and risk losing others. Sitting around and doing nothing could have devastating consequences." She narrowed her icy stare at Daphne. "We've lost three of our own. I was there when it happened. This was an orchestrated attack designed to cripple, confuse, and frighten us. And I fear more is coming."

Daphne did not avert her eyes. "And what exactly do you suggest we do? We don't know who did this. We have only the ramblings of a man we don't know who says he flew in from Eudora. Whose only connection to us is through Royce Fletcher, who is supposedly the next High Child of a planet we've never been to and will likely never go to. How do we know what's real? You trust Ramsey and the Fletchers, but what do you really know about any of them? How do you know they're not the cause of all this? Maybe this supposed 'High Child' is making a play for power here and is using this madness to do it?"

Morgana stood motionless, her mouth open.

Anderson, one of the older members who was expected to retire soon, spoke. "Have you gone completely senile?" Despite his frail appearance, he exuded a quiet strength.

Daphne crossed her arms. "Not at all, Anderson, but I'm thinking the rest of you have." She huffed. "We all know the Ramseys, but you have placed too much trust in the Fletchers. We were living a peaceful existence until they came along. If you ask me, I say we banish the lot of them."

A wave of heat traveled up Morgana's back and neck. This would have been the time Drake would have said something scathing, diverting attention, and allowing Morgana time to think. But Morgana didn't have that luxury anymore. "Are you really this stupid? Or has all that time in the sun impaired your brain function?"

Daphne leaned forward, her eyes narrowed. "This is a spray tan. I don't spend time in the sun."

Morgana straightened. "Then maybe you need to get outside more. Maybe get to know your fellow Grays and Reds. Because if anyone doesn't belong around here, it's you."

The room went quiet. After a few seconds, Anderson cleared his throat. "Perhaps we need to take a quick break until calmer heads prevail."

Daphne stood. "All I'm saying is what you are all afraid to voice." She raised her hand. "If someone is truly after us, they don't want anyone in this room. They want the Fletchers, and maybe the Ramseys too, now that they're all buddy-buddy. So, I'll say what you won't. You want to stay safe, then let this Burke, if he really exists, have them. Banish them. Then we can all get back to what we were doing. If this man is as bad as you say he is, then that's our only course of action. If we choose to fight and defend, then we lose. We can't defeat this man and you know it. And if he doesn't exist, and the Fletchers are the true enemy, then we've taken care of that threat as well." She furrowed her brow at the surprised faces. "You know what I'm saying makes sense. And if it doesn't, then you're risking the lives of everyone here, and possibly your family's lives too." She smacked her hand on the table. "And if any of us dies, I won't be held responsible." She glanced at Morgana. "Will you?"

Morgana opened her mouth to speak, but no words emerged. She had no idea how to appeal to a madwoman. She tried to think, but before she could answer, the doors to the room burst open and Ramsey, Declan, and Royce stomped into the room, a flustered Jenkins behind them.

"I'm sorry, ma'am," said her personal assistant. "I tried to announce them." Jenkins glared at the men.

"We don't have time for announcements, Jenkins," said Ramsey. "My wife almost died and my best friend is dead. I think you telling everyone 'We're here' is pointless. Don't you?"

Jenkins breathed hard, and his face went red.

"It's okay. Jenkins," said Morgana. "Let it be. It's been a hard day."

Jenkins deflated a bit and finally offered Morgana a nod and Ramsey another glare before leaving the room.

Morgana sat, glad for the diversion. "How are Sarah and Eve?"

The mention of their loved ones seemed to take some of the ire from them. "They're both going to be fine," said Royce.

"Thank God," said Randolph. "I'm sorry about Leroy and Olivia, Ramsey. I know how close you were to them."

Ramsey went still, but then just as quickly responded, his voice gruff. "Thank you. I appreciate that." He cleared his throat. "But that's not what we came here to talk about."

Daphne, still standing, faced them. "Do tell. I can only imagine."

Royce tensed. "Daphne, if I recall?"

"Yes," she answered.

Ramsey recalled his encounters with Daphne in the past. "Have I ever told you you're my least favorite Council person?" asked Ramsey, his voice unwavering.

She squinted.

"I've never liked you either," said Royce. "So why don't you sit down?" His ominous tone left nothing to speculation.

Daphne hesitated, but finally relented and sat. Morgana sat too, glad to have a moment to think. "So, gentlemen. What's on your minds?"

Ramsey cocked his head. "What's on our minds?"

"I think you know," said Declan.

Morgana rubbed the bridge of her nose, wishing she had some aspirin. "Take a seat. I wish I could tell you we've made some progress."

"I don't need a chair. I need answers," said Royce. "We need to find Burke."

"We realize that," said Randolph. "Any idea how?"

"What exactly does he want?" asked Benjamin. Sitting back, his large belly strained the buttons on his bright yellow Hawaiian shirt. "Maybe that will help us figure out what to do next."

"He wants the Fletchers," said Daphne. She tapped at the table. "The High Children."

"I don't think it's that simple anymore," said Declan. "That may have been his original intent when he came the first time, but he failed and now believes we've slighted him. He's holding a grudge. And if he takes out a few others along with the Fletchers, then even better."

"He wants to make us pay," said Ramsey. "We aided in his defeat before, and he's taking it personally." He started to pace. "He didn't succeed, but he'll be back to finish the job." He stopped and clutched the side of a chair. "And we need to be ready. We can't let him hurt anyone else."

Daphne shifted in her seat. "And what exactly would you have us do? Throw a party and invite him over?" She tapped her finger again. "Perhaps this is more of a 'you' problem than a 'we' problem. None of us are on the target list."

Royce set his jaw. "Not yet, at least. But perhaps that could be changed."

Morgana raised her brow. "It could be just as simple as that."

"What, throwing Daphne to the wolves? Works for me," said Ramsey.

"No," said Morgana. "Giving him a reason to come to us." She sat back, thinking.

Talbot, one of the newer and younger members of the Council, spoke. "What are you thinking? Using them as bait?" His salt and pepper hair was slightly out of place, as if he'd jumped out of bed the moment the meeting had been called.

"My sisters will not be bait," said Royce.

"Think about it, Royce," said Morgana, standing from her chair. Pushing a fallen tendril of hair behind her ear, she walked over to a smaller table which held a silver teapot, tea bags, and ceramic cups. No one had touched it, but she took a moment to pour herself some tea. "He wants you and your family, and he went after the Ramseys as well, plus we've lost a member of the Council. This was an attack against all of us, whether some of us want to believe that or not." Holding her cup, she glanced at Daphne, who smirked. "He didn't finish the job. He'll be back. We give him an opportunity to show his hand and hope he takes it."

Declan stepped forward. "All due respect, Morgana, he's not stupid. Us throwing a gathering and hoping he attends seems obvious. He'll know. He's not going to waltz in here and ask for tea."

"And even if he did, how do we get rid of him?" asked Ramsey. "We'll still be at a disadvantage. Wondering when, how, or if he'll strike. We still have to determine how to take him down."

"And I don't like putting my family, or anyone else's at risk again," said Royce. "We've been through enough."

"Perhaps there's a better way?" Talbot stood and walked to the table beside Morgana, reaching for the teapot. He rifled through the tea bags. "No Earl Grey?"

Morgana removed her tea bag and placed it on the saucer. "No." Talbot, since his induction into the Council, had demonstrated a reserved and laid-back demeanor, but when he'd offered his advice, it had always been sound and wise.

"Pity." He made his tea.

"What are you thinking, Talbot?" asked Ben.

Talbot turned toward the group. "Based on what I've heard about this man, I think we're overthinking it."

"What do you mean?" asked Ramsey.

"He's egotistical, arrogant, and used to getting what he wants. When he came here before, he planned for a simple job. It wasn't. The Fletchers and a band of Grays handed him a defeat. He went home with nothing. Now he's back. He waited for us to let our guard down and tried again. He's dealt us a severe blow, but he still didn't succeed. His ego will tell him we are weakened and afraid. He'll expect us to cower. We need to let him believe that. In short, we need to turn the tables. Make him feel confident again. Let him get comfortable." He bobbed his tea bag in his teacup.

"And how do you propose we do that?" asked Declan.

"We do what Morgana proposes. We throw a party. Only we don't wait to see if he comes. We invite him personally."

A hush settled over the room.

"And when he does, we cower?" asked Morgana.

"I won't be cowering," said Royce.

"You miss the point," said Talbot. "We defer to his ego. Make him feel in control. Give him exactly what he needs. Fear, sadness, desperation. He'll eat it up, bask in it. He'll still plan to finish his task, of course, but we'll act before he can."

The room went quiet again.

"Act? Act how? That's still the question," said Declan.

Talbot took a sip of his tea. "You want to tell them, Morgana, or should I?"

Morgana held her cup, studying it before placing it back on the table.

"Tell us what?" asked Daphne.

Morgana paused. "There is a way to defeat him," she said. She put her hands on the back of her chair.

"How?" asked Ramsey. "Are we finally going to hear what this plan of yours is?"

Morgana thought back, wondering what to say. In her experience, directness was the best approach. "Thillium."

"Thillium?" asked Randolph. "What's Thillium?"

"Thillium is a poison," said Talbot. "Extremely toxic to Red-Lines, and not so great for Gray-Lines either. It affects the nervous system and shuts down vital organs, including the heart and lungs. Muscles seize up, and nerve endings fire off all at once as the body shuts down. It is a particularly painful way to die."

"I've heard of it," said Anderson. "In my studies of our history, it was a potent plant grown on Eudora, but extremely rare. But if I remember correctly, like any other drug, it was an illegal substance, for obvious reasons." He scratched his head. "But that plant does not exist here. And even if it did, it wouldn't survive. It's just as sensitive as the Red-Lines it kills. Where could you possibly find a source?"

Morgana looked at Talbot, who took a sip of his tea. "The serum," said Morgana.

"What serum?" asked Randolph.

Ramsey stilled. "Not that serum?"

Declan narrowed his eyes and straightened. "You're kidding. You didn't destroy it?"

Royce shook his head. "Would somebody tell me what you're talking about? What serum?"

"We told you about it," said Ramsey. "It's the serum that was sent from Eudora to destroy us decades ago. The one that Varalika died for and ultimately resulted in Sarah's birth and her role as part Red, part human." He looked at Morgana. "That serum was supposed to have been destroyed."

"You told us it was," said Daphne. "You and Drake said it was taken care of." She frowned and gripped her fingers together. "Did you lie to us?"

"Not completely," said Morgana. "Most of it was."

"Most of it?" asked Estelle. "Morgana, what is going on here? Why keep it? Why lie?"

"Why destroy all of it?" asked Talbot. "By keeping some, they could study it. Find out exactly what was in it. Maybe learn something from it."

"And how do you know about it?" asked Randolph.

"My company did the studies. Covertly, of course. We saved one canister. The rest was dumped. And now it is safely stored in a very private vault. It is very secure."

"I can't believe you didn't tell us this," said Daphne. "This goes against every rule we have. You should be stripped of your position. I move we banish Morgana from these proceedings. She can't be trusted."

"Oh, do shut up, Daphne," said Ben. "We can talk about rules later. Now that we know we have it, the question becomes, what can we do with it? Are you saying there's Thillium in the serum?"

"Loads of it," said Talbot. "One sip is all it will take."

Everyone quieted as the idea sunk in. Ramsey was the first to speak. "So we bring Burke in, make him feel superior, cower before him, let him think he has the upper hand, slip him the poison, and he drinks it and dies. That's the plan?"

Morgana added some cream to her tea. "Precisely."

Chapter Eight

HANNAH SAT BESIDE THE hospital bed, watching Sarah take slow and steady breaths. Her friend had been moved out of recovery thirty minutes earlier and was settled into a private room. Eve had been moved also and was on the same floor, only two doors down. Hannah had notified Ramsey, and he was on his way back to the hospital after an apparently interesting Council meeting. Declan had told her he would explain when he saw her. She'd also informed Charlotte, Ramsey's mother, who'd taken Ethan and Rosie to her house. She'd been relieved to hear her daughter-in-law would be fine and planned to bring the kids up to the hospital the next day.

She yawned and looked at the clock. It was almost one a.m. Her head throbbed. Her doctor, after giving her twenty stitches in her forehead, had told her to go home and rest, but she couldn't do that until she knew everyone was okay. Visiting hours had ended at eight p.m., but Hannah, being a nurse herself, had some sway at the hospital, and the night staff had made some exceptions for her, Gillian, and Adam. Gillian was staying in Grayson's room, and Adam was sitting with Eve.

Hannah eyed the couch and debated lying down on it when Gillian poked her head into the room. "You awake?"

Hannah nodded her weary head. "Yes. Apparently, so are you."

Gillian entered the room and sat in an empty chair. "Can't sleep."

"It's a hospital. Nobody sleeps well in a hospital. Including the patients." She noted Gillian's heavy lids. "Why don't you go to our place? Declan and I have a guest room. Get some shuteye."

Gillian shook her head. "I can't. I need to be sure Grayson is okay. That concussion of his is severe. They keep waking him to check on him. He barely remembers his name." She observed Sarah. "How is she?"

"Seems fine. Doctor said she came around briefly in recovery, but she's been out since." She pulled the sheet up higher on Sarah. "How's Eve?"

"About the same. Adam's with her. Won't leave her side." She sighed. "Royce should be here soon."

Hannah rubbed her eyes. "They must be exhausted."

"We all are. It's been a hellacious day."

"To say the least."

Adam poked his head into the room. "Hey."

"Hey, Adam," said Hannah. "Come in."

Adam, his hair disheveled and his scrub shirt wrinkled, entered and sat on the couch.

"How are you? How's your arm?" asked Gillian.

"Never mind me. I'm fine. It's Eve, Sarah, and Jasper I'm worried about."

Hannah turned in her seat. "Jasper? How awful of me. I forgot. Declan told me he'd appeared right before the explosion. How is he?"

"Out of it. Rambling." He sighed. "Which may be a good thing for us. He keeps talking about his ship and his pills. Doctors think he's hallucinating. But we know otherwise."

"His pills," said Gillian. "He needs them to survive. I remember Royce telling me about that the last time Jasper visited. Do we know where they are?"

"If we could find his ship, that would help."

"He arrived injured, didn't he?" asked Hannah.

Adam leaned forward, his elbows on his knees. "Everything happened so fast. I don't recall if he was injured, or just sick, although he had a black eye. He's got contusions and broken ribs, but I don't know if that's because of the explosion or something else. All I know is if we don't get those pills, he won't make it long."

Hannah glanced at Sarah. "What if she comes around? Could she help him? Heal him?"

Adam paused. "It couldn't hurt. I don't know how long-term it would be, but it might stabilize him and keep him going long enough till we can locate the ship."

"Did the doctors say when to expect her to gain consciousness?" asked Gillian.

"She'll likely sleep through the night," said Hannah. "Maybe if she's awake tomorrow and strong enough, we could find an excuse to wheel her into Jasper's room." She touched her bandage, wishing she could scratch her stitches. "How much longer can Jasper hold out?"

"I'd say within forty-eight hours, he'll start to decline rapidly. Let's hope Sarah comes around before then."

"That should be plenty of time," said Gillian. "If we could get Eve up, she could help, too. If we know the vicinity of where to look, she could probably locate the craft."

"How so?" asked Hannah. Declan had told her about Eve's abilities. "By communicating with the animals?"

"Yes, and with the Earth," said Gillian.

"The Earth?" asked Hannah.

"She doesn't do it often, but when she does, it's impressive. When we were younger and after our Shifts occurred, there was a lost dog in the neighborhood. It belonged to a friend of Eve's and she was distraught. After getting more information, Eve went to the area where the dog had disappeared. It was a few wooded acres, and she literally placed her palms on the trees and on the ground. She touched rocks and roots, and before we knew it, she'd located the dog in an old sewer drain. I was amazed. I think she was too. She might be able to do that with Jasper's ship."

Adam checked the clock. "Well, let's hope time doesn't run out. We're cutting it pretty close as it is."

"Time is running short, isn't it?" said a male voice.

They all turned. A man stood at the door to the room. He was tall, with black hair pulled back into a ponytail. His jaw was shadowed, and his facial features were sharp and edged, much like his physique.

Hannah didn't recognize him, but Adam stood from the couch. "What are you doing here? Get out."

Hannah and Gillian stood. "Who are you?" asked Gillian.

The man smirked.

"It's Burke," said Adam.

Ice cold hit Hannah in her chest. She didn't know if it was from fear or from the energy the man exuded. "What do you want?" she asked. She thought of Declan, wondering when he would arrive.

Burke put his hands in his pockets. "Just checking in on the patients. Seeing how everyone is doing." He shrugged. "Sorry to hear about Leroy and his wife. Oh, and Drake too."

"Son of a bitch," said Adam. He stepped closer, putting himself in front of Hannah and Gillian. "If we weren't in a hospital right now ..."

He smirked. "You'd what? Hurt me?" He took a few steps into the room and walked right up to Adam. Adam didn't budge. "What you fail to understand is while you hold back because of where you are, I have no such reservations."

Adam sucked in a breath and doubled over as if someone punched him in the gut. He dropped to his knees and gasped for air.

"Adam," said Gillian, dropping beside him. "Stop it. Leave him alone."

Hannah held her ground. She'd never been one to cower. "Is that what you like? Bullying others? Hurting people you don't even know? There were children in that house."

Burke stopped staring at Adam and offered Hannah a malicious smile. Hannah heard Adam let out a breath.

"You're a feisty one," said Burke. "For a Gray." He glanced at Sarah in the bed. "You're Declan's mate?"

"You didn't answer the question," said Hannah.

He grinned. "Pity she was hurt," he said, watching Sarah. "She would have made an excellent gift to our new leader. Roma would have taken great interest in her." He sighed. "I wouldn't have minded having her around, either. Perhaps Roma would have given her to me."

Gillian stood. Adam had uncurled, as if the pain had subsided, but he held his belly.

"You've done enough damage," said Gillian. "Leave us alone."

Burke grinned. "One of the High Children. I was aiming for you too, plus that annoying brother of yours. Poor Eve, though. She's vulnerable right now. It would be so easy to walk down to her room ..."

Adam grunted and attempted to stand, but an unseen force shoved him backward and he hit the wall hard. Air whooshed out of him, and he gripped his stomach again.

"Stop it," said Gillian.

Hannah didn't move, unsure of what to do next. "You came here to finish the job? You plan on killing us?"

Burke took his hands out of his pockets and folded his arms. "It's tempting. But no. Not yet. Right now, I have a message. For Ramsey and Royce. I need information. Royce knows something and his presence has been requested. I don't like it. I'd rather just kill him. That was my plan. But, like everyone else, I take orders from another. So, if he cooperates, maybe I'll spare his sisters. And if Ramsey doesn't intervene, maybe I won't take his family from him."

Hannah dropped her jaw. "Take his family? What do you want with Ramsey? He's done nothing to you."

"He's a Gray who lacks respect. What other reason do I need?"

"Royce will never agree to help you," said Gillian.

Burke's eyes roamed over Gillian. "I doubt that."

Gillian grimaced and gripped her head. Hannah heard her moan.

Burke spoke to Hannah. "You tell them what I said. Royce's cooperation and Ramsey's acquiescence. Or I finish the job I came here to do. Can you tell them that for me, Hannah?" He reached out, and Hannah made a defiant effort not to move. He touched her long hair and trailed it through his fingers. A shiver went down her spine. "How did these Grays attract such desirable mates? Where I come from, they'd be working the fields, and you'd belong to a Red."

Hannah's insides curdled. "I'll tell them." She glanced at Gillian and Adam, both still in pain. "Now let them go."

He dropped his hand, his smile still on his face. "I like you Hannah."

Gillian and Adam relaxed. Adam uncurled, and Gillian straightened, holding her head, but her face was pale.

Burke turned and walked to the door. Looking back, he said, "I'll be in touch." And he was gone.

Chapter Nine

ROYCE CRACKED HIS EYES open. Someone was nudging him. He blinked, trying to remember where he was, and grimaced when an ache traveled down his stiff back. Everything seemed muffled, and he shook his head.

"Royce, you awake?"

His sister Gillian's face came into view. Along with that came the memories of the previous day. He instantly sat up, his back protesting. "What is it? What's wrong?"

"Did you sleep here all night?" She waved at the waiting room.

Assessing there was no immediate threat, Royce relaxed and stretched. His shoulders were tight, and his neck hurt. "Yes."

"What for? Ramsey told you there was plenty of space at his mom's."

He sat straighter, his foggy brain slowly clearing, and he recalled returning to the hospital. They'd heard of Burke's visit and his assault on Adam and Gillian, and his threats. Royce had almost put his fist through the wall. The man had threatened his family again, and Royce hadn't been there. Ramsey and Declan were equally angry. Declan had immediately arranged for security at Eve's and Sarah's doors, not that they'd be able to stop Burke, but they had to do something.

"I'm not leaving. If that bastard Burke shows his face again, I'm going to be here." He rubbed his face. "How's Grayson?"

Gillian sat beside him. "Sleeping comfortably. They may release him later today."

"Good."

Gillian sighed. "You can't slay all the dragons, you know. We talked about this last night. After what was discussed at your Council meeting, this situation could benefit us."

"That man being around you or Eve benefits no one. Until he's subdued, none of us are safe." He massaged his neck. "What time is it?"

"Eight o'clock. I can't believe you slept in these chairs."

"I can't believe I slept."

"You were exhausted. We all were."

"Ramsey go home?"

"Once Declan's security arrived, he went to his mom's. He wanted to be there when the kids woke up. Declan and Hannah went home too. They'll all be back soon."

"Adam?"

"He stayed with Eve."

"Fool should have gone with Declan and Hannah."

"Sounds like someone I know."

Royce ticked his brow up at his sister. She raised her brow back at him.

"How's Jasper?"

"Not good. We need to get those pills."

"I know." He stood and arched his back.

"Where are you going?"

"I want to check on Eve. And Jasper. Make sure they're okay. Then I need some coffee. And some food. Declan's security still here? They stay all night?"

"They did. Declan says they're two of his best." She stood beside him. "So, what are you going to do about Burke? About his threat?"

"We'll talk about it more when Ramsey and Declan get here. But let's just say I won't be telling Burke anything." He stepped closer. "And he won't be touching you or Eve."

She aimed a worried gaze at him. "You're not going to do anything stupid, are you? I mean, I know you want to lure him in, but he's still a dangerous man. I know you worry about us, but we worry about you too." She grabbed his forearm and squeezed it. "I need you to be around." She paused, her brow wrinkling. "My child needs his uncle."

Royce stilled. "Your what?"

"You heard me."

His mouth slowly opened. "Are you pregnant?"

Her lips curled up, and she nodded. "I am. Three months. Gray and I were going to say something at dinner, but, well, that didn't happen."

Royce shook his head, trying to absorb the news. "I'm going to be an uncle?"

Her smile grew. "Yes."

Stepping forward, he wrapped an arm around her waist and lifted her, twirling her around.

She squealed. "Put me down."

He set her on the ground and gave her a hug. "Congratulations, Gilli. I'm so happy for you." Pulling back, he saw the tears in her eyes. "What's wrong?"

She blinked. "It's just ... all this. The explosion. Sarah and Eve. Leroy and Olivia." She wiped an eye. "So many mixed emotions. It's hard to express joy amid such tragedy."

He squeezed her shoulder. "I'm just glad you're okay. You are okay, right? The doctors checked you out?"

She nodded. "I'm fine. The baby's fine."

"Then that's all that matters. I know what's happened is hard to process, but we'll get through it. I'm going to be damn sure of that. That little bundle of joy will be born safe and secure. I promise you." He wished he knew how to make her feel better, but words seemed to fall short. "Does Eve know?"

"No. You're the first."

"She's going to be ecstatic."

The tears threatened again. "I'm just glad she's alive. When she was hurt, I thought ..." She sniffed.

"I know. It was terrifying."

She raised her hand. "Sorry. My emotions are all over the place."

He put an arm around her and pulled her close. "Come on. Let's go check on Evie. Maybe if we're lucky, she'll be awake and we can tell her the news. And if not, I'll buy you a cup of coffee."

"Decaf for me." She sniffed again. "That's a deal."

Royce followed her out the door, thinking of Burke and his threats, and of Gillian's pregnancy, and what could have happened. Inwardly, his belly clenched, and his chest tightened. If Burke showed his face again, nothing would stop Royce from ripping the man's throat out.

• • • • • • • • • •

Two hours later, they all sat in the commissary, most with a cup of coffee in hand. Ramsey studied the group, noting they all looked as tired as he felt. None of them had slept well. He'd made it to his mom's around two-thirty a.m. and had returned to the hospital by eight. He'd been there to see the kids in the morning and reassure them that mommy would be home soon. His mom wanted to bring them to the hospital to visit, but Ramsey told her no. After what had happened with Burke, he wanted them as far from danger as possible. He wondered if he should send them away.

"I thought they'd be awake by now," said Hannah. "The doctors don't see anything abnormal."

Declan stabbed at the eggs he'd ordered. "You think it's because they're Reds? Maybe they need more time."

"Maybe." Hannah sighed. "I guess I shouldn't be so impatient. They probably just need rest."

"I saw the day nurse this morning," said Gillian. "She said their vitals were normal. Nothing unusual."

"I wish they'd wake up too. I'd love to talk to my wife." Ramsey shoved his plate back. He'd ordered a bagel and cream cheese, but he'd only taken a few bites.

"You're not the only impatient one, Hannah," said Gillian. "But if they don't wake soon, we have to think about Jasper."

Royce grunted and sipped on his third helping of coffee. "I wish there was some way to figure out where he may have landed."

"How's he doing?" asked Ramsey.

"He slept last night," said Gillian. "But his fever's up, and he's still rambling. Doctors think he has a virus of some sort. They're giving him antibiotics."

Ramsey groaned. "Lot of good that's going to do." He leaned forward and stretched his shoulders. "Does he have protection, too?"

"Yes," said Declan. "I've got Jones at his door. Good man. Mary will take the day shift for Sarah and Tyler for Eve."

"They know what they're doing?" asked Royce.

"They do," said Declan. "One glimpse of Burke, and I'll know." He raised his phone.

"You think he'll come back?" asked Adam, raising his head. He'd been sitting at the corner of the table, his head on his folded arms. Ramsey thought he'd been dozing.

"He said he would," said Hannah. "Said he'd be in touch."

"What does that mean, though?" asked Adam. "He'll come back here? He'll invite us to the local bar for a drink?"

"I don't know, but maybe we should discuss that," said Ramsey, thinking of Sarah and wishing he could see her beautiful eyes. The last thing he wanted to do was discuss Burke. Between Leroy and Sarah, it was all he could do to keep his thoughts straight.

"You mean the Council's plan to poison him?" asked Hannah, lowering her voice. "I can't believe Morgana and Drake kept that serum."

"It was smart. Without it, we'd have nothing to use against Burke," said Declan. He observed the room. "Let's all keep our voices down."

Ramsey checked the area. It was quiet, save for a family a few tables away and a few patrons getting coffee. No one sat nearby. "We're okay."

"So, how do we get him to drink it?" asked Adam.

"The man wants to talk to me," said Royce. "The logical answer would be to use me to get to him."

"No," said Gillian. "I don't like that. It puts you at too much risk."

Royce patted her wrist. "I understand your worry, but we're all at risk already. If he wants to barter, then let's barter. When he gets in touch, then we bring him in. Meet with him."

"We could use the Council. Tell him to come to a meeting," said Adam.

"No. Too many loose ends. That loon Daphne being one of them," said Ramsey. He picked at his bagel, debating taking a bite.

"We need some place smaller. Some place where Burke won't feel threatened," said Declan.

"He won't feel threatened no matter where he is," said Adam. "The man has an ego bigger than this hospital. The Council meeting might feed that, make him feel important that they're all gathered because of him."

"True, but Ramsey's right. Daphne's a loose cannon. I don't trust her," said Royce. He stared at his empty cup. "I need some more coffee."

Declan stood. "I'll get you some. I need more, too. Black, right?"

"Yes. Thanks," said Royce. "What about Morgana's house?"

Declan paused. "Not a bad thought." He walked to a nearby table, which held three large coffee thermoses.

Ramsey considered it. "It's more intimate than a big Council room. Morgana would be there, which would appeal to his ego."

"We could invite a couple of other Council members, make it look more official," said Declan from the coffee stand. He finished filling the Styrofoam cups and brought them back, handing one to Royce.

"You think Morgana would care it's in her home?" asked Adam.

"Morgana?" asked Ramsey. "She's done much stranger things there. She won't blink an eye."

"Plus, I think keeping Daphne out of it would appeal to her right about now," said Declan.

Royce sipped his drink and grimaced.

"Hospital coffee for you," said Declan.

Royce took another sip. "So, when Burke gets in touch, we invite him to Morgana's. Tell him I'll be there."

"I'll be there too," said Ramsey.

"He wanted you to not intervene," said Hannah.

"So I'll sit in the back of the room and act mollified. That will play to his ego," said Ramsey. "But I'm going."

"We should all be there," said Adam.

"Is that really necessary?" asked Hannah. She took Declan's hand. "If Burke suspects something's up, he could lash out and kill everyone."

Adam reached out and picked up Ramsey's bagel. "You mind?"

"Help yourself."

"I don't think he'll do that," said Adam. He slathered some cream cheese on the bagel.

"Why not?" asked Hannah.

"He's had ample opportunity to take us out. We're all sitting here in this hospital. It wouldn't be hard." He held the bagel. "I know him. He's an evil man, but he's ambitious. He's here on orders. The initial plan may have been to kill us, but something's changed. Now he wants to talk to Royce. And he wants Ramsey kept at bay. They think Royce knows something. And Burke will play the part until he gets what he wants from you." He nodded at Royce. "Once he does, then I would consider all agreements null and void. Then he'll kill us." He bit into the bagel.

"What's changed, though? Why does he suddenly think I know something?" asked Royce. He eyed Gillian's half eaten omelet. "You going to finish that?"

"No." She held her stomach. "I'm feeling a little queasy." She slid the plate over.

Royce nodded. "Thanks." He picked up his fork. "But what does he think I know?"

"My guess is Jasper has that information," said Adam. "He came to warn us."

"Jasper told us Burke was here. That we were all in danger. He didn't mention Royce specifically," said Declan.

"He didn't exactly have time to explain anything," said Adam, adding more cream cheese to the remains of the bagel. Ramsey pondered whether to ask Adam if he wanted any bagel with his cream cheese, but he didn't have the energy for it. "Plus, he was out of it. He wasn't well. It looked like he jumped on that ship and took off with no prep whatsoever." He stopped. "It was like—"

"He was running from something," finished Royce, through a mouthful of omelet. He swallowed. "That would explain a lot."

"You think he was running from Burke?" asked Ramsey.

"Burke was ahead of him," said Adam. "No. He was running from someone else." He put the knife down. "Someone further up the chain. Someone who could give orders to Burke. Tell him to hold off on the killing. Tell him to get the information they need." He put the cream cheese slathered bagel down too. "The information they didn't get from Jasper."

Declan swiveled in his seat, facing Adam. "You think they were torturing Jasper to get information?"

"Maybe," said Adam. He stared at Royce. "But he got away and managed to get here. To warn us."

"But since Jasper's here now," said Hannah, "wouldn't Burke come after him to get the information? He's only a few floors down."

Everyone went quiet. Ramsey admitted it was a good question. He tapped his finger on the table. "Maybe Burke doesn't know he's here."

"How could he not know?" asked Declan.

"Think about it," said Ramsey. "Jasper grabs a ship, disappears. They don't necessarily know where he's headed."

"Couldn't they track the ship?" asked Hannah.

"Not if you disable the tracking mechanism," said Adam. "That would be easy for Jasper." He popped the last bite of cream cheese bagel in his mouth.

"But he's right here in the hospital. He'd be easy to find," said Gillian.

"But on a different floor," said Ramsey. "Not near Sarah or Eve. And we've checked in on him, but most of our time has been spent with Sarah and Eve."

"And he came into the hospital after everyone else," said Declan.

"But couldn't Burke sense him?" asked Gillian. "They're both Reds."

Adam pushed the empty plate back and wiped his face with a napkin. "Burke's not looking for him. Plus, he's got other things on his mind. Jasper's sick too. His energy is scattered. Not focused. Makes it harder to pinpoint."

Royce drained his terrible coffee and put the cup down. "You really think Burke doesn't know Jasper's here? No one from the mother ship has alerted him?"

Adam nodded. "Seems that way."

"How long is that going to last?" asked Ramsey.

"Well, if we don't get him his pills, it won't matter much," said Adam.

"His pills," said Hannah, sitting forward, staring blankly.

"Hannah?" asked Declan. "You okay?"

She looked over at him. "If Jasper needs pills, so does Burke, right?"

Ramsey eyed Declan and Royce.

"Yes, he does," said Adam.

Royce picked up his fork and moved the remains of the omelet around on his plate. "Burke has pills Jasper needs." He stared off. "And he wants something from me."

"So, we trade," said Declan.

"We trade," said Royce.

"You can't trade without giving away Jasper's location," said Hannah.

"That might not matter, if Burke thinks Royce will tell him what he needs to know," said Declan.

"Trade the pills for what though?" asked Ramsey. He glanced at Royce. "What do you supposedly know?"

"We don't actually trade anything. We kill him first," said Declan.

"But that begs the question," said Ramsey. "What did they want from Jasper? And why do they think Royce knows it too? What would make Jasper risk his life to warn us?"

Royce went quiet and held his empty coffee. He stared at the table.

"Sarna," said Adam, leaning forward. "They want Sarna and Greta."

Royce crushed his Styrofoam cup.

Chapter Ten

VEE SAT AT A small table, holding her own stale coffee and listening. She'd arrived at the hospital, prepared to follow up on the investigation and ask some more questions about the explosion. She'd stopped at the rooms of two of the victims. She'd been surprised to see someone posted outside each of their doors. She'd talked to them, but they'd only provided their names, and not much else, saying just that they were there to make sure the patients were being watched while the family stepped out.

The only other person around had been a nurse in Eve's room. She'd informed Vee that the family had gone to eat breakfast downstairs. Vee had stopped at Jasper's room on the way down, hoping to speak with him, but he'd been sleeping. Someone had been standing at his door as well. And by Jasper's pallor, he appeared to be doing worse. There was one other injured victim, Grayson Steele, who was still in the hospital. She knew who he was from her research—a wealthy and famous entrepreneur married to Gillian Fletcher. She'd found his room, which also had a man outside, but the doctor had been in with him, so she'd said she'd return later. Walking down the hall, she was happy at least one person was conscious and could speak with her.

Making her way down to the commissary, she thought back on her earlier conversations with the Fletchers and Ramseys, and now, knowing what looked like security was watching the injured, she knew these people believed there was more going on than just a gas explosion. The question was why. There was nothing so far to point to this act being deliberate.

Not that a gas explosion wasn't unusual and life-altering. They'd lost loved ones, which could make people react in uncertain ways. During their first conversation, the tall one, Royce Fletcher, had been definitely angry, and she'd sensed it had been about more than just a random tragedy. And she wanted to figure out what.

Entering the café area, she'd seen the group sitting in the corner across the room. Watching them, she walked into the buffet area and ordered a coffee. The cashier had handed her a cup and pointed her toward a small table with large thermoses. There were a few of these tables placed around the room. Luckily, this one was not near the group in the corner.

Once she had her coffee, she decided to observe for a while instead of walking up and interrupting them, as she had in the ER the previous night. Sometimes, observing could tell you more than being direct. She moved closer until she was within a few tables of the group and sat behind a support beam, facing away from them, so she could make the plausible excuse that she had not known they were there. They were in deep conversation, though, and had not even glanced her way.

She drank her coffee, wondering how they could call it that. The cream and sugar she'd added had not killed the bitter aftertaste. Holding her cup and taking small sips, she listened. She was close enough that she could hear small snippets of conversation. She reached into her jacket and pulled out her notepad and a small pencil, writing what she heard.

The first word that got her attention was "Burke." They'd mentioned that name before. She put a question mark next to the name. It was something to follow up on. Was this the person they believed was responsible for the explosion? Continuing to eavesdrop, she wrote a few other things. "Morgana" and "council"? Morgana was the name of another person present at the explosion who was on her list to speak with later today. Was she a member of some sort of council? It sounded as if she had some clout with the group. They also mentioned Jasper and pills, which was what Jasper had said to her when she'd found him. Was Jasper sicker than she realized?

She cocked her head when she heard Royce Fletcher talk about trading with Burke. Something about information. One of them, she thought she recalled his name as Declan, stood to get more coffee. She turned away, hoping he hadn't seen her.

The names Jasper and Burke were mentioned again, and she wondered what the connection was. Were they somehow responsible for the explosion? She perked up when she heard the word "ship." Jasper had mentioned a ship when she'd found him. Tapping her pen against the pad, she considered how strange all of this was. There was definitely more about this group than anyone realized.

Again, she heard the word "trade." It had something to do with Royce and information. Then, she distinctly heard the names "Sarna and Greta." Who were they? She wrote the names down.

The group went quiet for a moment, and she hoped they would continue. A small child sitting with a mother on the opposite side of her let out an ear-splitting shriek when he dropped his fruit roll on the ground. All eyes went toward the sound, and when she glanced over, she saw the one named Declan staring at her. He mumbled something, and she felt sure it was something to the effect of, "Heads up. We've got company." More heads swiveled in her direction.

She tipped her head in their direction and stood, putting her notepad away and walking over to them.

"Officer Chappell, was it?" asked Declan.

"It is," she answered. "Good morning."

"I wish it was," answered John Ramsey. He appeared a little less lost than he had in the waiting room the previous day. "How can we help you?"

Watching them, she got the impression they were closing up on her and banding together, as if they were a pack of wolves protecting their young. "I came by to see how your family was doing. I'm glad to see they're better."

"They are. Hopefully, they'll wake soon," said one of the women. She was familiar, but Vee couldn't recall who she was.

"How is Jasper?" she asked. "I stopped by his room, but he's still ill?"

"You stopped by his room?" asked Royce, narrowing his eyes. He was apparently still angry.

"I stopped by each of their rooms, looking for all of you." She paused. "I'm curious. Why do you have someone posted by each of their doors?" There was a distinct pause, and she sipped the remains of her coffee. "You worried about something?"

"We just lost three people to an explosion and four others are injured. What's wrong with taking a few precautions?" asked Ramsey.

"Precautions against what? You think they're still in danger? After a gas explosion?"

Royce swiveled toward her. "Do you have any productive questions? What we choose to do with our people while we're not with them is none of your damn business."

She caught the phrase *our people*. That was interesting.

Declan stood, frowning at Royce. "I know it may seem odd to you. I understand that. But we're dealing with a lot right now, and it's not so much security as you call it, but more that we just want someone there to keep an eye on them. We can't be present all the time."

Vee had been a police officer for five years, and she'd learned when to sense bullshit. "Of course. It's just not something I've seen before."

"Well, now you have," said Royce. Declan cleared his throat, and Royce raised a brow at him before looking back at her. "Did you say you had some questions for us?"

"Yes," she said, accessing her notepad. "Was there anything suspicious going on that would lead you to believe this might have been deliberate? Anyone mad at you? Did you piss off a neighbor? An angry relative? Anything like that?"

Declan answered. Obviously, he was the go-to guy. "Have you heard from the fire department? Did they determine if it was more than a gas explosion?"

"No, not yet." She waited.

Declan nodded. "I am not aware of any angry relatives or pissed neighbors." He glanced at the others. "Anybody else?"

Everyone shook their heads.

"What about angry people in general? You didn't mention that. Anybody like that?"

Declan stared. She could almost hear his mind ticking. He hadn't expected her to realize he'd bypassed that snippet of the question.

"Who doesn't have someone who's mad at them?" asked John Ramsey. "I ticked off the cashier the other day at the grocery when she double charged me for apples and wouldn't give me my money back. People get angry all the time."

"You think the cashier blew up your house?"

"What kind of question is that?" asked Royce. He pointed. "This man just lost his best friend and almost his entire family and you're going to be a smart-ass?"

"Royce ..." The woman beside him put her hand on his arm.

"I apologize," said Vee. "I don't mean to be flippant, but I think you see my point. If someone deliberately did this, and I'm getting the impression that's what you think, then there would have to be a high level of animosity between you and him or her. An angry cashier doesn't fit the bill. And I think you know that. So, if you're worried enough to post look-outs, or security, or whatever you want to call it, outside your family's hospital doors, then I have reason to believe you think you're still in danger. And it's my job to make sure you're safe. So, if you know of a threat, I'd like to know so we can bring this person to justice." She held her notepad, ready to write.

Nobody spoke. They didn't trust her. She could see it on their faces.

"We appreciate that," said Declan. "To be honest, we're not exactly sure what to think. It hasn't even been twenty-four hours yet. We've barely slept, and our family is still not out of the woods. We posted people outside the doors because it gives us some sense of security over this insanity. Maybe this was just an accident, and maybe it wasn't, but until we know for sure, we'd like to err on the side of caution. But is there someone angry enough at us that would warrant this level of cruelty, and who would target children? No. I don't even comprehend that level of evil."

"But if there is, he better watch his back," said Royce.

"Mr. Fletcher," said Vee. "I would advise you not to take matters into your own hands. If this was a deliberate act, please let the police handle this. Otherwise, you may find yourself on the wrong side of the law."

"No one is going to do anything," said Declan. "As you said, we don't know for sure what happened. But if we have more information that you may find of interest, then we will certainly let you know. Right?" He eyed the group.

"Of course," said Hannah.

"Yes," said the other woman. It occurred to Vee that this must be the other Fletcher sister named Gillian.

"If I sense the cashier is seeking revenge, you'll be the first to know," said Ramsey.

Royce shrugged. "Whatever you say, Officer Chappell." It was about as sincere as an inmate's declaration of innocence.

Vee studied the names on her paper. There were more questions to be asked, but now was not the time to ask them. Perhaps there was a better way to get answers.

"When your family is able, I'd like to talk to them," she said.

The other man finally spoke. She couldn't remember his name. "They won't tell you anything different. They probably won't remember anything." He grabbed a paper napkin and crumpled it in his hands.

She flipped through her notepad. Adam. His name was Adam. "That may be the case, but I'd still like to determine that for myself."

"Of course," said Declan.

She closed her pad and put it away. "One other thing."

Sighing, Declan answered. "Yes?"

She paused for effect. "Morgana and this council. I'd like to talk with them too. Maybe they might shed some insight on your friend Jasper and this ship he mentioned."

Declan paled and his mouth opened, but nothing came out.

Bingo, she thought. She'd taken a risk, and it had paid off. There was definitely more to this group than met the eye. Explosion or no explosion, and she wanted to know what it was. "Is that a problem?"

"I–I don't see why," Declan stammered.

"That's fine," said Ramsey. "We'll have Morgana get in touch. She'd be happy to speak with you." He sat back in his seat.

Cool customer, she thought. Much cooler than yesterday. "Thank you." She took a step back. "I'll be back soon, to check on your family, and hopefully speak with them when they're up for it."

"Can't wait," said Royce.

She nodded, turned, and left. This group was going to be a hard nut to crack, and she suspected this Morgana would be the same. What she needed was someone willing to talk.

Reaching the elevator, she hit the button and wondered what she was doing. Her only assignment was to follow up with the victims and wait for the fire department's report on the explosion. Barring that, there was little else for her to do. These people and their secrets, assuming there was nothing illegal going on, were none of her or the department's business. But something about this group intrigued her, even if their precautions turned out to be only the result of post-traumatic stress.

Thinking about it, she had to ask herself how far she was willing to go. If this was only a gas explosion, then case closed. She'd be reassigned. But until they knew for sure, then she'd keep digging.

The elevator opened, and she stepped inside. Using her cop's instinct, she knew who she needed to talk to. Making up her mind, she punched the button to Jasper's floor.

Chapter Eleven

THE NURSE WALKED DOWN the quiet corridor, peering into rooms as she headed toward the two patients she sought. There was little activity that morning. The soft murmurings of TVs and beeping from machines in nearby rooms were all she heard as she neared her destination.

Finding the first door, she saw the man standing outside. He nodded at her, and she nodded back. Stepping into the room, she saw no one else. The nurse on duty had mentioned the family had gone to breakfast. Approaching the bed, she studied the woman lying in it. Eve Fletcher. The sheets were pulled up to her neck, but her thick red hair spilled out over the pillow. She appeared to be sleeping peacefully. The nurse observed the machines, which monitored Eve's heart rate and blood pressure. Little had changed since the previous night. Eve had survived a nasty injury and delicate surgery, but appeared to be recovering.

Pulling back the sheet, the nurse took Eve's hand and held it. Pausing a moment, she closed her eyes and went still, allowing her mind to go quiet. She stood that way for a while, knowing she had little time. She still had to access the other woman's room before the family returned. Taking a deep breath, she stood silently until she'd accomplished her goal, then let go of Eve's hand and pulled the sheet back to cover it.

Aware of the time, she headed for the door, but looking back, she smiled. This really was too easy. All she had to do was keep these women from waking. Burke had told her to do whatever was necessary, just not get caught. She'd wondered how she would do that, but quickly realized that a nurse's uniform had given her easy access to wherever she needed to go. All she had to do was avoid the family, especially one man in particular, but that had not been difficult.

Pleased with her progress, she opened the door, nodded again at the man posted outside, and headed to Sarah Ramsey's room.

· · · • • • • • · · ·

Vee stopped at the intersection of two hallways and peered around the corner. Just a few steps away was Jasper's room, and outside of it was the man watching the door. Vee pondered stepping up to him, flashing her badge and gaining access, but she knew he'd be on the phone in a minute to the family downstairs. If this was going to work, then she needed uninterrupted time with Jasper, assuming he was well enough to speak with her. She debated her options when an orderly with a tray of utensils entered the hallway, just as a nurse stepped out from behind the main desk. The two collided and the objects on the tray fell and scattered across the floor, making a loud clatter.

The man at the door turned to help, and Vee didn't hesitate. She stepped out into the hallway, passed the trio stooped low to collect the fallen items, and entered Jasper's room. No one saw her.

Once inside, she waited, wondering if the man would double check the room since he'd been distracted, but after several seconds, she released a held breath and focused on Jasper, who appeared to be resting quietly, although he took shallow breaths and his face was pale.

Vee walked closer and again second-guessed herself. What the hell was she doing? Sneaking into a sick man's room to question him about ... what? Ships? Fake explosions? Secrets of the family downstairs? She could hear her sergeant's voice in her head. This was lunacy. These people were traumatized and dealing with lost and injured loved ones. Of course, they were acting strangely. Wouldn't she in that situation?

Feeling foolish, she started to leave.

"Wait." Jasper's voice was quiet and raspy, but there was a degree of strength behind it.

She paused and turned back, surprised to see his eyes open, although barely. "Jasper?" She moved closer. There was a chair nearby, and she pulled it closer and sat in it. "You all right?"

He watched her with weary eyes, and she wondered how long he would remain conscious. "Who are you?"

She scooted the chair closer. His hand was above the covers, and although she knew she should remain professional, she felt strangely compelled to hold it. She settled for touching his wrist. "My name is Vee." He moved, and his warm fingers encircled hers and a strange energy fluttered through her. "Do you remember me? We met in the Ramsey backyard after the explosion." He made no acknowledgement. "Can you talk?"

He shifted in the bed and grimaced, but he kept his eyes on her. "Yes. I can talk." He swallowed, and she knew his throat was dry. There was a cup of water beside the bed. Letting go of him, she reached for it and held it up to his mouth to let him take a sip from the straw.

The water helped, and he audibly sighed. "Thank you," he said, his voice a little stronger.

She put the water down. "You're welcome." His hand reached out, and she realized he was seeking her. She took it again and the strange energy returned. It traveled up her arm and down her chest and bloomed in her gut. She'd never felt anything like it. She was sure she was blushing.

His face appeared a little less pale, and she wondered if he was feeling it too.

"You're pretty," he said. His eyes closed but slowly opened again, and she wondered if he was hallucinating.

Ignoring the compliment, she moved forward with her questions. This man intrigued her even more than the others. "Can I ask you a question, Jasper? Can you tell me about your ship? Where is it?"

"My ship?"

"Yes. Can you tell me about it? You mentioned it yesterday."

He pulled up the covers with his other hand and shivered. "It's in the woods."

"Where?"

"Not far from the house."

She assumed he meant the Ramsey home. "How far?"

He went quiet, and she was worried she was wearing him out, but he finally answered. "About five miles, maybe ten. It's sort of a blur. Northeast, I think." He coughed softly, and his eyes closed.

"Jasper? You still with me?" She squeezed his hand, and his eyes opened.

"I need my pills," he said.

She leaned closer. "Pills? What pills? Where are they?"

His voice was barely a whisper. "Ship. They're on the ship. Can't survive without them."

"Why not? How sick are you? Can't the doctors give you a new prescription? You're in a hospital."

"No." He coughed. "Don't exist."

She furrowed her brow. "What doesn't exist?"

"The pills."

"Jasper, you're not making any sense. How can the pills you need not exist? You obviously have some."

"They're on my ship."

"I know. So tell the doctors."

"I can't." He shifted and grimaced again. She touched his forehead and despite his paleness, she could tell he was burning up. Unexpectedly, a kernel of fear crept through her. Could this man die?

"Jasper." She searched for what to say. This was not how she had envisioned this encounter. "Tell me what you need. I want to help."

He swallowed and moaned. "You can't help me."

"Why not?"

"Because you're not like me."

"What do you mean? We seem pretty alike." He closed his eyes. "Jasper, hold on. You can trust me. Why aren't we alike?"

His eyes barely flitted open, and he watched her. "Because you're human."

She pulled back. He was definitely hallucinating. "And you're not?"

His head shook. "No."

"What are you then?"

He blinked and his eyes closed again. "Eudoran."

She paused. "What's that? A country?"

"A planet. Eudora." He spoke softly, his voice losing strength.

She played along. "Where's that?"

"A long way away. I landed here."

"On your ship?"

"Yes."

"And are you sick because you need the pills? Are these pills from Eudora, too?"

He swallowed and moaned. Every movement seemed to be painful for him. "I shouldn't be telling you this. It's against the rules."

"What rules?"

"About revealing ourselves."

He started to push down the covers, but she reached over and pulled them back up. "Jasper, I'd say you're in a position to break the rules, so don't worry about it. Your secrets are safe with me. Tell me about the pills."

He opened his eyes, and she noticed they were bluish gray. "You remind me of the women from home."

Her jaw dropped. "You mean big eyes and a large head?"

Despite his misery, he chuckled. "That's a fallacy. We don't look like that. I don't look like that." His face furrowed. "Do I?"

In her mind's eye, she pictured Jasper as a healthy male, and that strange heat bloomed again. What the hell was wrong with her? "No. You don't look like that."

His brow relaxed. "Good." His eyes drifted.

"The pills, Jasper. Tell me about the pills."

He coughed again and turned slowly on the bed to face her. HIs grip on her hand increased. "I can't survive without them. Earth's frequencies are too harsh."

His voice grew stronger, and that weird energy heated her arm and chest. She wanted to take off her jacket because she was sweating. Tugging on her shirt to cool off, she tried to understand. She didn't know what she had expected, but it hadn't been this. Jasper was obviously on some powerful drugs. She decided to see how far he would go with this.

"If you're from Eudora, when did you arrive?"

He was quiet, and she wondered if that was all she was going to get from him when he answered. "Two nights ago. I think it was around midnight your time. Hard to be sure, though. I was out of it."

Vee opened her mouth to ask another question but stopped. Thinking back, she realized that was the same night she'd been out with Larry and seen the small craft in the sky. She'd been searching for it when she'd received the call about the explosion. Recalling the location, she realized she'd been about six, maybe seven miles from the Ramsey's home. Northeast.

She stared at the man holding her hand. His blanket had slid down when he'd turned, and she reached over and pulled it back up. His eyes never left hers, and that energy bubbled and churned, only it had moved into her belly. She held her breath as the heat increased. He pushed down the covers she'd raised as his cheeks turned pink, and she realized the warmth was affecting him too. The urge to get up and leave the room and never look back occurred to her, but the pull in the pit of her stomach wouldn't let her. Despite the warning bells, she leaned closer. "Who are you?" she whispered.

His thumb slowly moved over the back of her hand. "I told you who I am." He took a deep breath and released it, and looked almost serene. "You make me feel better."

His words and his touch were an electric shock to her system. She'd come in here to question this man, and now—now, what—she was attracted to him? She pulled her hand away despite the desire to keep it there and stood, wondering where she'd lost her professionalism.

The heat vanished and her chest returned to normal, but her belly still churned. She pulled at the flaps of her jacket to cool off. Looking at him in the bed, she saw his paleness return, and he seemed to visibly shrink in the bed. He pulled the covers up.

"You don't believe a word I've said, do you?" he asked. His weariness returned, and he coughed again.

She stood there, remembering why she was there. How had she gotten so off track? "It doesn't matter what I believe. All that matters is that I figure out what is going on here. Your friends seem to think this explosion was deliberate. Is that what you think, too?"

He shivered. "Yes. It was deliberate. Why do you think I came here?"

She scratched her head. All of this was crazy. What was she supposed to tell her sergeant? "Let me get this straight. You came from another planet to save these people? You knew they were in danger. But this planet is toxic to you. You can't survive without your mystery pills, which are apparently on your ship, which crashed in the woods near the Ramsey home."

He nodded. His strength appeared to be rapidly diminishing and his eyelids looked heavy. Had her touch really helped him that much? "Close enough," he whispered.

Vee stared. No matter how much she wanted to believe him, she had to put her police hat on. "Who is this person who tried to kill the Ramseys? What's his name? Is he from another planet too?"

Jasper looked defeated. "Why don't you believe me?"

Her heart pounded, and she resisted the urge to take his hand again. Had she really been buying into this 'I'm from another planet' fallacy? "Jasper, you're sick and in the hospital. The doctors are trying to help you. You're on medication. I'm sure when you're well, you'll look back on this story and laugh. We both will. But if it's true that this accident is deliberate, then I need to find the man responsible. But to be honest, you are obviously not well enough to give me the answers I seek, and I apologize for bothering you."

His blue-gray eyes were back to being half-slits, but he still watched her intently. His gaze made her uncomfortable, and she turned to leave.

"I don't believe you either."

His voice was so quiet she'd barely heard it. She looked back. "What do you mean? What's not to believe?"

He smiled softly. "I held your hand. I felt your curiosity and your interest. You went looking for my ship. You're a seeker and have been for a long time. You also like my eyes." He blinked. "You want to believe me, don't you, Vee?"

She stood stock still, unsure she'd heard him right. How had he—

The door opened, and Royce Fletcher walked in. His face dropped, and he looked from Vee to Jasper. "What in the hell are you doing in here?" He went to the bed. "Jasper? You okay?"

Jasper closed his eyes and didn't answer. Vee stood like a frightened mouse in the room, still flattened by Jasper's words. "I–I wanted to ask him a few questions."

Royce leveled a hard stare at her. "Get out." His voice was so frigid, Vee was surprised not to feel a frigid blast of air against her skin.

Nodding, she turned and left.

· · • • • • • • ·

The nurse held Sarah's hand and eyed the clock. Time was running short. It had taken longer than she thought to access the room. The day nurse, whose name tag read "Gloria," had been with Sarah, and then the doctor had stopped by. She knew the family would return soon, but she had to complete her task or risk Sarah waking. This daytime visit was proving trickier than the previous evening's. Between the family and the medical staff, accessing Sarah and Eve's rooms without drawing suspicion was proving more difficult. She was going to have to talk with Burke about that. If she was going to this amount of trouble and risking discovery, he owed her a bigger piece of the pie.

Continuing her task, she thought of Burke and his plans. The man definitely didn't like these people, but they were a means to an end, and once he got what he wanted, he would discard them like he did everything else. Not that she cared. She had no concern about what happened any more than he did, and Burke was her meal ticket. She knew an opportunity when she saw it, and if doing Burke's bidding would gain her some clout with Roma, then so be it. Conscience was not her strong suit, nor did she regret not having one. She wondered how people walked around with so much guilt and regret.

A few more minutes passed, and the nurse returned Sarah's hand beneath the covers when the door opened and Sarah's husband, John Ramsey, and the woman named Hannah entered. They stopped when they saw her.

"Is everything okay?" asked the husband, who walked to the opposite side of Sarah's bed. "Any change?"

The nurse smoothed the sheets. "No. No change. Still resting comfortably." She turned to leave and almost ran into Hannah beside her.

"She should have come around by now," said Hannah. "How are her vitals? Any change?"

The nurse stepped around Hannah. "No. Like I said. No change." She walked to the door.

"Why hasn't she woken up?" asked the husband.

She reached the door.

"Wait," said Hannah.

The nurse paused and turned back. "Yes?"

"I saw Gloria earlier. I know she's our day nurse, but I don't see a name tag on you? Are you on this floor, too?"

"Yes. I'm assisting on this floor today." She started to leave again, but Hannah stopped her.

"What's your name?"

Hesitating, the nurse opened the door. "Alice. You can call me Alice." Before Hannah could ask another question, she left the room.

Chapter Twelve

RAMSEY HELD SARAH'S HAND, willing her to wake. He'd been there since the previous day, sitting with her, watching and waiting. The only time he'd left had been to catch a few hours' sleep and check on his kids at his mom's. Hannah and Declan had been there, too. Adam, Gillian, and Royce wandered between Sarah and Eve's rooms. Grayson had been released from the hospital the previous day and he'd stopped by before Gillian had taken him back to a hotel room they'd booked near the hospital. Morgana had come by in the evening to check in as well, hoping there'd been some progress, but there was none to report. Sarah and Eve continued to lie in bed unchanged, like Sleeping Beauty waiting for her Prince Charming, but no matter how much Ramsey kissed his wife, she refused to wake. The doctors were stumped. They couldn't understand it either.

Looking at the clock, he saw it was almost noon. His stomach grumbled. He'd skipped food that morning and his body was complaining. He was not good at eating when he was stressed. He could hear Leroy's voice in his head. *You need to take care of yourself, Sherlock. You're no good to anyone if you don't.*

Thinking of his best friend, a wave of emotion engulfed him. He missed Leroy. Wiping at his eyes, he recalled Morgana telling him she was taking care of the funeral arrangements and as soon as Sarah and Eve woke, they would hold the ceremony for Leroy and Olivia. He hadn't said much about it. It was too difficult for him. He hoped his friend understood.

There was a soft knock on the door. It opened and Royce walked in. "Any change?"

Ramsey sniffed and a kernel of anger flared. "Does it look like there's a change?"

Royce stepped to the side of the bed. "Nothing with Eve, either."

"What the hell is going on here?" He stood and scratched at the stubble on his jaw. "Something's wrong."

Royce eyed him. "You think the doctors aren't telling us something?"

"I don't think they know either."

"They talked about doing more tests if they don't wake soon."

"This isn't about more tests. This has to have something to do with who they are."

"They're half-Reds. They should recover faster than most."

Ramsey kicked his chair. "I know that. Don't you think I know that?" He put a hand on the wall and dropped his head. "Sorry," he sighed.

"No apology necessary."

The room went quiet.

"Any sign of that nosey policewoman?" asked Royce.

Ramsey popped his head up. "Who?"

"What's her name? The woman who took it upon herself to question Jasper. Officer Chappell, I think?"

"No. Haven't seen her."

Royce grunted. "Good."

Ramsey pushed off the wall. "Damn it. I wish there was something I could do. If Sarah was up and around, she could help, but she's the one who needs the assistance this time, and there's no one here for her."

Royce crossed his arms. "That's what sucks about being the healer. There's no one to take care of you when you need it."

"What about Gillian? You think she could do something?"

"She tried with Eve. Said she felt a strange blankness. She saw and felt nothing."

"Nothing? That makes no sense. She should feel something. They're still alive. They still have energy coursing through their bodies."

Royce rubbed his eyes. Ramsey knew Royce had been sleeping in the waiting room in case Burke returned. "I know. I don't understand it either."

"How's Jasper?"

"Rambling. Feverish. I hoped he would give me some information about his ship, but all he keeps saying is 'She knows. Ask her.' I have no idea what he's talking about and he won't elaborate."

Ramsey leaned over and put his hands on the side of Sarah's bed. "So, until Burke makes contact, we have no way of getting pills for Jasper."

"None. I asked Gillian to talk to Jasper, but that didn't work, either."

"You said Officer Chappell spoke with him?"

"She snuck into his room. I know that much, but as far as if she got any information out of him, your guess is as good as mine. I'm not too worried about it, though. If he spouted off about being from another planet, it only sounds like the ramblings of a sick man. I'm not even sure why she wanted to talk with him."

"She suspects something. She's digging for answers."

"Let her dig. She's only making the hole deeper."

"Maybe."

There was another knock on the door, and Ramsey looked up as Adam poked his head in the room. "Can I come in?"

"Of course," said Ramsey. "How's Eve?"

"Same." He walked in and stopped at the foot of the bed, but his eyes held a distant look. He stared at Sarah for several seconds, but said nothing.

Ramsey glanced at Royce.

"You okay, Adam?" asked Royce. "Maybe you should go get some shut-eye."

Adam continued to stare for a few more seconds, but then blinked his eyes and looked at Royce. "I feel the same thing in here."

"Same what?" asked Ramsey.

"It's the same in Eve's room. There's a familiar presence. I can't put my finger on it."

Royce's brow furrowed. "It's probably one of us."

Adam shook his head. "No. It's not. This is a different familiar. Like from Eudora familiar."

Ramsey straightened. "In the rooms? In both rooms?" He thought about it. "Burke was here. Is it him?"

"No. That energy has faded. This is someone else."

Ramsey walked closer and so did Royce. "Are you saying someone else from Eudora has been here?" A flicker of hope sprouted in Ramsey.

"Who?" asked Royce.

Adam ran a hand through his hair. "I don't know. It's not strong enough for me to identify, but it's definitely present."

"What about Jasper?" asked Royce. "Anything in his room?"

"No. I looked for it, but it's not there."

Ramsey eyed Royce. "Our theory may be correct. If someone from home is snooping around, they don't know Jasper's here. At least not yet."

"But who is it?" asked Royce. His eyes widened at Ramsey.

Realizing Royce was thinking the same as him, Ramsey nodded. He remembered Jasper's words when he arrived. "That could explain Sarah and Eve."

Royce cursed. "Why didn't we consider that? Jasper mentioned Burke wasn't alone. He's working with someone."

"But who?" asked Adam. "We've been here the whole time. We've seen everyone come and go from these rooms. How have we missed this person?"

"Have we?" asked Ramsey. "I didn't get here until after eight this morning. Sarah was alone prior to that."

"I slept in an empty room. Were you with Eve the whole time?" asked Royce.

"No. I went down for coffee and food early," said Adam.

Royce grunted. "There have been opportunities."

"Plenty," said Ramsey. "Especially if they're dressed as a hospital employee. It wouldn't be hard." He walked to the door and opened it. Mary, Declan's security, stood outside. "Mary, what time did you start this morning?"

"I came on at seven. I relieved Travis."

"You see anybody suspicious? Someone who didn't fit in?"

"If I had, you would have known about it."

Royce stepped up from behind. "What about medical staff? Nurses? Doctors? Anyone enter Sarah's room this morning?"

"Yes. A couple of nurses."

Ramsey tensed. "A couple? Who?"

"Gloria started her shift around the same time I did. She was there. Then another nurse came in about an hour later."

"What other nurse?" asked Royce. "You see her before?"

"Yesterday morning. She came in then too."

"What was her name?" asked Ramsey.

"Don't know. I didn't see a name tag."

Adam stepped between Ramsey and Royce. "What did she look like?"

Mary thought about it. "Petite, slim. Curly blonde hair. Pinned up though. Pretty."

Royce froze and looked at Adam, his jaw taut. "Shit."

Adam nodded. "Exactly."

"What?" asked Ramsey. "Who is it?"

Royce, his eyes dark as coals, and hands clenched, almost growled. "That bitch, Desde."

• • • • • • • • • •

Vee stepped through the foliage and pushed a branch away from her face. Wiping her sweaty forehead, she sat on a rock, pulled out her water bottle, and took a swig. Catching her breath, she studied the sky. It was a cool day, but the sun was out. She was off duty until that evening, so she'd decided to take a hike in the woods to clear her head. After the events of the previous two days, she needed it. Her talk with Jasper had confused her more than helped her, and she'd barely slept. Thoughts of pills, ships, and aliens swirled in her head, plus that strange feeling that had come over her when she'd held Jasper's hand. She couldn't shake it. It was almost as if she missed it, or rather, missed him. She hated to think that was why she hadn't slept. How could she be attracted to a sick man in a hospital bed? It made no sense.

Even worse, her sergeant had called and preliminary results from the fire department regarding the Ramsey incident were pointing to a gas explosion. No funny business was suspected. She'd been reassigned to a stolen bicycle case reported by a prominent family in the neighborhood. Hanging her head, she kicked at a stone on the ground. She no longer had any reason to talk with the Ramseys or Fletchers, but that's all she wanted to do. Those people had secrets, and although they were none of her business and she didn't suspect anything illegal, she wanted to know what they were.

She recapped her water bottle and stood. Looking at her phone, she gauged where she was and how far she needed to go. Even though she was no longer on the case, what she did with her free time was her choice, so that she happened to be hiking in the woods six miles northeast of the Ramsey home was not a coincidence. She was farther out from where she'd been hiking on the day of the explosion, but she had been slightly off in her original direction. If Jasper was correct, she had to be near his landing site, if there actually was one. The woods were becoming thicker, and she was now off the trail, but she still had a cell signal and knew where she was. Pushing deeper into the trees, she tried not to think about what she was doing. Was she seriously searching for an alien spacecraft? Did she really believe the ramblings of a delirious man? The nickname "VT" bounced in her brain. There was a reason Vee was walking through this forest. Jasper was right. She wanted to believe. She couldn't just sit at home and wonder. She had to know the truth, and when she wandered around in the trees for a while and came up empty, then she would be satisfied, but until that happened, she had some searching to do.

Continuing to walk, she monitored her surroundings. The thicker coverage of trees blocked the sun, and the air became cooler. There was less foliage, but being off the trail, she had to watch her step as she avoided rocks and roots. About thirty minutes later, she stopped. Jasper had said five, maybe ten miles. She was now close to seven miles out. Looking around, though, she saw nothing unusual. The trees swayed in the wind and there was the occasional hoot of a bird, but that was it. Nothing around her indicated the presence of a downed ship. But what exactly would that look like? If he'd crash landed, there would be debris, wouldn't there? Scorched earth or damaged tree trunks? A hole in the dirt? She kept walking. If Jasper was off though by a few miles in his calculations, or wrong in direction, then the ship could be anywhere. She'd need a drone to find it. Or she could keep walking and hope she got lucky. Eyeing the time, she decided to keep going.

Another fifteen minutes passed. Nothing in the forest indicated a downed craft. She stopped and leaned back against a tree. No wonder people talked about her behind her back. It was no surprise she was considered strange by her coworkers. Her interests had left Vee with few friends and even fewer dates. After her father had died, there was no one Vee could confide in about her off-duty pursuits. She had a few acquaintances through her MUFON connections. Meeting up with them once or twice a year was fine, but they were serious devotees who spent most of their working hours searching and researching, and Vee couldn't afford to do that. She still had to make a living.

Sighing, she debated going home. She needed time to shower and eat before clocking in for her shift that night. Her stomach rumbled, and she pulled a granola bar from her pack. Opening it, she stared off into the woods, wondering what was next for her. Was she doomed to stay in this town forever, searching for bicycle thieves and watching the skies at night, hoping to see what she'd seen so many years ago on a clear night with her father? Munching the bar, she realized the answer was yes.

A bird flew overhead and cawed. Vee was not a birdwatcher, but it looked like a robin. The bird perched on a branch and sat for a few seconds. Vee finished her snack and decided to head home and call it a day when something fell at her feet. She suspected the bird had dropped a twig or whatever it was using to build a nest, but when she looked closer, she saw that it was shiny. She stooped and picked it up. The bird cawed again and flew away.

Vee stared at the object, not sure what to make of it. It was short and thin and round like a pencil, only thinner and metallic. It looked like a ball-point pen, but it was not as long and there was no ink. She turned it in her hand, wondering what it was. The tip of it depressed, and she pushed on it. The quiet forest filled with an immediate *whoosh* sound. It was hard to describe. It was like the sound of wind rushing through an open door or a wave building before it crashed against a shore. She pushed it again and heard the same noise. The woods went still, as if even the trees were listening.

She turned toward the sound. About fifty yards away, she saw a small clearing. She'd passed it on her way here, but nothing about it had caught her attention. Walking up to the edge of it, though, she looked closer. It wasn't an extensive area, but it was big enough to hide something. Problem was, there was nothing there. But Vee noticed some things that looked a little odd. The surrounding trees were damaged. There were a few broken branches and some trunks were scarred or possibly burned. The minimal grass in the area appeared depressed, and there was a broken rock on the other side of the clearing. She supposed something could have been there, but it was now long gone.

She glanced at the strange object again. What was this thing and what had that weird sound been? Turning, she looked back into the woods and depressed the button again. The sound returned, only this time much louder and from behind her. She swiveled back toward the clearing and dropped her jaw. Sitting right in front of her, looking slightly damaged and listing to the right, was what could only be described as an alien spacecraft.

Chapter Thirteen

DESDE WALKED DOWN THE hallway and stopped at Eve's hospital door. Nodding at the security man stationed at the entrance to Eve's room, who nodded back, she went inside. She'd been watching and waiting for an opportunity, and when Adam left and she knew Royce was with Gillian downstairs in the cafeteria, she made her move. Approaching the bed, she stared down at Eve, who slept peacefully. She wondered when Burke would give her the go ahead to kill Eve and Sarah. She was itching to do it, but he'd told her to hold off. The time wasn't right, so she waited, knowing the payout would be a good one. Desde was ready to relish in Royce's grief. That man had cost her everything. She'd returned to Eudora with nothing. No baby and nothing to show for her efforts. Her mother had called her a failure, and she'd had to resort to currying the favor of various high-powered Council members to maintain the lifestyle she'd grown accustomed to, bribing and threatening and sleeping with them as necessary to get what she wanted. But none of them came with the status and favor that carrying the High Child's baby would have provided. Every night, she thought of Royce Fletcher and how she would exact her revenge.

When Roma had summoned her and mentioned Burke's new mission to return to Earth to complete the destruction of the Fletcher family, she'd jumped at the chance. She couldn't get here fast enough. Plus, Roma had offered her a juicy payoff for her efforts. It was a win-win.

She slipped her hand underneath the blanket and found Eve's, taking it in hers. Closing her eyes, she summoned the energy, focusing in on Eve and suppressing Eve's natural ability to heal and wake. It was requiring more effort each time as Eve slowly gained strength. It was the same with Sarah. Burke was going to have to act soon. Desde figured she had two, maybe three, days before she would be unable to prevent them from coming around.

Concentrating, she was interrupted when the door opened. She quickly dropped Eve's hand and opened her eyes. Sarah's husband, the one everyone called Ramsey, stood in the doorway.

"What the hell are you doing?" he asked. He was no longer the sad and grief-stricken victim.

Desde faced him. "Just checking in to see how she's doing. Unfortunately, she seems the same."

"I wonder why that is?" he asked. He continued to stare at her as if she were prey. "What do you think, Royce?"

The air shifted and Desde blinked as little pixels of light coalesced in the corner and quickly formed into the shape of a large man. Royce, arms crossed, with a sneer on his face, came into view as Adam rounded the corner behind Ramsey. Desde squared her shoulders. The idiots had figured it out.

"Get away from her," said Royce.

"I knew it," said Adam. "Desde. I could smell you a mile away. You need to work on cloaking your stench better."

Desde smiled and narrowed her eyes. "It was never my strong suit, but then I didn't think it would require much effort, considering who I was dealing with. You guys aren't exactly, what do they say here, a crackerjack team."

"What have you been doing to them?" asked Ramsey. "Why are you keeping them unconscious?"

"I have my orders. Much as I hated to follow them. If it had been my choice, I'd have killed them the first day. It would have been so easy."

Royce, his face as hard as the tiled floor, stepped closer, along with the other two, and the door shut. The security man outside did nothing. He must have been the lookout for any wayward doctors and nurses. "I think I told you to get away from her."

Desde crossed her arms. "Don't tell me you still have hard feelings, dear Royce? I mean, you and I have fond memories together. Don't you remember?" She moved toward him. "Or would you like me to remind you?" She trailed her eyes over his body, lingering in spots.

"Hard feelings?" asked Adam. "I know what happened to you after you returned to Eudora. Your failed attempts to carry the High Child were no secret. You were disgraced before the Council."

Desde's stomach curled. "What would you know about it? You're just an errand boy doing Roma's bidding. No different from me. You were just pathetic enough to fall for one of them. Or is that just what you're telling everyone? Maybe you're just as conniving and waiting for your opportunity, just like me. Word is you were Roma's favorite. Maybe you two even had a little fun together."

"That's a load of crap and you know it," said Adam. "But I do honor the High Child, who's standing right here."

Desde flicked her gaze toward Royce. "Seems he's lacking in his ability to take power. It's a problem for him, although I enjoyed our special time together. That's the one area where you are more than well equipped."

"Shut up," said Royce.

"What?" She cocked her head. "Am I bringing up painful memories?" She raised a brow. "Or maybe pleasurable ones? Tell me. How much did you tell Sarna about our time together? Does she know how much you liked it when I..."

A chair slid across the room and launched into the air, heading straight for her. Desde raised her hand, and the chair was deflected into the wall, where it hit hard, leaving a mark in the drywall before it fell sideways to the floor.

"You really are a lovely woman," said Ramsey. "I can't imagine why Royce, and everyone else, hates you."

"I have my moments," she said, still looking at Royce, but then she directed her attention toward Ramsey. "Your wife has an impressive energy. I'm surprised she fell for a Gray. She could have done so much better on Eudora."

Ramsey didn't frazzle as easily as Royce. "Thankfully, she's half-human. Makes her a little more level-headed. You full-blooded Reds seem to be a little unstable." Ramsey raised his hand. "So how about we cut to the chase before Royce and Adam here put your head through the wall? Why are you doing this? Where's Burke? He wants to meet, then let's meet. Why the games? And why try to kill all of us, including my children? What is it you want that warrants this level of destruction?"

Desde pushed the IV stand back and out of her way. "You really have no idea, do you?"

"That explosion killed people. Good people. But for what?" asked Adam.

"Because you exist." Desde explored her options for escape. She couldn't hang out in this room forever. "Burke also doesn't like losing. Especially to a line of Grays. Getting rid of you and killing the High Children at the same time is a bonus for both of us." She reached up and pulled the pin out of her hair and her curly locks spilled over her shoulders. "I don't like losing either. If I can garner Roma's favor by coming to assist Burke and help kill the man who killed my unborn child, then that's fine with me."

"You never cared about that child. You just wanted what it could gain you," said Royce.

She shrugged. "What's wrong with that?"

"Where's Burke? Obviously, something has changed. He could have killed us all by now and left. What's the hesitation?" asked Adam.

"Just like me, he has orders, too. He's following them. But don't worry. At some point, he'll get back to what he came here for."

"We don't go down so easily," said Royce. "We'll be ready for him."

Desde laughed. "You're cute, Royce. But so naïve. He'll take you all down. But not until he gets what he wants."

"Which is what?" asked Royce.

"I think you know."

Royce scoffed. "You'll get nothing from me. If you think I know something, you're wrong."

She shook out her hair. "You know more than you realize." She glanced at the clock on the wall. "Much as I am enjoying this time together, I have to go."

"You're not going anywhere," said Royce.

"Aren't I?" she asked. She watched the three of them puff up, as if increasing their size would somehow intimidate her. "I think you need to get out of my way."

"Watch the door, Adam," said Royce. The knocked over chair rattled.

"You ever considered just coming peacefully?" asked Ramsey. "It'll be a lot easier on the walls."

"You obviously don't know me very well," she said. The chair flew up and hit Royce in the side. Royce grunted, but barely moved. The chair bounced down against the ground and broke apart. A piece of a broken wooden leg shot through the air and grazed past Desde's cheek as it was redirected and flew into Royce's midsection. Royce doubled over and grabbed his belly.

"Obviously, I don't." Ramsey ducked as the chair leg zipped upward and barely missed his head, just as the door blew open and hit Adam in the back. He was knocked forward and almost fell onto Eve's bed before he was lifted into the air and violently thrown into Royce. Both men fell to the floor in a pile.

Desde stared at Ramsey. "I'll be on my way now."

Ramsey glared. "Apparently so."

The door slammed shut on her, and Desde laughed. "Oh, Royce. I admire your determination."

Adam sat up. "That wasn't Royce."

The chair leg flew back around and hit Desde on the back of the head. The impact knocked her to her knees.

"That was," said Royce. "I hope that hurt." He shook out his hands. "My skills are improving."

Desde touched the injury and felt the warm blood on her fingers. The wound throbbed. "Not bad," she said, standing. "Not bad at all."

Royce got to his feet, but before he could respond, there was a loud crack and he fell to the ground again with a pain-filled shout. He grabbed his leg below the knee.

"But I'm still better." She smiled, and as Royce writhed in pain, she left the room, pushed the security man away from her, and without touching it, slammed the door shut behind her.

Chapter Fourteen

A soft wave dragged against the shore, and the sun slowly rose, bringing the light with it. It was quiet and peaceful, and Sarah sat in the sand and closed her eyes, enjoying the warmth against her face. She'd been here for some time, listening to the sound of the surf. Many times, she'd been ready to stand and leave, but something held her back, like a weight sat on her shoulders, pressing her down, and she'd settled back into the sand.

This time felt different, though. She'd managed to rise and walk down the beach toward a distant doorway. In her heart, the doorway was home, and she couldn't wait to reach it. She didn't understand why she'd been here so long. It wasn't like her to spend so much time away from her husband and children. The doorway beckoned, and she started to run, eager to return. Reaching the threshold, she stopped, breathless, and reached for the knob, when a hand extended outward and touched her own. Turning, she saw Leroy standing beside her, his big grin flashing brightly at her.

She smiled back. "Leroy, what are you doing here?"

"Hello, Sarah."

There was something different about him. A bright soft light surrounded him, and his usual vibrant energy seemed magnified, but it was lighter, almost weightless. "I came to tell you something."

The door was so close. "It's time to go home." She tugged at his hand. "Come with me."

He smiled at her. "I can't. Olivia is waiting for me. And you know she doesn't like it when I'm late."

She looked around. "Where is she?"

"She's already on the other side."

"Then let's go." She tugged his arm.

"Not that door, Sarah. Another one. Listen. When you return, there are things you will face that will be hard, but you will be okay. You and Sherlock won't be alone."

She scrunched her face. "What do you mean? What's wrong?"

"No matter how bad it may seem, you will never be alone. Tell Sherlock that."

"Why don't you tell him?"

He squeezed her fingers. "I have, but it helps if it comes from you. He gets in his head too much. And it's hard for him to hear me."

"I don't understand, Leroy."

"I know you don't, my dear, but you will." He let go of her hand. "Just remember, you're stronger than you think. You all are." He leaned in and kissed her cheek. "I've got to go now."

"Wait. Where are you going?"

He turned and walked down the beach. "Tell Sherlock I'm sorry." He threw out his hands. "But this was just too good to pass up. Remind him I love him, and I'm never far away. Same goes for you." He waved at her. "See you." The farther he walked, the harder he became to see, until he completely faded from her view.

Sarah stared at the water and sand, missing Leroy's vibrant energy and trying to understand the ache in her heart. But remembering her loved ones, she turned back toward the door, grabbed for the knob, and with no hesitation, opened and stepped through it.

· · · · · · · · · ·

Sarah opened her eyes. The brightness of the room made her blink, and she heard the soft murmur of voices. Focusing, she saw images on a TV on the far side of the room, but the volume was low. A news show played, and the two anchors spoke to each other, laughing intermittently.

Looking around, she saw machines to her left and the IV in her arm, and she realized she was in a hospital. To her right was a dark head of hair nestled beside her—her husband, who was sitting in a chair next to her bed. He was holding her right hand.

She tightened her fingers around his. "Hey," she said softly. Her voice barely worked, but it was audible.

His head shot up, and she saw his red eyes and tired face with a few days' worth of stubble on his jaw.

"Sleepyhead," she whispered.

He stared at her, open-mouthed. "Sarah," he finally said, squeezing her hand. His eyes turned shiny. "Thank God." He pushed up and kissed her forehead, then buried his face in her neck. "Thank God."

His warm skin against hers brought her fully awake. But she sensed his pain when he shuddered, and she felt a wet tear trickle down her neck. She raised her other hand and put it against the back of his neck, soothing him. Her memories surfaced. An explosion. The house. A searing pain in her side, and a split-second fear for her children before everything went blank. Her heart thumped. "The kids?" she asked.

He reached up with his free hand and hugged her. "They're okay. They're safe." But his emotion did not abate. His hot tears slid down her skin. "I–I was so scared."

She could only imagine what he'd been through, but there was something more. Closing her eyes, she remembered her dream. Leroy. The beach. His fading energy. And she knew. "I'm so sorry, honey. I'm so sorry." Her own tear slipped down her cheek.

His breath hitched. "Leroy ... and Olivia." He squeezed her harder.

"I know." Pulling him close, her own tears running down her face, she held him while he wept.

"I love you," he said, his voice cracking.

She stroked his hair and held him. "I love you too."

****

An hour later, after a doctor's visit, Ramsey sat with Sarah, still holding her hand. He'd filled her in on everything that had happened since the explosion, and she was quiet but eager to see her children. Ramsey had called his mom, and she was planning to bring the kids to the hospital that evening. After Burke's visit, he'd asked her not to bring the kids until Sarah was awake and he felt it was safer. The doctor had been pleased with Sarah's progress and planned to release her the next day. Ramsey couldn't wait to have them all under the same roof again.

There was a knock on the door. "Come in," said Ramsey.

Royce stepped inside, trying his best to maneuver on crutches. "Hey, Sarah. How are you?"

Sarah pushed up on the raised bed. "I'm good, thanks. I hear that Eve's awake too."

"Doctor's with her now. So's Adam. He won't leave her side."

"I know the feeling," said Ramsey.

"How's your leg?" asked Sarah.

Royce grumbled. "It's nothing. It's fine."

Ramsey raised a brow. "He doesn't want to talk about it."

"I don't blame him," said Sarah. "Where's Gillian?"

"She and Grayson are on their way. They're excited to see you."

"How's Grayson? I heard he was injured."

"He's okay. He's lucky it wasn't worse."

"Jasper is here?"

Royce shook his head. "He is. He came to warn us at significant risk. We need his pills, but don't know where to find them. He's declining. His fever is high, and he's hallucinating. As much as I dread it, I'm hoping this meeting with Burke happens soon. We're running out of time."

Sarah adjusted her pillow. "Maybe I can help him."

Ramsey patted her hand. "You're recovering yourself. Let's not push it."

"I feel fine. The doctors are just being cautious."

"You should be too. I want you to take it easy."

Sarah stroked his skin with her thumb. "I know you're worried, but I'm not going to let Jasper die if I can help him." She pointed at Royce. "I can help you, too. Find me a wheelchair."

Royce raised a brow at Ramsey, who sighed. He knew when his wife had made up her mind. "You heard her."

Royce nodded. "I'll be right back."

Ramsey sat on the side of the bed. "You're sure about this?"

"I am. I have to do something."

He pulled her covers up. "You almost died. I think you've done enough."

"You know what I mean. I want to see Grayson, too."

"Sarah."

"I won't overdo it. Besides, it will benefit Gillian. She needs that right now. Between Grayson, Eve and ..."

"And what?"

She shrugged. "Nothing. It's just a lot for a pregnant woman to deal with, as you know."

"She's pregnant?"

Sarah nodded. "I sensed it at the dinner. But don't say anything. I'm not sure who they've told."

Ramsey opened his mouth but didn't speak.

"How's Morgana? How's she dealing with losing Drake?"

"I don't know. But I'm sure it's not easy."

"Poor woman. I know she cared for him a great deal. I need to call her. Once I'm home, we should invite her over for dinner."

Ramsey grimaced. "How about lunch? It's going to take some time for me to be comfortable with dinner plans again."

Sarah squeezed his hand. "Lunch, then."

The door opened and Royce came with an orderly who wheeled a chair inside. "Your chariot awaits," said Royce.

****

Down in Jasper's room, Ramsey wheeled Sarah up to the bed.

"Help me up," she said.

He stood beside her and helped her stand. Royce pulled the chair back, and Sarah sat beside Jasper. He was pale and beads of sweat dotted his forehead, but when she took his hand, his skin was ice cold. "Jasper? Can you hear me?"

He moaned and his eyes blinked, but he looked at her. "Who are you?" he whispered.

"I'm Sarah. I'm here to help."

He coughed and moaned. "Where am I?"

"You're in a hospital."

He closed his eyes. "Where is she?"

"Where is who?"

The coughing grew worse; he struggled to breathe. He tried to talk, but none of what she heard made sense.

"Jasper, I'm going to put my hands on your chest. Try to relax." She wasn't sure if he understood her or not, but she placed her hands on him and closed her eyes. She wondered after her injuries how running energy would affect her, but the usual powerful flow of movement returned and flooded through her and into Jasper.

Several seconds passed, but she didn't feel the usual relief. Jasper continued to lie in the bed, looking drawn and ill. Worse, he didn't feel any different to her.

"What is it?" asked Royce.

"You okay?" asked her husband. "Don't overdo it."

Sarah pulled her hands back. "That's strange. I feel his sickness and I know he's receiving what I'm sending, but it's not helping."

"That's a first. Isn't that a first?" asked Ramsey.

She nodded. "It's certainly different." She looked at Royce's leg. "Come here."

Royce hesitated, but then hopped over to Sarah. Sarah reached down and put her hand on the cast, feeling the usual rush move through her again and sensing the change in Royce. After about a minute, he let out a breath and visibly relaxed. "That feels much better."

Sarah pulled back, and Royce put weight on the leg and stood on it. "Much better."

"Yeah, well, don't let the doctor see that," said Ramsey. "You're going to have to leave that cast on until we get home."

"So apparently, it's not me," said Sarah, taking Jasper's hand. "It's him." She closed her eyes, intent on trying everything. In her mind's eye, she scanned Jasper, looking for anything that might explain why he wouldn't recover.

Opening her eyes, she sat back.

"Anything?" asked Ramsey.

"It's odd. I think part of it is bigger than me. Being on this planet is disabling. I can't stop that. Even if I helped him, I think he would only decline again."

"But can you slow it down?" asked Royce.

"I tried, but I don't think it did a lot of good. His energy is so scattered; it's hard for me to zero in on exactly what's wrong. It's like he's half here and half somewhere else." She cocked her head, thinking.

"I know that look," said Ramsey. "What's on your mind?"

She spoke to Royce. "Has there been a woman around? Did he come with someone?"

Royce's brow furrowed. "Not that I'm aware of. The only other visitors are us and doctors and nurses. Oh, and that nosey cop."

"Nosey cop?" asked Sarah.

"Officer Chappell. She's been investigating the explosion," said Ramsey. "She snuck into Jasper's room to ask him some questions."

"She found Jasper in the backyard," said Royce.

Sarah squinted. "A police officer comes into a barely coherent man's room to ask him questions about an explosion? What exactly was she hoping to find out?"

"Good question," said Ramsey.

"Huh," said Sarah. "Interesting." Jasper moaned again.

"If you can't help him, how long do you think he has?" asked Royce.

Sarah stared at the sick man and sighed. "Maybe forty-eight hours?"

Royce's eyes widened. "That's it?"

"Unfortunately, yes. It's only speeding up."

"Hell." Royce leaned over the bed. "Jasper, where the hell is your ship?"

Jasper made no response.

"I know exactly where it is," said a female voice from behind them.

They all turned. Sarah saw a petite woman with short, wavy, black hair wearing a police uniform standing in the open door.

None of them spoke. The woman rested a hand on her fully equipped belt. "In the woods, seven miles northeast of your destroyed house." She nodded at Ramsey.

"Excuse me?" asked Royce.

Ramsey snickered. "What are you talking about?" He glanced at Sarah and Royce with wide eyes before looking back at the officer. "Ship? What ship?"

"I think you've been smoking a few illegal cigarettes, Officer Chappell," said Royce. "And you're having one hell of a colorful dream."

Sarah pointed. "You're Officer Chappell?" She studied the woman and raised an eyebrow at Jasper. "I see."

"You come back to bother him some more?" asked Royce. "He mentioned the Loch Ness Monster a few minutes ago. Maybe you should follow up on that, too."

The policewoman opened her jacket and pulled out a small clear canister. She shook it, and several tiny white pills rattled inside. "And I suppose this is make believe too?" She tossed the container onto Jasper's bed.

Ramsey and Royce didn't speak but stood, slack jawed.

Sarah eyed the container and smiled. "Oh. I like her."

Chapter Fifteen

"I STILL DON'T UNDERSTAND how she found that ship," said Declan. They'd all gathered in Sarah's room as Jasper slept peacefully after receiving his pills.

"Jasper told her," said Royce.

"The man was out of it. Why did she even believe him?" asked Adam. "I can't believe she located it."

"And why didn't he tell us where the ship was?" asked Eve. "Why tell her?"

"He likes her," said Sarah. "They connected." She pushed up on the bed.

"I think we're all too worried about it. She's curious, that's all. It's not like she's going to run to the police station and report us," said Ramsey.

"What did you tell her?" asked Declan.

Ramsey threw out his hand. "What did you expect us to tell her?"

"We gave Jasper some pills," said Royce. "Then we told her that there were things about us that were better not discussed with anyone else."

Declan shook his head. "Great. Another human who knows about us. That's not good."

"We're really not as bad as we're made out to be," said Grayson. Gillian smiled.

"Sorry. No offense," said Declan.

"So, what now?" asked Eve. "What about Burke? Are we still waiting to hear from him to set up this meeting?"

"We don't need the pills for Jasper anymore, so there's no need to bargain. We just need to get him to a place where we can kill him," said Royce.

"By drinking the poison?" asked Gillian.

"Yes," said Declan.

"What about Desde?" asked Adam. "We have to deal with her too."

"One bad guy at a time," said Ramsey. "Hopefully, if we take care of Burke, she'll simply go home."

"I doubt that," said Royce.

"Maybe we can take care of both of them at the same time," said Declan.

"I hate this talk," said Sarah. "I wish there was another way."

"Me too," said Ramsey. "But unfortunately, it's them or us."

The room went quiet until Declan's cell phone rang and he answered. "Morgana?" He listened and his face furrowed. "Really?" He eyed Ramsey. "Tonight? With the full Council?" He sighed. "Ok. It'll be tricky." He paused. "We'll be there." He hung up the phone.

"What is it?" asked Ramsey.

"Burke. He called Morgana. He set up the meet. It's tonight. With the full Council."

"I thought we were going to try for Morgana's house?" asked Ramsey.

"She tried. He said no."

Ramsey scowled. "When?"

"In one hour. We have to go now," said Declan. "Morgana's made arrangements to get the tampered serum. She'll have it ready."

"Then let's go," said Royce, stepping away from Eve's bed. "Let's take care of this."

Ramsey stood. He gave Sarah a quick kiss and held a look with her before he nodded and headed toward the door. "I'm ready when you are. It's time for Burke to face his fate."

****

Morgana poured herself a drink. The tea had been replaced with Scotch, and she took a healthy sip.

"You okay, Morgana?" asked Talbot. He stood beside her and drank from his own drink. "You ready for this?"

Morgana set her drink at her seat at the table. "I'm ready. But a little fortification never hurt anyone."

"Here, here," said Talbot, raising his glass.

"He's late," said Declan, checking his watch.

"He's making us wait," said Royce. "Showing us who's in charge."

"Remember, we use that to our advantage. He expects us to cower, to be afraid." Talbot walked back to the conference table and put his drink down.

"We should cower. That man will kill us all if he suspects what we're doing," said Daphne.

"Not if we kill him first," said Ramsey. He pointed at the bar. "It's the bottle on the right?"

Morgana sighed. "For God's sake, Ramsey, please try to remember which is the poisoned one and which isn't. It's the one on the left."

Ramsey leaned against the wall. "I'm kidding. Just trying to lighten the mood. It's getting a little tense in here."

"You honestly think this is going to work?" asked Estelle. "He may not want anything to drink."

"It has to work. What other options do we have?" asked Randolph.

"This whole scenario is absurd. Who are we? The Justice League?" asked Ben.

"I agree with Ben. Why don't we give the man what he wants?" asked Daphne.

"Because once he gets what he wants, he kills us," said Declan. "You okay with that?"

Daphne hesitated.

"I think she is," said Ramsey. "As long as she survives."

Morgana sat and rubbed her temples. "Daphne, as soon as this is over, I will be initiating dismissal proceedings to remove you from the Council.

Your utter disregard for the safety of our people is grounds for ejecting you."

Daphne's eyes widened. "Ejecting me? I think I am the only sane one in the room. The safety of our people is all I'm thinking of. By doing this, you risk all of us. Not just a few."

"You believe the death of a few is justified if it saves the whole?" asked Stephens. It was a rare question from the typically reserved councilman.

"Exactly. Why risk all of us?"

"What makes you think he'll stop with the Fletchers?" asked Talbot. "We'll know who they are and see what they've done. Besides, once you bow to tyrants, you will forever be owned by them. I suspect these people are no different. They might disappear for a while, but the moment they recognized a use for us, they'll be back, wanting something else, and threatening the people we love. We cannot allow that. We make our stand now, or we don't make it at all."

"Here, here," said Morgana. "Besides, we've already taken a vote."

"I didn't vote for this," said Daphne.

"You were the only one. Majority rules," said Anderson. "Talbot's right. It was only a matter of time before our people returned. It's unfortunate that it had to be this way, though. Things have obviously changed on Eudora, and not for the best."

"If we could get the proper High Child on the throne, then maybe we could change all that," said Ramsey.

Royce huffed. "How about we deal with Burke first, before we make me a High Leader?"

Declan checked his watch again. "Maybe he's not coming?"

"He's coming," said Royce. "Why else gather us all in one place, other than to—" He went still.

Ramsey's eyes widened. Morgana stopped in mid-sip.

"What?" asked Talbot.

"You don't think ..." Declan looked around the room. "Would he?"

"What?" asked Ben.

"Blow us all up?" asked Morgana.

"He already tried it once." Ramsey bent low and looked under the table.

"We need to get out of here," said Daphne, standing.

The doors opened, and Jenkins walked in. "Your guest has arrived." A tall man with long, dark hair pulled back in a bun entered the room. He wore black pants, a long-sleeved shirt and a blue jean jacket. The room went quiet. Morgana thought he looked like a middle-aged man trying to look twenty years younger. Her heart picked up its beat, and she stood. "I presume you are Burke?"

The man stopped in the middle of the room, and Jenkins left and closed the door behind him. Burke eyed the group. "I'm glad to see everyone here. Sorry I'm late. Had a few lingering tasks to deal with." He put his hands in his pockets. When no one said anything, he smiled. "What? You were thinking I was going to kill you all with another bomb?" He chuckled and glanced at Ramsey. "Sorry about the house."

Ramsey glared. "The house? You killed my best friend and almost killed my wife and children."

Burke shrugged. "That wasn't the plan. Next time I'll do better."

Ramsey launched himself at Burke, but Burke raised a hand and Ramsey flew backward and hit the counter of the bar, his side taking the brunt. Morgana held her breath as the bottles swayed, but didn't fall. Ramsey fell forward, holding his ribs. Breathless, he spoke. "I'm going to kill you."

Declan leaned next to him. "You okay?"

Ramsey waved him off with a grimace. "I'm fine."

Declan faced Burke. "What is it you want?"

Royce stepped closer. "I know what he wants. Me."

Burke turned. "As a matter of fact, I do."

Royce loomed over Burke. Burke was tall, but Royce was taller. "I've been here the whole time. Why go after innocent people? People who are no threat to you."

"My plans changed unexpectedly. Getting rid of you and your sisters was my primary objective, but adding in the Ramseys was a bonus." He glanced at the Council. "Grays need to learn their place. I find a show of force can be quite effective."

Morgana's chest constricted. She gripped her glass. "You have no say here. No one from Eudora has been to Earth in quite some time. We live peacefully and rule with fairness and equality. There is no reason for that to change."

Talbot cleared his throat. Morgana got the message. She was doing a poor job of cowering at this man's feet.

"You're wrong about that," said Burke. "You have had a few visitors over the years. Your father, for one," said Burke, regarding Royce. "Which is how we got into this mess. And your Uncle Galen, who has never returned home."

Royce shrugged. "Maybe he got lost."

"Royce is lousy with directions," said Ramsey, slowly standing and holding his side. "Must run in the family."

Burke smiled. "I'm sure." He glanced down at Royce's leg. "How's the injury? I heard about your encounter with Desde. She can be dangerous when threatened." Royce didn't move. "But it looks like you're all healed up."

"Desde's not as tough as she thinks," said Royce.

"That or your lovely wife is up and around," Burke said to Ramsey. "Glad to hear it. She's a powerful Red. I'd hoped she'd survive. Maybe once this is over, she'd consider a visit to Eudora. It really is lovely this time of year."

Ramsey stepped forward, but Declan put a hand on his chest. "Don't. That's what he wants."

"Can't you find a woman of your own?" asked Royce. "Surely Desde is all over you. She loves the easy marks."

"Present company, included?" asked Burke.

Royce frowned. "I sent her on her way, just like I will with you."

Talbot stood and walked to the bar. "Gentlemen, this is getting us nowhere. We can bicker for the rest of the day, but for what purpose? Mr. Burke here obviously has something to tell us. He's a powerful man who needs something. I suggest we listen to him. Maybe we can find a resolution to his problems without anyone else getting hurt." Morgana held her breath as he picked up the bottle on the left and poured himself a drink, and then poured another glass. He handed one to Burke. "How about a drink before we begin the proceedings? Something to calm the nerves?" He held the drink out.

Burke paused. "I didn't come here for a drink."

"Have you ever had a good earthly Scotch? You might be surprised." Talbot held the glass.

Burke eyed the glass. "Maybe." He stepped forward and took the Scotch from Talbot. "Once I get what I want, maybe we'll toast the group." He put the Scotch down on the table.

"Tell us what you want," said Randolph.

Burke walked past the table and studied a painting on the wall. It was an abstract Morgana had purchased at a local art fair. "Royce and I need to have a chat. He has information I need to know."

Royce walked to the table and sat sideways, his long legs jutting out. Burke's drink was next to him. "What could I possibly know that's so important to you?"

Burke turned away from the painting. "You have a child. We need to know where it is."

Royce went still, and Morgana saw him clench his fists.

"A child?" she asked. "What could you possibly want from a child?" She returned to the bar and added more Scotch to her glass. She poured it from the left bottle.

Burke raised his hand. "Surely this is not difficult. The lineage. It's another High Child. We seem to be collecting them," said Burke. He moved to the table and sat in the empty seat next to Royce, facing him. "Pretty logical that we need to get rid of them." He reached for the glass of Scotch in front of him and swirled it.

Royce's face went flat. "You wasted a trip. I can't help you."

Burke grinned. "I figured you'd say that."

"You figured right. Even if I knew where they were, I'd never tell you. But I suspect you knew that, too."

Ramsey stepped away, leaned against the bar, and held his ribs, his face unreadable. Morgana hoped he was calming down. If he attacked again, she worried Burke would be too distracted to drink his Scotch, or worse, would kill Ramsey.

Burke continued to swirl the drink. "Which is why I have a contingency plan."

Royce narrowed his eyes and Morgana sat straight, fearing what came next.

Burke sniffed the drink. "Your sisters, of course."

Royce's face paled, and Morgana sensed the amount of energy it was taking for the man to stay in his seat. He didn't move, though, and Morgana silently willed him to keep cool and follow the plan.

Royce spoke with an edge in his voice. "I can't tell you what I don't know. I didn't even realize I had a child until after she was born."

Burke crossed one knee over the other. "You know it's a girl?" He snickered. "Good ole' Adam. Our little double agent. Rushing to tell you everything. How is he, by the way? He must be off protecting Eve, I'm sure. Although she is much stronger than him. I wonder if he realizes that?"

"I need a drink." Ramsey poured himself a beverage from the bottle on the right and knocked it back. "Royce, you want anything?"

Morgana watched him, eyeing his movements. She understood his motives. Ramsey was buying time, trying to slow things down and give Royce a moment to think. She raised a brow when she saw him quietly slide a drawer on the bar open, his body blocking Burke's view. Her heart thumped faster.

Royce didn't move. "No."

"It's a child," said Estelle. "You can't possibly harm a child."

"That's not my choice," said Burke. "I simply need to find it."

"It's not an 'it,'" said Randolph.

Talbot cleared his throat again. "Let the man talk. Is that all you want? What happens after you get the information?"

Burke put his drink down and tapped on the table. "I will report back the information to my superiors."

"And then what?" asked Declan. He moved closer.

"I wait to hear what they want to do next."

"Next?" asked Ramsey, turning away from the bar and stepped around Declan. "The only answer we want to hear is that you and Desde pick up your souvenirs and go home. You've been here long enough."

Burke ticked up a brow. "We'll leave when we choose to leave. As Grays, you have no say in the matter."

"Are you saying you might stay?" asked Daphne.

"It wouldn't be my choice, but again, I'll follow the orders I'm given," said Burke.

"What about Royce and his sisters?" asked Declan.

Burke paused, and Morgana waited, suspecting the answer and response. "I'll be honest. I have been given permission to spare your sisters if you cooperate, but you will still have to die." He picked up his drink and sniffed it again. "It smells like Brinf. A good bottle on Eudora costs a healthy paycheck."

"I'm supposed to tell you where my daughter is and then you kill me? That's the deal?" asked Royce.

Daphne stood. "If you and Desde agree to leave the rest of us alone, I say it's a deal." She looked at Morgana. "Pour me something. I say we drink to it."

Morgana paused. "I think perhaps we should reconsider that deal."

"She's right," said Talbot. He stood and walked to the bar. "You prefer bourbon, right, Daphne?" He poured from the bottle on the right. "Sorry, Royce, but if it means protecting our people, then we have no choice." He handed Daphne her drink. "Morgana? What do you think?"

"This is madness," said Anderson.

Morgana studied the group. They all watched her with bated breath. She faced Burke. "We have no guarantees you will leave after this. How can we be sure you're a man of your word?"

Royce smacked his fist on the table. "Are you serious? You all are going along with this?"

"It means saving your sisters and the rest of us," said Declan. "It's better than we hoped for. You know how powerful they are. But I don't want the child harmed, and I agree we need Burke's word that he and Desde will leave Earth once they have the information." He looked at Burke. "Can you guarantee that?"

Burke sat back. "I guarantee nothing. But I can take it to my superior. If Royce willingly gives us what we want, we can make this as painless as possible." He leaned forward and nodded at Royce. "For you as well. I promise I'll make it quick." He snickered. "You're lucky Desde doesn't know you sired a child with Sarna. You'd be dead already, and she would have taken her time."

"She doesn't know?" asked Royce.

"That information is on a need-to-know basis. And she doesn't need to know. For obvious reasons. She can be unstable."

"She's not the only one," said Royce.

"This is ridiculous," said Ramsey, throwing out a hand. "You're going to hand Royce over to the wolves? What's the matter with you people?"

"You saw what he did to your house," said Declan. "You want to live in fear of that again? You want to worry about Sarah and the kids the rest of your life?"

"What about Eve and Gillian?" asked Ramsey. "They'll never forgive us for this."

"I'm sure they'd rather be angry than dead," said Daphne. "We'll have a big funeral for you, Royce. Your sacrifice won't be forgotten."

Royce set his jaw. "That's very kind of you, Daphne." He glanced around the room. "Is this what you all want?"

Everyone went quiet. Royce looked at Ramsey, whose face fell. Shaking his head, Ramsey walked to the wall behind Burke and leaned back against it, his head down. Morgana heard him mumble. "I can't believe this."

Daphne raised her drink. "On our planet, we drink to celebrate. I say we drink to this. Let's make it official."

Morgana hesitated, but then raised her glass. There was a hushed silence in the room, but then, following Morgana's lead, everyone else did the same.

Burke nodded at Royce. "You don't have a drink."

"You'll forgive me if I don't toast my demise."

Burke held his Scotch. "I insist."

Royce stared silently.

"I'll get him one," said Declan. He walked to the bar and picked up a glass.

"Pour from the left one," said Burke.

Morgana's belly flipped, but she made no reaction. There was a brief hesitation from Declan, but then he picked up the left bottle and poured.

"I take you to be a Scotch man," said Burke. He cocked his head. "Right?"

Morgana swallowed as she observed the two men. Royce never took his eyes off Burke. Declan placed the drink in front of him. Royce picked it up and swirled the amber colored liquid in the glass.

Ramsey pushed off the wall. "Royce, you don't have to do this."

Morgana sat like a block of ice in her seat, willing Burke to drink.

"Yes, he does," said Daphne. She raised her glass, knocked back her drink, and slammed it back on the table.

Burke held his glass and Royce held his. The room was silent.

"I'm curious," said Burke. "Everyone who's taken from the left bottle is waiting. I wonder why that is?"

Morgana shifted in her seat. "Perhaps we've already had a few before you got here. Best to keep a clear head."

"Royce hasn't," said Burke. "Have you?"

Royce's steely stare didn't waver. "No."

Burke smiled. "If you're willing to drink, I'm willing to drink." He paused. "But you first."

The side of Royce's lip rose. "You worried?"

"Are you?" Burke lifted his glass and clinked it against Royce's. "To your death."

Royce hesitated, but then raised his own drink. Morgana thought her heart was going to pop out of her chest. He wasn't really going to drink it, was he?

"To yours," said Royce. And as he lifted the glass to his lips, Ramsey stepped forward, his hand removing an object from his pocket. He raised it, and Morgana glimpsed the needle just as Ramsey plunged it into Burke's neck.

She jumped out of her seat, and Daphne screamed. Talbot uttered a curse as Royce reared up, kicked Burke's chair and knocked Burke backward and onto the ground. Declan ran forward. Burke, eyes wide, reached for the needle and yanked it out of his neck, but the poison was already taking effect. Morgana watched as the man seized and fought to breathe.

Royce kneeled beside him. "How's that for a Gray, you son-of-a-bitch?"

Burke twitched and made a grisly moan. Ramsey never flinched. Ben and Estelle looked away, and Daphne remained in her seat, her hand on her mouth. Morgana held her stomach and was glad she'd skipped dinner.

Burke gasped, and his lips turned blue. Ramsey finally moved, kicking the syringe out of Burke's grasp, and kneeling beside the dying man, who clawed at the rug. "That's for Leroy, and my family." He leaned closer, gripping Burke's hair and pulling his head back. He met Burke's wild gaze. "I hope it hurts like hell."

Declan put a hand on Ramsey's shoulder. "John. It's done. He's dying."

Burke twitched again, his face taking on a purplish hue. He took one last hitch of breath and then went still, eyes open.

"My God," said Stephens. "What did you do?"

Declan leaned over and put his fingers on Burke's neck. "He's dead."

"What was that?" asked Estelle.

"A syringe loaded with serum," said Talbot. "A contingency plan." He almost shot back his drink, but then realizing his mistake, he put it down, looking a little green.

"A what?" asked Daphne. "No one mentioned this." She looked at Morgana. "Did you know?"

Morgana sighed. "I did. It was a last resort."

"What have we done?" asked Anderson.

"We killed the bastard," said Royce. He got to his feet as Ramsey got to his. "You okay?" he asked Ramsey.

Ramsey stared at the dead man, his eyes slightly glazed. "Much better actually."

Royce picked up the syringe. "Nice follow through." He tossed the syringe onto the table.

"I thought so," replied Ramsey, standing, but a little shakily.

"This is outrageous," said Daphne.

Ramsey spoke, his face pale. "You know what you can do with your outrage, Daphne? You can shove it up your—"

Declan took him by the arm. "Easy."

Ramsey deflated and nodded.

"He knew, didn't he?" asked Ben. "About the poison in the drink?"

"He suspected something was up," said Declan.

Morgana collected herself. She smoothed her jacket and took a deep breath. "You took the syringe when you were at the bar?"

Ramsey glanced at Burke's body and shuddered. "Yes."

"You knew he wasn't going to drink?" asked Talbot.

"I couldn't be sure," said Ramsey. "I felt we needed to prep the back-up plan."

"Good thing," said Royce. "Especially when I'm about to down poison."

"How did you know John had the syringe?" Declan asked Royce.

"I saw him slide it into his pocket."

The room went still as the adrenaline kicked in and the ramifications of what they had done settled in. Morgana noticed her fingers tremble and clenched them.

"So now what?" asked Estelle. "We can't just leave him there."

Declan pulled out his phone. "I'll make some calls. We'll get it taken care of."

Relieved the deed was done, Morgana returned to the bar. "Anybody else need one?" She heard the door to the conference room open. Reaching for a bottle, she turned. "Jenkins, I asked for no interruptions—"

"Jenkins is not available," said a woman who walked into the room.

Morgana stopped and stared, as did everyone else. The stranger stood in the entry. She appeared to be around Burke's age and was of average height with ruler straight, reddish blonde jaw-length hair. She wore a brown pencil skirt with a black jacket and heels. She looked like she was there for an interview.

She met the gazes of the others in the room. "He won't be available for a very long time, unless you like dead people to make your appointments and answer your calls."

Morgana put down her glass as a cold finger of fear stretched up her spine. Despite the woman's small size, she exuded a presence far more powerful than Burke's.

"Who are you?" Morgana finally managed to ask, trying not to imagine what had happened to Jenkins.

She moved slowly into the room. "I am Andolina. I am Burke's superior and a member of Roma's inner circle. And as of now, I am the new leader of this Council. Under my authority, this group is disbanded, until I say otherwise." She ignored the shocked sighs and exclamations and looked at Royce. "You have something I want."

Royce began to speak when he doubled over and fell to the ground, holding his belly and grimacing.

Andolina stepped over Burke and loomed over Royce. "And I'm going to get it."

Chapter Sixteen

VEE SAT IN THE hospital chair, wondering what she was doing. After returning Jasper's pills, she'd been called in to assist with a hit-and-run near the local high school. A teenager had been sideswiped by a car and the driver had sped off. The teenager was in surgery for a broken leg and she'd found herself back at the hospital again to talk with the victim's family. It seemed she couldn't avoid the place.

After reassuring the parents, she'd planned to leave. Reports had to be completed and after the last crazy few days, she had planned to go home and fall into bed early. She was tired, and to be honest, questioning herself. Had she really found a spaceship in the woods and talked to the man who'd arrived in it? Was the whole family in on it? Were they all from some faraway planet, living among humans on Earth? It was one thing to see a UFO buzz by you in the sky, but this was taking it to another level. Maybe it was better to listen to the chatter in her head and avoid these people.

Mentally, she questioned if this was some elaborate hoax. Were her coworkers going to jump out at her at any moment and say, "Gotcha, VT. We knew you'd fall for it!" But that hadn't happened, and really, were they that capable? It was hard enough for them to organize their paperwork and keep track of their car keys. How could they plant a spaceship in the woods? And one that could turn invisible?

Vee rested her forehead in her hands. After talking to the teenager's loved ones in the ER, she'd ignored her logical self and found her way back to Jasper's room, expecting to see a protective ring around him, but surprisingly, no one was there. A different security man was posted outside the door, but once she told him who she was, he allowed her inside. If he told the family, she didn't care. The big secret was out. What else could Jasper possibly tell her?

Sitting beside the bed, she ran her fingers through her hair and massaged her scalp. The beginnings of a headache made her think she should have followed the plan and gone home to bed. Jasper was sound asleep, although looking much better than before, which pleased her. Maybe those pills had really helped him.

Groaning, she sat back. She was startled when she caught him watching her.

"Hello," he said. His voice was quiet, but stronger than before.

She squirmed in her seat, suddenly uncomfortable under his gaze. "Hi."

He shifted in the bed and did not appear to be in any pain. His face held a boyish look, like it was Christmas morning. "You came back."

She rested her elbows on her knees. "You remember me?"

"Yes. You took my hand."

She looked at everything but him. "You were a little out of it at the time."

"I may not remember the words, but I recall the energy."

Energy? That was a strange term to use. She played with her fingers, wondering again why she was there. "You feeling better?"

"Much better." He adjusted the covers on the bed. "You found the pills?"

She recalled the ship in the woods. "I did."

"I'm impressed. I thought the ship was well hidden. It's designed not to be found."

Chuckling, she sat back and bounced her knee. Nervous energy coursed through her, and she felt off balance, like the slightest shove would knock her off her chair. Shaking her head, she told herself to pull it together. She was a police officer. She'd dealt with some of the strangest and lowest dregs of humanity. This was a simple conversation. Granted, it was with an alien, but still a conversation. "Guess I was lucky. Although it is my first spaceship. Normally, all I find is arrowheads."

He smiled, and she warmed. She took off her jacket and put it on the back of the chair.

He blinked tired eyes. "You must have questions. Is that why you're here?"

That sounded like as good an excuse as any. "You might say that, but your friends didn't seem too eager to answer them."

"They're skittish about outsiders, with good reason."

"Where are they now?"

He reached for the controller and hit a switch. The bed slowly raised. "I've been sleeping. They're probably up with the others. I'm not the only one in the hospital." The bed at a higher angle, he relaxed against it. "Hopefully we'll all be out soon, though."

"Those pills really saved your life?"

He nodded. "They did." He glanced at her chair. "Why are you sitting so far back?" He waved. "Pull up closer. It's easier on my neck."

Vee didn't think she was that far back, but she obliged him and pulled the seat forward so that she was more in his line of view. The moment she did, that strange off-balance feeling became stronger. It was like there was a magnet between her and Jasper. She couldn't figure it out. Was that what he meant by energy?

"Let me have it," he said, once she was situated.

"Excuse me?" Her cheeks warmed.

He smiled again. "You said you had questions."

"Oh. Yes." She stared at the side of the bed, trying to think. "You're from outer space?" It sounded ridiculous, and she waited for his declaration of absurdity.

"Yes. I am."

She took that in. "And the rest of the group?"

"Not from outer space, but their roots are."

"Roots?"

"We all originate from a planet called Eudora. The group here are descendants from a community that arrived here many years ago and never left."

Could this be true? "And that's your ship in the woods?"

"I crash landed. I was in a hurry." He stared off. "I took some risks and was reckless."

"I take it that's not your normal style."

"No. It isn't." He shifted again in the bed.

"Why are you here?"

He thought about it, and his brow furrowed.

"You okay?"

He settled. "You know how long it's been since you left? Where is everyone?"

"Your family?" She thought about the car crash and the subsequent interview. "It's been a few hours since I was here earlier. Not sure what time they left your room, though." His attention seemed diverted, but she continued. "Why were you reckless?"

Her question made him refocus. "I was running out of time."

"Why?"

He pushed up. "Can I use that phone? Do you know what room they're in?"

She felt the discord bubble up. It was like ice against her skin. Something was bothering him. This energy thing had merit. "What's wrong?" she asked.

"I need to get in touch. Find out what's going on."

The door opened, and a man walked in. Vee recognized him as Adam, one of the men from the explosion. He stopped short. "What are you doing in here?"

Vee opened her mouth, but Jasper spoke first. "Never mind that. She's fine. What's going on? What's been happening?"

Adam paused, as if debating whether to throw her out. "I brought you some more pills." He shook the small canister Vee had found on the craft and doled out four white discs. "Here." Jasper took them and popped them in his mouth. "How do you feel?"

Jasper swallowed. "Forget about me. How is everyone else?"

Adam frowned and nodded at Vee, but Jasper waved him off. "Don't worry about it. I trust her."

Vee's heart thumped. He trusted her? He barely knew her. But something in her chest expanded, and she stopped short of smiling.

Adam hesitated, studying Vee, but then sighed. "Didn't Royce tell you? We lost three people in the explosion. There were injuries, but everyone's out of the woods. We should all be out of this hospital tomorrow."

"Good. Where's Royce?"

Adam paused, and Vee suspected he wasn't quite ready to bring her into the circle of trust, but Jasper kept waiting. "He, Ramsey, and Declan left about an hour ago to meet with Burke."

"What?" asked Jasper. He pushed back the covers, and Vee got an eyeful of lean, muscular legs. He stood and pulled at his IV pole. "I need to get rid of this thing."

"What are you doing?" asked Adam. "You're in a hospital. You're still recuperating."

"Nonsense." He pulled at the tape and removed the needle.

Vee stood. "I don't think you should do that." She grabbed a tissue and handed it to him when the puncture bled.

"It's not the first time I've done something I shouldn't, and it won't be the last," said Jasper, dabbing at the blood. "Where are my clothes?"

Adam shook his head. "Don't ask me."

"They probably cut them off you when you came in," said Vee.

"I don't suppose you picked up my suitcase when you grabbed the pills?" he asked her.

"Sorry. I wasn't looking for your laundry."

"Doesn't matter. I didn't actually pack." He pulled the sheet off the bed and wrapped it around him. "This will do for now."

"What exactly is it you're planning?" asked Adam. "If you're going somewhere, you need a wheelchair."

"That's one thing I hated about these hospitals," said Jasper. "Too many rules." Holding his sheet, he walked to the door. "We're going to see the others. Are Eve and Gillian here?"

"Yes. So are Sarah and Hannah. We're waiting to hear from Royce."

Jasper pulled the door open. "You can fill me in on who's who on the way." He glanced at Vee, who still stood there, wondering what was going on. "You coming?"

Vee considered what to do. She could say no, leave, and never look back. This whole alien thing was absurd. These people believed they were from another planet. Why would she want to get involved? But then she thought of her dad, and their late-night sky watching, and all the dreams she'd had of one day finding what she searched for. Plus Jasper's sexy legs were a big plus.

She took a step forward, knowing she might regret it one day. "Yes."

Adam stood with his mouth open. "I don't think that's such a good—"

"Let's go," said Jasper.

****

Sarah, sitting in her wheelchair, stared at the clock on the wall.

"How long's it been?" asked Eve.

"Too long," said Grayson. "We should have heard something by now."

"Not necessarily," said Gillian, who paced at the foot of Eve's bed. "Any number of things could account for the time. Let's not overreact."

Hannah stared out the window. "That's one thing I've learned from Declan. Never assume anything." She stepped away and crossed her arms. "That doesn't help with the worry, though."

"How much longer should we wait?" asked Eve. "And what do we do if they don't call? Go down there and barge into the meeting?" She pushed herself up in the bed. "I can't wait to get out of this hospital."

Grayson moved his arm and shoulder. "I still can't believe I have no pain. That's incredible. How do you do that?"

Sarah continued to watch the clock and didn't answer. She pulled out her cell phone.

"I told you she could heal, honey," said Gillian. "Same way I can feel and know things."

"They should have been here by now," said Sarah. She punched a number on the phone and raised it to her ear.

Hannah pulled out her cell and stared at the display as if willing it to ring.

"I know," said Eve. "That's what I said." She glanced at Gillian. "How are you so calm over there? Aren't you getting or sensing anything?"

Gillian patted her belly. "I'm trying to stay cool. Getting all worked up is not good for me or the baby."

Eve narrowed her eyes. "I'm still mad at you for not telling me sooner. You're three months pregnant and the whole time nobody knew."

"Sarah knew," said Grayson.

"She guessed," said Gillian. "I never told her."

"I'm still mad," said Eve.

Sarah hung up the phone.

"Nothing?" asked Grayson. "Ramsey doesn't answer?"

"I'm going to call Royce," said Eve. She patted the bed. "Where's my phone?"

"I'm not calling John," said Sarah. "I'm calling my mother-in-law, Charlotte. She's not answering."

"Considering she's got two children to wrestle, she's probably running late. I'm sure she's on her way," said Gillian.

Sarah nodded and sighed. "I'm sure. She's notorious for not keeping her phone charged or just not hearing it when it rings." She rubbed her neck. "I'm just tense and worried. I won't relax until this Burke is gone and I know John is safe."

"And this Desde person. What about her?" asked Gray.

Not finding her phone, Eve sighed. "She's just as evil as Burke."

"One problem at a time," said Gillian. "We'll figure it out. We always do."

"You all right?" asked Gray. "You keep pacing. You want to sit?"

"No. I'm just–I don't know. Restless." Gillian shook her hands. "Like I have too much energy or something."

"I wish I felt that way," said Eve. "I just want to get out of this bed."

"I'm going to walk a little," said Gillian. "Go down to the cafeteria or something. Get a snack. You want anything?"

"You want me to come with you?" asked Gray.

"No. I'm fine," said Gillian. "Stay here. I just need to get out, use the restroom, maybe get something to drink."

"I'll take a chocolate milkshake," said Eve.

"You always eat when you were stressed," said Gillian. "I'll get you some yogurt."

Eve snorted. "I don't want a yogurt. I want some ice cream. And if they don't have that, get me a cookie or a brownie."

Gillian picked up her phone and put it in her pocket. She gave Grayson a kiss. "I'll look for some trail mix."

"I don't want any trail mix," said Eve, but Gillian had disappeared through the door.

Sarah dialed Charlotte's number again. Listening, she heard it go straight to voicemail. Worried, she hung up the phone.

"I'm sure they're on their way," said Grayson.

The door opened, and Adam entered.

"How's Jasper?" asked Eve, sitting up. "And where's my phone?"

"It's in the drawer," said Adam. "And you can ask him yourself."

"I'm fine," said Jasper, who walked in still wearing a hospital gown with a sheet wrapped around him. "I brought a friend."

Sarah sat up when the female police officer who'd found Jasper's pills entered the room. "Officer Chappell?"

"I told him to stay in bed," said Adam, aiming his thumb. "And I definitely told him she needed to stay out of this."

The officer paused inside the room, looking uncertain.

"It's okay," said Jasper, holding his sheet. "She found the ship. I think at this point it's safe to say she's in the loop."

"In the loop?" asked Adam. "Royce is going to be so pissed."

Jasper looked in the closet. "Anybody have any clothes I can wear? This sheet and gown aren't going to cut it."

"I can get you something," said Gray. "I've got some clothes back at the hotel."

"I can have Declan pick up something too, on his way back," said Hannah. She watched the phone. "If he'd just call."

"That would be great. Thanks," said Jasper. He pointed. "Hannah, right?" She nodded. "And you're Grayson Steele? Gillian's husband?"

Grayson offered his hand, which Jasper shook. "I am. Gillian stepped out for a second, but she'll be back in a minute."

Jasper swiveled. "And you're Sarah? Married to John Ramsey. You're half Red-Line?"

Sarah shook his hand. "I am. Nice to meet you."

He turned. "Eve Fletcher? Royce's sister?"

Eve raised her fingers. "And your half-sister. That's me. Gillian and I heard about you and what you did for Sarna. I'm glad to hear she's okay."

"She's alive and well. But that doesn't mean she's safe. Greta, too."

"Royce's daughter?" asked Sarah. "What's going on, Jasper?"

Officer Chapell shuffled on her feet. "You know. Maybe I should go."

"Probably," said Adam.

"No. You should stay. We may need you," said Jasper.

"Considering what we're dealing with here," said Gray. "Adam's probably right."

"I just, um, not sure what to think about all of this," said the officer.

"I can imagine this must be shocking," said Sarah. She thought back to the time when she had learned who she was and how she had reacted. "For obvious reasons, we can't tell people who we are. It can be difficult for people to understand."

"That's an understatement," said Grayson. He walked over to the officer. "I had to adjust as well. I married one of them."

The officer shook her head. "This is just so hard to believe. I'm still questioning whether all of this is true." She looked around. "I mean, you all seem so normal."

"We are, for the most part," said Hannah.

"Except for the moving furniture thing," said Gray. "And the talking to animals. Oh, and don't lie to my wife, because she'll know. It's really annoying."

"Moving furniture?" asked the officer.

"Officer Chappell?" asked Sarah.

"Please, call me Vee."

Sarah glanced at Jasper and saw him staring at Vee. "Vee, I know it's a lot to take in, but if Jasper trusts you, then I trust you."

"What?" asked Adam.

"I trust you too," said Eve. "There's a reason you're here."

Adam pointed toward Vee. "Just be forewarned. Everything you hear or learn stays with you. You go tell your friends that you've just made some new alien acquaintances, we close ranks, and you're out. You understand?"

"I don't really have any friends." Vee stood still, eyes wary. But she met Jasper's gaze and seemed to relax. "You're sure you want me to stay?"

The empty chair in the corner slid across the room and bumped gently into the back of Vee's knees.

"Have a seat," said Jasper.

****

Royce doubled over in pain. Searing hot pokers stabbed into his chest, and he fought to breathe.

"Enough!"

He was coherent enough to hear Morgana's voice. Grabbing at the ground, he gasped when the torture suddenly ended, and he went limp.

"You understand what I mean now?" asked Andolina.

"What do you want?" asked Ramsey. "Did you send Burke to kill my family?"

Royce struggled to push himself off the floor. His muscles felt like jelly. He managed to get to his knees.

"I couldn't care less about you and your family, but Burke held a grudge. That was always his weakness." Andolina stared at Burke's lifeless body. "But it became useful when I realized there was a new High Child."

"Royce is on Earth," said Declan. "There is no way for him to assume his rightful place from here. Roma can keep everything she has with no threat from us."

Andolina stepped to the table and picked up Burke's empty glass. The contents had spilled when Ramsey injected him. "You know there's another. Royce knows there is another. Jasper would not give us the information, so we came here. We know you were given a letter."

Royce began to breathe more easily when Andolina squatted next to him. "Your woman gave birth to a child. I want that child." She touched his shoulder, and it felt like a drill bit biting into his skin. Royce's face contorted, but he held still. "Where is Sarna?"

Royce fought the pain. "I don't know."

The drill bit stopped, and Andolina stood. "Very well."

Royce shook his head, trying to clear it. Still shaky, he got his feet under him and stood. He had to hold a chair for support.

"Sarna and Greta can't hurt anyone," said Morgana. "If they are in hiding, let them stay there. Roma is obviously a powerful woman. Why is she worried enough to send a team to Earth?"

The glasses on the table rattled and began to spin, then flew off and hit the walls, shattering. The glass in Andolina's hand also flew upward and broke into pieces. Andolina didn't flinch. "Who are you to question me? You're nothing but a Gray, sitting here in a pitiful show of power, with a Council vacant of wisdom and ability. I have no idea how such weakness endured for so long." She moved to the head of the table. "Not anymore. This community is now reclaimed and back under Eudoran influence. You no longer do as you wish. You now do my bidding." She cocked her head. "And you will do it with pleasure."

"Excuse me?" asked Talbot.

"That's preposterous," said Randolph.

Morgana stayed quiet.

"I'm sorry," Ramsey stepped forward. "Andy, is it?"

Declan's brow furrowed. "John."

Ramsey ignored Declan. "I don't know who you think you are, but we didn't ask for you and we don't want you. And as far as I can see, we've been doing just fine without Eudoran influence. In fact, the more Eudoran influence we get, the more we get screwed. So why don't you take your skinny, offensive Red-Line ass back to your messed-up planet? And while you're at it, put some lavender on your travel pillow. Maybe you'll relax, and it will make that stick up your butt a smidge more comfortable. Although I'm guessing it's big, so don't expect miracles."

Declan closed his eyes, and Royce admired Ramsey's perhaps ill-advised advice. He couldn't help but chime in. "Actually, I think she's going to need a lot more than lavender." He paused. "Maybe some morphine?"

Something shoved Royce's chest, and he was lifted off the ground. He flew across the table, catching only a brief glance of Council members dodging him as he slammed into the wall at the back of the room. His head took the impact, and warm liquid dripped down his face. Something heavy was leaning against him, and he saw it was Ramsey, laying on his side and holding his chest.

Royce wiped the blood trickling down his cheek and tried to sit up. Ramsey sucked in some air and pushed back against the wall. "I think we pissed her off," he said with a cough.

Royce wiped his bloody fingers on his jeans. "I think she was pissed way before she ever got here."

Daphne pointed at them. "You two need to shut up. You'll get us all killed."

Andolina flicked her eyes toward the councilwoman. "You should listen to Daphne. Perhaps not everyone here is ill-mannered and disobedient."

Royce realized maybe Daphne was right. "I can't tell you what I don't know. But I think you realize I wouldn't sacrifice them to you. I'd die first."

Andolina stood taller. "I admire your loyalty. You're much like your father. But it will serve you as much as it served him. His death was for nothing. Roma still gained power. Just like your death will ensure it."

Every muscle in Royce's body went numb. "His what?" His heart thumped, and it was hard to breathe. "My father's dead?" He pushed himself to move, making a trembling effort to stand. His muscles did not want to engage.

Andolina smiled. "I wouldn't worry about it. You'll be right behind him. But first, I want the letter."

Royce's numbness disappeared. "Why don't you go f—"

"Royce." Morgana rose from her chair. She'd fallen into it when Royce sailed past her. "Stop." She spoke to Andolina. "There has to be another way. You know Royce will not reveal the location of his loved ones."

Ramsey finally got to his feet with a groan. "I think Andy here just wants to have some fun. She's obviously run out of people to torture on Eudora." He winced and arched his back.

Andolina paused, as if considering her options. "I am here to give you the opportunity to avoid more bloodshed. Burke promised he could deliver, but he failed." She gave Burke's body an annoyed stare. "So, I came prepared. You will give me what I ask for. Maybe your own pain does not concern you, but I know someone else's will."

Royce, his mind still wracked by the knowledge of his father's death, tried to put it to the side. "What do you mean?"

Andolina walked to the front of the room, near the entry. "You might want to check in at the hospital, Royce. Make sure everyone is okay."

The blood in his body seemed to pool in his chest. "Don't go near them."

Andolina smiled. "Remember. I gave you the chance to prevent all this."

Ramsey picked up his phone. "I'll call."

"That's good," said Andolina. "Contact Charlotte first. Check in on the children."

Ramsey stopped tapping on his phone and his face went white.

Andolina stopped moving, her face flat. "What? No jokes?"

Ramsey held the phone, then hit a button and listened.

"I'll call Hannah," said Declan.

"This is madness," said Anderson.

"Ramsey's children have no part in this mess," said Morgana. "How can you involve them? They've been through enough."

Andolina waited as Royce debated what to do. "You can stop all of this, Royce. Simply tell me what I need to know."

Ramsey hung up. "Mom's not answering."

Declan ended his call. "The kids are not at the hospital. Sarah's been trying to reach them." He paused. "And Gillian's gone missing. She went to the cafeteria and hasn't returned."

All eyes went to Royce, who stood like a dead tree. His chest constricted, and he felt the blood drain from his face.

"You have my children?" asked Ramsey, who didn't look much better.

Andolina did not acknowledge him, but continued to wait for Royce's response.

Royce forced his legs to move and walked up beside Andolina. "You want the letter? I'll get it, but I'm going with you. You hurt Gillian or anyone else, and you will regret it. Burke's death will be a birthday party compared to yours."

Andolina smiled and held the door. "After you."

Chapter Seventeen

RAMSEY SEARCHED HIS MOTHER'S house frantically, calling for Ethan and Rosie, but no one was home. He heard Declan yelling for them in the backyard, but he knew it was too late. His children and mother were gone.

Footsteps on the porch alerted him, and he ran to the door just as Sarah ran in, with Hannah behind her. She fell into his arms and they clung to each other. "We left the hospital," said Sarah, breathless. "Where are they?"

"It's okay," he said, his own breath ragged. "We'll find them. I promise."

She pulled back, struggling to keep her composure. "What happened?"

Eve, Grayson, and Adam entered the house, with Jasper and Officer Chappell behind them.

"Where's Royce?" asked Eve.

"He went with them...or her," said Declan, who appeared from the back of the home. "There's nothing out back. No sign of them." He and Hannah hugged.

"He did what?" asked Eve.

Declan explained the events to the group. Sarah paced, wringing her hands.

"How could she just take Gillian from the hospital?" asked Grayson, looking pale. "She would have put up a fight." He punched a number on his cell and listened.

"It had to be Desde," said Jasper. "She likely threatened to harm you or Royce and Eve to get her to cooperate. Just like Andolina did to Royce."

Grayson cursed and hung up the phone. "We have to do something."

Ramsey frowned and pointed. "You want to tell me what she's doing here?" He looked at Officer Chappell, who stood in the back of the room.

Jasper took the officer's elbow and guided her forward. "I insisted she come. She could help us."

"Help us how?" asked Ramsey. "By calling in the cavalry and making this a sideshow with the public?"

"If I call in a missing person's report, then more people are out looking for your family members. It could help," said the officer.

"And what do we tell them, Officer Chappell?" Ramsey asked.

Vee shook her head. "It's Vee. I feel at this point we are on a first name basis."

Ramsey kicked a chair. "And what do we tell them, Vee? To look for two Eudoran women and their silver spaceship? Last seen in the woods, but could be invisible. No known plates?" He walked to the mantel and rested his hands against it, dropping his head.

"I wouldn't go that far, but we could at least issue an Amber Alert. If your children are not on a spaceship, as you say, but in someone's home or walking down the street, they could be found." She turned and faced Jasper. "The same for your siblings."

Ramsey uttered an epithet and swiped the books and candles off his mom's mantel to the floor. A picture of his mother and her grandchildren hit the ground and cracked. He swung around. "Who do you think we're dealing with here? This is not your run-of-the-mill child abduction. Things go wrong and these people will kill my kids." He stepped closer. "I don't need some innocent bystander putting their lives at risk. And I don't need you getting in the way of my children's safety because you think you can help. You have no idea what we're up against."

"John." Sarah walked up to him and put her hand on his arm.

"Agreed," said Grayson. "I want my wife back. Alive and well."

"This isn't her fault," said Jasper. "I brought her here and whether you want to admit it or not, I think she can help us. We don't have to report it, but she knows this town and she can access information we can't."

Ramsey narrowed his eyes. "Jasper, is it? You show up five minutes too late to my house before it gets blown to bits, taking my best friend and his wife with it. Now my kids and their grandmother are gone, and Royce and his sister are missing. As far as I can tell, you bring a lot of trouble with you. How do I know what side you're on?" He took another step. "Maybe you even led them to us?"

Jasper didn't move.

"John, you're upset—" said Declan.

"I'm upset?" asked Ramsey. He snickered. "Upset would be a relief."

"I tried to get here in time," said Jasper. "But Burke was ahead of me. I left as soon as I was able—"

"Which wasn't soon enough, was it?" asked Ramsey.

Jasper stiffened, but stayed calm. "I came to warn you. To warn Royce. I know what they want."

"How did you even know where I lived?" asked Ramsey.

"Come on," said Adam. "I know Jasper. He is not a traitor. He despises Roma and her cronies just as much as I do. He's the one who sent me here, remember?"

Jasper folded his arms. "I knew where to find you because Sarah healed me. That day in the hospital when I'd been hit in the head." He nodded at Sarah. "You don't know this, but I was very aware of your presence. Your energy leaves an indelible mark. I simply followed it. Plus, being a half-sibling to Royce, Eve, and Gillian helps. All of them together make them easier to find."

Sarah, still holding her husband's arm, recalled that moment in the hospital. It was the day she'd met Royce and Sarna. "You remember me?"

"I do."

"But why look for us?" asked Ramsey. "Why not go to Royce's cabin in the woods?"

"Because I knew of Burke's plans. He meant to harm all of you. It was a logical choice."

"Pretty damn fortunate choice if you ask me," said Ramsey, his voice low.

"Honey," said Sarah. "Don't take it out on him."

Ramsey spoke to Vee. "My advice? Get the hell out while you still can." He waved a hand at Jasper and glowered. "And don't get involved with a home-grown Eudoran. They only bring death and destruction. It's only a matter of time before he'll hurt you, too."

Vee stepped back from Jasper, as if she'd been caught stealing. Jasper didn't move, but his face spoke volumes.

Sarah put herself between her husband and Jasper.

"John," said Declan. "Listen—"

"Shut up, Declan," said Ramsey. Sarah gently guided him away from Jasper.

"You're overreacting," said Adam. "I know you're upset. We all are, but Jasper is not betraying us. He's helping us."

"You better be right," said Grayson.

Ramsey shot back as Sarah continued to push him away. "When your kids are missing, you tell me who's overreacting."

"Adam, leave him be," said Eve, holding his elbow. "We're all on edge. I'm scared too."

Sarah put her arm around Ramsey and directed him to his mother's bedroom. She shut the door. "Sit down."

"I don't want to sit." He paced the room, restless, wanting to hit something. "They took our children." He grabbed a paperweight off a small desk and threw it, leaving a substantial dent in the drywall.

"I know." Sarah's eyes welled up. She put her arms around his waist. "This is not your fault."

He stopped and his head fell. "I should have protected them. I left them alone and vulnerable." He rubbed his temples. "I should have known this could happen." His voice was a whisper. "I'm so sorry."

Sarah wiped a fallen tear from her cheek. She enfolded him in her arms, and he clung to her. "You couldn't have known. None of us could have."

His hands gripped her back, and his breath hitched. "If something happens to them..."

She squeezed him. "That's not going to happen." She stroked his neck. "Remember who our children are. They are not incapable."

He pulled back and sniffed. "They're just children. They shouldn't have to fight for their own survival." He blinked watery eyes. "No matter who they are."

Sarah straightened, wanting to dissolve into her own tears, but she knew her husband needed her strength. "Remember? Trust destiny."

He moaned and rested his forehead in the crook of her neck. "I hate destiny." He pulled her closer. "I just want my kids back."

Sarah held him. "Me too. But we can't fall apart. If we want them home, we've got to keep it together. They're counting on us. So is your mother. So are Royce and Gillian."

He let go of a deep shuddered sigh. "I don't know what I'd do without you. I love you so much."

She squeezed her eyes shut, and a tear escaped. "I love you too." They held each other for several seconds before Sarah pulled back, wiped her face, and met her husband's gaze. "You okay?"

He set his jaw. "I'm surviving."

"Good." She took a deep breath and blew it out. "Now let's go get our children."

****

Declan stared at the closed door. Hannah moved beside him. "What are we going to do?"

Grayson ran a hand through his hair. "I have contacts. One phone call and I can get plenty of help. None if it has to go through the police. We can keep it quiet."

Declan stepped over and picked up the cracked picture frame and put it back on the mantel. "It doesn't matter who you get. Guns and military training will not defeat these people. You know that."

Grayson's face fell. "My wife is missing. She's pregnant. I think I've done a decent job of keeping my shit together until this point. But I'm about to make Ramsey's outburst look like a romp in the playground if we don't come up with something more than 'that won't work.' We can't just sit here and do nothing."

"I agree," said Adam. "Jasper, what do you think?"

Jasper paused. "Andolina wants Sarna and Greta. That's why she took Gillian. She took the kids as an extra incentive for us to stay out of her way."

"Royce went with her," said Declan. "What happens when she gets what she wants?"

Eve sat in one of the living room chairs. "Royce will never sacrifice Sarna and his daughter. I know why he went with her. He'll be looking for a way to get Gillian out of there."

Declan walked over to the sofa. "Royce doesn't know where Sarna is. I think Andolina knows that. She wants the letter Sarna sent to Royce. Why?"

Adam sat beside Eve on the arm of her chair. "She may think it provides clues to Sarna's whereabouts." He shook his head. "How did she find out about the letter?" He looked at Jasper. "Only you, me, and Sarna knew about it."

Jasper frowned. "Unfortunately, there was someone else. I had security watching Sarna, and I dispatched one of them to bring me the letter. They had no way of knowing who it was from or to, but it would not be hard to deduce. I suspect he was paid handsomely for the information." He looked away. "I am not immune to stupidity."

"We can play the blame game later," said Declan. He sat on the couch. "We need to figure out what to do."

Grayson paced. "If Andolina gets what she wants, what happens to Royce and Gillian?"

Declan watched Jasper, suspecting he knew the answer. Jasper answered flatly. "She will kill them both." He looked at Eve. "Then she will probably find and kill you as well."

Grayson cursed again. The room went quiet. "What about the kids?" asked Hannah. "Ethan and Rosie?"

"I would like to think she would release them," said Jasper. "Andolina is a monster in many respects, but even she has her limits. She's just using them to keep your friend Ramsey in check. It's a good bargaining tool, since we know she plans to kill the Fletchers."

Grayson stopped pacing. "So we know where we stand. Now we need to figure out what we can do to find her and get our people back."

"Andolina is strong. She will be difficult to defeat," said Jasper.

Declan stood. "We aren't defenseless."

Vee stepped forward. "I still think an Amber Alert would be wise."

"It couldn't hurt," said Grayson.

Declan thought about it. "I see your point, but if Desde is holding them, then that puts anyone who sees them at risk. It puts the kids at risk too. If Desde feels threatened, I worry she could take matters into her own hands."

"Desde does not sound like someone who's going to take the kids out for ice cream," said Hannah. "She'll keep them hidden."

"Desde thinks only of herself," said Jasper. "She will use whatever means necessary to ensure her survival. Andolina may have her limits, but I'm not sure Desde does."

"Hell," said Adam. "How do we beat them?"

Jasper walked over and picked up bits of debris from the mantel off the floor. "We have to find them first. Once we do that, then we figure out what's next."

"How do we find them?" asked Eve.

Jasper put the broken remains on the coffee table. "We could do something similar to what I did to find you. Follow the signal."

"We don't have a connection to Andolina and Desde," said Adam.

"No. But you have one to Royce and Gillian. And the Ramseys certainly have one to their children."

"That's a Red-Line skill," said Adam. "Not everyone can do it."

"Eve is a Red-Line," said Jasper. "So is Sarah."

"Partial," said Eve. "And between me, Gilli, and Royce, I'm probably the least powerful."

"Don't assume anything," said Jasper. "Certain circumstances can bring out abilities you never knew you had."

"I'm willing to try anything," said Eve.

"We just need a place to start," said Jasper. "A thread to follow."

"What do you mean?" asked Declan.

Adam stood from the chair and walked over to the wall, leaning against it. "Energy leaves a trail. If you can find a strong enough marker, that may be all you need."

"What about the Council meeting?" asked Grayson. "Andolina was there and Royce left with her. Start there."

"No. Andolina will cover her tracks well. And Royce did not know where he was headed, plus he was in a high state of emotion. Not focused. That stream has long since faded." Jasper rubbed his jaw. "But..."

"But what?" asked Eve.

"How did she know about the Council meeting?" asked Jasper.

"Burke must have told her," said Declan. "He arranged the meet up."

Jasper squinted. "That would not be like Burke. He came down here to lead the mission. Roma sent Andolina as back-up to ensure it was complete, and to provide the needed assurance that Burke and Desde did what needed to be done. Normally, Andolina does not do the dirty work."

"So, what changed?" asked Adam.

"That's pure conjecture," said Grayson. "Burke could have been filling her in on everything."

Jasper cocked his head. "Did she say anything, or do anything, that may have sounded out of place?"

The bedroom door opened, and Ramsey and Sarah stepped out.

"You two okay?" asked Declan.

Sarah nodded. "We'll be better when we get our children back." She looked around. "Any ideas?"

"Jasper was asking about the Council meeting," said Hannah. "Ramsey, you and Declan were the ones there. Did Andolina do or say anything to make you take notice? Something that didn't make sense to you at the time?"

Declan noted his brother didn't look much better than when he'd entered the bedroom.

Ramsey cleared his throat. "Other than the part where she threw me across the room, threatened my family, and casually discarded Burke like he was shit on her shoe? No. Not at all."

"There was something," said Declan. He pointed. "When she knocked you backward. Remember?"

"Vividly," said Ramsey. He rubbed his back.

"Daphne told you and Royce to shut up," said Declan.

"Nothing new there," said Ramsey.

"And Andolina said we should listen to her. We should listen to Daphne," said Declan.

His brother paused, but then his eyes narrowed.

"She knew Daphne's name?" asked Jasper.

"She did," said Declan.

"No one else used Daphne's name while she was there?" asked Eve.

"No," said Ramsey.

"It's a stretch," said Hannah.

"It's a stretch I'm willing to follow," said Grayson.

"Where does Daphne live?" asked Adam.

Declan accessed his phone. "I can find out." He dialed a number, listened for a moment, then cursed. "No one's answering." He hung up and tried again.

"I can try Morgana," said Ramsey, pulling out his phone. "She'll know."

"You think we should involve her?" asked Declan, trying to call again. "That's one more person we might put at risk."

"I don't care if she's at risk or not," said Ramsey. "Morgana's always been skilled at taking care of herself." He swiped at his cell's screen.

"I can get the address," said Vee, stepping forward. "I just need a last name."

Ramsey stopped, and Declan put his phone down.

"That's a good idea," said Adam.

Jasper nodded, and Declan gave her the last name. Vee stepped back and dialed a number.

"What happens once we have the address?" asked Eve.

Ramsey walked to the entry and picked up his car keys. "Daphne better hope to hell she's got answers, or her current problems are going to be minor compared to the shitstorm she's about to face." He gripped the keys. "She'll wish she never met me."

"Should we all go?" asked Declan. "I think a small group would be better."

"I'm going with John," said Sarah. She walked up beside him.

Jasper sat on the couch. "I'll stay. Eve, Adam, Grayson. I'd like you to stay too." He glanced at Vee on the phone. "She'll stay as well."

Grayson blanched. "I should go. This is my wife. If that woman knows something..."

"You'll be the first to know," said Declan. He grabbed Hannah's hand. "You're human, Grayson. It's better you stay here. Hannah and I will go with John and Sarah. We'll talk to Daphne and let you know what she says."

"What does being human have to do with anything?" Grayson picked up his jacket.

"Grayson," said Jasper. "I need you to stay. You may be able to help."

Vee hung up the phone. "Got it. She's actually not too far from here."

"Give Ramsey and Declan the address," said Jasper. "We're staying put."

Vee looked at Declan, her face unsure.

"You know too much as it is," said Declan. "Besides, you're a police officer, and I'm pretty sure my brother's on the verge of some illegal activity."

"You bet your ass," said Ramsey.

"So you stay," said Grayson. "But I go." He headed toward the door.

"You want to find your wife?" asked Jasper.

"Is that a trick question?" said Grayson.

"Then what I'm about to show you could be more effective than finding Daphne. She may not know a thing."

Grayson stopped, his brow furrowed.

"You all have a connection to these people," said Jasper. "Eve to her siblings and you to your wife. That's critical and there are ways to use that. Let them go talk to Daphne. That has merit, but we can also be helpful here. Maybe even more so."

Grayson paused, closing his eyes. He groaned.

"Trust me," said Jasper. He spoke to Declan. "Go. Let us know what you find out."

Ramsey took the address. "Come on."

Chapter Eighteen

ROYCE SAT ON THE floor in an empty room. White walls and a gray-tiled floor were the only colors in the small space. It was quiet. The only thing he could recall about getting here was waking up on his back. His last memory was getting into the rear seat of a black SUV with tinted windows. That was it. He didn't even know who was driving the car. He had some sense there was someone else present besides Andolina. A man may have been in the driver's seat, but he couldn't be sure.

His arms and legs felt heavy, and he wondered if he'd been drugged. Slowly, he tested his limbs and stood. Everything worked as before. But his head felt like someone had poured gravy in his ear.

There didn't appear to be any entry point into the room. He didn't see a door or any exit in the ceiling or floor. It was all white tile. He walked around, feeling the walls, looking for any weak points, but found none. He thought of Gillian. Was she nearby?

"Hello?" he asked, but his voice echoed back at him. He pounded on the tile. "Anyone here?" There was no answer. He paced for several seconds. This didn't look like the inside of any building he'd been in before. He was about to bang on the tile again when there was a whoosh and a portion of the wall slid open, revealing a narrow door-way. Andolina entered the room wearing the same outfit, her hair still stick-straight. Royce assumed he'd not been out long, unless Andolina wore the same outfit every day.

She stepped farther into the room and the door closed behind her. Royce thought of Star Trek and the doors that closed on the Enterprise. It wasn't much different. Was he on her ship? Was Gillian here too?

"Where's Gillian?" he asked.

"We'll get to that," she answered. "Where's the letter?"

Royce paused, considering his options. "You'll get nothing from me until I know she's safe."

The side of her mouth ticked up. "Such the big brother."

Royce didn't answer. Seconds passed before she stepped back. "Very well." She crossed her arms. "Open it."

A panel on the opposite side of the room slid open. It revealed another chamber, much like Royce's, but this one had a small white sofa and Gillian was sitting on it.

"Gillian..." Royce ran toward her but stopped when he saw the barrier separating him from her. He banged on the glass. "Gillian." She did not react.

"She can't hear you," said Andolina. "She's in a soundproof room and all she can see is the same white walls. She has no idea you're there."

Royce smacked the glass again, but to no avail. Gillian put her elbows on her knees and pushed her hair back. The good news was that she was unharmed. He turned toward Andolina. "Let her out."

"In due time. First, I want the letter. Where is it?"

Royce hesitated. "I don't understand why you want it. There's nothing in there that says where Sarna is. It's useless."

Andolina walked along the border of the room. "That's where you're wrong. You still lack the knowledge of what's possible. Your father could have taught you a few things."

Royce ignored the mention of his dad. He didn't need grief clouding his focus. "What happens to them if you find them?"

"*When* I find them." She leaned back against the wall. "I'll inform my superior. But I think you know."

"Your superior? Roma?"

"Your half-sibling."

Royce set his jaw. "Wish I could meet her."

Her lip ticked up again. "I'm sure you do."

"How'd you end up becoming her servant?"

She smiled fully then. "You're stalling."

"Just a question." A stabbing pain hit him in the belly, and he went down on his hands and knees.

He heard her heels click against the floor. "You'll find if you cooperate, this will all go a lot more smoothly. There's no need to suffer."

Royce held his stomach and grimaced. "I want you to let go of Gillian."

"No."

Royce groaned as the pain sharpened and twisted. It was hard to breathe.

"The letter."

Royce gritted his teeth. Sweat popped out on his skin. The agony moved into his chest, and he slid and fell sideways into the fetal position.

Andolina squatted beside him. "Pride never saved anyone. You're just drawing this out."

He tried to talk, but it was difficult to form words. "Go to hell." It was barely a whisper.

She waited, and Royce shut his eyes against the agony. He almost screamed when the pain dissipated and was gone as quick as it came. Royce went limp and a cold trickle of sweat ran down his back. He sucked in a deep lungful of needed air.

"Hurts, doesn't it?" Andolina asked. She stood and walked toward the glass. Gillian stood and pounded on the tile as he had done. He couldn't hear it, though. She made no indication that she could see anything other than the walls around her.

"You're stubborn, like your father," said Andolina. "I wonder if your sister is too."

Royce reached out. "No," he said, but his words fell on deaf ears as he watched Gillian fall to the floor, gripping her belly.

Andolina grinned.

****

"Sit with us," said Jasper to Grayson. He moved to the side of the couch. He waved at Vee too, who still seemed to be hesitant. He patted the seat beside him. Grayson hesitated, and Jasper couldn't be sure if he was angry or sad. Probably both.

Finally, Grayson sighed, came over, and sat on the other end of the couch. Vee sat in the middle.

"I hope you know what you're doing," said Gray. He threw his jacket over the arm of the sofa.

"What are your plans?" asked Adam.

"How are we going to help find them?" asked Eve.

Jasper clasped his hands together. "It's called Sensing on our planet, or that's the closest translation. On this planet, you would call it remote viewing. It's a more advanced skill, but not as difficult when there's a lot at stake."

Grayson swiveled on the couch. "Are you kidding me? Remote viewing?"

"I've heard of it before," said Eve. "I've always wondered if that was possible."

"Is this where you try to connect with your loved ones? See where they are?" asked Adam.

"Yes."

"That's ridiculous. That will never work," said Grayson. He muffled a curse. "I should have gone with them."

"Actually, I believe the military has used remote viewing," said Vee. "Not that they'll admit it. But I understand they've had some success with it."

"This is absurd," said Grayson. "We need to be talking to Daphne."

"You're sitting in a room with three Eudorans, one of whom just flew in on his spacecraft, and you call this absurd?" said Vee.

Grayson opened his mouth, but nothing came out except a sigh.

"I say we give it a shot," said Adam.

"Humans have abilities they don't give themselves credit for," said Jasper. He pointed between him and Adam. "We are only who you will become."

Grayson dropped his head. "I don't know if I should laugh or cry."

Jasper sat forward. "Neither. Just listen. All of you have connections to Royce, Gillian, and even the children, although the Ramseys have a better shot at finding them. But we can use this to our advantage." He paused. "All you need to do is quiet your mind and pay attention."

Grayson groaned.

Jasper ignored him. "We need some paper and some pencils."

Vee stood. "I saw an office. I'll go look."

"Thanks." He sat on the floor in front of the coffee table. "All of you sit."

Eve and Adam followed his lead and sat on the carpet. Grayson raised a brow, but then finally agreed and sat beside them.

Vee returned. "I found a notebook and some pens." She ripped off pages and gave everyone some paper and something to write with.

"Sit beside me," said Jasper, motioning to Vee. He knew there was little she could do during this exercise, but he liked having her there. She sat next to him. "Now, take a deep breath and go quiet. Clear your minds."

He waited as Eve and Adam both went still and did as he asked. Grayson shook his head, but finally did the same. He smiled when he saw Vee was doing it too.

He allowed a minute or two to pass until he felt the energy in the room calm. Then he closed his eyes as well. "Take your time with this. Go slowly, but focus in on your loved one. See them in your head. Feel their presence."

He focused in on Royce. He didn't have the connection that Eve had, but the man was still his half-brother and they shared an energetic thread.

"Relax. Just be with them. Allow your mind to guide you and your heart to open. Breathe deeply."

He heard the sound of inhalation and went deeper, sensing that the others were doing the same.

"When you're ready, pick up your pen and write whatever comes to mind. Words. Shapes. Sounds. Colors. Names. Whatever you see. Discard nothing."

Jasper took another deep breath, and an image of Royce slowly coalesced in his mind. Continuing to focus, Jasper watched Royce begin to walk. Jasper picked up his pen and wrote. He heard others do the same.

They sat that way for what seemed like several minutes. Jasper couldn't be sure of the time. He continued, his pen hovering above the page, writing what he saw, when he heard a loud gasp.

"Eve," said Adam.

Jasper opened his eyes. Eve was pale and holding her stomach.

"What's wrong?" asked Adam.

She panted. "Pain. They're in pain."

"Who's in pain?" asked Jasper.

Eve let go of her stomach and some of the color returned to her face. "Gillian and Royce. I felt it."

"What else did you see?" asked Jasper.

She shook her head and closed her eyes. "I don't know. I just … they're scared."

"White," said Grayson. "I saw white. Everywhere."

"I don't know if this means anything, but I saw trees," said Vee.

"There's a ship. In the woods," said Adam. "I saw it. It's big. Much bigger than a usual transport craft."

"Where?" asked Grayson.

"I don't know," said Adam.

"Did you see anything?" Vee asked Jasper.

Jasper sat back, recalling his vision.

"What?" asked Adam.

Jasper stood and walked to the foyer. "I saw a white bag."

"A white bag? What the hell does that mean?" asked Grayson.

Jasper picked up the white plastic bag he'd brought back with him from the hospital. He'd found it in the closet in his room. It contained his tattered clothes they'd removed from him and his shoes. He hadn't bothered to look any further. Grayson had found some clothes for him to wear and he'd thrown the bag in the entry when they'd arrived at Ramsey's mother's house.

In his vision, he'd seen Royce pick up the bag. Jasper had asked an unspoken question. *What are you trying to tell me?* Royce had only smiled.

Holding the bag, Jasper rifled through it, throwing out his dirty clothes, socks, and shoes. At the bottom, he saw it. It was a white envelope. He pulled it out.

"What is it?" asked Adam.

Jasper opened it, feeling a little unsteady. Inside was a white sheet of paper, along with a small picture and another set of folded papers, looking much more worn, as if they'd been opened and closed several times. On the white sheet was a note.

You kept this safe for me once before. I need you to do it again.
R.

Jasper knew exactly what it was. Sarna's letter to Royce.

· · · · · · · · · ·

Ramsey pounded on the door. "Daphne!" He pounded again.

"It's late," said Sarah. "She may be in bed."

"It's not that late." He punched the bell several times and was about to knock on the door again when the lock turned and it opened.

Daphne stood there, still in her make-up, but she wore a robe. "What are you doing?" Ramsey pushed his way past her. "Excuse me. You can't just barge in."

"Your excuses are over Daphne," said Ramsey. Sarah, Declan, and Hannah followed him.

Daphne tightened the sash around her pink robe. "How dare you? The Council will hear about this."

"What Council?" asked Declan. "It was disbanded by Andolina."

Her jaw dropped. "You're not taking that seriously, are you? That woman doesn't care about us. As soon as she gets what she wants, she'll be back home before you can say Earth. She has no interest in our issues or our Council."

"That's where you're wrong," said Ramsey. "She's taken an interest in our children."

Daphne rolled her eyes. "She won't hurt them. She's just using them. Then she'll let them go."

Ramsey walked up to her and put his face close to hers. "You know where they are, don't you?"

Her eyes widened. "I most certainly do not."

"Don't lie to me." Ramsey took her by the elbow and pulled her toward her living room. She squawked all the way. Once he got her there, he pushed her into an overstuffed chair.

"This is madness," said Daphne, gripping the armrests. "What is the matter with you?" She looked at Sarah. "Do you know what's going to happen to all of you once I tell the Council? Once I tell the police?"

Ramsey tried to control his rage. He wanted to punch this woman, and it was taking all of his control to stay cool. Sarah put a hand on his arm, and he instantly breathed easier. How she could project soothing energy to him at a time like this, he didn't know.

"Daphne," said Sarah. "We have no interest in harming you, but if you know anything about where Ethan and Rosie are, then you need to tell us.

My husband is on the precipice of great destruction, and to be honest, I'm not far behind him."

"But I can't tell you what I don't know," said Daphne.

"Andolina knew your name," said Declan. "She used it at the meeting. How is it you're on a first name basis?"

Daphne froze. The color left her cheeks.

Ramsey clenched his fists. "What do you know?"

Daphne didn't answer.

"Just tell us," said Hannah. "I'm sure there must have been a reason why you would put innocent children at risk."

Daphne pulled back. "I would never harm a child. I didn't think..."

Ramsey stepped closer. "You didn't think what?"

Daphne's face fell and for the first time, Ramsey believed the woman was scared.

Sarah squatted beside the chair. "Tell us what you did, Daphne."

"I–I–He came to my house," she sputtered.

"Who came to your house?" asked Declan.

"Burke." She looked away from Ramsey.

Ramsey's heart thumped in his chest. "When?"

If it was possible to look like a ghost, then Daphne did. "Five days ago."

"Five days?" asked Hannah.

"That was right before the explosion," said Sarah.

Ramsey was sure his own face was ghostlike. "Before the explosion?" He clenched his jaw. "What did you tell him?"

She sat up and spoke with more vigor. "He told me what he wanted. Royce. That was all. He wanted the High Child."

"And you gave Royce to him? You gave all of us to him?" asked Declan.

"He didn't want all of you," she yelled. "He told me he wanted to keep this simple. But if he couldn't find Royce, then he would have to do it the dirty way. Said he would go through each of you until someone told him where Royce was. He said he would kill Royce's sisters, then he would have no choice but to harm your families. He told me if he had to, he'd destroy the Council. Nothing would be off limits." She shook her head. "I knew Morgana was going over to your house the next day. That you were having a big dinner with the Fletchers. So I told him Royce would be there."

Ramsey's heart stopped and everything went white. He thought of Leroy and Olivia and Drake. His wife and children.

"What have you done?" asked Declan.

"You killed them," said Hannah.

Daphne went rigid. "I didn't kill anybody. I didn't set the bomb. He was only supposed to find Royce—"

"I'll kill you," Ramsey grabbed her by the shoulders and yanked her up. Daphne screeched.

"Ramsey!"

The shout stopped him cold. Everyone looked toward the voice as Daphne punched at him with little effect.

Morgana stood in the foyer, watching the scene. Talbot, the other councilman, stood beside her. "Let her go," said Morgana. Her steely eyes never left his.

Ramsey tried to breathe. "This woman is to blame for everything. She knows where my children are." He tried not to shake Daphne, but he was only somewhat successful.

"Then I suggest you not kill her." Morgana walked into the room. Her hair was pinned up, and she still wore the same navy-blue pantsuit from the Council meeting, but she had added a navy and white pinstripe scarf. She looked like she'd just stepped off the tarmac of a private jet.

"She told Burke everything," said Sarah.

"I heard," said Morgana. "I see all of you were also curious about how Andolina knew Daphne."

"Now we know," said Talbot. He wore a wrinkled gray suit and looked like he'd just stepped off a red-eye flight.

"I did nothing wrong," said Daphne, squirming in Ramsey's grip.

Ramsey pulled her closer. "You what? That man almost killed my entire family. Leroy and his wife are dead because of you."

She squawked again. "He didn't tell me that was his plan."

"Why didn't you warn us?" asked Sarah. "You could have told us he was coming."

Daphne stopped squirming. "And what would you have done? You would have told Royce. He would have hidden, and Burke would have come after all of us."

Ramsey fought the urge to throw her across the room. "He did come after all of us. Don't you see that?"

"You're hurting me!" screamed Daphne.

"You think this is painful?" asked Ramsey. "I'll show you pain..."

"Ramsey. This accomplishes nothing," said Morgana. "You can take out your anger later. You can borrow my cardboard cutout of her and obliterate it if you wish. Right now, we have to find your children."

Sarah put her hand on his arm. "She's right. I'd love to throttle her too, but we can't."

Ramsey gritted his teeth. He envisioned shoving Daphne into a pile of sharp instruments and watching her writhe in pain, but knew it was pointless. Forcing himself to take a breath, he shoved Daphne back into the chair. Daphne fell into it with a gasp and the chair tilted backwards.

"Then somebody better get her to talk, because if I have to do it, she's gonna find out what it's like to be inside a burning home." He lowered his voice and glowered. "With no way to escape."

Daphne sat up. "How dare you—"

"Be quiet, Daphne," said Morgana. She pulled off her scarf and laid it on the couch. "I suggest you consider your next words carefully. Unless you prefer to be medium rare before this day is done."

"Try well done," said Ramsey.

Daphne huffed. "I don't know anything."

Morgana stepped in front of Ramsey, blocking Ramsey's path to Daphne. Ramsey thought that was smart. He moved back, and Sarah put her arm around him.

Morgana crossed her arms and faced Daphne. "You may think that, but I'm sure Burke must have told you something that might be of some use. Think. I know it's not your strength, but try anyway."

Daphne curled her lip. "You've always thought you were so high and mighty. I've tried for years to get you replaced as head of the Council."

Morgana leaned down, putting her hands on the arms of the chair. "I know, Daphne. Why do you think you failed?"

Daphne scowled and leaned back.

"Tell us about Burke's visit. What did he tell you?"

"Nothing about taking the children. He didn't mention them."

"He may not have spoken of it specifically, but any detail may be important. Don't assume anything."

Daphne wrung her hands. "He said he would kill Royce, but he told me he would take him to his ship first."

"Ship?" asked Declan. "Where?"

"He didn't say. It's not like he had a map."

"What else?" asked Morgana.

"Once he had Royce, he and his associate would take care of it. He said they would do it quick."

"His associate?" asked Talbot.

"Desde. He called her Desde."

"And where is this Desde?" asked Morgana.

"How should I know? I assume on his ship, waiting for his return."

"That's going to be a long wait," said Declan. "With Burke gone, Desde will be reporting to Andolina now."

"Undoubtedly," said Morgana, straightening. "Andolina arranged to have Gillian taken and for Desde to find the children. Desde likely took Ethan and Rosie to Burke's ship to wait. It's the most logical place."

"How do we find that?" asked Talbot.

They all regarded Daphne, who dropped her chin. "Well, don't look at me."

"We draw her out," said Declan.

"What do you mean?" asked Hannah.

Declan thought about it. "Based on what Royce told us about Desde, we know she's vain, vapid, and power hungry. She'll stop at nothing to get what she wants. If we can offer her something, we may be able to bring her out into the open. Expose her."

"What could we offer her that Andolina can't?" asked Ramsey.

The room went quiet as they considered the question.

Sarah stepped forward. "What about me?"

Ramsey held his breath. "Absolutely not."

"Why you?" asked Morgana. "How would that benefit Desde?"

Sarah regarded Hannah. "You told me what Burke said. That he considered bringing me back to Eudora as a gift to Roma. Maybe Desde would be just as interested."

Ramsey's body temperature took a nosedive. "There is no way in living hell we are using you as bait. It's too dangerous."

"It's not a bad idea," said Talbot.

Sarah faced him. "If it can bring our children back, it's worth it."

Ramsey shook his head. "Or I could end up losing all of you."

"Desde's not dumb. She'll smell a trick from a mile away. She'd have to believe it," said Declan.

"We are not doing this," said Ramsey.

Declan's face softened. "Listen. I know this is scary, but if Desde goes for it, and she ends up bringing Sarah back to the ship, it would be like breadcrumbs leading us straight there. Sarah's not helpless either."

"That's what I'm afraid of. Desde will take precautions to ensure Sarah is subdued," said Ramsey. He took Sarah's hand. "She could hurt you."

Morgana raised a brow. "If Desde is power hungry, like Burke, then this might work."

"If she thinks she has the upper hand, that could be her downfall," said Hannah.

"Sarah..." Ramsey didn't know what else to say.

Sarah cupped his face with her hand. "You would do it in a heartbeat. I wouldn't like it, but I would trust your judgement. Now you have to do the same for me." He put his hand over hers. "I'll be okay, and so will our kids. I promise."

Ramsey knew she couldn't guarantee that outcome, but he knew his wife. If she'd made up her mind, she was going to do it, especially if it meant protecting her children. He groaned and pulled her close. "I don't want you to do this."

"I know. But I have to. This is Ethan and Rosie. We have to do whatever it takes to get them back."

He bit his lip, knowing she was right. His throat tightened. "You better come back to me," he whispered in her ear.

"I will," she whispered back.

"There's just one problem," said Declan. "How are we going to find Desde? It's not like we have her cell phone number."

"Actually, we might," said Talbot. He nodded at Morgana, who pulled a small silver square object out of her pantsuit pocket.

"We found this in Burke's jacket," said Morgana. "It's beeped a few times. It's similar to something Adam used when he came to Earth. We think it's a communication device."

Declan stepped close, took the object and studied it. "Well, that's helpful. Anyone know how to work it?"

"I'm sure we can figure it out. But the bigger question is who is going to offer Sarah to Desde? Who is Desde going to trust enough to even consider it?" asked Talbot.

Morgana regarded Daphne. "I can think of one person."

Chapter Nineteen

"No. Stop. Leave her alone." Royce tried to stand, but his legs had no power. He watched in misery as Gillian curled into the fetal position, holding her belly. "I'll tell you," he screamed. "I'll tell you where the letter is. Just stop."

Gillian's tension eased, and she went still. Royce dropped his head to the ground. "Don't hurt her anymore."

Andolina leaned over him. "I didn't have to hurt her. Nor you, for that matter. You just chose to be stubborn." She sighed. "That's a strong trait in your family. Roma has it too."

He lifted his head. "You're doing all of this because my sister is worried about losing her precious seat on the throne?"

"Basically, yes." She straightened and walked back to the wall. "Plus, we can't have a half-human take power. It's unheard of. Your ascension risks many people in important positions. It would tip the balance in ways you would not understand. Plus, by keeping you away, I improve my position and standing. As you say on this planet, it's a win-win."

Royce struggled to get up, but his limbs were shaky. He kept an eye on Gillian who was still lying on the ground. "And what about my father? Was his death at another's hand?"

She moved around the room, aimlessly running her hand along the wall. "Your father was a popular leader, but he was weak. Galen knew that. Your father confided in him, and it was his downfall. It was only a matter of time before he would be ousted. He could have prevented it, but that stubborn trait, plus his love for his family, was what brought him down."

Royce got his wobbly legs under him and stood. Sweat trickled down his back. "Jasper told me last year that he was sick."

"He was, and rightly so. He was being poisoned."

Royce swayed. "What?"

"He figured it out eventually, but not before it was too late."

Royce's heart thumped. "How can you live with yourself? How can Roma?"

She rested against the white tile. "Not that hard, really. Now, let's get back to business."

"What about Jasper? He's Roma's brother. He knows what you're doing. How do you plan to handle him?"

She cocked her head. "Jasper. Probably the most stubborn of all of you. We tried unsuccessfully to get him to reveal Sarna's location, but he kept quiet. I'm impressed he survived. He's quite loyal to you."

Royce recalled Jasper's unexpected and disheveled appearance in the Ramsey's backyard. "What happens to him after this?"

"Since he's her brother, Roma will likely have him banished. He's been a thorn in her side for a long time."

Royce walked over to the glass where he could see Gillian. She was slowly uncurling and seemed to be okay. "What happens to her once you have the letter?"

Andolina paused. "I have my orders."

Royce put his hand on the wall. "There's no point in giving you anything if you're going to kill her."

"Which is why I have been given permission to spare her. Eve, too, provided you cooperate. As long as they remain on Earth, they will be safe. Unfortunately, I cannot provide the same protection for you."

"I don't care about me. I just don't want her and Eve harmed."

Andolina nodded. "I've never been fond of killing pregnant women. So, do me and yourself a favor and tell me where Sarna's letter is."

"What about the Ramsey children?"

"They will be released as well."

"And Sarna and my daughter? What happens to them?"

Andolina hesitated. "Roma wants their location. What happens after that is out of my hands."

Royce swiveled toward her. "I'm supposed to sacrifice the woman I love and my child to you?"

She studied him. After a moment, she stepped away from the wall and approached him. "I have some sway. I will try to have them banished. But I cannot guarantee anything. It's the best you can hope for."

He looked back and saw Gillian stir and push up. She was shaky, but managed to get back up on the couch. She held her head and rubbed her stomach. Royce's heart broke when he saw her wipe a tear off her cheek. He took a deep breath. "Fine. I know who has the letter."

"Who?"

Guilt weighed him down and he slumped. "Jasper."

Andolina's brow furrowed. "Jasper is on Eudora."

"You might want to check with your superiors. He escaped and found his way here. He came to warn me. Unfortunately, Burke arrived first."

"Jasper is here? On Earth?"

"Yes."

She chuckled. "Jasper never ceases to surprise me. He has more lives than all these earthly cats of yours." She paused. "You understand he must not refuse me, or I cannot guarantee the safety of anyone."

"He won't refuse you."

"Where is he?"

"Last I saw, he was in the hospital. I put the letter in a bag with his belongings. You'll have to figure the rest of it out on your own."

Andolina squinted her eyes, gauging his truthfulness. After a few seconds, she stepped away. "Very well. Let's hope he cooperates."

"I want Gillian and the Ramsey children released once you have it."

"You have my word. And I'll make it quick for you. You won't suffer."

Royce closed his eyes. "If you have any say in it, then protect my daughter. I don't care what you do with me."

He heard nothing for a moment, then only footfalls on the tile and a whooshing sound. He opened his eyes and saw she was gone.

· · · · · · · · · ·

Vee knocked softly. She stood outside the door to the main bedroom, which she assumed belonged to Ramsey's mother. Glancing into the living room, she saw Eve and Adam sitting on the couch, talking softly. Eve still held her stomach, as if she still felt the ghostly pain. Grayson had stepped outside for a moment, needing air. He was restless, and Vee worried he would do something rash, and probably would have already, if he knew what to do or where to aim his anger.

She knocked again. Jasper had disappeared into the room shortly after finding the letter. She'd given him some time, but the longer she stood there, the more out of place she felt, like a bowling ball at a Ping-pong game. Why was she here?

She heard a soft "come in" and opened the door. Stepping inside, she saw Jasper sitting at a desk. He held folded papers, slid them into an envelope, and put them into an interior jacket pocket. She closed the door. "The natives are getting restless out there. Is everything okay?"

"I read the letter. I know why she wants it."

Vee closed the door and held up a hand. "Listen. Before we get any further into this, I'm going to leave."

He stood. "No. You should stay. Your position, familiarity, and knowledge of this town make you a powerful asset."

"I'm a police officer. There are about a million rules I've broken since I found those pills. There are children missing, plus Grayson's wife." He stepped closer and that familiar tingle she had first felt at the hospital buzzed louder. She couldn't figure out why it wouldn't go away. "I have to follow my instincts."

"And what are your instincts?"

"To report this. To tell my superiors what is happening here. If this goes bad, it will be my fault."

"No. It won't. And those aren't instincts. That's just logic. Do you really think if you tell them they'll be able to help?"

She opened her mouth to speak, but then had to consider the question. "They may not be able to find this Desde person, but it's more eyes looking. You don't know where they are. If she brings them out into the open, somebody might see them. There's also Gillian Fletcher to consider. Her husband is a powerful man. One word from him could bring in the cavalry. That would help too. I'm surprised he hasn't done it already."

He sat on the bed and patted the space beside him. "Sit down."

Cautious, she sat, but a comfortable distance from him.

"I know all of that sounds perfectly reasonable and makes sense. But we're not dealing with your basic human kidnapper. Desde has a variety of talents and if she feels threatened or backed into a corner, she'll use them. What do you think would happen if your police force found her and tried to bring her in? She could fling them across the room, break their bones, crush their throats, take their weapons. It puts your people at risk, as well as the kids. The same for Gillian. Grayson knows that. His people are no match against Andolina. Plus, I don't believe they wish to harm the children. Once they have what they want, they'll let them go."

She shook her head. "I've been doing this job too long. I've seen plenty of times where nothing went as planned."

He was quiet for a moment, then reached over and put his hand over hers. Heat traveled up her arm, and she almost pulled away. "Ask yourself something," he said. "How did you find my pills? They were in the woods on an invisible other-worldly craft. Was it logic or something else?"

Vee thought back. His questions were only confusing her more. "It wasn't logic."

"No. It wasn't." He paused. "You trusted your gut, and it led you in the right direction. It's hard for people to do, but it's going to be crucial for us. I've found through all of this that it's been the moments I've trusted my inner guidance that are the most powerful, even when things are at their worst." He squeezed her fingers and the tightness in her shoulders eased. It was a strange sensation. "I know this is a lot to process. You're talking to someone from outer space whom you've just met and you're questioning everything. It's why we can't reveal who we are. Most won't accept it and will fear it. But, as you may have figured out by now, there are some of you who kind of like us, and we found and Binded with them, which is how we find ourselves in this situation."

"Bind?"

He smiled. "When Red-Lines take a mate. Sort of like marriage, but not really."

There was so much swirling in her head, she didn't know what to say. "I just think—"

"Stop doing that. That's why you're confused." He stood and pulled on her hand. She stood beside him. "What does your heart tell you? Listen to that."

Her heart was thumping, and she didn't want to talk to it, because she suspected what it might say. *Stay. Trust him. You have a place here.* But she didn't want to believe it. Too many times she'd been called crazy for following her heart, and she didn't want to go through it again. The only one who'd truly understood her had been her father.

"You have a place here, Vee," he said. "I think you know that." She startled when he'd repeated her own inner thoughts back to her. "I don't know why, but you found your way to us. That wasn't logic, that was fate. I think that's been your path all along."

"But why? Who am I? What do I have to offer?"

He smiled again, and her heart flipped. *God. What was the matter with her?* "You don't know? You have more skills than you realize. You're highly intuitive, Vee. I suspect you're picking up on things right now that are surprising you. It's happening to me too. I didn't expect..." He rubbed his thumb over her palm.

She swallowed, and her cheeks warmed. Could he hear her heart beating? Or was his heart beating as fast as hers? Just the thought made her think it was true. Did he have feelings for her? But they'd just met. And he wasn't from Earth. *Hell. She was falling for an alien.* What would her dad think about that?

She took a deep breath. "I don't know what to believe."

He took a step closer. "Maybe I should take my own advice. We should both trust our instincts."

She watched in slow motion as he reached out with his free hand and touched her cheek, then trailed his fingers down her jaw and to the back of her neck, where he pulled her closer. Her heart racing, she thought she should resist, but the pull was too strong. Leaning close, his face stopped near hers, his lips only inches away. His breath fanned against her skin, and he smelled like almonds. A need so strong swirled in her belly, making it hard to breathe. It took all her strength not to jump into his arms. Taking his advice, she stopped thinking and moved closer. Their lips brushed together when there was a loud pounding on the door. Vee jumped back.

Grayson's voice traveled. "Hello? What's going on in there? Are we just going to sit on our asses all day?"

Chapter Twenty

RAMSEY SAT IN THE passenger seat of Declan's car, watching and listening. The seconds ticked by as fast as a sloth uncurled from sleep. He questioned for the millionth time what he was doing. Using his wife to bring out the bad guys brought up too many hard memories he'd tried to forget. He didn't know which was worse, almost losing Sarah to another evil Red-Line a few short years ago or losing his kids now. They were equally devastating. And now she was risking her life again.

He sighed, and Declan looked over from the driver's seat. "She'll be okay. She's a smart lady, and she can handle herself."

"Would you say that if this was Hannah?"

Declan raised a brow at him. "Probably not, but you'd be telling me the same thing."

Ramsey thought of Leroy, who'd given him similar advice in the past. He missed his friend's calm presence. He needed it right now.

Hannah leaned forward from the back seat. "You'd be a basket case and you know it." She patted Ramsey on the shoulder. "But he's right. Sarah knows what she's doing. This will work."

A male voice came over a walkie-talkie that Declan held. "There's a car approaching from the west."

They turned and saw a dark sedan coming down the street. It slowed in front of Daphne's house and pulled into the driveway. The windows were tinted, and Ramsey couldn't see the driver. The car idled in front of the house.

Once they'd decided to move forward with the plan, despite Daphne's initial reluctance, they'd managed to figure out Burke's "phone" if that's what it was called. After calling and talking to Adam, they'd accessed a panel, and punching a few buttons, there'd been a beep, then static, and a female voice had answered. Daphne had handled the conversation well. Confirming it was Desde, she'd mentioned Burke's untimely demise and his interest in Sarah. Desde seemed to have no reaction to Burke's death, so she either already knew or it was confirmed she was a psychopath. Daphne inquired if Desde valued Sarah as much as Burke. There'd been a pause, but then she'd shown interest. She wanted to meet. Not wanting to waste time, Daphne had provided her home address and told her to come in two hours. After the phone call, they'd come up with a plausible story, and Declan called in his crew. They'd contacted Grayson and given him an update. Within an hour, they'd installed a couple of listening devices in Daphne's house and had a man on the street. Morgana and Talbot were in Talbot's car down the road, listening as well.

Several seconds passed, and Ramsey saw the back door of the idling car finally open. A woman with long, curly, blonde hair emerged from the back seat, wearing slim black pants, a snug fitting red V-necked shirt, and a black leather jacket. Her heels were at least four inches high.

"Apparently, she likes earthly shopping," said Hannah.

"I wonder where she gets the earthly money?" asked Declan.

"Probably better we don't know," said Hannah.

Ramsey held his breath as Desde approached the front door and rang the bell. The sound of a door chime traveled through Declan's phone. It was clear and easy to hear.

Daphne answered the door. By then, it was after ten o'clock, but Daphne had changed out of her robe and reapplied her heavy make-up. Apparently, this sort of situation required it.

"Come in," said Daphne. Her voice traveled clearly.

They watched Desde walk inside and the door shut behind her.

"Here we go," said Talbot's voice over the walkie-talkie. Ramsey forced air into his lungs.

They heard footsteps on Daphne's tile floor. "I must admit, your phone call intrigued me," said Desde.

"I'm sure it did," said Daphne. "I suspect I was the last person you expected to hear from."

"Burke mentioned he'd spoken to you. But I'm curious. How did you know to contact me?"

Ramsey waited to hear Daphne's answer. This was the part that was tricky, making sure their cover story was plausible. If Desde smelled deception, she'd be gone, and would likely leave somebody dead in her wake.

"I'm a member of the Council. I know a lot of things, including your involvement with Royce Fletcher. The man hates you."

Ramsey heard a faint laugh. "Most men do," said Desde. "But he was one of my more memorable conquests."

"I don't doubt it."

There was a brief pause. Ramsey tapped on the car door panel until he heard Desde speak. "I'm curious. What's in this for you? Why give up one of your own?"

"Have a seat," said Daphne. "I'm not stupid. I can see the writing on the wall. You and Andolina are powerful women. Burke was powerful too."

"Burke was stupid. He should have known better. To be honest, it's better he's gone. Too many roosters in the henhouse. Is that your saying?"

"Close enough."

"Andolina is different though," said Desde. "She knows what she wants, and she gets it. I'm the same way. Burke just wanted to impress Roma."

"Isn't that what you want?"

Another pause. "Easy, Daphne," said Declan. "Don't piss her off."

"No. It's perfect," said Ramsey. "It's exactly what Desde likes. Directness."

Desde spoke. "He wanted to get her in the sheets. He'd always had a thing for her, and she knew it. Used it, too. Men are always so weak when it comes to sex. I just want power. Like Andolina."

"Which is why I got in touch," said Daphne. "Andolina disbanded our Council. I've been trying for years to get rid of that hag, Morgana, and now I have a shot. I figure if I show a little good faith, maybe you'll put in a good word for me. I give you Sarah, and you make me head of the new Council."

Another moment of quiet ensued. "She's good," said Talbot over the line.

"Too good," said Morgana. "Remind me to banish her when this is done."

Declan smiled.

"Interesting," said Desde. "I suspected there was corruption in your group. You couldn't all be sunshine and rainbows. I'm glad to see I was correct."

"You are," said Daphne. "I'm tired of the status quo here. Plus, Sarah's husband Ramsey is a pain in my ass. This might shut him up for a while."

Morgana's voice returned. "On second thought, maybe we'll keep her."

Ramsey grabbed the walkie-talkie and clicked the button to speak. "She better pray this goes well."

Desde's voice returned. "I find that men usually are, especially the good-looking ones."

Daphne made a scoffing noise. "I find him to be quite unattractive."

The walkie-talkie clicked. "Maybe I'll give her my job," said Morgana.

Ramsey clicked the button again. "You're enjoying this, aren't you?"

"Immensely," came the response.

"Shhh," said Hannah. "They're talking."

"I like you, Daphne. You remind me of me," said Desde.

"I was going to say the same thing about you," replied Daphne.

"Maybe she's a little too good at this," said Declan.

"Okay," replied Desde. "I'll put in a good word for you and you give me Sarah Ramsey. I'll take her to Roma, and Roma can use her as she sees fit. A half-human, half Red-Line would be of great interest back home. We so rarely see such oddities. I know Burke liked her."

Ramsey rubbed a hand through his hair.

"She's a healer," said Daphne.

"It's unusual for a crossbreed," said Desde.

"God," said Ramsey. "What the hell are we doing?"

"Getting your children back from this witch," said Declan.

"Where is she?" asked Desde. "She's not going to just board my ship."

"She's in the bedroom, sleeping," said Daphne.

"At a time like this? With her children missing?"

The walkie talkie squawked. "Let's hope she buys it," said Talbot.

Daphne spoke. "She's a wreck. Completely blindsided by all of this. When she heard what happened, she blamed her husband. They got in a huge fight. Morgana called and spoke with her, told her what happened with Burke and Andolina at the Council meeting. Apparently, she mentioned me. Next thing I know, Sarah's at my door, demanding to know what was going on and where her children were, as if I knew anything. She was accusing everyone. I think she's gone a bit off the rails, if you ask me. But it gave me the idea. Why not use her for my own gain? I made her a cup of tea, added a little sedative to it, got her to rest, and called you."

There was a pause, and the slow click of heels on a hardwood floor could be heard. Ramsey imagined Desde walking around the living area, considering what to do next.

"What happens when she wakes?" asked Desde.

"You make her an offer. You'll release her children when she agrees to go with you."

"Who says I have the children?"

Ramsey held his breath.

"It's the only logical conclusion," said Daphne. "If you don't, then Andolina must, but I figured she was dealing with Royce and Gillian."

Ramsey bounced his knee up and down. This conversation was killing him.

"You're right. I do," said Desde. "But believe me, it's not an assignment I relish."

Ramsey let go of his breath. At least now they'd confirmed she had Ethan and Rosie.

Desde continued. "It's a good thing their grandmother is with them, otherwise I'd have drowned them hours ago."

Ramsey gripped the door handle and almost jumped out of the car, but Declan grabbed his arm. Ramsey cursed, but then let go and sat back.

"Children require patience and attention," said Daphne, "which is why I never had any."

Desde chuckled. "You are one of the sanest earthlings I've ever met."

"So, we have a deal?"

Desde stayed quiet.

"You think she'll go willingly?" asked Desde.

"You have her kids. She'll do whatever you say. You take her to them, show her they're safe, then let them go. You keep Sarah and return to Eudora and show her off to Roma. I become a head of the Council here and get Ramsey and Morgana out of my hair. Then, if you ever return, you know I'm here to provide you with whatever you need. It sounds perfect to me."

"I will have to ask Andolina. We didn't plan on bringing anyone back with us."

Ramsey shuddered. "Hell. If she talks to Andolina, Sarah could be screwed. She can't fight them both."

"Andolina will see right through this," said Declan. "Come on, Daphne. Think it through."

They waited for Daphne's response.

"Why bother her?" asked Daphne. "She's busy dealing with Royce. Wouldn't it be better to just show up with Sarah? I would think that would communicate that you're smart enough to handle things on your own. Plus, Sarah's presence only benefits Andolina. I would think she would appreciate you taking care of this." She paused. "But that's only my opinion. You know her better. Maybe you should ask permission first."

Declan nodded. "Good. She's appealing to Desde's ego."

"Only if it works," said Ramsey. His heart was thumping so hard, he wondered if it would hold out long enough to see this through.

It was quiet for several seconds. Ramsey didn't know how much longer he could wait. Finally, Desde answered. "Go get her."

A collective sigh of relief filled the car. The slight lift in spirits Ramsey felt was muted, though, when he realized Sarah would now be in Desde's hands. His tension ramped up again.

"She did it," said Talbot through the walkie-talkie.

Ramsey heard footsteps, but no voices. They had not placed a microphone in Sarah's room, so they would have to wait until Daphne brought Sarah to Desde. Time moved at a glacial pace. Ramsey was almost ready to launch himself out of the car and into the house when he heard Sarah's voice.

"Who are you?"

High heels clicked. "My name is Desde. I have your children."

"What?" asked Sarah, her voice shocked. "You took Ethan and Rosie? Daphne, what is going on here?"

Daphne responded. "You wanted to find your kids. Well, now you can."

"Where are they? Take me to them now."

"You might want to hear the conditions first," said Desde.

"I know who you are. I know what you've done. Why would you take innocent children?" asked Sarah.

"It seems you've answered your own question," said Desde. "Since you know me so well, then you know I don't do anything without it benefitting me. Daphne here has made a generous offer. You come with me, and I'll bring you to your kids."

"I'll do whatever you want," said Sarah, pleading. "I just want my babies back."

"You don't understand, Sarah," said Daphne. "In exchange for your children, you'll be going with Desde to Eudora."

There was a pause. "Hang in there, honey," whispered Ramsey to no one.

"She's doing great," said Declan.

"Eudora?" asked Sarah.

"My home, and now yours," said Desde. "You'll be all the rage. Like those freaks in your circus. You can assist Roma as needed, plus as a healer, you'll come in handy. She'll love it. And she'll love me for doing it."

"I am not going to Eudora," said Sarah.

"You are if you want your kids released," said Desde, her voice ominous.

"But I'm their mother. I can't leave them."

"Kids adapt," said Desde. "Most mothers suck at the job, anyway."

"Daphne, did you have a hand in this?" asked Sarah, her voice trembling.

"You want your children returned, don't you? Well, here you go," said Daphne.

"This is ridiculous. I'm not leaving my kids behind. How can you expect me to do that?" Sarah's voice raised, and Ramsey could sense her anger even from the car.

Desde spoke slowly. "You are welcome to remain, but it's either you or the children. Someone's going with me. It's your choice."

Ramsey raised his head. "What?" He looked at Declan. "Did she just threaten to take my kids to Eudora?"

Declan's face lost some color. "It's a threat to get Sarah to do as she wants. She's not serious."

"She doesn't even like them," said Hannah.

"Shit," said Ramsey.

"You would take Ethan and Rosie away? From Earth? Why?" asked Sarah. Ramsey could hear the despair in her voice.

"They have just as much appeal as you do. Maybe more so. In fact, I might fetch a nice price from some sweet couple who might want to raise them. What are they? Part Gray, human, and Red. Very unusual. In fact, that might be the better idea."

They heard the clicks of Desde's heels on the floor.

Ramsey was ready to fling the car door open. There was no way in hell this woman was going to disappear without telling him where his kids were.

Morgana's voice returned over the walkie-talkie. "Don't do anything stupid, Ramsey."

Ramsey grabbed the device and hit the button. "Don't tell me what to do."

"Let Sarah handle it," said Morgana.

"She's right," said Declan. "Just wait."

"I'll go with you," said Sarah. "I'll do whatever you want. Just don't take Ethan and Rosie. Please."

Ramsey's heart almost cracked. His own fears combined with Sarah's almost broke him. He leaned forward and held his head. He didn't know how much more he could take.

A quiet voice sounded in his head. *Sherlock. You always did worry too much. Relax. Remember? Trust Destiny.*

Leroy. His voice was clear and quiet, and Ramsey looked up, half expecting to see his best friend standing at the car window.

Desde's response traveled through the phone. "I figured that would help you decide. As much as I'd like the money those kids could bring me, you could bring me much more." There was a pause. "You ready?"

"I need to call my husband," said Sarah.

"You can call him later. Tell him where to pick up the kids. Let's go." Desde's footfalls traveled, and Ramsey envisioned them walking to the front foyer. "Daphne, I'll let Andolina know of your ambitions. I'm sure we can figure something out."

"I'd appreciate that," said Daphne. "You take care, Sarah. Good luck on your journey."

"You better hope I'm long gone," said Sarah, her voice low, "because if I'm not, you'll never see the inside of a council room again. You'll be lucky if you know your own name."

"She's been hanging around you for too long," said Declan to Ramsey.

Ramsey didn't answer because the front door opened. Desde stepped out with Sarah behind her. His wife did not look his way, which was good because he may have lost it. Watching Sarah get in the back seat with a woman like Desde was akin to watching his wife disappear into a burning pyre. He said another silent prayer for her safety.

What did I say, Sherlock? Stop worrying, said the ghostly Leroy.

Shut up. I don't want to talk right now, answered Ramsey.

You have a rock for a head, was the reply. *You never listened to me.* It was so like Leroy, it brought tears to his eyes. Ramsey blinked them back, watching the dark car with his wife inside back up, turn, and drive down the street.

Chapter Twenty-One

JASPER OPENED THE BEDROOM door, his emotions in a swirl. His half-siblings were fighting for their lives and he was trying to kiss Vee. Guilt settled over him, but the energy and heat generated from being in the same room with her would not dissipate. It had started in the hospital when he'd opened his eyes and seen her by his bed. There had been an immediate connection. Falling for an Earth woman had not been on his agenda for this trip, but he knew he shouldn't be surprised. Sarna had never planned to fall for Royce, and now she was the mother of his child. Destiny had a funny way of revealing itself.

Grayson stood there, red-faced and angry. "I just heard from the others. They've confronted Daphne and are planning on using Sarah to find the kids."

Jasper stepped past Grayson and into the living area. "They're doing what they have to do. Desde may find that two angry parents may be more than she bargained for."

Vee came out of the room too. They made brief eye contact, but she looked away.

"The question is, what are we going to do?" asked Grayson. "Our viewing session didn't exactly offer an array of clues to follow."

"I wouldn't say that," said Jasper. "We know Andolina wants this." He pulled the letter out of his pocket. "She'll come looking for it."

"Does the letter reveal Sarna's location?" asked Grayson.

"Not specifically, no," answered Jasper.

Grayson threw out his arms. "Then what good is it?" He paced behind the couch.

"Gray," said Eve. "Try not to worry. We'll get her back."

He stopped. "You said she was in pain."

Eve's face had regained some of its color, but she still looked fatigued. "It's gone now. It didn't last."

"She's pregnant..."

"I know. But I also know that Gillian is strong. So is Royce. They'll take care of each other."

Grayson made a sad chuckle and gripped his forehead. "I hope you're right."

Jasper held up the letter. "It may not have a physical address, but Sarna's energy is all over it. There's even a picture of her and Greta."

"Great. It's full of positive vibes. Maybe a fortune teller will help," said Grayson.

"That's exactly it," said Jasper. "There are people who can do that." He spoke to Eve. "I hear you read animals and objects."

"I do," she said. "I can get feelings and emotions, but I've never discerned a location before."

"You want to try?"

Eve hesitated, her face uncertain, but she reached out. "Let me see it."

Jasper handed her the letter, still in its envelope. She took it, holding it in her hand and closing her eyes. Vee sat on the couch, and Jasper joined her. Grayson remained behind the sofa, but watched with interest.

Eve took some deep breaths and went still. After a minute passed, she spoke. "There's a farmhouse. In the country. I see some animals. It's far away. Not near a city."

"Good," said Jasper. "Keep going. Do you see anything nearby?"

Eve sighed. "Trees. I see a lot of trees. Wait. There's a road." She scrunched her eyes. "It looks like a two-lane highway. But no cars."

"Take your time," said Jasper. "Keep focusing."

Grayson came around the couch and sat in a chair.

"There's a fence around the property. Gray and white." She paused and shook her head. "I feel sadness. Loneliness."

Jasper sat forward. "Try not to focus too much on the emotion. The letter's full of it. Look only at the flatness of it. Meaning the non-emotional parts, if that makes sense."

Eve made a soft smile. "She's feeding the animals."

"Who?" asked Adam.

"A woman. Dark, straight hair. I think it's Sarna." Eve's face softened. "A baby is crying."

"That's good. You're zeroing in on them. Try to get a location," said Jasper.

Grayson watched intently, his elbows on his knees.

"There's a sign on the road," said Eve. "Not at the farmhouse, but across the street."

"What does it say?" asked Jasper.

Eve cocked her head. "I can't read the writing, but there's a picture of an animal. It looks like an ostrich. Its feathers are fluffed out, like it's about to fly."

Jasper nodded. "That's very good, Eve. You're a natural."

Eve opened her eyes. "Is that where Sarna is? On this farm?"

"Hard to say, but Sarna always did like the country. I'm not surprised she's around animals."

"You don't know where she is?" asked Grayson.

Jasper clasped his hands together. "That letter was written a while ago. There's no telling if Sarna is still there or not. She stayed with me until she had Greta, but it became too dangerous after that. I was an obvious target and was being watched. She had to leave."

Eve smoothed the letter, still in its envelope, and put it on the coffee table. "If there's no guarantee that Sarna is still there, then what good is the letter?"

"It's a start," said Jasper. "She could still be at the farm, but if she isn't, it's a good lead. Once you have a starting point, it will make it easier to find her. There will be other objects there that can be read. It will become harder and harder for Sarna to cover her tracks, which is why it's important to keep this out of Andolina's hands. If she gets it, it will only be a matter of time before Sarna is found."

"We're not giving her the letter?" asked Grayson. "What about Royce and Gillian?"

"We'll have to find another way," said Jasper. He stood. "I know this may be bad timing, but I'm starving. Is there anything in this house to eat?"

Grayson jumped out of his seat. "Eat? My wife could die, and you're hungry?"

Eve stood along with Adam. "Nobody's dying," said Eve. "Andolina wants the letter. She won't do anything until she gets it."

Adam held his stomach. "I could eat too."

"This is ridiculous," said Grayson.

Vee left the sofa and walked over to Grayson. "I know it may seem callous, but I've seen people neglect their needs when they're stressed and worried. They get run down, and when the time comes when their loved ones need them, they're depleted. It's late. It's been a long day. You should eat something too. Keep up your strength."

Jasper walked into the kitchen. He recalled the last time he was in one and his unsuccessful attempts to make breakfast. He opened the refrigerator, and Adam joined him. He pulled out a carton of eggs. "You know how to make these things?"

Adam took the eggs from him. "Look for some butter."

Jasper eyed the shelves. "What exactly is butter?"

Vee and Eve came in from the living room. "Find anything?" asked Eve. Adam held up the eggs.

"I'll make some coffee," said Vee.

Jasper watched the door. "Where's Grayson? He needs to eat, too."

"He's sitting on the couch. I think he's trying to call Gillian again," said Eve. She rifled through the pantry and found some coffee grounds and handed them to Vee. "He's understandably upset. How are we going to get Royce and Gilli back without giving away the letter?"

Adam opened and closed drawers until he found a skillet. "I'd like to know the same thing."

Vee added grounds to the filter, then picked up the pot and began to fill it from the sink. "Before I go any further with this, I need to change." She looked down at herself. "I'm still in my uniform. If I stick around and plan to keep a low profile, this won't work."

Jasper found a yellow bar called butter and took it out of the fridge. He handed it to Adam. "You're probably right." He rather liked her in her uniform, but he kept that thought to himself.

"Mrs. Ramsey is around your size. I bet she has something you can wear in her closet," said Eve. "I doubt we'll have time to swing by your place."

"Not anytime soon," added Jasper.

Vee added the water to the machine and flipped the switch. "I'll go look. Coffee will be ready soon."

"So, what's your plan?" asked Adam, as he added butter to the skillet. "How do we get them out of this mess?"

Vee left the kitchen and Jasper made a significant effort not to watch her leave.

Eve placed some salt beside the skillet. "If the others are successful in finding the kids, what happens then? If Desde isn't subdued, she'll go straight to Andolina. That puts Gilli and Royce at even greater risk."

Jasper saw an apple on the counter and picked it up. "The children were another diversion for us to pursue. Andolina wants us scattered, scared and divided. And it's worked. What we need to do is stay together and not let her mental games get to us. The longer we wait, the more she expects us to break. It favors her. We can't let that happen. Plus, I have a plan."

Adam added the eggs to the hot skillet. They sizzled and Adam stirred them. "What plan?"

Vee returned to the kitchen, her face anxious. "We have a problem."

Jasper stopped before he took a bite of his apple. "What?"

She held up a small piece of paper with writing on it. "Grayson's gone, and so is the letter."

·········

Royce dreamed of Sarna. They were laughing, and he was holding her, his arms wrapped around her shoulders. She stretched up on her tiptoes, whispering naughty words in his ear, and he smiled, ready to comply. A baby's cry interrupted, though, and they stopped and looked toward the sound. There was only emptiness, but the cry grew in strength. Sarna pulled away, calling for her child. He tried to follow, but the more he walked, the farther away she became. He called her name, but she didn't hear him. Finally, in the distance, he saw her holding Greta, who settled her head into Sarna's neck. He ran, determined to reach them, but with every step, they faded away until they were gone.

He awoke with a start, eyes blurry and body aching. Blinking, he looked around, seeing white walls and tile. The memories returned. He was lying on the floor on his side, facing the wall where he could still see Gillian. She was sleeping on the white sofa. He rubbed his eyes, wondering how long he'd been out. It surprised him that he'd been able to sleep, but the previous days and hours were a blur and he'd rested for very few of them.

He sat up, groaning. Sleeping on a hard floor did nothing for his back. He stretched and arched, trying to get the kinks out. He wondered how long he'd been out and what time it was. There was no way to know in the small, windowless space. Watching Gillian, he stood. His belly rumbled.

Not long after Andolina had left him, he'd heard a quieter whoosh, and he'd looked to see a small tray slide into the room through a narrow slit in the wall. On it was a cheeseburger and some water. At least they'd given him something decent to eat and not some strange Eudoran plant food. He knew from Sarna and Jasper that Eudorans did not eat meat. Gillian had also been given food, and he'd watched her enjoy her own burger as he polished off his. He wondered why they would feed a dying man, but he had no answers. Probably just out of habit. Or a last meal sort of thing. After his dinner, he'd tried unsuccessfully to bang on the wall to get Gillian's attention, but she continued to stare blankly, while taking bites of her food. It wasn't long after that he must have fallen asleep.

Stretching his arms, he took a few steps and walked up to the transparent wall, watching Gillian rest. He put his palm against it, feeling the coolness against his skin. He closed his eyes, wishing he could talk to her. In his mind's eye, he pictured her stirring and sitting up, knowing somehow he was there. She stood slowly, head tilted, listening and standing. She moved to the wall and touched it. His eyes still closed, he imagined her sliding her fingers along the clear glass, sensing his nearness, until finally, her hand slid over his, separated only by the soundproof tile.

Sighing, he opened his eyes and almost jumped. Gillian stood right in front of him, doing exactly what he'd pictured. She stood at the wall, her arm outstretched and palm over his, with only the transparent tile between them. Her eyes were wide, as if touching something delicate and new for the first time.

"Gillian?" he asked. She made no response, but her hand remained. He realized what was happening. She'd sensed his inner communication and had followed it. He and his sisters had always shared a unique connection, and apparently soundproof walls were not a deterrent. Instead of speaking, he projected his energy, pushing it outward and through the barrier, seeing it reach and permeate her skin.

Her eyes closed, and he saw her mouth a word. *Royce*. She'd said his name. His excitement bubbled up. He was communicating.

A wave of warmth engulfed him, and he smiled. She'd projected her own energy, and it had found him. He took a second to breathe it in, and then he focused, projecting his thoughts through his body and out through his fingers. He waited to see if she'd respond. Within a few seconds, she did. A rush of energy met his, meeting in the middle between their fingers. He pushed harder and so did she. The pressure mounted. Vibrations rippled up his arm, and his skin tingled. After another minute of their combined strength, the wall between them began to tremble. Royce could feel the material between them weaken. He concentrated more and sensed Gillian's response as she increased her own outflow.

The material between them shook more. Tiny cracks formed beneath their hands and splinter outward, weaving a spiderweb of thin lines that reached farther and farther, until one of them widened and split. Royce took his other hand and pushed. The wall in front of him cracked, split some more, and opened. Bits of what felt like plastic hit the ground, making a soft sound against the floor. It wasn't glass and there were no sharp shards. He pushed harder, made a bigger hole, and reached through.

He grinned when Gillian took his hand.

·· · ●·●·●·· ·

They sat at the dinner table eating eggs. "We have to find him," said Adam.

Jasper pushed his plate back. Rushing after Grayson, hungry and late at night, seemed futile. "You try calling him again?" he asked Eve.

Eve nodded. "Yes. He's not answering."

Vee sat across from Jasper, holding her cell, wearing a pair of jeans and a long-sleeved navy sweater. She'd left her uniform in Mrs. Ramsey's room. "I hope to hear something soon. I'm calling in a favor to do this, so it's taking a little longer than usual. As long as his cell phone stays on, though, my contact at the station should be able to find him."

Eve pulled the paper Vee had found on the coffee table toward her. *Trust me* was written in Grayson's scrawl. "If he gives Andolina that letter, Royce is a dead man."

"This is his wife," said Adam. "I understand where he's coming from."

"You'd risk my brother to save me?" asked Eve.

"In a heartbeat," said Adam. "And you know he'd agree with me."

"That bothers me. I would never want to sacrifice Royce for my survival. I couldn't live with myself," said Eve.

"I'd rather have one of you alive instead of both of you dead," replied Adam. His cell rang. "It's Declan." He answered and listened, nodded his head, made a few 'okays,' and hung up. "They followed Sarah and Desde to a hotel. Now they're just waiting. It looks like they may be there for the night. They'll keep us posted."

"That sounds like Desde. Staying at a hotel. Probably getting room service and a massage," said Jasper. He stood from the table and picked up the apple he'd never gotten around to eating. "My guess is she's in for the night. Better to make the exchange during the day."

"I hope they're careful," said Eve.

"As far as Grayson goes, though, we need to figure out where he's headed." Jasper started to take a bite when Vee's phone rang.

She answered, asked a few questions, and wrote on a piece of paper. Hanging up, she said, "They found him. He's at the park."

"The park?" asked Eve. "What park?"

"Primrose. Out on the west side. Just sitting there."

"That's not too far from the Ramsey's house," said Adam. He stood from the table. "Let's go."

Jasper stared at a brown spot on his apple. "Wait."

Vee started to get up but paused. "What is it?"

"How long has he been there? At the park?"

Vee raised a brow. "My guy says he's been there since they pinged his phone. Not long."

"Then we can't waste time," said Adam.

"Hold up." Jasper rubbed the brown spot with his thumb. "Not yet."

Adam's face furrowed. "Why not? We know where he is."

"I think he anticipates that," said Jasper. "Think about it. The man's a tech giant. He makes his living staying ahead of the trends. He knows Vee can track his phone. He's not stupid."

"Then why..." Eve tapped at the table, her eyes questioning. "Wait a minute. Is that why he wants us to trust him? He's following Sarah's lead, isn't he? He's planning to lead us to where they are."

Jasper walked to the sink and rinsed his apple. "That's what my gut tells me. It's what I would do. My guess is he was contacted. He has the most at stake. Maybe someone answered when he called Gillian. 'Bring the letter or your wife dies.' He does what they ask, but he trusts we'll follow."

"Why not tell us that?" asked Adam.

"Because we would argue," said Eve. "The man makes a living going on pure instinct. It's what made him rich."

"What happens if they meet him at the park?" asked Vee.

"Grayson will demand to see Gillian. He's not going to give them anything until he knows she's safe. Maybe Royce, too. If he's smart, he'll ask to see both," said Jasper.

"There's no way Andolina is going to bring Gillian and Royce with her to see Grayson. Too much room for error," said Adam.

"Exactly. Which is why she'll bring Grayson to them," said Jasper. "And we'll be right behind him. So we wait."

"Why not go to the park and watch from there?" asked Vee.

"Too risky. Andolina will be cautious. She'll have her radar on. Better to wait until he moves, then follow the ping." He grabbed a paper towel and dried the apple. "There's just one problem."

"Only one?" asked Eve. She sighed and pushed her hair back.

"What?" asked Vee.

"Andolina's not stupid. She's not like Desde. She won't trust Grayson. If she's smart, she'll toss the cell. Or worse yet, Grayson could jump the gun and give her the letter. Then that's it. Of course, if Grayson's successful, then this might work, and we could follow and find Gillian and Royce, but then we have to deal with an angry Andolina, and that's a whole other issue. Finding them is one thing. Getting them out is another. She could end up killing all of us."

Everyone went quiet. Vee sat back in her chair. Eve closed her eyes and groaned.

"You really are a beacon of hope, aren't you?" asked Adam.

Jasper took a bite of his apple.

Chapter Twenty-Two

GRAYSON BLINKED HEAVY LIDS. He'd been sitting in his car, staring at the playground jungle gym, for an hour, when his phone rang, and he answered. "I'm here."

It was a woman's voice. He assumed it was Andolina. "You have it?"

Grayson took his time. "Let's just say I know where it is."

There was a pause. "You like to take risks with your loved ones?"

He breathed deliberately. "I'm not going to give you anything until I get my wife back. How stupid do you think I am? You get nothing until I see Gillian and Royce, alive and well."

"The deal was for your wife, not her brother."

"You think my wife will ever speak to me again if she knows I gave Royce up? I need to see them both, upright and breathing, or I burn the letter."

Another pause. "Wait there. Someone will arrive in the morning."

"The morning?" The line went dead. He hung up. The swing set hung in stillness, and the park was bleak and quiet. It was as spooky as sitting in a cemetery after midnight. He hoped a security guard wouldn't drive by and see him. A strange man, all alone in the dark, near a park playground, would incite too many questions. The last thing he needed was to be hauled off to jail. Hoping for the best, he pulled the lever on his seat and pushed back. If he was going to be here tonight, he might as well get comfortable.

He thought about Eve and the others. They would be angry, no doubt, but he suspected they already knew where he was, if Vee knew how to do her job. He hoped they understood his note and would stay put for now. So far, it looked like they'd gotten the message. If they could just wait and watch, he could lead them right to Gillian and Royce. He pulled up Eve's number on his cell for the hundredth time, but didn't punch the call button. He worried it would tip off Andolina. Like she would hear and discover what he was trying to do, and he couldn't risk Gillian's safety. He didn't even text them. If this was going to work, he had to be the lone wolf, separate from the group, willing to do whatever it took to get Gillian back. If Andolina had any way of checking his phone, it could show no indication of his plan. That's what he'd told himself, at least.

So he stayed where he was, got settled in his seat, and closed his eyes. His stomach rumbled, but he ignored it. He had bigger things to worry about, one of which was what to do when he got to Gillian. He would be expected to turn over the letter. Would Andolina keep her word? And if Gillian was released, what about Royce? Gillian would not leave without her brother. But Gray also knew Royce would want to keep Gillian safe. If he gave Andolina the letter, though, he would be risking the life of not only Royce, but also Royce's lover and child.

He rubbed his tired eyes. Thinking back, he remembered what had happened when the siblings had encountered their Uncle Galen a couple of years earlier and how he'd almost lost Gillian then, too. When threatened, Gillian, Eve, and Royce could be a formidable team. Could they do it again? If Eve joined up with them, would they be able to handle Andolina?

The questions swirled, and his phone buzzed. This time it was a text, and it was from Eve.

I hope you know what you're doing.

Sighing, he stared up at his car ceiling and wondered the same thing.

•••••••••••

Not far away, Ramsey also blinked tired eyes. The light had gone off in the hotel room twenty minutes ago, and he wondered how Sarah was faring. They didn't have a microphone on her, so they couldn't hear anything, but the locator in her shoe transmitted a blinking soft light on a map on Declan's phone. He doubted she was sleeping.

He wondered again why Desde would sleep in a hotel, but he figured there was a good reason. He'd hoped to have his children back by now, but apparently Desde needed her rest.

Declan sat in the driver's seat, his head resting on the cushion. Hannah had laid down in the back seat. They'd told Morgana and Talbot to go home. There was no point in both cars remaining. They would call as soon as there were any developments.

"You should try and rest," said Declan. "Tomorrow could be a long day."

There was a discarded food wrapper on the console and Ramsey put it in a paper bag with the rest of the trash. Morgana and Talbot had brought them some hamburgers before leaving. "I'll rest when my wife and children are safe."

Declan tapped the steering wheel. "Have you thought about tomorrow?"

"That's all I can think about."

"We didn't have much time to go over the plan."

Ramsey picked up a fry from a bag in his lap. He hadn't eaten much, and the fry was cold. "I'd hardly call it a plan. It's more of a 'let's cross our fingers and pray this works.'"

"The problem is, we have no idea where Desde is taking Sarah. It could be in a public place which might play to our advantage, or someplace secretive, which could make this much harder."

"It'll be somewhere private," said Ramsey. "As much as Desde loves to flaunt her power, I think she'll want to stay under the radar for this. It will be easier if she doesn't draw the wrong kind of attention."

"We'll need to buy time, so we can call in the cavalry. If we can do that, we should be able to keep Sarah safe."

Ramsey dropped the uneaten fry back in the bag, untouched. "It's the 'should' part I don't like. This could go bad in a heartbeat." He crumpled the bag with the rest of the fries and added it to the trash. "What happens then? Do I watch my wife disappear into the sky with a crazy Eudoran? You know I can't do that."

There was a shuffling from the back and Hannah poked her head between the seats. "If Ethan and Rosie are safe, Sarah won't go with her willingly."

"That's what I'm afraid of," said Ramsey. "This could get ugly before the cavalry gets directions. I doubt they'll be much help anyway, to be honest."

"Safety in numbers," said Declan. "It's not perfect, but if one of them can bring Desde down, then we have to try. We can't do it on our own."

"Are they going to use the tranquilizers?" asked Hannah.

Declan shifted in his seat. "Yes. They'll be loaded with the poisoned serum. One hit and she'll drop like a rock."

"There's too much room for error," said Ramsey. He imagined Desde lashing out, hurting Sarah and his children as he watched, helpless. Or watching Sarah and his children disappear into the sky while he screamed from below. It made him want to puke up his hamburger. "She could sense them from a mile away."

"Or she might not," said Declan. "Her ego and the thrill of getting what she wants makes her overconfident. She underestimates us. That's her weakness."

"And what about the others?" asked Hannah. "Gillian and Royce are still in trouble. What about them?"

Declan checked his phone. "According to Jasper, they've got a plan of their own. I've let them know about the cavalry. If they can get a location, they can call Morgana to send reinforcements. Hopefully—"

"This plan of theirs is better than ours," finished Ramsey. "If Andolina gets wind of any of this, tomorrow could be a terrible day." He dropped his head back and stared at the ceiling.

"Or a very successful one," said Hannah.

"And Cinderella lived happily ever after," said Ramsey. "But somehow I doubt that. That prince was sketchy, if you ask me."

"Andolina's the problem. How do we get her to leave?" asked Declan. "And not come back?"

"She wants the letter," said Hannah.

"And Royce dead," said Ramsey.

Declan rubbed his stubbled jaw. "Maybe there's a way for her to think Royce is dead."

Ramsey bobbed his head up. "If you can pull that off, then I'll buy you a steak dinner."

Declan dialed a number on his cell. "I'll hold you to that. In fact, if …no, when everyone gets home safely, you treat us all. Booze included."

"You're on." Ramsey watched the hotel room with the dark windows where he knew his wife was staring at the ceiling, much like he was. He prayed that by this time tomorrow, he and his family would be together again. "It'll be the best dinner I've ever had."

· · ◦ ● · ● · ● · ·

Sarah Ramsey stared upward, blinking. She was in a dark hotel room, listening to the whir of the fan above. Desde slept in the bed next to hers, breathing softly. After arriving at the hotel, Desde had ordered a light meal, but Sarah had eaten little. She'd asked numerous times why they couldn't go to her children, but Desde never provided an answer, saying only to be patient. Desde had made a comment about enjoying one last night on Earth on a comfortable bed, instead of a lumpy tube, so Sarah knew Desde had plans to leave tomorrow and assumed she'd be leaving with Andolina.

That meant that tomorrow would decide their fate, Royce and Gillian included.

Closing her eyes, she prayed for the millionth time for the safe return of her kids, for her husband, herself, and everyone else. Despite their plans, the next day was a giant question mark, and she had to prepare. She pushed back the covers and studied her hands. She'd been blessed with the gift of healing and had used that gift with great benefit over the years, but she'd never guided that ability in any other way. Her abilities were meant for helping, not hurting. There had been one time she'd unleashed some powerful energy on another, but it had been during her Shift, when energy levels could be unpredictable. She remembered little of that time. Most of it had been told to her by John. The only other time had been to ward off another evil Red-Line with ill intent, so she knew it was within her, but would it be enough? Or would it only anger Desde more and risk the lives of everyone she loved?

She sighed and rolled to her side, thinking of her husband, whom she knew was outside, watching. He wouldn't sleep tonight either. Envisioning her children in her arms, warm and soft, giggling and wiggling, Sarah smiled softly. She couldn't wait to feel that again. The smile vanished though as the fear returned. It was going to be a long night.

Trust destiny. The whispered words popped into her head, but in Leroy's voice, not her husband's. *Trust yourself.* Memories of Leroy's boisterous personality and his love for her, John, and the kids made her eyes well, and she knew he was near. He would be there tomorrow, watching over them, and that brought her comfort.

Feeling some measure of resolution, she closed her eyes. Despite Leroy's advice, she worried. Tomorrow would decide not just the fate of her family, but their entire community.

As much as she trusted destiny, she prayed it had a big ace up its sleeve.

•••••••••••

Royce and Gillian sat on the white sofa. Not long after Royce had punched through the wall with his hand, they'd made a hole big enough for him to step through. Nothing had made him happier than to wrap his sister in a bear hug and know she was okay. Apparently, she felt the same because she didn't want to let him go.

Realizing their time was short, they sat and talked, discussing what they knew and how to prepare. The next person to walk through that door could be there to kill them. Their options were few, and they argued, but in the end, they decided. Royce hoped it would work. His sole desire was to get Gillian out to safety, and he would do whatever it took to get her there.

Putting his arm around her, he pulled her close, and she put her head on his shoulder. All they could do now was wait.

Chapter Twenty-Three

VEE SAT ON THE back porch of Charlotte Ramsey's home. The sun was coming up, and the soft light brightened the yard. Yellow flowers bordered the fence, and there was a patch of grass with a swing set. Sipping her coffee, she pushed back and forth on her patio chair, rocking slowly, listening to the sound of distant traffic. She'd called in to work, telling them she was taking a personal day. It wouldn't matter. She had about six weeks of unused time coming to her. They were probably happy she was using it.

Grayson had not moved during the night. She'd kept her phone with her in case something changed. Everyone had, at some point, found a place to lay their heads. Adam and Eve had slept in the master, and she had stayed in the guest room. Jasper had taken the kids' room. They'd not been alone since their near kiss, nor had they discussed it. Vee still wondered what had happened. How had she gone from ticketing speeders and hunting bike thieves to chasing extraterrestrials and falling for one of them?

She shook her head and sighed. It was why she was out here now. Normally an early riser anyway, she took the opportunity to sit quietly and think. There was a lot to consider. What would today hold? Should she involve the police? How far would she need to go to protect these people? What happened afterward? What about Jasper? What about Jasper? What about Jasper?

Crap. She couldn't get the man out of her mind. "Shut up already," she said out loud, and shut her eyes.

There was a shuffling sound, and she heard a man's voice. "Sorry. Is this a bad time?"

Turning, she almost spilled her coffee. Jasper stood outside the back door, holding his own coffee mug. "No. Sorry. Just talking to myself."

"You mind if I sit?"

There was a chair beside her. "No. Not at all." She picked up her rocking motion.

"You're up early," he said.

"I usually am. I like the morning."

"Me too. It's quiet." He took a sip from his mug. "I'm guessing there's been no change."

"No. He's sitting in the same place. Assuming he and his cell are still together."

Jasper nodded. "I hope so."

"What happens if it isn't?"

He put his drink down on the patio table. "I think whatever's going to happen will happen soon. If there's no change in an hour, we'll have to risk going out there and hope we don't alert Andolina."

"What if he's gone?"

He made an awkward chuckle and shook his head. "I don't know. I might be able to track him myself, but it will be harder because he's human, and to be honest, it's not my strength. We'll just have to figure that out if it happens."

She played with the rim of her cup. "Declan said something about a cavalry? You didn't go into much detail about that."

"With good reason." He shifted in his seat. "As a police officer, you may not like it."

"I think I should know what to expect. Are you worried I'll call in my own cavalry?"

"You might be tempted."

"Would it help?"

"No."

She nodded. "Then I won't call." She took a sip of her coffee. "But I would like to know the plan."

He pushed back in his seat. "Listen, I know there's a lot going on right now, and we can discuss it, but before things start moving, and people start waking, I'd like to ask you about yesterday."

She tensed and rocked faster. "What about it?"

He smiled, and her cheeks warmed. She wished she had control over that. "I wanted to kiss you."

She cleared her throat. "I noticed." She kept rocking.

"I would have too, if we hadn't been interrupted." He leaned forward. "I know things are moving fast. I didn't expect this either." He paused and held up a hand. "Never mind all that. What I'm trying to say is I'm thinking of kissing you now. Would you have any objections?"

She stopped rocking. Stomach flurries threatened to spread, and she gripped her mug. "Listen Jasper. I don't know what's going on here. I just met you. We don't know each other. We're from two different planets. And from what I can gather, I feel fairly certain our lives may be at risk today." She put down her drink. "I think that this is not the best time for us to be getting together. I mean, think about it. Do you really think I'm someone you'd want to get involved with?" Her hands splayed in the air as she spoke. "This whole thing is crazy."

He studied her. "You know what's crazy? I have a father who's in love with a woman from another planet. Someone he had three children with. But he left her for duty and married my mother, who also married him for duty. They spent many years together, each pining for someone else. I held a grudge thinking my dad had betrayed my mother, but now I know better. He did what he felt was expected of him, and because of that, sacrificed love. I saw the heartache he carried every day. And even though he had me and Roma, whom he loved, he also pined for his first family." He hesitated, and Vee could see the sadness in his eyes. "I won't do that, Vee. I can't ignore what I feel in my heart or worry about what anyone else thinks or about what they expect. My dad was indescribably strong to endure that torture. I'm not."

Vee didn't know what to say. Plus, the way he looked at her made it hard to talk. "I'm sure you're a lot stronger than you think. And maybe this whole 'long distance relationship' thing may have some appeal. But let's think this through. What are you going to do, travel back and forth to see me? And I think we're getting ahead of ourselves here. We still have to survive today. Which we need to talk about. This whole cavalry thing has got me on edge." He stood from his chair, and she kept rattling on. "I'm a police officer. I should be doing my job. I've broken several rules." He leaned over her, and she leaned back, still talking. "I could lose my job. And let's not forget, there are children who are in danger. And Gillian. And Royce." He came in closer and put his hands on her armrests. "What if something happens to any of them? I'll never forgive myself. Nor will you. Are you listening—" His lips descended over hers and everything finally went still. Her mind stopped whirling, and her heart hit the gas. Forgetting about all her complaints, she froze for a second, but then opened her lips over his and kissed him back. Something warm and soft moved through her, like walking in the front door of your home for the first time after a long trip. They held that way for a moment, his lips against hers, soft and tender, but then the warmth turned to heat and the kiss slowly deepened. His breath fluttered against her cheek as it picked up in speed. He slanted his mouth over hers, and his tongue explored hers and grazed against her lips.

Vee's body reacted. The feelings moving through her were indescribable. She'd kissed men before, but that had been like her first sip of coffee. Not bad, but it needed some cream and sugar. This was like her first full-on tequila shot—heat and shock hitting her all at once, making her body flame and her heart flip.

She reached up and pulled him in. She wasn't thinking anymore, only going on pure instinct. The kiss sizzled, and their tongues darted and retreated. Her breathing was rapid fire. There wasn't enough oxygen, and she needed more.

His arm came down, wrapped around her waist, and he pulled her out of the chair. She held onto him and her body pressed against his. He moaned and pulled her closer. Her arms went around his neck and she moved her mouth against his, tasting and touching him. His hands roamed down her back to her butt, where he squeezed and pushed her against him. The sensation was mind blowing, and Vee moved her hips against his. Nothing made sense and everything else went blank. All there was, was him. She was fire, and he was gasoline. She heard a soft keening sound and realized it was her. She had no idea she could make that sound, but Jasper was drawing things from her she never knew existed.

She pulled away briefly and spoke against his lips. "What is happening here?"

He was breathless. "You're as amazing as your sunrise, and just as beautiful." He rubbed his nose over hers and brought his lips down again, fanning the flames higher.

Vee held him, running a hand through his hair as his hands explored her back and moved up to her neck as he held her tighter. She didn't want it to stop. Her body felt like warm molasses, all gooey and sweet, and she wanted to pour herself all over this man. She imagined him in bed, his naked body over hers, and her mind almost short-circuited. Was sex supposed to be this good?

"I want you, Vee," he said against her lips. "Desperately."

"I want you too." She wasn't sure how she managed to talk. She appeared to have lost control over most of her body.

And then her phone rang.

He groaned, pulling back from the kiss.

Vee tried to focus. Her phone. There was a noise. It was ringing. "Hell. That could be about Grayson." She disentangled herself from Jasper, who reluctantly let her go.

He sighed as she pulled the phone from her back pocket, took a calming breath, which she was still trying to regulate, and answered. "It's Vee."

A male voice spoke. "He's on the move."

• • • • • • • • • •

Ramsey breathed deeply, smelling Sarah's hair. Peaches, he thought. It smells like peaches. He ran a tendril through his fingers, and she rolled over, smiling, her eyes bright after a night's sleep. Her hand trailed down his waist, and he leaned close and nuzzled her neck, grazing his lips against her soft skin. She was so beautiful.

Something nudged him in the arm. He tried to ignore it, but the nudge became a punch and he opened his eyes. Sunlight made him squint, and he tried to get his bearings. "What is it?" he asked, his voice raspy.

Declan spoke. "Movement. Sarah and Desde are leaving the hotel."

Memories swarmed back, and he sat up, his mind sharpening. "Is she okay? How long was I out?" He rubbed his eyes.

Declan held binoculars, and he handed them to Hannah in the back seat. "Not long. Maybe two hours." He started the car.

"I can't believe I slept. You should have woken me."

"You needed your rest," said Hannah from the back, peering through the binoculars. "You don't want to greet Ethan and Rosie looking like the boogeyman."

"I looked like the boogeyman every day for the first year of their lives," said Ramsey. "They should be used to it." He held out his hand, and Hannah handed him the binoculars. He looked for Sarah and saw her standing outside the SUV she'd been in the day before. Desde appeared after a few moments, along with the driver. He was male, tall, and had dark hair. None of them recognized him, so they could only assume he was there on orders to assist as needed. Maybe he was a lowly Gray, serving the high and mighty Reds. There was no way to know.

They got in the car, and Ramsey watched them back out, turn away from the hotel, and join the early morning traffic fray, which was starting to pick up speed. Ramsey lost sight of the car. "Damn it. I don't see them."

Declan joined the traffic. "It's okay. We don't want to be too close, anyway. We can see her here." He pointed to the screen on his phone where the red circle pinged on a city street not far ahead.

Ramsey watched the circle, hating that it was his lifeline to all he held dear. His dream played in his mind, and he imagined nuzzling Sarah's neck again. "Did you call Morgana?"

Declan shot out a thumb. "Hannah's calling."

Ramsey nodded and monitored the red circle. *Hang in there, baby,* he thought to himself. *We're coming.*

·•••••••••

Grayson walked through the trees, following the path. He'd been walking for twenty minutes, holding the phone as he waited to hear what to do next. He was grateful he'd had a portable charger in his car. None of this was going to work if his battery died.

He'd been dozing when the call had come in. Soft sunlight had brightened the horizon when he'd answered. All he'd heard was a female voice saying, "Follow the trail ahead until you get a phone call." Then the line had gone dead.

It didn't make sense at first. Follow the trail? What trail? And then he saw it. He was parked in front of a sign. Looking at it closely, he read, *Mt. Justin Trail Head.* There was an arrow pointing off to his left. He saw the narrow dirt path winding away from the park. He wasn't sure why it was called Mt. Justin. The area was hilly, but certainly not mountainous.

He'd left the car and started walking. The day promised to be a beautiful one. The air was crisp and cool, and a light breeze ruffled his hair. If he hadn't been walking to save his wife's life, the jaunt would have been an enjoyable one. If they'd been at their beach home, they'd have taken a long walk in the sand. He thought again of Gillian and remembered when she'd told him she was pregnant.

He'd been in his office downtown, talking on the phone with his business partner and best friend Cooper about an upcoming client meeting. Cooper had been out of town, schmoozing with the clients at the time when Gray's door had burst open and Gillian had rushed in, her face flushed as if she'd been running.

Before he even had time to speak, she'd taken the phone out of his hand, said, "He'll call you back, Cooper," and hung up the phone. It scared him at first, but her bright smile and shiny eyes told him this was good news. She'd flung herself into his arms, and kissed him, oblivious to his open door and his curious and surprised assistant, who stood there gawking.

If they'd been alone, he would have taken advantage and pulled his wife into his arms, but aware of the eyes on them, he pulled back and smiled. "To what do I owe this great pleasure of seeing my lovely wife out of the blue?"

She was breathless with excitement and started jumping up and down. "I'm pregnant!" Her cheeks were a cherry red and her eyes were shiny with tears. "We're going to have a baby!"

Grayson stood frozen for a moment, but then his assistant yelled, "That's awesome!" and Gray came out of his trance. "Really?" he'd asked. "A baby? A little Gillian?"

She'd nodded. "Or a little Grayson."

Pure joy pulsed through him. Just seeing his wife's happiness was enough to bring him delight, but to know he was going to be a father brought an indescribable emotion. He'd told her before they'd married, after their broken Binding and her miscarriage, that it didn't matter whether they had children, and it was true, but now that it was here, he couldn't have been more thrilled. He'd pulled her into his arms and kissed her again, not caring who saw it.

Thinking back on that moment, Grayson dodged a low-lying branch and kept walking, hoping and praying that after this journey he would have his wife and unborn child back. Glancing at his phone, he saw he had four bars. It was plenty of juice, provided they didn't make him walk for hours. He hadn't considered cell phone coverage, but these days, if he was within range of a nearby city, he should maintain a decent signal.

He trudged deeper down the trail, moving farther and farther away from the park. With any luck, Vee and Jasper were tracking him now, and help would not be far behind. Once he got to Gillian, he was going to have to figure out how to buy time. The key was the letter. The longer it took for them to get the letter, the better. At the same time, though, he couldn't drag this out for too long. They had to believe he could deliver. Again, he went over his plans, but knew most of this would depend on what happened when he got to Gillian. At that point, anything could change.

He passed a huge, knotted overhanging tree when his cell rang again. He answered and heard the same female voice saying, "Turn east at the tree. Follow the sun," before she hung up again. He did as asked and turned left. Now he was off the path. Pushing back branches and stepping over roots and overgrowth, he was thankful someone knew where he was, otherwise he'd be lost. He was a city boy. Stick him in the middle of a pile of buildings and traffic, and he'd be on his way home within the hour. Out here, he could be within fifteen minutes of his house and never find his way back.

He wondered how these people knew his location. Could they track his phone as well? If their technology was more advanced, then it would be easy. And if that were true, the likelihood of success decreased with each step. They would be able to detect help coming as well.

There was nothing he could do about it, though. He had to push through and hope for the best. And if he failed, and Gillian didn't make it, then he would die fighting the bastards who did it. He and Gillian would either walk out of the woods together, or not at all. He was not coming back alone.

Chapter Twenty-Four

Adam pulled into the space beside Grayson's car. Jasper stepped out, and the rest followed. He peered inside the windows of the empty vehicle.

"Anything?" asked Eve.

"Nope. Nothing." He glanced at Vee. "Anything from your friend?"

Vee shook her head. "He's still on the move. About a mile northeast of here. In the woods."

"Declan knows where we are," said Adam, studying his cell. "He's sending reinforcements to our location. They're on the move as well. Following Desde."

Jasper studied the woods, considering the next move.

"Should we follow?" asked Eve. "Or wait for the others?"

Vee lowered her phone and cocked her head. "Has anyone considered we could all be heading to the same place? What if the kids are with Gillian and Royce?"

Jasper leaned against the car. "I think it could be very likely." He tried to think like Andolina. How would she handle Grayson? What would she do once she got Royce's letter?

Thinking of the letter, he pushed off the car and tried the door. It was unlocked, and he opened it. Searching the vehicle, he saw nothing and closed the door. "There's no letter. He took it with him."

"Or he stashed it somewhere on his way to the park," said Eve.

"Where?" asked Vee. "He doesn't live in the area. He stayed in his car all night. Where do you stash a letter around here?"

They surveilled the park and street, looking for any place to conceal an envelope. Adam checked under the car in case Grayson had taped it underneath the carriage. "Nothing here," he said.

"He probably has it on him," said Jasper.

"If that's true, Andolina will know it. Then Royce, and maybe all of them, are dead," said Adam.

"Maybe not. Grayson is human. She's not used to humans. Not as easy to read. That may save him," said Jasper. He raised a brow at Vee.

"What?" she asked.

"Just an idea," he replied. "One that might work, if you're up for it."

· · • • • • • • · ·

They drove for several minutes, the red dot pinging. Moving farther from the bustle of the city, they drove toward the outskirts and the traffic gave way to quiet county roads and wooded areas.

Ramsey recognized their surroundings. It was a favorite for campers and hikers. The gentle rolling hills and old heavy trees were an outdoor enthusiast's playground. The pinging slowed and then stopped, and so did Declan. Pulling up to a rutted turnoff, he waited and watched.

"You know this place?" asked Ramsey.

"I've hiked in the area," said Declan.

"The Red Rhinestone trail is about a mile west. We hiked it last year," said Hannah.

Ramsey studied the road. "What about this place? Is it a trail?" He looked for a sign but didn't see one.

Declan studied his phone. "It is, but according to the web, it's closed. It was damaged in a flood last summer." He hit a button, and his brow furrowed. "She's moving again."

Ramsey wanted to open the door and chase after Sarah. "Where? There's nowhere to go."

"It's much slower. They're on foot."

"I'll text Morgana," said Hannah. "Tell her where to send the team."

"What are we waiting for? Let's go," said Ramsey.

"I want them to get a decent distance before I pull in. I don't want them to see or hear us."

Hannah poked her head between the seats. "What if they're not all gone?"

"What do you mean?" asked Declan.

"What about the driver? What if he stayed back for some reason?" asked Hannah.

Ramsey tapped his fingers on the dash. "I guess we'll wing it."

"That's about as good a plan as I can think of," said Declan. He pointed at Hannah. "I don't suppose I could get you to stay behind?"

"Why would I do that?" she asked.

He sighed. "I don't want to worry about you if I'm going to have to go up against somebody."

"Well, I don't want to worry about you if you end up fighting a Red-Line. Maybe I can help," said Hannah.

Declan twisted in his seat, raising a brow. "You're sure?"

"You know I am," said Hannah, her tone leaving no room for argument.

"You two ready?" asked Ramsey. His knee bounced, and he gripped the car door handle in nervousness. "Odds are the driver went with them, anyway." He wished he could see through the trees and know Sarah was safe. "It should be long enough. Let's go."

"You heard him," said Hannah. "Let's go."

Declan slumped his shoulders, but turned back in his seat and put the car into drive. Slowly, he drove down the dirt and pebble road. The car bounced, and dust billowed up behind them. The trees became thicker, and they crossed a small stream. Once past the water, the woods opened into a small clearing with a few parking spots. A trailhead was marked at the spot of a narrow path leading deeper into the trees. The SUV was parked in front of it.

Declan slowed, and Ramsey saw nothing other than the vehicle. "We're safe. No one's here."

Declan parked the car beside the other and killed the engine. Ramsey opened the door and stepped out. It was quiet, save for the occasional melodic bird song or the whacking of a woodpecker. He closed the door behind him.

Declan and Hannah exited also, and Declan opened the SUV and looked inside.

"Anything?" asked Ramsey. He studied the path. It was rocky, making footprints impossible to see.

Declan closed the door. "Nothing."

Ramsey listened for anything other than birds but heard only the wind. "You ready?"

Declan nodded. "As I'll ever be." He looked back. "You sure you don't just want to hang back by the car?"

Hannah raised a brow. "You know me better than that."

Declan shrugged in a gesture of defeat. "I do. As much as I love your warrior spirit, right now, I wish I'd married a wimp."

Hannah rubbed his back. "Hang in there, honey. I'll get you through it."

Ramsey stepped onto the trail and started walking.

· · · • • • • • • · · ·

Morgana put down her phone, walked to her picture window, and stared out. Everything was in play. Sarah was on the move, with Ramsey following, and Jasper and his group were tracking Grayson. Talbot had the information and was ensuring the teams had the serum. Now all they could do was wait.

She thought of Drake, wondering what he would be doing or saying if he were here. Nothing positive, she knew. The man could expect thunderstorms with the presence of one puffy white cloud, but she still missed his stabilizing presence. Despite his grumpiness, he'd been her rock in past crises. She imagined him sitting on her red couch, his clothes wrinkled and his hair uncombed, detailing everything that could go wrong, and she smiled. For some reason his complaints had given her confidence it would all work out.

It was important to believe that now. So much depended on what would happen today. If this failed and they lost people, her role as a councilwoman and leader would end. Not because of any vote, but because she would remove herself. It would be hard to lead people you had failed, despite the odds against them.

And if Andolina's threats had any merit, she would be ousted anyway and replaced with a Eudoran headpiece. Someone there on orders, who cared little about her or the well-being of her community.

Sighing, she turned, and her phone beeped. Glancing at the text, she saw it was from Talbot. She picked it up.

Team is on the move. Two on Grayson. Two on Sarah.

She typed. *They have everything they need?*

Fully equipped. We should know something soon. Stay put and I'll let you know when it's over.

She wrote back. *Keep me posted.*

Putting the phone down, she sighed and went back to the window. *Soon,* she thought. But soon was relative. It could be an hour or twenty-four hours before she heard anything.

Thinking back, she remembered a day spent with Drake last year. It had been beautiful and cool, and despite the one cloud in the sky, she'd convinced Drake to go hiking with her. Normally one who enjoyed the outdoors, she found it difficult with her schedule to often spend time in nature. But it had been a rare day of freedom, and she'd pestered Drake until they'd made it to a trail outside the city, in an area not far from where Ramsey was now. The trees were old, and moss-ridden, and the streams had been low and rocky, and they'd walked for miles. Drake had even smiled a few times. It had been a good day.

Recalling that hike, Morgana paused. Still staring, but seeing nothing, she cocked her head. She turned from the window and picked up the phone, staring at the screen. She scrolled through the messages, rereading them, finding the one from Hannah.

After reading it, she slipped the phone in her pocket and stood there. Drake's voice rang in her head, telling her to do the exact opposite of what she was considering. She ignored it, which is what she normally did when it came to Drake. *This has disaster written all over it,* was his only response.

Morgana turned, walked out of the room, and down her front hallway. She made her way to a front coat closet, opened it, and, pushing back her long coats, she bent low and pulled out her hiking boots.

Chapter Twenty-Five

GRAYSON WALKED FOR ALMOST an hour. Trees, roots, and branches were thick enough in some areas to block his path, but thin enough in others to provide an easy trail to follow. It was slow going as he dodged brambles and thorns, careful to avoid poison ivy.

He was beginning to wonder if they'd left him out here to wander forever, lost in the emptiness of this strange world. A bird cawed, and his stomach rumbled again. He wished he was at a hot dog stand on a city street, with Gillian beside him, ordering her usual with relish and mustard. He could go for one of those dogs now.

He checked his cell. The battery was at sixty percent, and he still had a signal. Not strong, but still usable. He wasn't sure how much longer that would last.

As if on cue, it rang. He stopped and answered. "Yes?" He wiped a trickle of sweat from his forehead.

"Turn north. Go to the clearing." The line went dead.

Grayson stared at his phone. "What?" He looked north. All he saw were trees. "What clearing?" His frustration was rising. "Gillian?" he yelled into the trees. There was no response. Where the hell were they bringing him?

Groaning, he followed their instructions and kept walking. If they kept him going for another hour, he didn't know what he would do. Were they just moving him around in circles? Was this just all a big distraction while they took Gillian farther and farther away? Thinking the worst, he considered whether he should dial the caller back and tell them all to go screw themselves and if they wanted the letter, they could come and get it, when he pushed past a big shrub and stepped into a large treeless space.

He stopped. There was only dull brown grass flattened against the ground inside a wide circle, almost fifty yards across. He'd passed a few other grassy areas on his journey, but nothing this big.

Maybe in some other time, some hard-working farmer had used it for grazing or growing crops, or whatever it was they did out in the middle of nowhere. But right now, it was empty and forlorn, like an unused theater stage. He didn't hear the birds anymore, either.

He slipped his phone into his pant pocket and waited. Sliding his jacket off, he hung it on a low-hanging branch and walked farther into the space. He had no doubt this was where they wanted him.

"Hello?" he yelled. Listening, he heard no response. "Anyone here?"

The wind rustled the surrounding foliage, but that was all he heard. Spying a nearby fallen tree, he sat on the rotting trunk and waited.

A few minutes passed. Getting antsy, he checked his watch. He debated getting on his cell, but he didn't want to use the battery any more than he needed to. Wondering if Vee was tracking him, he swiveled, studying the area behind him, acutely aware of the quiet. The movie *Deliverance* popped into his head, and he shivered. He turned back and froze when he saw a woman walking toward him. He looked around, wondering where she'd came from. Scanning the area, he saw nothing.

He stood as she approached. Seeing her up close, he assumed this was Andolina. Her stick-straight brown hair was parted to the side and hung in a bob to her chin. She wore navy pants and a comfortable long-sleeved white shirt tucked in at her narrow waist. She looked like she was about to go to a Sunday brunch with her friends and enjoy some mimosas.

She stopped in front of him, saying nothing.

A chill ran through him. This woman had Gillian. He took a deep breath and calmed himself. "Strange place to hang out. You ever consider a downtown hotel?"

Her expression didn't change. "I prefer as little contact with humans as possible."

He nodded. "I get that." He couldn't help himself. "We tend to prefer friendlier, non-violent aliens. The big heads are a plus, too."

"You prefer your mate had a big head?"

The mention of Gillian made his pulse quicken. "I like her just the way she is. Alive." He paused. "Where is she?"

"Where is the letter?"

"I'm not giving you anything until I know she's okay. I want to see Royce, too."

She squinted. "The arrangement was not for Royce. Only for her."

"Like I said, I can't tell my wife I bargained for her safety and not for her brother's. I'd like to keep living. Besides, he's not a threat, he just acts like one. It's one of his less admirable traits. Once you have the letter, just leave him behind. There's no way for him to claim what's his."

She walked to a tree and looked up at it. "Unfortunately, he's what you all like to call a 'loose end.'" She turned and leaned against the tree. "I'm sure you don't leave any of those when you close one of your big deals, do you?"

Her knowledge of his business dealings made him raise a brow. "You've done your homework."

"Every good businesswoman does. This is just a job. It's as simple as that. Nothing personal. You understand?"

He took a few steps into the clearing and wondered again where she'd come from. "I do. Dotting the i's and crossing the t's is important if you want to succeed. I know greasing the wheels can go a long way to ensuring long-term relationships."

She pushed off the trunk. "I'm not even supposed to be here. If Burke had done his job, I'd be on my way home. But now I have to clean up his mess."

"You have more in common with female humans than you realize."

She stepped closer. "The letter."

He held his ground. "Not until I see Gillian and Royce."

"Do you have it?"

"I know where it is."

She studied him. He got the strange sensation she was probing him. "Is it nearby?"

"Maybe."

"In your car?"

"Again. Where's Gillian?"

She set her jaw. "I could kill you right where you stand."

"You could."

Her eyes narrowed. "Are you carrying it? I could search you."

He hesitated. Negotiation was a skill he'd honed over the years. Knowing the subtleties of bargaining with aggressive adversaries had made him a lot of money. This woman was no different, although she had his wife. He'd have to be careful. Losing this deal would cost him more than he was willing to give. Raising his arms, he said, "I'm all yours, but be careful. I'm ticklish."

She studied him but didn't move.

He dropped his arms. "Gillian? You have her, don't you?"

The question made her square her shoulders. "Of course. You doubt that?"

He picked up on her irritation, as if she didn't like her abilities questioned. Maybe he could use that against her. "We're out in the middle of nowhere. I don't see her. Maybe she escaped? My wife can be hard to handle. Maybe I should check..." He reached for his phone.

Her face hardened. "She has not escaped." She paused. "I'll show you."

He put his phone back.

Andolina stepped away and pulled a silvery device from her pocket. It was about the size of a small billfold. She depressed a button.

For a moment, nothing happened, but then Grayson heard a slight swooshing sound. It got louder, and Grayson stared in disbelief as a large metallic ship materialized in the clearing, taking up about half of the area. Now he knew why the grass was flat. The craft had a tubular middle with two additional oval sections attached on either side. It was wide and tall, supported by two V-shaped legs. There were no windows, although Grayson saw an outline of a door on the oval section closest to him.

Openmouthed, Grayson heard another whoosh as the door slid open and a ramp slid out and descended to the ground.

Andolina put the device back in her pocket. She turned toward the craft but looked back at a stunned Grayson, who didn't know what to say.

"Let's go see your wife," she said, and started walking.

· · · ● · ● · ● · ·

Sarah slipped on a rock but caught herself.

Desde looked back. "We're almost there."

Sarah didn't answer, but glanced behind her, wondering how far back her husband was. They'd been walking for a while and the sun beat down from above. The day had warmed, and Sarah felt sweat trickle down her back. They'd followed the trail for the first thirty minutes, but then had moved off of it. It had been nothing but forest, shrubs, roots, and streams since. She'd ripped her jeans on some brambles, and had a few scratches from some low-hanging branches, but her energy level remained high. Every step brought her closer to her children.

The driver walked with Desde, but neither of them said much. Desde had changed into more suitable clothing that morning, wearing jeans and hiking boots. Her hair was up in a messy bun. The driver had glanced back at Sarah once, but that had been the extent of his engagement.

Since Desde had said they were close, Sarah began to wonder about the exchange. If they planned to keep her and release Ethan and Rosie, then who was going to take the kids back to safety? Did they plan to let Charlotte find her way back on her own?

"Once we're there, what happens?" she asked. "I want to see my kids."

Desde kept walking. "You will."

"How will they get home?"

"They have legs, don't they?"

Anger bubbled up. "They're children. You expect them to walk through this by themselves? Even with their grandmother?"

Desde scowled. "I don't know why children on this planet are so coddled. You'd do them a favor if you expected more from them."

"I don't think asking my three-year-old twins to walk through miles of woods with an older woman with bad knees is going to toughen them up. They're more likely to get lost. I'm not going to leave them knowing they're not safe."

Desde snickered. "You'll leave when I say you leave. You take orders from me now. Don't think because you're some sort of unique hybrid that you'll get any favors from me." She sneered. "Remember that."

Sarah bit her tongue. If she hadn't known that John was somewhere behind her, ready to rescue her and their kids, Sarah would have told Desde to shove her favors in a dark place. Deciding to continue her docile role, she didn't speak.

They walked for ten more minutes, and Desde pulled something from her pocket. It looked like a cell phone. She stared at the screen for a moment, touched a button, then pointed. "That way."

They veered off again, pushing through even thicker foliage. A bird cawed in the distance and Sarah swatted another wayward branch away from her face. "How much longer?"

Something sharp slammed into her stomach and she fell, holding her belly. It felt like someone had shot her with an arrow, but there was nothing there.

She heard Desde's voice. "You will speak when spoken to. You will walk until I say stop."

Sarah looked up. Desde stood over her, her face sharp. The driver watched, his face impassive. Perhaps he'd had to deal with this treatment as well.

"Tell me you understand," said Desde.

Sarah dropped her head. The pain was easing, and she attempted to straighten. "I understand."

"Look at me when you say it," said Desde.

Sarah tensed, but came up on her knees and made eye contact with Desde. "I understand."

Desde's eyes flared. "Good." She swiveled and started walking. "Now stop talking."

Sarah got back on her feet and followed. She prayed that once they reached their destination, she'd be able to get her kids to safety before she threw Desde into a tree. Taking a deep breath, she knew she had to control her anger. Desde was a powerful enemy and would fight back. There would be no point in challenging her if it meant leaving her children motherless.

The sun rose higher as they moved through the woods. Sarah slipped off her jacket and tied it around her waist. Continuing to glance behind, she saw nothing. A nugget of doubt blossomed when she considered no one was following. Was she on her own? What if they'd lost the signal? How would she get her children out? If it meant leaving to protect them, would she do it?

Sarah pondered these questions and more, feeling her anxiety build. For a moment, she wanted to cry, when Desde stopped. Sarah, lost in her thoughts, stopped too, and froze. In front of her, in a large clearing, stood a ship, bright and shiny in the sunlight.

Chapter Twenty-Six

GRAYSON STEPPED UP ONTO the metallic ramp leading into the interior. His footsteps clanged as he walked, and his stomach rolled. Gillian was here, and he was about to see her. His mind whirled with anxiety. What would he do once he had her? Would he see Royce too?

Entering the craft, Grayson stared at the walls of the ship. There wasn't much to it. Just a short anterior room with five closed doors, one in front of him and two on either side. All his space movies had left him expecting to see something like the Millennium Falcon or the Starship Enterprise, but this was far less impressive. Andolina continued to walk. Her footsteps echoed off the walls. Grayson waited to see someone or something else, but it was quiet.

They passed the first set of doors and Andolina stopped in front of the second one on the right, just before the entryway ended. She waved her hand over a small screen beside the door and it swooshed open, much like the doors opened in the movies. *At least something is accurate*, thought Grayson.

With the door open, Grayson saw a small room with more white walls, and just beyond the doorway, the armrest of what looked like a white sofa. He followed Andolina inside.

· · · ● · ● · · ·

Sarah stopped and stared at the large ship. It stood about six feet off the ground, with two large sections attached to a tubular middle. Four large support beams descended from the bottom to prop it off the ground. The driver and Desde stopped too, and Desde checked her device. "She's here," she said. "She's on the other side." She tapped on the screen and spoke to the driver. "She's not answering. Go find her. Tell her we're here. I'll take care of Sarah."

The driver glanced at Sarah before walking out of the woods and beneath the craft toward the other section. Looking closer, Sarah noticed a lowered ramp on the far end of the ship.

"Are my children here?" she asked.

Desde continued to tap on her screen. "You ask too many questions." She slid her device into her pocket. Sarah heard a noise and saw a second ramp on their side of the ship descend. "I'll have to fix that." Desde started walking.

Sarah followed, hope bubbling up that she was about to see Ethan and Rosie. Desde turned, her face stony. "You stay here."

Sarah stopped short. "But—" The sharp pain returned, and she dropped to her knees, holding her belly.

"Be quiet." Desde swiveled back and headed toward the ship, leaving Sarah kneeling in the dirt. All Sarah could do was watch her walk away because it hurt too much to breathe.

As the distance grew between her and Desde, the pain subsided until eventually she could draw a breath with ease. Slowly, she stood and saw Desde disappear into the craft. She waited silently, reminding herself to breathe. Desde knew Sarah wouldn't run. Not with her kids still in danger. Glancing behind her, she wondered if John was somewhere close. She prayed help was nearby. Hours seemed to pass, and she paced until finally there was movement and a woman appeared at the top of the ramp. It was Charlotte, her mother-in-law. Behind her were Ethan and Rosie. Charlotte took their hands and led them down the ramp.

Sarah's heart raced, and she took off in a sprint. "Ethan! Rosie!"

Ethan pointed. "It's Mommy," he said, smiling.

"Mommy, Mommy!" said Rosie.

Charlotte dropped their hands, and the kids ran down the ramp.

Sarah got to them at the bottom and swooped them up into her arms. "My babies." She nuzzled her face into their necks and kissed their heads. Tears sprang into her eyes. "How are you? Are you okay?"

"We had ice cream," said Rosie.

"I want more," said Ethan.

"You did?" asked Sarah, crying and kissing their cheeks. She saw Charlotte, who'd joined them. "You okay? They didn't hurt you?"

Charlotte shook her head. Her face was pale, but she appeared to be in good health. "No. They treated us well. Nobody's hurt. The kids kept asking about you and John. I did my best to allay their fears."

"Where's Daddy?" asked Rosie.

"I want Daddy," said Ethan.

Looking past Charlotte, Sarah saw Desde appear at the entrance of the ship. She didn't say anything, just stared down at them.

"Oh my gosh," Sarah said, holding them close. "I missed you two so much." She wiped at her tears.

"We missed you too," said Rosie.

"I cried," said Ethan.

"You did?" asked Sarah. "That's okay. I cried too."

"I didn't cry, Mommy," said Rosie.

"You didn't?" asked Sarah.

"No. Nana said you'd come," said Rosie.

"You're both very brave," said Sarah.

Desde crossed her arms, and Sarah realized her time was short. She spoke to Charlotte. "Listen, I need you to take the kids to safety."

Charlotte frowned. "What do you mean? What about you?"

"You have to trust me," said Sarah.

"I want to go home, Mommy," said Ethan.

"Me too," said Rosie.

"I know, babies. I know," said Sarah. She kissed their foreheads and smelled their hair. The thought of letting them go brought a new threat of tears, but she swallowed it back. "Grandma's going to take you home. She'll take you to see Daddy. You want to do that?"

"Yes," said Rosie. She squirmed, and Sarah loosened her hold. "You have to do something for me. Can you go with Grandma to go see Daddy?"

"I want you to take us," said Ethan. He pulled on her hand. "Let's go."

Forcing back her tears, Sarah pushed his hair off his face. He needed a haircut. "I know, sweetheart. But Daddy can't wait to see you. He misses you so much."

"Let's go Mommy," said Rosie.

Swallowing the lump in her throat, she pulled Rosie in for a hug. "I'll be right behind you. I promise," she whispered into Rosie's ear. She reached over and pulled Ethan close. "I love you both so much." It was hard to breathe. All she wanted to do was hold her kids and make sure they were safe. She hugged them tighter.

"Mommy, you're squeezing," said Ethan.

Sarah released her hold. "I'm sorry, baby. I'm just so happy to see you."

"Is Daddy going to get us?" asked Rosie.

Finding it hard to breathe, Sarah kept her face placid and tucked her daughter's hair behind her ear. "Yes, sweetheart. He's looking for you. But you need to help him find you. I need you to go with Grandma, okay?"

"Wrap it up," said Desde from above.

Sarah's heart thumped, and she fought hard to hold it together. She pulled Ethan and Rosie in for another hug and kissed them. "You need to go now. Go with Grandma. She'll take you to Daddy."

"You too, Mommy," said Rosie.

Sarah tried to answer, but her throat closed.

Charlotte leaned down. "Come along, darlings. Mommy needs to talk to this nice lady for a minute, then she'll be along. Don't worry." She took their hands. "Let's go see Daddy."

Sarah nodded, thankful for Charlotte's help. She managed a shaky breath, stood, and pointed. "It's about a thirty-minute walk to the trail. Just go straight west. You should see the path soon." She paused as a tear escaped and ran down her cheek. She wanted to tell Charlotte that John was following, but she couldn't risk Desde picking up on it. "Be careful."

Charlotte nodded. "You too. I don't know what's going on here, but just be sure you come home. These children need their mother."

Sarah hugged her mother-in-law and gave her a quick kiss on the cheek. "I'm working on it."

Charlotte tugged on the kid's hands. "Ready? Who wants more ice cream?"

"Me, me!" They said in unison.

They walked away from the ramp and toward the woods. Sarah's vision blurred with tears. "I love you," she said, her nose running.

"Are we going through the trees?" she heard Ethan ask Charlotte.

"Can we see a squirrel?" asked Rosie.

"Yes, Ethan," said Charlotte, "We're walking through the trees. And yes, Rosie, keep your eyes out for a squirrel." She glanced back at Sarah as she guided her grandchildren into the woods. Sarah listened to their muffled voices and watched as they slowly disappeared from view. Holding her stomach, she wanted to throw up. Watching her children walk away was the hardest thing she'd ever done.

Slow footsteps came up behind her. "It's difficult now, but you'll get over it," said Desde.

Sarah wiped her nose and brushed away a tear. She hated this woman.

"Pull yourself together," said Desde. "It's time to go home."

"This is my home," said Sarah. Her breath hitched, and she tried to stop crying.

Desde stared toward the trees. "Not anymore." She turned to walk back up the ramp. "Let's go."

· · · ● · ● · ● · · ·

Grayson walked into the white chamber and saw nothing other than a white couch and a cracked wall with a big, ugly hole in it. Looking through the broken remnants of the tile, he could see another white room that looked similar. "Looks like your ship has some structural issues." He put his hand beside the damage and patted it. A hanging piece of the structure fell off and broke apart on the floor. "I have a foundation guy if you need one."

Andolina seemed frozen in place. Without a word, she turned and walked back into the hallway. Grayson's heart raced. Gillian had been in this room. He could smell her perfume. And he could only deduce that Royce had caused the damage. Had he done it to save Gillian? Grayson tried to think. Had they escaped? He turned to follow Andolina when the door slid shut in his face, cutting him off. Running up, he slammed his palm against it. "Hey!" he yelled. He searched for a button or a keypad, but there was nothing. He banged on the door and yelled again, but there was only silence.

· · · ● · ● · ● · · ·

Royce slowly dropped the unconscious man to the ground.

"Is he all right?" asked Gillian.

Royce stepped over the man. "He's breathing. That's all I know."

"You're not cloaked anymore."

"I realize that. It's not that easy to stay cloaked when you're fighting for your life."

"What do we do now?"

Royce surveyed the room. They appeared to be in a supply closet. There were metallic objects of all shapes and sizes secured to the walls and shelves.

A few of them appeared to resemble hammers, wrenches, and screwdrivers, but there were other objects he could not identify.

They'd gotten in here on pure luck. While waiting in the white room, he'd cloaked himself, and when someone had arrived to bring Gillian food, Royce had tackled him, putting him into a chokehold until he'd collapsed. Once out of the room, though, he and Gillian had no idea how to get off the ship. They were in a hallway with nothing but doors, none of which would open. Realizing they couldn't stand there forever, he'd dragged the unconscious man out of the room and swiped the man's hand over the various screens. This was the first door that had opened, and they'd dragged him inside and closed the door behind them.

"We've got to figure out how to get off this thing," said Royce. "You have any idea where this ship is located?"

"We're in the woods," said Gillian. "A good distance away from anything of consequence. We're unlikely to be found unless some random hiker walks by."

"We can't rely on that." He thought about it. "We're going to have to either wait it out or venture outside again."

"But we don't know how to get out of here. We can't get the doors open."

Royce grabbed what looked like duct tape and bound the unconscious man's hands and mouth. "I know. We'll have to wait. When someone shows up, we make a break for it."

Gillian's jaw dropped. "Are you crazy? How are we going to do that?"

"I'll cloak myself again. Then go out there and watch for access. When we get an opportunity to get out, I'll give you a signal and you get the hell out of here. You head into the woods and get help."

"What about you?"

"I'm going to be sure we don't have anyone following us. We won't get far if we're being chased."

"I'm not leaving you behind."

He tossed the tape to the side. "Gillian, you're pregnant. You've got to get off this ship, and the sooner the better. Besides, they want me, not you. And they'll use you against me, and I'll die before they hurt you."

"Royce—"

He pointed. "Don't argue with me. We have to do it this way. You know that."

Gillian scowled. "There is another way. You and I together make a formidable team."

"You don't know that. We don't have Eve with us. We can't be sure the two of us alone will handle Andolina."

"You expect me to run off, knowing they'll kill you? How am I supposed to live with that?"

"Happily, knowing that you and your child are alive. Name the kid after me if you want. Just don't question it. This is about survival. Don't spend one day of regret about it, because I'll come back and haunt you if you do."

"That's not funny, Royce."

"I'm not laughing."

They paused. "There has got to be a better way," said Gillian.

"If there is, let's hope it shows itself."

She walked over and hugged him, burying her head in his shoulder. "Please don't die," she said into his shirt.

Royce hugged her back, gritting his teeth. "I'll do my best. I promise." The thought of saying goodbye broke his heart. "You tell Evie what I said about the whole haunting thing. The same goes for her. Mom, too."

She nodded into his chest but wouldn't pull away.

He rubbed her shoulders. "Come on. The fat lady hasn't sung yet. There's still hope."

She stepped back but held his hand. "I love you, you big jerk."

He smiled, feeling his heart swell. "I love you too, twerp."

Before he could cloak, the door to the room slid open. Royce grabbed Gillian and pushed her behind him.

Andolina, her back straight and her face relaxed, walked into the room. "There you are," she said. "I assumed you didn't go far." She raised a brow at the unconscious man, then glanced around Royce and spoke to Gillian. "Your husband's here. Would you like to say hello before he dies?"

Chapter Twenty-Seven

"Stop," said Adam. "This is the location of Grayson's last signal." He slipped his cell phone into his pocket and put his hand on the trunk of a nearby tree. "We're in the middle of nowhere. I don't see anything."

"Maybe something happened," said Eve, walking up behind him. "Maybe the signal was lost." She kicked at a fat root. "How are we supposed to know where to go from here?"

Jasper stood quietly, his head cocked as if listening.

"You got any ideas?" asked Adam.

"Where's Vee?" asked Eve. "Is she going to know where to find us?"

Jasper squinted. "She knows these woods better than we do. She'll be fine."

"I'm still not sure why we separated," said Eve. "Isn't there safety in numbers?"

"Sometimes," said Jasper. He continued to study the area.

"What are you thinking?" asked Adam. "How do we explain our complete failure in finding Grayson?"

Jasper turned and took a few steps into the trees. "On the contrary, I'm thinking this is the perfect place to land a ship. And..." He moved into the foliage, and Adam and Eve followed.

Adam pushed back some branches and dodged some thorns before stepping into a large clearing. He dropped his jaw when he saw a large metallic ship sitting in the middle of the forest. Eve bumped into him, and he heard her gasp.

"And all we need is a place to land it," said Jasper, quietly. He raised his arms and directed Eve and Adam back into the brush.

Adam stepped back and squatted below a thick vine. Eve joined him. Jasper made a shushing sound and stooped low behind a branch. They watched the ship for a few seconds, but saw no movement.

Adam spoke in a whisper. "Do we wait for the cavalry? They should be on their way."

"Do you see Gray?" asked Eve, wiping a trickle of sweat from her forehead.

"Probably on the ship," said Jasper.

"Which means Gillian and Royce must be here too," said Eve. She sighed, and Adam could feel her worry.

Jasper pulled out his own cellphone like device, tapped at it, and put it away. "This is the tricky part. We have to wait. Hopefully Adam's right and help will be here soon, because timing is critical."

"We can't wait forever," said Eve.

Jasper pulled his water out and took a sip. "We go in too soon, we could get your siblings killed. We go too late," he paused, "basically, same scenario."

"So, how do we know?" asked Adam.

Jasper watched for a moment, then spoke to Eve. "I know you can read objects, but how good are you at reading your brother and sister?"

Eve's face scrunched. "Gillian's the intuitive one. Not me."

"That's not exactly true," said Adam. "You don't give yourself credit. You pick up on much more than you let on."

"You read Royce's letter pretty easily," said Jasper. "I need you to do it again, but with Royce and Gillian. Can you do that?"

"You mean pick up on their thoughts?" asked Eve.

"Exactly," said Jasper.

"It's not something I've practiced," said Eve. "I prefer to keep other people's thoughts at a distance."

"Well, now's the time to try," said Jasper. "I need you to go still and listen. They're not far. Quiet your mind and see if you can find out where they are and what's going on. The more information we have, the better. And if you can, communicate to them we're here. Hopefully, they'll be able to pick up on your signal. Once we know more, we can make a better decision as to what to do next and when to move."

Eve took a deep breath and nodded. "Okay."

She sat on the ground and crossed her legs. Closing her eyes, she breathed deeply and went still.

· · • • • • • • • · ·

Ramsey stepped around some poison ivy and squatted low beside a thick bush. Declan and Hannah followed. They made as little noise as possible as they moved, not wanting to bring any attention to their presence. Ramsey knew his wife was somewhere ahead of him. Declan had noted that Sarah's forward progress had slowed and stopped. Ramsey had to force himself not to sprint into the woods. Until he knew his kids were safe, he had to let this play out and allow Sarah to do her part. It was killing him to put her at risk, but they'd had no other choice.

Getting closer to the spot where Sarah's signal had stopped, Ramsey stepped carefully, keeping an eye out in front of him. He didn't want to walk straight into an ambush. Declan and Hannah were quiet behind him, but the closer he got, the more stressed he became. What would they do if the kids were not where they were taking Sarah? What if Sarah disappeared and Ramsey couldn't get to her? The terrifying scenarios plagued him, and he tried not to think the worst, but icy fear made his chest hurt.

Pushing through another dense area of foliage, Ramsey froze when he heard something. He looked behind him and put a finger to his lips. Declan and Hannah froze, too. They listened. After a few seconds, Ramsey recognized voices. Soft footfalls and crunching leaves accompanied the sound and whoever it was made no effort to be silent. As the noises grew louder, he crouched low, ready to launch himself at whoever was headed their way. There was no time for them to hide or retreat.

His stress level at its max, Ramsey waited and prayed that they wouldn't be discovered, but as his ears tuned in, he heard what sounded like a child. He swore he heard, "It's a squirrel," in a high-pitched voice.

Declan punched him from behind and Ramsey looked back. His brother pointed with wide eyes. "It's them," he said, just as Ramsey heard a female say, "That's a bunny rabbit, Rosie."

Ramsey's heart dropped. It was his mother. Without thinking, he scrambled out of the woods. Pushing past a heavy branch, there stood his mother, holding Ethan and Rosie's hands, directing them through the trees.

"Mom!" he yelled.

Charlotte Ramsey jumped and turned. "John? Is that you?"

Ramsey raced toward his mother and kids.

"Daddy!" said Ethan.

"Hi, Daddy," said Rosie.

Ramsey dropped to his knees and pulled his kids into his arms. There were no words to describe his relief. Tears welled up in his eyes, and he hugged them tightly. "Thank God," he said into Rosie's hair. His voice quivered and his body shook.

"Are you crying, Daddy?" asked Rosie. She pulled back and patted his cheek. "Don't cry."

"Mommy says boys cry all the time," said Ethan, his eyes wide. "It's okay, Daddy."

Ramsey wiped his eyes. "Are you all right?" He checked them for any injuries. "Are you hurt?"

"We're all fine," said his mother.

"Grandma's taking us for ice cream," said Rosie. "You want some?"

Ramsey smiled. "Not right now, sweetheart."

Declan and Hannah came up behind them. "You're okay," said Declan. "Hi, Rosie. Hi, Ethan."

"You want some ice cream, Uncle Declan?" asked Rosie.

Declan kneeled beside her. "Maybe later, honey. Right now, your daddy and I have to find Mommy."

"She's on the ship with the mean lady," said Rosie.

Ramsey sniffed and stood. "What happened? Where's Sarah?"

His mother's face paled. "She stayed behind. Told us to go. Said you were looking for us. I took the children away. I didn't know what else to do."

Ramsey put his hand on her shoulder. "You did the right thing, Mom. It's fine. Where's the ship?"

She pointed. "Straight that way. About ten minutes. You can't miss it." Her eyes had dark circles beneath them, and her face was taut. "What are you going to do?"

Ramsey squatted next to his children. "Ethan. Rosie. I need you to do me a favor. Can you go with Grandma? I need you to listen to her. She'll take you back to the car and out of the woods. Can you do that?"

Hannah joined him. "I'll go too. Let's see how many squirrels we can find." She smiled and nodded at Ramsey.

Ramsey smiled back wearily. "Thank you," he said. He knew it would be hard for her to leave Declan.

Hannah stood, holding Rosie's hand. "I'll show you where the car is, Charlotte."

"I saw three squirrels already," said Rosie.

"Those were birds," said Ethan.

"No, they weren't," said Rosie.

"Hush, children," said Charlotte. "No arguing. Let's follow Aunt Hannah. She knows where to go."

John gave his mother a hug. "Be careful."

"I will," she said. "Don't worry about the kids. We'll get them back safe."

Hannah hugged Declan. "You be careful too. Don't do anything stupid," she said.

Declan nodded and kissed her. "Don't worry. Just get the kids to safety. We'll be right behind you."

Hannah held his hand. "Don't you dare lie to me."

Declan nodded. "I know better than to do that."

"I love you," said Hannah.

"I love you too," he said.

Hannah let go of Declan, and Ramsey saw her swallow. Reserved, she looked at Ramsey, her eyes pensive. "And you..." She paused and Ramsey waited. "Go get your wife. Bring her back safe. I'm not getting ice cream without her."

Ramsey held his breath. Every nerve in his body was on edge. "You can be damn sure of that."

With a quick turn, Hannah stuck a smile on her face and guided Rosie into the woods with Charlotte and Ethan behind her. "Last one there is a rotten egg."

They headed through the trees, and Ramsey listened as his children babbled about birds and squirrels, and he wished Sarah was with them so they could all go home. He turned away. "You ready?" he said to Declan.

"As I'll ever be," his brother replied.

Ramsey broke into a jog, heading toward the ship.

Chapter Twenty-Eight

Sarah followed Desde into the large craft. She paid close attention to her surroundings. Every detail would matter if she planned to get out of here. John was on his way, and as much as she needed to get out of this alive, she had to be sure he didn't get himself killed, either. She would use whatever she could to her advantage.

There wasn't much to see. Desde walked into a small antechamber with one door ahead of her and one on either side. Sarah was reminded of the game show *The Price is Right*. Did the contestant want door number one, two, or three? Desde swiped her hand over a console on the wall. The door on the right slid open.

"This will be your place for the time being. Until we're ready to leave. Then we'll prep you for the long sleep back." Sarah could see a small, sparse room with a white couch and chair. "There's a bathroom on the other side. It's not much, but none of the rooms on this thing are anything special. I'm sick of white. I can't wait to get back home. Get in my big bed with my soft sheets. You'll like it there. It's much more comfortable."

Desde stood at the entrance, waiting for Sarah. Sarah hesitated, wondering what to do. If she entered that room, would she ever get out? Were her children far enough away to be safe if she tried to run? The questions swirled. Where was John? Did he know where she was? Fear made her stomach churn, and her thoughts wouldn't settle. "Where will you be?" It was the only thing she could think to say.

"It's not your business, but I'll give you some leeway here until you learn your place. I'm across the way." She pointed to the door opposite Sarah's. "It's not much different from yours, but it's bigger."

"This ship is large. This can't be all of it," said Sarah.

Desde half-smiled. "It's not. That over there," she pointed to the middle door, "leads to the rest of the ship. Where Andolina rules the roost." She said it with a sneer. "Right now, she calls the shots, so I do as she wants." She paused. "For now, at least."

"Does she know I'm here?" Sarah wanted to keep her talking.

"What she knows or doesn't know is not your concern. Just keep your mouth shut and do what I say and everything will be fine. I know what I'm doing."

"What about Royce and Gillian? Are they here?"

Desde narrowed her eyes. A sharp twist of pain hit Sarah in her midsection, and she buckled to her knees. "I told you to stop asking questions."

Sarah began to slide toward the opening of the small room, and she held out her hands to stop her movement. "Wait. Please." It came out as more of a whimper than a shout. Her progress halted just outside the door.

Desde crouched beside her. "You should know who you're dealing with. Sarna messed with me, and she paid the price. And when I find her again," she paused. "Let's just say that bitch will pay for what she did to me."

Sarah bit her lip in pain, but risked another question. "What did she do?"

Desde glowered. "If it hadn't been for her and Royce, I'd be the mother of the High Child. Not the puppet of Roma's cronies."

"Then Roma would have been threatened by you."

"I would have never hidden. I would have told everyone who I was. Roma would have had no choice but to make a place for me, or face ousting by the Council. Plus, I like money. I have no interest in politics or change. I simply want to live the life I've grown accustomed to. Sarna is different. She likes to politicize her position and use her connections to oust Roma and put Royce in place. Roma is not going to allow that to happen. Nor am I."

The pain eased enough for Sarah to take a deeper breath. "But Sarna has a child by Royce. You can't kill a baby, no matter what the politics are."

Desde went quiet. Her body turned rigid and her face lost its color. "What did you say?"

Sarah realized her mistake. It had not occurred to her that Desde did not know about Greta. She didn't know what to say. Did none of them know about Greta? Maybe Roma and Andolina knew, but Desde clearly did not.

Desde glowered. "That's impossible. She could not have sustained a pregnancy after..." She stared off and Sarah wondered what she was remembering. By the twisted look on her face, it wasn't good.

"Get in your room," said Desde.

"But—" Sarah couldn't finish her sentence before the pull on her body returned, and some unseen force dragged her the rest of the way into the chamber. Her side hit the wall, knocking the air out of her. She caught a quick glance of Desde walking away before the door slid shut on her.

· · • • • · • • · ·

Gillian stepped out from behind Royce. "Grayson is here?" Royce tried to push her back, but she held her ground.

Andolina smiled. "He's came to save you. Very courageous of him. I traded the letter for your life." She eyed Royce.

"The letter? Grayson found Sarna's letter?" asked Royce.

"Yes. And as soon as I hand over your sister, I'll have it. Then you and I will say a final goodbye, and I'll go home, find Sarna, and take care of her too." She leaned against the doorway. "Another successful mission in the books. Roma will be pleased."

"What about Gillian and Eve?" asked Royce.

"They will be spared if Grayson brought me what I wanted. Assuming they will not pursue any interest in being High Child." She pointed at Gillian. "But that agreement is void should you change your mind. Same goes for any offspring you may have." Andolina's eyes dropped briefly to Gillian's stomach. "Remember that."

Royce considered what to do next. According to Andolina, Eve and Gillian were safe. "What about Jasper? What happens to him?"

Andolina paused. "Roma has a soft spot for her brother. But I am less tolerant. If he interferes, I'll take care of him too. Roma will grieve, but she'll understand. Sometimes retaining power means letting go of the people you love." She nodded behind her, looking out the open doorway. "I suspect he's out there now, waiting." She looked back. "He thinks I don't know that he followed Grayson. He should know better. Unfortunately, his chances aren't good." She spoke to Gillian. "Your sister and Adam are out there, too. You should probably warn them about the agreement if you want them to leave alive."

Gillian, despite Royce's attempts, stepped forward. "Then let me leave and I will."

"Not without the letter," said Andolina.

"Why go after Sarna?" asked Royce. "She has no claim to the throne."

Andolina raised a brow. "You know why."

Fear coursed through Royce. "You know about Greta."

"I have eyes and ears everywhere. It's why I get paid so well."

Royce fought every instinct he had to wrap his hands around Andolina's throat. "You would kill a child?"

Andolina crossed her arms. "Oh, I'm not going to do it. But I know who is."

Royce couldn't speak. All he wanted was to protect his family, but his options were dwindling.

"I don't understand," said Gillian. "Who could be so depraved as to kill an innocent baby?"

There was a swooshing sound, and Andolina turned to look as footsteps sounded on the metal floor. "You're back," she said.

A taller man with short brown hair and a fresh face appeared in the doorway. He nodded. "She tried to reach you, but when she didn't hear back, she sent me."

"I've been busy," said Andolina. "But there's been progress. We'll leave soon, but I have a job for you. There are others outside. I need you to make sure they stay off the ship. You do whatever it takes."

"Of course," he said, nodding.

Royce wondered who the 'she' was that the man was referring to when he suddenly understood Andolina's plan. "It's Desde, isn't it? You're going to make her kill Sarna and Greta."

Andolina frowned. "I won't make her do anything. Once she learns the truth, she won't even ask permission. In fact, if I forbid her to harm the child, she'll do exactly the opposite. You have no idea how much she hates you and Sarna. She's cunning and vengeful, which makes her useful, until I don't need her anymore." She addressed the man behind her. "Tell Desde I want to see her." She shot a knowing look at Royce. "There's something I need to tell her."

Royce gritted his teeth. If there was a way to stop Andolina, he was going to have to think of it fast.

"There's something else," said the man. "She didn't come alone."

"What do you mean?" asked Andolina.

"She brought one of them with her."

Andolina's eyes narrowed and her face dropped. "What? Who?"

"The hybrid. She plans to take her back with us."

Andolina set her jaw.

Royce shared a look with Gillian. He suspected he knew who they meant. Desde had Sarah. He thought of Ethan and Rosie. Had Sarah made a deal to save her children? It's what he would have done.

"Where are the children?" asked Andolina, her posture rigid.

"She's letting them go."

Andolina paused, her face flat, but Royce sensed the anger behind it.

"Maybe she's not as useful as you think," he said.

Andolina's dark eyes found his. "Her time will come." She flicked her angry eyes toward Gillian. "Let's get this over with." When Gillian hesitated, Andolina responded. "Or you can stay here and I'll kill Grayson where he stands. Letter or no letter. My patience is wearing thin."

Gillian took a hesitant step toward Andolina but offered Royce a wary glance.

"Gillian…" Royce held his breath. He ached to protect her, but he couldn't sacrifice her husband. "Remember what I said."

She nodded as she followed Andolina out of the room, but Andolina turned back. "You too," she said to Royce. "No need for you to cloak yourself when I have my back turned." She spoke to the man still beside her. "Send the message to Desde and keep watch. No one else gets on this ship who isn't already on it. You are authorized to use whatever force is necessary. Go."

The man walked away. Royce stepped out of the room and got a quick glance of the outside before the ship's door closed. He saw lots of trees and a lowered ramp before his view disappeared. At least he knew which way was out.

Andolina followed the corridor of doors that he and Gillian had crossed and went to the door of the room they'd left. It slid open with a wave of Andolina's hand. Sitting on the white couch was Grayson. His head popped up. "Gillian," he said, standing.

"Grayson." She ran into his arms, and he pulled her close.

Royce heard him whisper. "You okay?"

She nodded. "I'm okay," she said. "So's the baby."

He let go of a deep breath. "I was scared to death."

"I know," she said, pulling back. "But it's all right." She put her hand on his cheek.

"It's all right if he has what I want," said Andolina. "Otherwise this homecoming is going to be short-lived." She cocked her head. "So where is it?"

Grayson let go of Gillian, his face pale. He spoke to Royce. "I had to do it. I took the letter from Jasper. I was terrified. I had to protect Gillian."

Royce couldn't fault him for that. If their situations were reversed, he likely would have done the same thing.

Grayson regarded Andolina. "Just let us go. We'll keep Royce here. He'll behave. If he gets any grand ideas, we'll remind him of how nasty his enemies can be. You'll have nothing to worry about."

"We've gone way past that," said Andolina. "Now give me the letter. I've humored you for this long, so don't make me angry. We had a deal. You play with me and I will rescind the agreement." She walked into the chamber and got up close to Grayson, her eyes like darts. "Give it to me."

Grayson held Gillian's hand, but he let it go. With a glance at Royce, he said, "I'm sorry," bent over, and pulled up a pant leg. A tri-folded paper was in his sock, and he pulled it out. "You should have searched me." She ticked up a brow, and he handed it to her. "Here. Take it. Just let Gillian go."

Andolina took the papers and held them. Going still, she closed her eyes and, without opening the papers, stroked her fingers over it, as if petting a small bird. After a few seconds, her eyes opened, and she smiled. "Excellent. That wasn't so hard, was it?"

Royce's heart deflated, but he had one hope. "It says nothing about Sarna's whereabouts. You won't find her."

Andolina grinned. "You seem to think I'm stupid. You think I'd come all this way to read a love letter? This is much more than that." She waved the papers. "Sarna's energy is all over it. It's like a map, telling me exactly where to go. I suspect, once I'm home, that I'll find her within the week." She smiled and her teeth gleamed in the artificial light. "Greta too."

At the mention of his daughter's name, Royce's control vanished. Rage erupted, and he did the only thing he could do. He launched forward and tackled Andolina to the floor. He heard Gillian yell his name as he wrapped his hands around Andolina's throat and squeezed. She struggled for a quick second before a tingle in his belly became a jackhammer, and he was lifted and thrown off her. His body flew up and back out into the corridor, and he landed on his back, his head taking a hard hit. Gillian screamed and ran toward him.

"Get her out of here," yelled Royce to Grayson with a groan.

Grayson grabbed Gillian by the shoulders and tried to pull her away, but Gillian resisted.

"No. I won't leave him," she yelled as Grayson held her.

Andolina appeared at the doorway, her hair disheveled. She straightened her shirt, and still watching Royce, walked to a side panel in the corridor. Attached to it was a flat box. She put the letter in it and then turned her full attention to Royce.

Royce tried to sit up, but an invisible force held him down. He grunted, trying to move, but his body would not comply. A strange, heavy feeling moved up his legs, and he couldn't raise them. It was as if all his nerve endings were going on strike. A slow paralysis crawled up to his pelvis and traveled up his spine. White hot terror made him sweat, and he realized that this was it. Andolina was going to kill him, find Sarna and Greta, and kill them, too. He'd failed.

Controlling his fear, he managed to speak. If nothing else, he would protect his remaining family. "Grayson. Take Gillian now. Don't let her see this." Andolina didn't move, but her eyes told Royce everything. The paralysis moved up into his waist, and he knew his lungs were next. "Please," he said.

Gillian's face was streaked with tears as she tried to escape Grayson's hold. "Stop. Please don't kill him."

Grayson grabbed Gillian and pulled her back. "Gillian, we have to go."

Royce thought of the trees outside, wishing he could run into them. Sarna and Greta's faces flitted in his mind, and he reached out, wishing they could hear him. "I'm so sorry," was all he could convey before the paralysis moved up his belly and into his lungs, and his breath halted. Still able to move his arms, he gripped at the cold metal beneath him.

"No," said Gillian.

Fighting for air, Royce closed his eyes.

Chapter Twenty-Nine

RAMSEY CROUCHED LOW, AND Declan joined him. He was breathing hard from his run, and he tried to slow his breath. He didn't want to risk anyone knowing they were there. The ship sat quietly, its shiny hull gleaming in the sunshine. The size of the craft surprised Ramsey. He'd expected something small and fast, not big and imposing. But considering its passengers, he figured he shouldn't have been surprised. He suspected Desde liked her space.

Declan pointed. "Look. There's an open door. The ramp's down."

Ramsey nodded. Is that where they'd taken Sarah? "Can you see the other side?" He motioned toward the underside of the craft, which was raised on six-foot-high supports. "It looks like another ramp is down on the opposite end."

"I see it," said Declan in a whisper. "It's bigger. Maybe it's the main entrance." He studied the area. "How do you want to do this? I don't see anyone."

Ramsey considered what to do. "Morgana's sending support, right? They should be here soon."

"Theoretically, yes. But there's no telling when they'll arrive."

Ramsey couldn't afford to wait. If the ship showed signs of departure, he could lose his chance to save his wife.

"Any word from Jasper?" he asked.

"Not recently," said Declan. "But if they're trying to save Royce and Gillian, they've got their own can of worms to deal with."

Ramsey grappled with what to do. All that came to mind was what he always did. Trust his gut. "I say we take door number one."

"I'm right behind you."

Ramsey stepped out of the woods toward the ship.

· · · ● ● · ● ● ● · ·

Eve sucked in a breath. The images swirled fast, and it was hard to keep up. Gillian and Royce were standing in a room, talking. Gillian wrung her hands as Royce spoke to her. Then the picture shifted, and she could hear Royce in her head. *Sarna's letter.* Gillian's fear for Grayson and her baby coursed through Eve, and sweat popped out on her skin. Trying to follow the conversation, Eve frowned as everything went dark and then she saw them again. Gillian hugging Gray. Anger bubbling up from her brother. The letter. Sarna. Greta. The emotion was almost too much for Eve, and she struggled to keep her focus. Royce's fear for her and Gillian made her heart thump. Eve tried to reach out to him, but his thoughts were too jumbled, and she couldn't connect. Then white-hot rage enveloped her. So much so that she almost screamed, and then a terrible blackness joined it, making it difficult to distinguish between the two. She audibly grunted when the air was knocked from her and a fear she'd never experienced enveloped her and tightened its grip, making it hard to breathe. Tears spilled from her lashes as her body went numb, and she heard Gillian's shrieks of anguish. It was unbearable. Something pulled at her, and she was yanked from her vision and opened her eyes.

Adam was kneeling next to her, holding her elbow. "Eve," he said. "What happened? You're scaring me."

Jasper stood over her. "What did you see?"

Catching her breath, Eve jumped to her feet, wiping her face. "They're dying." Desperate, she ran out of the woods.

"Eve," said Adam.

"Wait," yelled Jasper.

But Eve ignored them. Her feet flew over the hard ground, jumping roots and dodging a prickly shrub, the images of her vision assailing her. Her siblings were going to die.

Clearing the trees, the ship came into view. The ramp they'd seen was still lowered, but the entrance to the ship was closed, and at the bottom of the ramp stood a man.

· · • • • • • • · ·

Desde marched toward the door that led to the ship's interior, intent on confronting Andolina. Waving her hand, the door to the central part of the ship raised. She walked through, and it closed behind her. Sarna had given birth to Royce's child? How was that possible? Her attack on Sarna should have ended any pregnancy and Sarna should have died as a result. Desde could live with Sarna's survival, but not the baby's. The High Child's baby was supposed to be hers.

She strode through a large chamber which housed the sleeping tubes and a round metallic table for meals. The front of the ship was on her right, and she passed the entrance to the pilot's chamber, where two main chairs and three passenger chairs stood vacant. Through the viewing pane, the wind rustled the treetops. The more she walked, the angrier she became.

Why had Andolina not told her? Perhaps she didn't know either, and if she didn't, then Desde would give her the news, and her plan would be to find that child and end its life. Preferably while Sarna watched. Then that bitch would know pain.

But somehow, she suspected Andolina had known. Heat flared through her as she considered what to do and say. Andolina had used Desde to do her dirty work and would no doubt take all the credit. Desde's imagination churned. Is this the real reason they'd come to Earth? Not just to kill Royce, but to also locate Sarna and her brat? It made sense. Roma would not want another potential threat to her throne. But why not tell her? Because they didn't trust her. Instead, they'd put Andolina in charge. Desde guessed what Andolina had planned. Once the Fletchers were dead, Andolina would use Desde's hatred to her advantage, finally telling Desde the whole truth and having her kill the High Child because she was too cowardly to do it herself.

Desde fumed as she passed to the other side of the ship, ready to confront Andolina and her lies. Reaching the door to the opposite section, she waved a hand, and the door slid open.

·· · ● ● · ● ● ● · ·

Grayson held onto Gillian, but her anguish ripped at his heart. He'd thought he was doing the right thing. It had made sense. Save his pregnant wife. Royce had wanted that too. The letter was his last concern. But now that he'd delivered it, his joy turned to misery when he realized Gillian was going to have to sacrifice her brother. It would be impossible. There was no way he could get her to safety while her brother suffered. The more he pulled on her, the harder she fought.

Royce made slow movements, but his efforts slowly weakened. His face stricken, his body began to succumb. Watching his brother-in-law dying in front of him, Grayson couldn't stomach it anymore than Gillian could. Gillian might live, but something inside of her would never be the same.

Spying the walls, he pulled Gillian close despite her struggles. "Gillian, you have to go."

"I can't," she said, sobbing. "She's killing him."

"Open the door," he yelled. Andolina, staring down at Royce, did not even acknowledge him, but he heard a rumble and a whir and saw the door begin to open. He said a prayer and hoped he was doing the right thing.

"I've got to get you out," he said to Gillian.

Royce had stopped speaking, but his mouth moved as he tried to breathe. Gillian was hysterical, but Grayson got in front of her and grab her by the arms. "Gillian. Leave now. Find your sister. Jasper too. They're out there. They can help."

Hearing her sister's name seemed to snap her out of it. Her eyes found his. "You have to help him." Tears rained down her cheeks and her nose was running.

He nodded and spoke forcefully. "Go get Eve. Now. Trust me."

They held eye contact, and he imbued every hope and prayer he had to get her to move. He had to get her away from the ship.

She hesitated, but his prayers must have worked because she broke free and ran for the door. Relief flooded him, and he turned, heading straight for an object he'd seen on the wall earlier, before Andolina attacked Royce. He didn't think twice or offer a second glance at Royce or Andolina. He knew the likelihood of success was low, but he wouldn't be able to look at himself in the mirror again unless he did something. He prayed Gillian would understand if he failed. Reaching the object, he pulled it off the wall from which it hung. It resembled a fire extinguisher, and it weighed about the same.

Gripping it in his hands, and pleased it had some heft to it, Grayson raised it high, and walking up behind Andolina, who ignored him as she sucked the life from Royce, swung it down on top of her head.

She went down hard, like a popped balloon, and didn't move.

· · · · · ● · · · · · ·

Ramsey ran into the clearing, looking around and hoping no Eudoran cronies emerged to confront them. He didn't see anyone, so he jogged up the ramp, trying to keep his footfalls quiet. Declan followed. Reaching the top, he saw a small area with three closed doors.

"Which one?" asked Declan, breathless.

There was a pounding on the door to the right and Ramsey jumped.

"Desde, let me out!" yelled a woman. "Where are you?" The pounding came again.

Ramsey's heart raced. It was Sarah. "That one." He ran over to it. "Sarah. It's John." He banged on the door.

There was a pause. "John? Honey? It's you?"

"Yes, sweetheart. I'm here. Hold on. Declan and I are going to get you out." He searched around the wall for a knob or a switch to open the door, but he didn't see anything.

"Be careful," yelled Sarah. "She may come back. Hurry."

"How do we open this thing?" asked Ramsey.

Sarah spoke from behind the door. "There's a controller on the wall. Desde moved her hand over it."

"Where?" asked Ramsey.

"There," said Declan. He walked over to a thin, square, metal panel with a screen mounted on the wall. He studied it and poked at the screen. Nothing happened.

Ramsey tapped on it, trying to get something to happen. Nothing did. "How the hell does this work?" He slapped his hand on it.

"This is not an old TV," said Declan. "Don't hit it."

"You have any better ideas?" asked Ramsey.

"They use energy. That's what probably makes it work. Hold on." He went still and closed his eyes.

Sarah spoke. "Did you find it?"

"Hold on, honey," said Ramsey. "We're working on it." He waited as Declan did his thing, but his impatience was growing. "Anything?" he asked Declan.

"Shhh," said Declan. "Let me concentrate."

Ramsey sighed and stepped away, trying to stay calm. If Desde returned, they were all screwed. He walked back to the door. "You okay?" he asked Sarah through the door.

"I'm okay. Where are the kids?" she asked.

"Mom and Hannah are taking them back. They're all right," he said. She didn't answer right away, and he imagined her nodding with her head against the door. "You sure you're okay?"

A quiet voice answered. "I'm scared."

His heart fell. "I know. Don't be. We're going to get you out of here."

"If she comes back..." Her voice trailed off. "Just know that I love you."

Ramsey bit his lip. He was not going to have this conversation. He was going to get his wife off this ship. Glancing at Declan, he saw his stepbrother still standing quietly, his eyes closed. Declan raised his hand and held it over the console. Nothing happened.

"I love you too," he said.

"If something happens, you get out," she said.

"I'm not leaving you," he answered.

"We have to think of our kids. We can't leave them parentless."

"I am *not* leaving you," he repeated.

"John, please," said Sarah.

"This is ridiculous," said Ramsey, his patience evaporating. "I prefer the old-fashioned way." He strode over to Declan, whose hand was still raised. "You had your shot," he said to his brother. "Now it's my turn."

Declan's eyes opened. "No. Wait."

Ramsey ignored him and slammed his fist down on the panel. Nothing happened, and he hit it several times.

"Stop it," said Declan.

On the last hit, the screen cracked. Ramsey stopped assailing it and put his hand down.

"Great," said Declan. "Now you've—"

All three doors opened.

Chapter Thirty

Vee stepped through the dense foliage and pushed her way past a wayward branch. A twig caught her hair, and she plucked it out. Checking her phone again, she verified the coordinates Jasper had given her. She was close. In fact, she should be there. Stepping past a dead tree, she saw a grassy area and ran toward it, her recognition returning. Reaching the area, she saw nothing but patchy brown grass surrounded by trees, but she knew this place. Reaching into her jacket pocket, she pulled out the silvery object that resembled a fountain pen. It was the object she'd found in the forest what seemed like years ago. Clicking it, the spacecraft slowly materialized—Jasper's ship.

Jasper had given her the directions to return. She hadn't been aware of how close they were until she'd raced through the woods, realizing she was coming at it from the back end. Checking her phone, she could see the slow blinking blip of Jasper's current location. The blip moved slowly on the screen, and she wondered if they were close to reaching Grayson. She studied the blip. If she finished her task here, then she could meet back up with them relatively quickly if she ran.

But before she could do that, she had to finish here. The small ship sparkled in the sun, and she ran up to it. She clicked the pen again, and a door slid open and a small ramp appeared just as it had on the day she'd found Jasper's pills. She took a breath and tried to not to think about the insanity of this situation. She was about to access an alien craft to help save a group of aliens from destroying another group of aliens. She wondered if perhaps she was lying in a coma somewhere and that at any moment she would wake in a hospital, realizing she'd been in an elaborate dream state. It hadn't happened yet though, so she kept going.

She jogged onto the ship and remembered what Jasper had told her. She took a right and accessed the cockpit. It was two chairs and a console of buttons, dials, and screens that sat below a window that looked out at the trees. Everything was quiet, and the ship was dark and dusty, like a vacant home long since abandoned.

She pulled the paper from her pocket and sat in one of the chairs. Her heart pumping fast, she studied Jasper's diagram and started punching buttons. The console whirred to life and green lights illuminated the cockpit. Vee took a breath, praying she knew what she was doing. Following Jasper's instructions, she completed her task, hoping she'd done everything correctly. Nothing had blared at her, so she took that as a good sign. Checking her watch, she saw the blip. It had stopped. Jasper wasn't moving. Was that good or bad?

She took one last look around, taking a few seconds to appreciate where she was. Her dad would never have believed it. She was sitting in the cockpit of an extraterrestrial craft. Would she ever see it again, or was she about to wake up from her coma? Running her hands over the panel, she felt the rush. She'd never felt so alive. It was like every cell in her body had suddenly turned on, and she had the brief thought of trying to fly this thing. She imagined raising it from the ground and traveling to Jasper's location, where she could hover over them, and rescue Royce and Gillian. She'd save the day. It was an invigorating thought, but a short-lived one. She'd more likely crash into a tree.

Flipping a switch, she saw the lights dim and wink out, and the instrumentation went dark, save for one button, which Jasper told her would remain illuminated. It blinked softly on the dim panel, like a distant ship at sea. Sighing, Vee left the cockpit, stepped off the craft, and closed the door. With a click of the pen, the ship disappeared before her eyes.

She felt strangely sad, as if she missed the ship, knowing she'd likely never return, maybe because she knew Jasper would leave on this craft and disappear from her life.

But she didn't have time for melancholy. Thinking of Jasper, she studied the blip again, which remained in the same place as before. Making a quick deduction in her head, she ran into the woods. If she pushed it, it wouldn't take her long to reach them.

····•·•••··

Morgana made her way through the trees. She moved easily, despite her age. She'd never been a couch potato, preferring to move instead of staying still. In her line of work, exercise had proven to be an excellent stress reliever, and she had plenty of stress to reduce. Being out here now, despite the circumstances, already made her feel better. The sun was out, and the day was warm. Holding her walking stick, she stepped off the trail and into the dense woods. She took a moment to check her phone and pinpoint where she was headed. Talbot, despite his disagreement with what she was doing, was sending her clear directions. The same ones he was giving the team armed with the serum. Familiar with the area, she'd parked off the side of the road near a neighboring trail. It would require some rugged hiking, but she'd get to Jasper and Declan faster than if she'd taken an easier path. Hopefully, the teams were ahead of her, and by the time she arrived, this would all be over.

Based on her experience, though, she knew that nothing ever went according to plan. But she also knew that could be a good thing. Sometimes, the wrong thing could lead you in the right direction. She trusted that would be the case again.

She walked for several minutes, and beads of sweat ran down her back. Continuing to check her phone, she adjusted her direction, and kept walking, periodically stopping to take a swig of water. She was close, based on the map, and paused to double check her coordinates.

A noise made her look up. A bird flew away, and Morgana turned, listening. Footfalls. She could hear someone running through the woods. She didn't move, unsure of what to do. Was this someone she knew, or was she about to encounter trouble? There was nowhere to hide, and even less time to do it. All she could do was wait.

Morgana heard the intruder moving through the trees, making no attempt to be silent. Whoever it was, they weren't worried about being found.

She stood still as the forest grew quiet again. The footsteps halted, and she heard only the wind. She considered moving when there was the snap of a branch and Morgana jumped at a figure running out of the foliage. It was a woman. Small of stature but moving fast and paying little attention to her surroundings. She stopped short when she almost stumbled into Morgana as she cut through the trees. Morgana didn't move as they studied each other. The smaller woman was breathing hard, and her sweaty hair was stuck to her cheek. She brushed it back as her breathing slowed.

Morgana realized the woman's face was familiar, and she tried to place it. Frowning, Morgana remembered the explosion. She thought once again of Drake. "Officer Chappell, if I recall," she said.

The woman's eyes widened.

"You may not remember me..."

"You're Morgana..." She paused. "Sorry. I don't remember your last name."

Morgana ticked up a brow, impressed. "No need. Morgana will do fine. I take it you're not out for your daily jog, officer."

The woman checked her watch. "Call me Vee. And hell no. And I doubt you're out here to bird watch."

"Hell no," replied Morgana.

"Good," said Vee. She paused, and gave Morgana a good look, as if appraising her. Morgana returned the gaze.

Vee didn't hesitate. "So how about we go find your people?"

Vee obviously knew a lot more than Morgana realized, but Morgana didn't care. She liked this woman. "After you, Vee."

Chapter Thirty-One

Eve ran at a sprint toward the ship. Adam called her name, but she kept going, terrified for her siblings. She had to help. Gillian's desperation and Royce's anguish made anything less impossible. Reaching the ramp, she stopped when the man at the bottom stepped in front of her. She'd seen him, but her fear had kept her going.

"You may not enter," said the man.

"Get out of my way," said Eve. She tried to sidestep him, but he raised an arm and blocked her. She half expected to be invisibly shoved back, but she felt no force rush out from him. Perhaps he was not as powerful as Andolina or Desde.

"My family is in trouble. Either kill me or let me pass," said Eve.

Adam ran up behind her. "Eve, wait." He stopped next to her.

Jasper ran up beside Adam. The three of them faced the man on the ramp, who didn't move, but his eyes widened.

Jasper spoke first. "Anso?"

The man squinted. "Jasper. I should have suspected you'd be leading this rebellion."

"I had no idea you'd risen in the ranks," said Jasper. "Working with the Reds, now are you?"

"It's lucrative," replied Anso.

"You're a Gray," answered Jasper. "It's not lucrative. It's slavery. Money doesn't change that."

"Money changes everything." Anso raised his hand again as Eve attempted to move past him. "I'd leave now if you want to live."

"Her brother and sister are in there," said Adam. "They need help."

"It's too late for them," said Anso.

"No, it's not," said Eve. "Let me pass." She shoved past him, and he grabbed for her, but Adam shoved him back.

"Don't touch her," said Adam.

Eve didn't stop to look. She ran around Anso and up the ramp, half expecting to be tackled. The door to the craft was closed, though, and she didn't know how to open it. She scanned the area, desperate to gain access. Looking back toward the ramp, she was surprised to see Adam on the ground, holding Anso in a headlock. "Open this door!" she yelled.

Jasper stepped past the two men on the ground and approached Eve. "There's a panel on the side..." He stopped when the door shuttered, creaked, and began to open. Eve put her hands on the door, as if she could somehow make it open faster. It rose slowly past her ankles and made it to her knees. She dropped to the ground and was ready to crawl through it.

"Gillian," she yelled. "Royce." The door continued to rise.

"Eve!" Gillian's voice sounded from inside the ship.

The door rose higher, and Eve entered the ship. Her sister ran up, and Eve embraced her, but she still felt her sister's panic.

"Royce," Gillian yelled, pulling back. "She's killing Royce."

Jasper ran past them, and Eve followed. They were in a small antechamber that brightened as the door opened. Eve caught sight of her brother lying on the ground, looking pale. His eyes were shut. Grayson stood over Andolina, holding a heavy metal object. He looked just as pale, his clothes were dirty, and his hair was askew. He breathed heavily. Blood dribbled down the side of Andolina's head as she lay unconscious.

"Grayson," yelled Gillian, and she ran over to him.

Jasper ran to Royce's side, and Eve joined him. Jasper put his hand on Royce's shoulder.

"Royce?" asked Eve.

Jasper lightly jostled Royce. "Royce? Can you hear me?"

Gillian ran over. "How is he?"

Eve put her fingers on his throat, terrified at what she would do if she found no pulse. Anchors of weight dissipated when she felt a light, thready response. "He's alive."

"Thank God," said Gillian.

"We've got to get him out of here," said Jasper. "Andolina won't be out for long." He shook Royce again and then went still, closing his eyes.

Eve glanced over at Andolina. "What did you hit her with?" she asked Grayson.

Grayson shook his head, dropping the object. "I have no idea. But it did the job."

Gillian kneeled next to Royce. "Royce, wake up."

Jasper remained with his eyes closed, and then he reached out and touched Royce's chest. Royce's eyes shot open, and he gasped, sucking in a deep breath and coughing. He held his side and groaning, rolled sideways, and took several choking breaths. "What the hell was that?" he said in a garbled whisper.

"A little jolt to get you moving," said Jasper.

"Are you all right?" asked Eve, holding his arm.

He nodded at her, still looking pale. He choked out a few words. "I'm okay." The effort to say them brought on a new coughing fit.

Jasper pulled on his elbow. "Can you stand? We've got to get you up."

"Where's Gillian?" Royce sputtered.

"I'm right here," said Gillian. "I'm all right. So is Grayson."

Royce nodded. It took him a few seconds, but moving slowly, he attempted to get to his knees. He groaned with the movement.

"Keep an eye on Andolina," said Jasper. "If she's coming around, use that tank on her again. Otherwise, we won't get far."

Grayson picked up the heavy object he'd put down. "I'll be ready." His face fell. "If I was brave enough, I'd kill her right now."

Royce gingerly rose to his feet as Jasper bolstered him. Eve came around and let him lean on her until he got his footing. Royce eyed his sisters. "You both should have left. I told you not to come back for me, Gillian."

"We're not leaving you," said Eve.

"You're risking your lives. Both of you go now. I can catch up," he said. He scowled at Grayson. "You should have gotten Gilli out of here."

Gillian scowled back. "He's the reason you're alive."

"Your life is more important than mine. He should put you first," said Royce.

"Would you shut up and start moving," said Jasper. "I'd move you myself, but you're too damn heavy."

Royce winced as he walked. "Everything hurts."

They made slow progress, but found their way to the top of the ramp. They stopped when Adam ran up to meet them. "Everyone all right?"

"Where's Anso?" asked Jasper.

"He got away. I tried to hold him, but he's slippery," said Adam.

"He didn't hurt you, did he?" asked Eve, still helping Royce.

"No," said Adam.

"Help us with Royce," said Jasper.

Adam took Eve's place, and he and Jasper helped Royce down the ramp. Eve watched Royce gain strength as he walked, and Jasper and Adam supported him less and less.

"I hope you have back-up," said Royce.

"We do," said Adam. "They should be here any minute."

"We've got to get back to the woods," said Eve. "That will give us some cover. Maybe we can get out of here."

"When we get down the ramp," said Jasper, "you all head for safety. I'm staying here."

Royce stilled. "Why?"

"Someone has to deal with Andolina. If it means taking the helm of the ship and flying her out of here, then that's what I'll do. If we leave her here, she won't stop until you're dead. You'll never be free."

"She'll kill you," said Royce.

"Maybe not. If I can get moving before she wakes, then I may prevent that. If I can get her into a hypersleep, then the next thing she'll know is waking up on Eudora."

"What about Desde? And what about the Ramseys? We have to be sure their children are safe before we go anywhere." Royce's eyes widened. "The letter." He looked at Grayson. "Where's Sarna's letter?"

Grayson blanched. "It's on the ship."

"I've got to get it," said Royce, pulling free from Jasper and Adam's hold.

"Royce, wait," said Jasper, but Royce pushed away, and started back up the ramp.

Eve turned, ready to help her brother, when they all froze. At the top of the ramp, looking down at them, was Desde, eyes round with fury.

• • • • • • • • • •

Ramsey ran toward the door as Sarah stepped out of the room. She ran into his arms, and his heart thudded with relief. He had his wife back. Now, if they could return to their children, life might feel right again.

"You okay, Sarah?" asked Declan.

Sarah pulled back. "I am. Thank you." She gripped Ramsey's shirt. "How are you?"

"We're fine," said Ramsey. "Hannah, Mom, and the kids are headed back to the car. I want you to follow them."

Sarah frowned. "No. I have to stay with you. I can't leave."

"Sarah," said Ramsey. "Declan and I have to find out what's happening with the Fletchers and ensure Andolina and Desde are either dead or sent packing. If we don't do that, none of us are safe. But as you said, the children need a parent. If I don't come back..."

"Then you go. I'll stay with Declan," she said.

He shook his head. "No. Declan and I will do it. You're the one they want."

"Exactly. I'm the Red-Line. My sensitivities may help Declan. Plus, if they want me, then they won't harm me. They'll kill you on the spot."

"You'd rather be taken from your home to be a circus side show on another planet?" he asked.

"You know what I mean," she said. "Be logical about this."

"I am being logical. I'm not leaving my wife to battle two angry Red-Lines and sacrifice her to—to—"

"To what?" she asked. "To protect our children? I'd say that's the noble path. It's what a father would do."

"But not a husband." He paused. "You're my wife, Sarah. I can't leave you here."

She stepped close and took his hand. "I love you. And it's because of that, you'll do this. You know my abilities can be of value and may help to save Royce and his family. I have to use them if I can."

Ramsey was at a loss for words.

Declan cleared his throat. "I hate to interrupt this difficult conversation, but we don't have a lot of time."

"What do you think, Declan?" asked Sarah. "Should I stay or go?"

Ramsey glowered at Declan, who stood mute. After a pause, he checked his watch. "If the reinforcements would arrive, then the argument would be pointless. But you know our chances aren't good if it's up to only us. They're stronger than we are."

"Which is why I should go," said Ramsey. "If anyone is going to die, it should be me."

"That's ridiculous," said Sarah.

Ramsey tried to think of what to say to convince his wife to get off the ship and go home, but she was stubborn. "If I leave, and something happens, I'll never forgive myself. You're my wife. It's my job to protect you."

She squeezed his fingers. "We can discuss gender roles in survival situations at a later time. Right now, we have to do what makes sense. Our children need one of us."

"Our children need both of us," he said.

She smiled softly. "I agree. And I'll do whatever it takes to make that happen."

"Trust destiny. Remember?" asked Declan.

"You know Leroy's here with us," said Sarah. "He'll help too."

At the mention of his friend's name, Ramsey almost crumbled. "Sarah, I can't lose my best friend and my wife in the same week."

"Then you should both go," said Declan. "Let me handle this."

"No," said Ramsey and Sarah at the same time.

"Then we're at an impasse," said Declan.

"No, we're not," said Ramsey. He hesitated, debating his next words. "I'll go."

Sarah's eyes widened, and her mouth opened as if she wanted to say something, but she stopped herself. Biting her bottom lip, she hugged him. He hugged her back, holding her tightly. He smelled her hair. All he wanted to do was pick her up and take her home.

He let go of her and put his hand on her cheek, their eyes saying everything.

"I love you," she said.

"I love you too."

She stroked his hand, which lay on her cheek. "I wish ..." Tears sprang into her eyes.

He nodded. "I know ..."

"Kiss the kids for me. Tell them I love them," she said.

"You can tell them that when you're home."

She nodded and wiped at her eyes. "Okay." She choked on the word.

Ramsey's throat was so tight, he couldn't answer. He looked at his brother. "Declan, you watch out for her."

Declan sighed. "I still think you should both go. I can take care of myself."

Sarah took a deep breath and shook her head as if to clear it. "You can't go alone. It's not fair to Hannah."

Ramsey took a step, pulled Sarah close, and kissed her. She returned the kiss, lips slanted over his. He savored the taste of her, not caring if his brother watched. He was all too aware that these could be his last moments with her. Her arms went around his neck and he pulled her body against his. His heart beat in time with hers, and he ached to hold her longer.

Breaking the kiss, she buried her head in his neck, and her hot tears moistened his skin. He steeled himself. The last thing they needed was for him to lose it, too.

He took a last whiff of her hair, attentive to the feel of her body as she pulled away from him. Sniffing, she let go of his hand and wiped her face. She stood straight, pushed her hair back, and glanced at Declan.

"I'm ready," she said.

Keeping his emotions in check, Ramsey nodded, winked at his wife, turned, and, without looking back, headed down the ramp.

Chapter Thirty-Two

DESDE STOOD AT THE top of the ramp, her long blonde hair hanging in ringlets down her back. Her eyes flared, and Jasper braced.

The impact came in seconds. He was flung backward, as were the others. He caught only a brief glimpse of Royce and Adam flying through the air. He hit the ground hard, making contact with a large tree root that arched from the ground. His head hit the trunk and a sharp pain made him gasp as he heard the crack of a rib giving way. Everything went blurry. Jasper curled against the pain. Laying against the tree, he breathed slowly. Regaining some balance, he managed to raise his head. Royce and Adam were at the foot of the ramp, both on their backs. Grayson lay below the ramp, as if he'd been flung off the side. Eve and Gillian were nowhere to be seen. Where had they gone?

Desde still stood at the top of the ramp, like a queen looking down on her pitiful subjects, wondering which would die first. Taking her time, she began to descend.

Jasper pushed up, fighting the pain in his side. He got to his knees, and using the trunk for support, got to his feet. He swayed for a moment, but the dizziness passed. Making a concentrated effort to stay upright, he took a couple of steps forward. He was happy he could stay on his feet.

Desde reached the bottom of the ramp and stood over Royce and Adam. She cocked her head, and Adam lurched and grabbed his arm in pain. Royce stirred and opened his eyes.

"Desde," said Jasper. "Stop."

Desde glanced his way and squinted. Jasper felt a twinge, and then heard another crack. Excruciating pain twisted in his side. He cried out and went to his knees, holding his ribs.

Royce sat up, his hand raised. "Wait. Stop. It's me you want. Not them."

Adam squirmed, his head in the dirt. He held his arm but was able to raise up on his good elbow. His face was pale and his forehead sweaty. "Eve," he said. "Where's Eve?"

Jasper, trying to control the agony with deep, slow breaths, noted that Grayson had not moved. He prayed the man was only unconscious.

Desde didn't speak, but stared at Royce with a look of malevolence.

Royce spoke, breathless. "What do you want?"

Desde half-smiled. "You know what I want. You're just not prepared for how I intend to get it."

Royce got to his knees. He held his side, much like Jasper did. He grimaced. "Where are my sisters?"

The half-smile became a full smile. Jasper's insides went cold.

"Desde, please," said Royce.

"Begging won't help you, Royce," said Desde. She looked around. "It won't help any of you."

Jasper sucked in a breath and grit his teeth against the pain. "Desde, listen..."

"Shut up, Jasper," she said. "Your time's up too."

A tentacle of heat slid up his spine and into his head, and fire exploded in his brain. He grunted, held his head and squinted against the daylight, which now blinded him.

"Stop," said Royce. "I'll do whatever you want. Just let go of Eve and Gillian."

"It's too late for them," said Desde. "They can't be saved."

"No," said Royce.

"Where are they?" asked Adam.

"Be silent, traitor," she said, and Adam cried out and held his head.

Royce, eyes wide and skin beaded with perspiration, held out his hand. "Tell me what you want."

Desde's shoulders came down as if some of her fury had abated and she had relaxed. She didn't answer, but Jasper sensed unseen communication.

Jasper saw movement and, looking up, spotted Andolina step into the sunlight at the top of the ramp. Blood dripped from her hair, down her temple and cheek, and onto her shirt, but she made no attempt to wipe it away. The coldness in Jasper's belly turned to ice.

Royce and Adam noticed her, too.

No one spoke, but Jasper heard a strange sliding noise. Gillian and Eve slid into view. Lying together on their sides, they were pulled from inside the ship to the top of the ramp. Reaching the edge, an unseen force shoved them over and they rolled down the ramp together. They came to a stop at Desde's feet, near Royce. Their eyes were closed, and neither moved.

"Gillian. Eve." Royce tried to move, but he struggled against an invisible assailant. He couldn't get to his sisters.

Jasper reached out with his senses, feeling for anything from the women, and from Grayson. He searched for any sign of life force emitting from them. He was weak, and his energy was low, but he was still capable. His fears grew as his search returned nothing. Holding his chest, he held his breath as his suspicions were confirmed. They were too late. Royce's sisters and brother-in-law were dead.

Jasper knew Royce sensed the same thing when the big man dropped forward, his head against the hard ground, his hands clawing at the dirt, digging narrow trenches. Opening his mouth, Royce wailed.

· · · · • • · • • • · ·

Morgana and Vee stopped, listening to the cry of anguish echoing through the woods.

"What the ..." said Morgana, breathless. "Who is that?"

Vee listened, and a chill crawled down her spine. Their time was running out. Praying it wasn't Jasper screaming, she ran faster. They had to be close based on the volume of that awful yell. Periodically, she glanced at her phone to see if Jasper had tried to reach her, but there was nothing from him. She picked up her pace.

Finally reaching the spot where Jasper was supposedly located, Vee dodged past a thick vine and stepped into a clearing. She froze when she saw a large ship, much bigger than Jasper's, twinkling in the sun. The ramp closest to her was empty. No one appeared to be around, although Vee couldn't be sure because she did not have a view into the interior of the ship. But Vee could see the other ramp, on the far side, had activity. There were people around the bottom, and she stepped back into the woods to conceal herself. From what she could tell, no one had seen her.

Vee heard footsteps and rustling as Morgana caught up to her. She was breathing heavily, and her cheeks were red, but she appeared to be fine.

"What is it?" asked Morgana as she came up next to Vee.

Vee pointed. "Look. Over there."

Morgana peered past the foliage. "Is that their ship? It's huge."

"They're down by the opposite side. At the foot of that ramp."

"I see them," said Morgana. "It's hard to make out what's happening."

"We need to get over there," said Vee.

"Any ideas what we're going to do once we get there?"

"Not really. No."

Morgana wiped a trickle of sweat off her brow with her sleeve. "Excellent. I find flying by the seat of the pants often works well."

"Let's hope so." Vee turned and headed farther into the woods to provide a little cover as they made their way toward the far ramp. Morgana followed, staying close behind. Vee tried to keep a line of sight with the ship as much as possible and tried not to think of Jasper. That wail still echoed in her mind.

Stepping under a branch, she stopped. Morgana stopped behind her.

"What is it?" she asked.

Vee put a finger to her lips and Morgana went quiet. Listening, Vee waited. She'd sworn she'd heard footsteps, and within seconds, her suspicions were confirmed. Someone else was out here. Morgana heard it too, and her eyes widened. Whoever it was, they weren't trying to be quiet. Maybe it was just a jogger or a hiker? Vee tried to imagine how they would explain this scenario if they were to happen across an avid exerciser. Nothing came to mind.

The footsteps quickened. Vee turned toward the sound and prepared to confront the unknown intruder when a man ran out of the trees and almost knocked her over. Vee dropped low and almost delivered a decisive uppercut to his groin when he dodged her and stopped. He was sweating, his shirt sleeve was torn and there was a scratch on his face. Vee, recovering from her fright, realized she recognized him.

"Ramsey?" asked Morgana.

Ramsey, breathing hard, raised a brow. "Morgana. What the hell are you doing out here?"

"I thought I'd offer my services." She looked him up and down. "It looks like you could use some help."

Ramsey looked at Vee. "You could say that."

"Where are the children? And Sarah?" asked Morgana.

Ramsey dabbed his face with his arm. "The kids are safe. They're with Mom and Hannah. Sarah and Declan are still on that ship."

"What's happening?" asked Vee. "Where's Jasper and the rest? We saw activity on the other side."

"I saw and heard it too. That's where I'm headed." He paused. "You're getting pretty involved in this, officer," he said to Vee. "You're risking your life. You could go home, act as if none of this ever happened."

"That's not my style," responded Vee.

"Suit yourself." He looked at Morgana. "Can you keep up?"

Morgana straightened. "I've made it this far."

"If you fall behind ..." he said.

"Don't wait for me, Ramsey. I can take care of myself."

"Have you heard from Talbot?" asked Ramsey. "We need help out here."

Morgana glanced at a cell phone in her hand. "Last I heard, they were coming. My signal's weak though, so I haven't heard anything recently."

Ramsey nodded and spoke to Vee. "You have any ideas about how to approach this?"

"Let's start with stealth," she answered. "Then evaluate once we get there."

"My thoughts as well. Let's go."

He jogged into the woods, and Vee followed.

· · · · · · · · · ·

Declan and Sarah took the open middle door since it led deeper into the ship. They stayed close and listened intently as they walked. "You sure you want to do this?" asked Declan in a whisper. "You can go. You won't hurt my feelings."

"I won't leave you alone. Hannah would kill me," said Sarah.

They were in a narrow corridor which soon widened and they entered a larger room. They stopped and looked around.

"That must be the cockpit," said Declan.

"This must be where they sleep," said Sarah, pointing toward some bed-like tubes.

Declan walked up to the ship's controls. It was screens and buttons, nothing that made any sense to him. Everything was dark. "See anything we might use to our advantage?"

"Nothing," said Sarah.

"If we keep going, we're going to have to confront them. I'd rather do it with some sort of weapon."

"What weapon is going to work on them, other than the serum?"

Declan pulled out his phone. "Speaking of that, let's see if I have any updates." He checked the display. "That's interesting. I'm getting an excellent signal on this ship." He punched a few buttons, trying to reach Talbot. Within seconds, a message came through. Declan read it and smiled.

"What is it?" asked Sarah. "Good news?"

"They're here. Our team has arrived."

"Really?" asked Sarah. "Where?"

"Outside the ship."

"Let's go, then. We can help."

Declan put his phone back in his pocket. He left the main area and continued walking, passing what looked like a dining area and moving into another corridor that led to the opposite side of the craft. Several feet in, they came to another closed door. Declan went quiet and put his hands on it.

"Anything?" asked Sarah, after waiting a few seconds. A muffled wail broke the silence. "What was that? It sounds like someone's in pain."

Declan opened his eyes. "This is where the action is. They're on the other side."

"Who?"

"Everyone, from what I can feel."

Sarah nodded.

Declan hesitated. "Sarah, once we step out there, there's no going back."

Sarah swallowed. "This has to be done. And I know I have to be here. Whatever's happening on the other side of this door, I'm needed. I can feel it."

Declan paused. "I know. I can feel it too."

"Our help is here, though. We have to trust we aren't alone."

"Sarah ..." Declan wanted to voice his thoughts but doubted whether he should.

"Yes?"

"You know John would never leave you."

Her face fell, and she shook her head. "He's out there, isn't he?" Declan hesitated. "Damn. He's so stubborn." She sighed and rubbed her temples.

"He loves you. I know I'd never leave Hannah in a situation like this."

She put a hand on his shoulder and squeezed it. "I know."

"Maybe he can meet up with our team. Show them where to go."

"I just hope he doesn't do something stupid," said Sarah.

Declan raised a brow. "This is John we're talking about."

She made a half-smile, and Declan leaned close to the door, listening. "You ready?"

"You can open it?" she asked.

"I think so. It's this thing." He pointed to a small square screen on the wall. "I was getting the idea of it before John busted out the other one."

Sarah took a deep breath. "Okay. I'm ready."

Declan hovered his hand near the device and stilled, focusing on gathering the energy. He directed it toward the controls and heard a click and then a swoosh, and the door slid open.

Chapter Thirty-Three

Andolina walked down the ramp and joined Desde at the bottom. Jasper bit his lip against the pain, not in his ribs or head, but at the loss of three of their own. It was impossible to comprehend.

"Thank you, Desde," said Andolina. She touched her bloody head and looked at her fingers, then rubbed the blood off on her skirt. "You may return to your quarters. I'll handle this." She narrowed her eyes. "And we'll discuss your unannounced guest as well once I'm finished here."

Desde narrowed her eyes. "I'm not going anywhere. And my unannounced guest is settled comfortably in her room. She's not going anywhere either."

Jasper's head throbbed, but he raised his head. Royce hadn't moved. He was on his knees, facedown in the dirt, his hands on his head. Adam was beside Royce, holding his ribs, his face pale, his eyes on Eve, looking as if all the goodness in the world had evaporated.

Andolina set her jaw. "I said return to your quarters. We will discuss this later."

Desde chuckled. "You'd like that, wouldn't you? For me to bow down and do as you say. But we have a problem. You lied to me. Sarna's not only alive. She had his child. Why did you keep that from me?"

Andolina paused. "I do not answer to you. You answer to me. I brought you here to assist with finding the High Child. We have succeeded. The mission is accomplished."

"We haven't found Sarna."

"We have," said Andolina. "I have the letter she sent Royce. It's only a matter of time before we find her now."

"A letter?" asked Desde. "How do you expect to find her with a letter?"

Andolina sighed. Jasper studied his surroundings, hoping for any way out while the women were distracted.

"You know how," said Andolina. "Our viewers will use the letter and the trace energy on it to detect and locate Sarna and her baby. It works quite well. Once we return, they'll be dead within the week."

"Her baby." Desde watched Royce. "What's the baby's name?"

"What does it matter?," Andolina said.

"How did you know Sarna had a baby?" Desde sounded almost melancholy.

Andolina sniffed in annoyance but made the effort to answer. "Roma's father, the former High Leader, told Roma. I suspect he hoped to appeal to her sense of family and spare her half-siblings and their offspring. After all, this is her niece we're speaking of."

Desde's face was flat, but her eyes were cold. "I should have been told."

Andolina faced Desde. "What for? You are not a member of the High Family, nor of the Council. I was only told since I was leading this mission. The only reason you're here is your history with this man." She pointed at Royce, who still lay face down in the dirt. "If I'd had my way, I'd have never brought you. You're reckless and arrogant. You put your needs above the mission. Roma disagreed, though. She thought your anger and desire for vengeance would come in handy. Perhaps it has, but your job is complete. I will handle the rest, and we will discuss other matters later."

Jasper sat back on his heels. The pain in his head had subsided. His ribs ached, but the pain was manageable. He studied the arguing women, wondering where this would lead.

Desde glowered. "And what happens when we return? Will you acknowledge my contribution to this victory in any way?"

Jasper tuned in, trying to reach Royce or Adam, but he got nothing. Something else flickered, and he turned toward the woods. There was nothing there at first, but then the signal grew, and he focused in on its origin. He squinted when he saw movement, and then, through the foliage, standing behind a tree, he saw Vee. She watched him, and he shook his head, trying to tell her not to move.

"Nothing happens when we return," said Andolina. "I will tell Roma of our success. The High Child is dead, and we will locate his offspring. You will go back to ... your latest conquest."

Jasper hoped Vee got the message. He didn't want her jumping into this mess and getting killed as well. Their only hope was the reinforcements.

Desde didn't move, but there was a swirl of something unpleasant in the air. Jasper got a whiff of the energetic odor, which resembled the early stages of rotting food, and he grimaced.

"You expect me to return home while you receive all the praise for this mission?" asked Desde.

Andolina smiled. "What did you think? That Roma would welcome you into her inner circle? You're naïve, as well as undisciplined. And if you think we're taking anyone back with us, you're misinformed. Bringing Roma a gift she did not request will not get you into her good graces. Roma will discard her, just as she will you."

Jasper held his breath. The fury emanating from Desde was so thick it felt like syrup. He wondered if Andolina felt it, too. If she did, she didn't seem to care.

"Now, return to your quarters. We will deal with your insubordination later." Andolina turned, dismissing Desde. "I will finish here. And then we can return home."

She turned her attention to Royce, who remained face down on the ground. He hadn't moved since his anguished cry. It was as if sensing the loss of his sisters had taken everything from him. Jasper doubted if Royce would even fight to survive.

Andolina didn't move, and then, without speaking, she lifted her hand.

Royce sucked in a breath and groaned. He held his head and curled into a ball, grimacing.

"Stop," said Jasper. He pushed up from the ground, just as a shriek emitted from Desde.

"Bitch," she yelled, launching herself at Andolina and tackling her to the ground. Andolina landed on her back with a huff as the air left her lungs. Desde swung her arms, striking Andolina in the face and arms, as Andolina raised her hands in defense.

The assault briefly paused, Royce uncoiled. Jasper ran over, grunting with the exertion, and kneeling next to him. "Royce?"

Adam moved as well. He crawled over to Eve's lifeless body.

Jasper glanced back at the two women, still fighting. Desde straddled Andolina and had wrapped her fingers around Andolina's throat.

"Royce, can you hear me?" asked Jasper. Jasper felt a hand on his back and he looked to see Vee. "Vee? No, go back to the woods."

Vee squatted next to him. "You need help."

Royce finally made a strangled noise. "Gillian. Eve. Where are they?"

Jasper heard a screech and glimpsed Desde flying backwards and landing hard on her side in the dirt. She lay still as Andolina got up, coughing and brushing the dirt off her clothes.

Jasper grabbed Royce's arm. "Royce, this is our only chance. We have to get you out of here."

Royce shook his head. "My sisters." He looked up, and Jasper followed his gaze. He spotted Adam holding Eve's hand, his head down. "No," said Royce.

Someone else squatted beside him. Jasper recognized John Ramsey. "How's Royce?" asked Ramsey.

"Not good," said Jasper.

Ramsey looked around. "Where's my wife?" asked Ramsey.

"Who?" asked Jasper. He took another glance at the fighting women. Andolina, hair disheveled, stood over Desde and raised her hand, but Desde reared up, her hand raised also, and Andolina grunted and fell to her hands and knees. Desde rose, walked up to her, and kicked her in the side.

Ramsey stared up at the ship. "There she is," he said, and then he was gone.

Jasper tracked Ramsey and saw Declan and Sarah emerge from the ship. They raced down the ramp. Sarah bypassed her husband and went straight to Eve and Gillian.

Declan stopped when he met up with Ramsey. He spoke and gestured toward the woods.

Desde, breathing hard, approached Andolina, who was getting back to her hands and knees while holding her ribs. Desde raised a hand again as Andolina sucked in a hard gasp and fell over.

Jasper spoke to Royce once more. "Get up. We have to go."

"He's right, Royce," said Vee. "You have to move."

Royce slowly sat up, his expression glum. "Not without my sisters." His eyes widened. "What is she doing?"

Jasper looked over to see Sarah squatting between Gillian and Eve, a hand on each of the sister's shoulders, her eyes closed.

Ramsey and Declan ran up to Jasper. "We have to get out of here," said Ramsey. "Our people are somewhere nearby. Declan will help you with Royce. I'll get Sarah."

Jasper spied the trees. "Where are they?"

Declan took Royce's arm. "Come on. Let's go."

Jasper pulled on another arm as they helped Royce up.

Desde was showing the upper hand. Rage played across her face as she sensed Andolina weakening and struggling to rise. Stepping closer, she reached out to touch Andolina when Andolina shot forward, pushing Desde back and knocking her to the ground with a primal yell.

Royce managed to stand as Jasper, wincing, got his shoulder under him. "Vee," he said. "Go find our people. They must be in the woods. We need them."

"Nobody's out there," she said.

"What do you mean?" asked Declan on the other side of Royce.

Before she could answer, Royce pushed against them. "Eve and Gillian. I'm not leaving them." He tried to turn back.

Andolina was up on her feet, watching Desde, who started to rise when an unseen force shoved her back against the ground. She struggled to get up as Andolina smiled down at her.

Royce's strength improved, and he broke free from Jasper's grasp. "Wait," Jasper yelled, but it was pointless. Royce ran over to Gillian and Eve. Sarah continued to sit between them, with Ramsey beside her. Royce dropped between them, his face in mute horror. "Please," he said. "Please." He took their hands in his.

Desde's struggle began to wane, and her red face turned purple. Andolina stared down at her, her expression flat, as if she poured hot water over an ant pile. Desde shook her head as her anger turned to fear and then terror.

Jasper ran over to Sarah with Vee beside him. Their time was running short. "Whatever you're going to do, do it now."

Royce didn't move, and neither did anyone else. Jasper shook his head. Desde's fight continued to diminish until she finally went still.

Andolina dropped her arm, stretched her neck, shook out her hands, and turned toward them.

"Vee," said Jasper. "Go now. You can still make it."

"Not without you," she answered.

Jasper's heart thudded. There was little he could do except wait and watch.

A figure emerged from the woods. Jasper squinted in the sun to see who it was. An older woman, tall and stately, despite her hiking gear, stepped out from the tree line. With her was a man, also older but younger than the woman.

Ramsey stood. "Morgana. Are they here?" He focused on the man. "Talbot?"

Andolina stepped away from Desde, as if discarding trash, and moved closer to the group. "Where were we?" she asked, straightening her clothes and brushing dirt from her hair.

Declan yelled. "Talbot, where are they?"

"Who's Talbot?" asked Jasper.

"One of our councilmen," said Declan. "In charge of the reinforcements."

Morgana stepped closer and as she neared, Jasper saw Talbot held her arm.

Andolina smiled at the approaching couple. She wiped the blood from her face. "Talbot. It's nice to see you."

Talbot let go of Morgana's arm. "Andolina."

Jasper's stomach dropped. He looked between the two as Declan did the same. "What is this?" asked Declan.

Morgana spoke, her face deflated. "There are no reinforcements."

Declan turned pale. "You were lying to us?"

Ramsey straightened. "Are you working with her?" He pointed toward Andolina.

Talbot raised his hands. "I'm sorry. But her offer was too good to refuse. Either you all die or the entire community. Morgana," he looked over at her, "you were willing to risk too much. I wasn't."

"And what do you get in return?" asked Declan.

Andolina dusted off her torn blouse. "He will be leading this community once we leave. And should we reclaim your people as our own, he will be Roma's earthly contact."

"You son-of-a-bitch," said Ramsey.

Talbot shrugged. "I'm sorry, Ramsey, but you knew the odds were against you as well as I did. I did the smart thing. I saved our people."

"You did the most cowardly thing you could do," said Morgana. "All you will achieve is to lead our community into subservience. They would never want that."

"You're so besotted with winning, you can't see you've already lost," said Talbot. "You'd rather sacrifice us all to save him?" He pointed at Royce.

"You miss the point completely," said Morgana. "This is not just about him. You're not saving anyone. You're condemning us."

"Are we finished?" asked Andolina, her jaw set. "This has taken far longer than I'd planned, and I am behind schedule." She smoothed her hair and glanced at Desde's lifeless body. "But at least I got rid of some baggage." Turning back, she grinned. "Let's get this over with."

Chapter Thirty-Four

Royce was inconsolable. Holding each of his sister's hands, he barely heard the conversation between Talbot and the others, although he was aware of Talbot's presence and what it meant. But it didn't matter. Nothing did. Gillian and Eve were dead. Which meant he was, too. He thought of his mother and his eyes filled with tears. How would she handle the loss of her children? He couldn't imagine her grief. If it was half as bad as his own, she would not survive the year.

Andolina said something, but he did not acknowledge her. All he cared about was lying in front of him. His head dropped, and he prayed. It was not something he did often, but now felt like a good time. Sarah continued to kneel between his siblings, her eyes closed. He wanted to believe she could help, but the lack of energy coming from Eve and Gillian did not encourage him. His hope fading, he heard Andolina speak again.

"Get up."

Royce assumed she was speaking to him, but he did not respond.

"Andolina, listen," said Jasper.

"There is no more listening," said Andolina.

"Just leave us," said Morgana. "Does it not occur to you that none of this would have happened if you'd left us alone?"

"Silence." Andolina threw out a hand and Royce saw Morgana drop to her knees.

"Be quiet, Morgana," said Talbot. "This will all be over momentarily. And then we can get back to our lives."

"This will never be over," said Morgana, wincing. "This is only the beginning. What you've done..."

Talbot argued. "If you hadn't interfered, then none of this would have happened. This is on you, not me."

Royce squeezed his sisters' fingers, realizing his time was short. He glanced at Sarah, who continued to work. "Take me if you want, but spare the others." His voice was a rough whisper. "They've done nothing but try to protect their own."

"They've done nothing?" said Andolina. "They colluded and killed Burke. And they attacked me. Their innocence was lost the moment they protected the High Child. Their actions are treasonous."

"Treasonous?" asked Ramsey. "How can we commit treason against a planet that abandoned us years ago? We were doing just fine until you people showed up."

"If anyone's committed treason, it's you," said Declan. "You are planning to murder the High Child. I suspect your people wouldn't be too happy about that if they knew."

Andolina narrowed her eyes, and Ramsey and Declan went down to their knees grimacing, both holding their heads.

A tingle fluttered through Royce's hands. He looked sharply at Sarah, whose eyes were clenched. She had to be aware of her husband's pain. Was the tingle in his fingers from that or was it something else? He watched his sisters, but there was no change.

Andolina spoke again. "I said get up."

The energy in his fingers tingled more. He spoke. "Let me say good-bye."

Her face went flat. "There's nothing to say goodbye to anymore."

Adam, who was on the other side of Eve, holding her hand, turned toward her. "Desde was right. You are a bitch." He let go of Eve's hand, and pushing up slowly while holding his ribs, he managed to stand on shaky legs. He walked directly toward Andolina, who didn't move an inch. "I don't care what I have to do, but I promise I will do whatever it takes to expose you for the evil, wretched, soulless person you are."

Andolina smiled. "Get in line."

The tingle in Royce's hands became a buzz. Glancing at Sarah, he saw her eyes were open, and she was watching him intently.

Andolina continued. "But since you feel so strongly about me, how about I give you another broken rib for your trouble?" She cocked her head, and Adam doubled over, falling back onto his knees.

The buzz turned warm, and heat traveled up Royce's forearms. He made an extreme effort not to show any reaction. The heat traveled into his chest, and Royce almost sobbed with relief. He could feel them now. Eve and Gillian's familiar energy coursed through him, although neither moved.

Andolina returned her attention to Royce. "Last time. I said get up. I want you to face me."

Royce took a deep breath and calmed himself. The energy was building at a rapid rate now, and he didn't know how Sarah was maintaining her weary façade. Everything was lighting up inside him.

"Let me say something," said Jasper.

"No," said Andolina.

Jasper continued with Vee beside him, holding his arm. "Tell Roma that I died at your hand. That you killed her brother. Make sure she knows that."

Andolina turned. "You think you're not expendable? Roma told me before I left that you were. She's not expecting your return. But I'm happy to relay the message, as I'm sure she'll be happy to receive it."

The sweat popped out on Royce's brow as the heat continued to grow. His heart thudded harder when Eve's finger twitched, and then Gillian's.

"I'm not asking again," said Andolina, her voice rising. "I want to see your face when you die."

Royce stayed where he was, dropped his head, and closed his eyes.

"Very well. How about I start with someone else?" said Andolina. "How about that one working so diligently on your sisters? I admire her confidence and strength. Maybe she should go first?"

Royce made eye contact with Sarah, just as Ramsey yelled, "No."

But Sarah was way ahead of Andolina. A surge of electricity flowed through Royce's body just as Eve and Gillian opened their eyes. Joy flooded through him, but he realized now was not the time for celebration. The energy between them swirled and intensified, and Eve and Gillian reached for each other as their hands connected, completing the circle. Sarah fell back from the trio, and before Andolina could wreak her punishment, a shaft of light emitted from each of the siblings as beams of energy shot from their midsections, met in the middle and then fired outwards directly at Andolina.

Royce allowed the raw power of their connection to grow. It was like the burst of energy he experienced after a hard workout, only this eclipsed it a hundred times over. If he hadn't been holding his sister's hands, he was certain he could have snapped one of the nearby tree trunks in half. He'd only felt this raw power once before, and he'd been saving his and his sister's lives then too.

The beam pierced Andolina at her chest and she stepped back, her hands rising to deflect the light. His sisters' gaining strength, they sat up, maintaining the circle, their gaze on Andolina.

Andolina squinted, but continued to push back. Royce watched with surprise as he witnessed the beam arcing away from her. It began to bend and deflect into the ground.

Royce and his sisters gathered and directed more energy, and the beam became brighter. Andolina faltered for a moment but then gathered her strength, the beam blasting the dirt. The battle between them appeared evenly matched, but it wouldn't be long before someone weakened. Royce continued his assault, as did Gillian and Eve. Andolina moved back more, her head turned as the light burned brighter. The beam was thick and luminous, and Royce knew they were stronger. They only had to wait Andolina out. He pushed harder.

The deflection began to curve less into the dirt as Andolina retreated, and Royce sensed victory was imminent. Royce noticed the sweat sliding down Andolina's bloody forehead as she fought to protect herself. She was tiring and would not sustain this battle. But she kept fighting, determined to survive. She stumbled, and Royce waited for her to go down when someone joined her. Royce widened his eyes when Desde, eyes wild, face red, and hair knotted and wild, stood beside Andolina, raised her hands, and helped deflect the beam.

As the two women fought back, the energy from the siblings began to wane. Royce glanced at Eve and Gillian and realized the energy required from them to overcome Andolina's, and now Desde's, defenses was limited. Were their injuries the cause?

Royce realized then that their time was dwindling. Without help, they were going to die.

········

Jasper stared in awe at his half-siblings. He'd never seen this before. He knew energy could be manipulated and directed, but never like this. The triplets used it as a weapon, pulling it into a giant ball of light and directing it at Andolina. The light was bright enough to make him squint. He pushed Vee back and held his hand up to shield his eyes. Andolina didn't go down easy, though. She fought back, showing more strength than Jasper would have guessed she had at that point. But her strength was diminishing. The beam was going to overtake her. Jasper waited for the eventual end, but was shocked when Desde stood. Her skin bruised, and her neck swollen, she joined Andolina, fighting beside her.

A gust of wind blew against Jasper's face, and a buzz rippled through the air, but Jasper was riveted on the scene before him. Could he help?

He didn't understand this power, but understood enough to know that he could not break the connection. Whatever was happening had to do with his siblings and their unique bond. Could he tackle Andolina and Desde? Doing so would put him in direct contact with the beam. Deciding he had to do something, he stepped toward them, but Vee pulled him back. He tried to pull away when the buzz in the air became a vibration and the ground rumbled beneath his feet. The wind blew harder, and he raised an arm as dirt kicked up in the air. He searched for the cause of the disturbance. Was it related to the beam of light?

The vibration increased, but the fight continued. Jasper realized that with Desde's added strength, the beam was easily deflected, and the two women would soon overpower the triplets.

The rumble became a roar, and a wicked gust blew his hair back. The battle played out as Jasper looked up to see a small ship landing beside the bigger one, close to them in the clearing. He stood in shocked surprise as it landed. It barely touched the ground when a ramp descended, and a man exited, jumping from it before it could fully extend. He hit the ground running and raced toward them. Jasper blinked, trying to believe his eyes. The large frame and agile gait were familiar to him, and his suspicions were soon confirmed as the man got closer. Standing in shock, Jasper realized it was his father. Carson Fletcher had just landed on Earth.

·· • • • • • • • ··

Royce tried to compensate for his sisters' weakening, but his reserves were also rapidly abating. With Desde's added power, there was little he could do. It would only be minutes, maybe seconds, before they would succumb. Sweat dripped off his nose and ran down his back, and his only focus was on pulling on whatever strength remained. Gillian and Eve were giving it everything they had. His own energy depleted, he prepared for the in-evitable when he felt a hand on his back. He feared it was Jasper trying to help, and he wanted to tell him to stop because it was pointless and would only result in injury, but he had no strength left. On the verge of collapsing, he gave it one final push when the hand dropped to his mid-back and a surge of strength ran through Royce's core. Everything went white hot, and his sisters engaged again, but with renewed power. The beam turned a brilliant silver, and it blasted from their circle with more power than he thought possible. Desde and Andolina were violently shoved back, their arms upraised. The beam enveloped them, and they fell, skin red, and their clothes charring with the heat. The surge of electricity running through Royce was thrilling. His strength tripled as he aimed the beam with all his fury and anger over what they'd done to him, his sisters, Sarna and Greta. He wanted to wipe them out. Destroy them. Make them feel the pain they'd inflicted. The women writhed in pain as they crumpled to the ground and went limp, but Royce couldn't stop. He wanted them dead and scourged from the Earth, never seen or heard from again.

A voice pierced the fog in his head. "Stop, Royce. It's over. They're gone." The hand on his back disappeared, and he felt a tug on his arm. "Royce. Stop."

His sisters let go of his hands, and the beam winked out as fast as it had arrived. The energy evaporated and Royce fell forward, breathing hard. Sweat slid down his neck and off his chin and he swallowed, his dry throat sticking. Reality hit him when he shook his head, trying to clear it, and looked up. Desde and Andolina were lying still on the ground. Their clothes were black, and their skin was blistered and burned. Their lifeless eyes stared blankly at nothing. The rage in Royce vanished. Now all he could feel was shock. But how? They'd been on the verge of losing when that hand had touched his back.

He heard Eve's voice. "Dad?"

Then Gillian. "Oh my God. Dad?"

Royce swiveled his head and went still. Gillian and Eve crawled over and enveloped the man in front of them, holding him tight in a bear hug. The man, returning the hugs, looked over at him and offered a weary smile. "Hi, son."

Chapter Thirty-Five

JASPER'S EYES FILLED, AND groaning, the tension of the last few days and hours left him. He held his aching ribs and watched as Royce moved slowly on his knees and reached out to their dad, who pulled him into a bear hug with Eve and Gillian.

"What just happened?" asked Ramsey.

"That beam. How? I've never seen anything like it," said Declan.

Jasper wiped his eyes. Watching the others, he saw them staring with surprise, except for one. Grayson remained unmoving beneath the ramp. Sarah quickly went to his side and gently rolled him over.

"Grayson." Gillian pulled herself from her father's grasp, stood, and ran to Grayson's side, dropping beside him. She cupped his cheek. "Grayson." She looked at Sarah, her eyes wide. "What's wrong?"

Jasper moved slowly with Vee's help. His father came over and pulled him into a quick hug.

"Are you okay?" asked his dad.

Jasper, despite his ribs, squeezed his dad before pulling back. "I am. But how?"

"I got your message. But we'll talk about that later." He broke away and stepped to Gillian's side, kneeling beside her. "Can you help him?" he asked Sarah.

Grayson was ashen, and Jasper couldn't tell if he was breathing. Sarah had her hands on his chest, her eyes closed, but she spoke. "He's alive, but barely. We have to move fast."

Tears streamed down Gillian's cheeks. "Please. Don't let him die."

Sarah's eyes opened. "Put your hands on him."

Gillian sniffed and put her hands next to Sarah's.

"Eve. Royce," said their father. "You too. Your energy will help."

Royce and Eve sat on either side of Sarah and put their hands on Grayson's midsection.

As they worked on Grayson, Vee took off her jacket and covered the faces of Desde and Andolina. Jasper gave her his jacket as well. With a last look at the women who'd caused so much suffering, he took Vee's hand and turned away.

"I should report this," said Vee. "There are two bodies to remove."

"What are you going to report?" asked Jasper. "Two aliens who won't return home?"

Vee didn't answer, and they watched as the group worked on Grayson.

"I'll take care of it," said Declan. "I'll make sure they're properly buried."

"Where are you going?" Morgana's voice boomed from nearby.

Jasper turned to see Talbot slinking back into the woods. Jasper pointed. "You run, and I'll follow. You won't get far before I drag you back here."

"And I'll be right behind him," said Declan.

"Get your ass back here, Talbot. You're going to face the firing squad on this one," said Ramsey.

Talbot stood uncertainly, but then, shoulders dropped, he sat on a rock, his hands on his knees. Morgana went to stand beside him.

Sarah and Jasper's siblings continued to work on Grayson. His father supported Gillian, with his hand on her shoulder and one hand on Grayson. Jasper stepped closer to watch. Adam stood behind Eve, doing his best to offer support.

Several minutes seemed to pass. The tears slipped down Gillian's cheeks, and her nose ran, but she didn't move. Occasionally, Carson would squeeze her shoulder.

Jasper was beginning to think it was too late when Gillian sucked in a breath and opened her eyes. "Grayson?"

Eve and Royce opened their eyes. "Did you feel that? I think he's coming back," said Eve.

"He is," said Royce. "He's growing stronger."

Carson leaned in and put his hand on Gray's shoulder. "Grayson. Can you hear us?"

Gillian patted his cheek. "Honey. Please wake up."

Sarah opened her eyes and sat back. "He's doing much better."

Royce and Eve removed their hands as Grayson's eyelids fluttered.

"Gray." Gillian shook his shoulder. "Can you hear me? It's Gilli. Wake up."

Grayson's eyes opened to slits, and the group all seemed to release a collective sigh. Gillian rubbed his cheek. "Hi." Another tear trickled down her face. "How are you?"

Gray looked around, blinking. He mumbled and coughed. "Why is everyone staring at me?"

Gillian smiled through her tears and buried her head in his neck. Carson patted her back as Eve, smiling too, turned and hugged Adam.

Carson stood also, along with Royce. They faced each other.

Royce let out a deep breath that must have released pounds of worry and fear. "I can't believe you're here. I thought ... Andolina told me you were dead."

His face fell. "I'm sorry. She used that, hoping to weaken you."

Royce dropped his head. "It almost worked."

Carson put his hand on Royce's shoulder. "You've always been stronger than you think."

Ramsey assisted Sarah as she rose from the ground. Sarah shook out her hands, and he pulled her close.

"Care to make the introductions?" asked Declan to Jasper. He stared at the small ship nearby. "That was quite an entrance."

"This is my ... our father," said Jasper. "Carson Fletcher."

"Wow," said Adam.

Grayson sat up slowly, still blinking and shaking his head. He rubbed his face. "What happened? Where's Andolina?"

"She and Desde are dead," said Gillian. She glanced toward the women whose faces were covered. "I can give you the details later, but we're safe. We're all okay."

Grayson grimaced when he saw the bodies. "I wish I could say I was sorry." He glanced up. "Did I hear right? You're my father-in-law?"

"The High Child?" asked Declan.

"Former High Child," said Carson. "I'm looking at the new one."

Royce made a weary groan. "I don't even know what to say."

Adam kneeled, his head down, then stood and stepped forward, his hand out. "It's an honor to meet you."

Carson shook his hand. "And you. Jasper told me what you volunteered to do for my son. You're a brave man and I appreciate it." He glanced at Royce. "I take it you succeeded."

"He did," said Royce. "I got the letter."

Grayson got to his feet delicately with a groan and Gillian's help. He briefly touched Gillian's stomach, and Gillian nodded, her hand over his. His face showing more color, he turned and held out his hand as well. "I'm Grayson Steele."

Carson took his hand. "I know. You married my daughter."

"I love her," said Grayson. "Very much."

Carson smiled. "I know you do. I felt it. On the pier."

Jasper didn't know what he meant. Gillian's eyes narrowed, as did Eve's. "On the pier?" asked Eve.

Royce frowned. "How do you know about the pier?"

"Dad?" asked Gillian.

Carson waved a hand. "Another story for another time. How about we talk about my impending grandad duties?"

Gillian's eyes widened. "You know?"

"I could tell when I held your shoulder," said Carson.

"Wonderful. It's about time we had some good news," said Morgana.

"You're sure you're okay?" asked Grayson. He glanced at the fallen women. "Something tells me they didn't go down easily."

"I'm fine," said Gillian. "Baby too. Thanks to Sarah."

Sarah stood back, her arm around Ramsey. "I only gave you the energy you needed. You did the rest. You're all stronger than you realize."

"I thought they were dead," said Royce. "Scared the hell out of me."

Sarah shook her head. "No. Their life signs were there, but suppressed, which is why you couldn't feel them."

"I will be forever in your debt for helping my children," said Carson.

"You brought Gray back too," said Gillian. "I know that was harder."

"Maybe," said Sarah. "But not so much that he couldn't be helped. Your energy helped with that too. Plus, I don't think he was ready to leave."

"I feel pretty good, considering," said Grayson, stretching.

"Speak for yourself," said Adam, holding his ribs.

Vee touched Jasper's side. "You're hurt too."

Jasper waved her off. "I'm fine. No need to worry about me. I've been through worse." He studied her face. "How are you? You've had a hell of a day."

"Don't change the subject," said Vee. "What's a few extraterrestrials, laser beams, and newly arrived UFOs? It's just another day in the life for me, but," she looked at Sarah and pointed at Jasper, "he needs help."

"Vee," said Jasper. "It's no big deal."

Carson walked over to Vee. "I don't believe we've met." He smiled, and Jasper noted the twinkle in his eye. "My name is Carson Fletcher." He held out his hand.

Vee took his hand. "Veronica Chappell, but most call me Vee."

"It's a pleasure." Carson shook her hand and smiled at Jasper. "Looks like there might be another human in the family." He winked and Vee blushed.

Jasper felt his own cheeks warm. "Like father, like son."

His father patted him on the shoulder.

"You said you got my message? Is that how you found us?" asked Jasper.

His father's smile dropped. "I heard what happened to you. What they did to get information about Sarna. I rushed to find you, but Roma told me you'd escaped, but that they were following you. I talked to some people, took a ship, and found my way here, but I was several days behind you. I could only hope I wasn't too late. Once I got here, I had no idea where to look. Andolina had cloaked her ship, and I assumed you had too. Your ship's signal popped up only hours after I arrived. You timed it perfectly."

"It wasn't me," said Jasper. "It was Vee."

"What?" asked Vee.

Jasper nodded. "That task I gave you on my craft," he said to Vee. "That alerted my father and sent him here. You saved our lives."

Vee's jaw dropped. "I doubt that."

"He's right," said Carson. "I wouldn't have found you without that signal."

"What task did you send her to do?" asked Adam. He leaned sideways as Sarah worked on his ribs. He sighed and stretched when she finished. "Thank you," he said.

Jasper started to answer when a rumbling shook the earth. The large ship vibrated as the ramp shuddered and began to retract.

"Get back," said Royce. He grabbed at Eve and Gillian as Ramsey, Sarah, and Declan jumped away from the edge of the large craft. The rumbling grew, and the engines whirred to life.

"Who's on board?" asked Declan, as the wind stirred his hair. "Who's driving?"

Jasper took a step away with Vee. He squinted as bits of dirt tossed by the gusts of the rising craft stung his face. "Anso. It's got to be Anso."

"Everybody get down," said Carson. "It's going to get windy."

Everyone ducked, hands raised, as the ship rose higher.

"Wait," said Royce. "The letter. Sarna's letter is on that ship." He ran forward as if he thought he could do something.

"Get down, Royce," yelled their father.

The ship ascended higher, and with a voluminous pop, it shot forward, disappearing and ejecting out a heavy blast of exhaust. Royce was knocked backward, and he hit the ground with a grunt.

Carson ran over. "Are you okay?"

Royce rose up, sputtering. "The letter. They can find Sarna with the letter."

Jasper shook his head. "No, they can't. They don't have the letter. They only think they do. I wrote that letter."

Royce grabbed his side as he got to his knees. "You what?"

Jasper dusted the dirt off his shirt. "I knew why Andolina wanted it. I rewrote it and gave it to Grayson. That's what Andolina had. The original letter is back at the house. It was my job to keep it safe, and I did."

"But Andolina said ..." said Royce.

"Andolina only thought she was reading Sarna's energy, but it was my energy on the letter. Andolina had her strengths, but she wasn't fluent in energy reading. She couldn't tell the difference. When they read it back home, they'll go straight to my house, but Sarna's not there. Hasn't been for a long time. It'll take them weeks, maybe months, to figure it out."

"That was smart," said Declan.

Royce's shoulders relaxed. "Thank you for protecting it," he said. "But I still don't like this. Anso can go back and make up any story he wants. If they don't know about Greta, they will now. He could make the search for her that much more important. Sarna can't run forever."

"It doesn't matter," said Carson.

"Yes, it does Dad. She's there and I'm here. Yet I'm still making things more difficult for her." Royce got to his feet and stared up at the empty sky, his eyes haunted.

"She's safe, son," said Carson.

"You don't know that," answered Royce.

"Yes, I do." Carson patted Royce on the arm and pulled on him, nodding back toward his small ship sitting alone in the large field.

Royce frowned, and looking back toward the craft, his eyes widened.

Standing on the ramp, with her black, shiny hair brushing her shoulders, stood Sarna.

Chapter Thirty-Six

ROYCE DIDN'T TRUST HIS eyes. He blinked, trying to be sure he was seeing clearly.

"I don't believe it," said Jasper.

"Who is it?" asked Eve.

"Sarna," said Royce, and he broke out into a run. Sarna jumped from the ramp and ran toward him. Reaching for him, she jumped into his arms, wrapping herself around him. Royce buried his face into her hair. She smelled like strawberries and peaches. "I don't believe it. You're here."

"Royce," she said, hugging him tighter.

The whisper of her breath tickled his neck, and his body came alive. Every ache and pain vanished. The feel of her against him erased every fear and worry in an instant. He pulled back and studied her face, pushing her hair back.

She was breathing hard, and she studied him. "I've missed you so much." She stroked his cheek.

He brought his lips up to meet hers and kissed her. Months of anger and doubt evaporated as he savored the taste of her. Memories of her warm body beneath his made his heart thump. He couldn't get enough of her, but another thought brought him back to reality. He pulled back, breathless. "Greta," he said. "Where's Greta?"

She smiled, let go, and slid down his body until her feet touched the ground. The sensation was electrifying. She pulled on his arm, and he followed her to the ship. They walked up the ramp, and Royce, still trying to comprehend Sarna's presence, entered the small craft. The interior was minimal, with only a cockpit containing four chairs on one side and four sleeping tubes on another. Sarna walked to one of them and hit a button. There was a whooshing sound as the cover lifted. Royce sucked in a tight breath when he saw a beautiful baby swaddled in blankets inside. Her chubby cheeks had a rosy hue, and she slept peacefully.

Sarna took his hand. "That's your daughter."

Royce couldn't speak, but a pressure rose into his chest.

"You want to hold her?"

The pressure grew, and Royce tried to make himself breathe.

Sarna sniffed, her own tears rising in her eyes. She rubbed his back. "Take your time."

A strangled sob escaped him.

She squeezed his fingers. "She's healthy and perfect. She's like her daddy."

Royce wiped a tear from his cheek. "She ... will she know me?"

Sarna dabbed her own eye. "I show her your picture every night. She knows you."

Royce finally took a normal breath. "She's so beautiful."

"That part she gets from me."

Royce smiled through his tears. "She certainly doesn't get it from me."

Sarna chuckled. "I wouldn't say that. Her daddy's pretty handsome."

At the sound of Sarna's chuckle, Greta stirred. Her fingers opened and closed, and her eyelids fluttered.

Royce reached down and put his finger next to her hand. Her tiny fingers wrapped around his. The sensation was unlike anything he'd felt before.

"Why don't you pick her up?" asked Sarna.

Royce stroked her tiny hand. "I don't want to hurt her."

"You won't hurt her. She's durable." Sarna scooted in and slid her hands beneath Greta, lifting her as the blankets fell away. Greta's eyes opened.

Royce took her and cradled her. Greta watched him with wide eyes, and Royce waited, expecting at any moment for her to cry.

But Greta didn't cry. Instead, she held out a chubby hand and touched his nose.

The pressure in his chest exploded inside him, and he allowed his tears to fall as Sarna cried too. He brought Greta closer and put her against his chest and shoulder. Her skin was soft, and she smelled like honey and bubblegum. She grabbed his longish hair and gave it a tug and babbled at him. He felt something wet and cold on his skin and Sarna wiped it off. "She's drooling a lot right now. She's cutting new teeth."

Greta's head popped up, and she patted at Royce's face. He smiled and sniffed through his tears. "She's the most perfect thing I've ever seen."

Sarna put her arm around him. "She is, isn't she? Until the next diaper change. Which you get, by the way. You have a lot to catch up on."

Royce nodded, smiling. "I'll take whatever time with her I can get." He cradled Greta in his arm. "Let's go show her off to the family." Royce put his other arm around Sarna. "You, too, by the way. I want you to meet my sisters."

Sarna fidgeted. "Was that them out there?" She played with her hair. "Do I look all right?"

"Stop worrying. You're beautiful."

Looking up at him, she rose on her tiptoes and gave him a kiss. "I missed you so much."

Royce pulled her close. "I can't believe you're both here. I never thought this moment would come. After you left with Jasper…"

She nestled her head against his shoulder and played with Greta's fingers. "I know. When I woke up and you weren't there, I was devastated. I cried for days."

Royce sighed. "Let's make sure that never happens again."

"Nothing would make me happier."

Royce took a deep breath, savoring this moment with his family. "I love you, Sarna."

She sighed back, her arms around his waist. "I love you too."

· · · ● · ● · ● · ● · ·

Vee paced the flattened grass in the empty field. Royce had disappeared into the small ship with the woman named Sarna.

"She's here?" asked Gillian. "You brought her?"

"I can't wait to meet her," said Eve.

"I couldn't leave her behind," said Carson. "It was too dangerous. Plus, she refused to stay."

"What about Greta?" asked Jasper. He winced as Sarah put her hands on his ribs.

"Easy," said Sarah. "It won't take long."

"Greta's here too," said Carson.

"How did you know it would be safe?" Jasper's grimace relaxed as Sarah worked on him.

"There was no one we trusted enough to leave her with. Sarna decided to take the risk. She felt, as I did, that being with Royce was the safest choice."

"You were lucky," said Ramsey. "You almost showed up too late."

"But they didn't. As always, fate intervened," said Morgana. She narrowed her eyes at Talbot, who still sat on the stump.

"Trust destiny," said Sarah, dropping her hands from Jasper. "Better?"

Jasper sighed. "Much. Thanks."

"I think we had some guardian angels too," said Declan.

"Some pretty powerful ones," said Ramsey.

Sarah embraced her husband. "Leroy was one of them."

Ramsey stilled, and Vee remembered that he'd lost his best friend in the explosion.

"I know he was watching over us," said Ramsey, kissing Sarah's cheek.

Jasper walked over to Vee. "You sure you're okay? You're quiet."

She nodded. "There's two dead bodies in the field, but like you said, I can't report it."

"Best if you didn't," said Morgana. She eyed Declan. "You have people who can take care of it?"

"I do," said Declan.

"I'd leave them to the birds. Let the animals have them," said Ramsey.

Adam kicked at a rock in the dirt. "I agree with you."

"While I agree they don't deserve a goodbye party, leaving them out here is not an option," said Morgana.

"Let's move over to the other ship. Away from this. We'll wait for Royce and Sarna," said Carson, extending his arm.

Vee and the rest made their way to the smaller craft and stood beside it.

"What's taking them so long?" asked Eve.

"You have to ask?" said Adam. "They haven't seen each other in over a year."

"We need to give them some time," said Grayson. "I know what it's like to be separated from the woman you love." He put his arm around Gillian.

"Me too," said Ramsey. "We may have to stay the night. You bring your camping gear, Morgana?"

"You should know, Ramsey, that I'm quite capable of sleeping beneath the stars," replied Morgana.

"That's right. I heard some stories from Leroy. You like your moonlight walks, don't you?"

Morgana pulled out her water and took a swig. "Clothing optional, of course," she answered.

"I'll be hiding behind a tree," Ramsey answered.

"Suit yourself," said Morgana. "You're welcome to join me, ladies."

"Sounds fun," said Eve. "I'm in."

"Excellent," said Morgana.

"If you're running around naked, then I'm not going anywhere," said Adam.

"How can you all make light of what you've done?" asked Talbot. He'd walked with them and now stood outside the circle. "You've murdered two of your own. Once the Council hears of this..."

"They'll hear of it," said Morgana. "All of it. Including your role. I'll leave out nothing."

"Go sit," said Declan. "You'll get your day in court."

Talbot opened his mouth, but then closed it, found a fallen log, and sat.

"There they are," said Gillian, nodding.

Vee looked to see Royce and Sarna stepping out of the craft, Royce holding a baby.

Jasper took her arm. "Can I talk to you?"

Vee watched as Eve and Gillian ran over to meet their niece.

Jasper pulled her away toward the trees as the rest met Greta and Sarna. "Listen, I know a lot has happened. You've witnessed more than you expected."

She fidgeted. "You could say that. If you'd asked me a week ago if I thought I would be here, well, I think you know the answer. I'm still not sure I believe it."

"I certainly did not expect everything that's happened, including meeting you."

Vee stared at her hands. "You were, still are, a surprise."

"This is probably not what you bargained for. Things have happened fast, and I know you don't know me or any of us very well. But I want to tell you something."

"What?" she asked.

He hesitated and took her hand. Her skin warmed. "I can't stop thinking about you. Ever since waking up in that hospital and seeing you sitting by the bed, you have been in my thoughts constantly. I know this is unexpected and if I had more time, I would spend every second I had showing you how amazing I think you are. But I don't have that luxury, so all I can do is tell you I feel fairly certain that I am in love with you."

Her face flushed, and she swallowed. "You are?"

"I am. And I'd like to know if you feel the same."

She stammered. "Jasper, this is a crazy time to be talking about this. There are two dead women in a field. Your dad is here with your sister-in-law and niece from outer space. We almost lost our lives. There's a lot going on. Can't we take it easy for a few days, chill out, and then talk?"

"We don't have a few days," he said, his face flat.

Her face furrowed.

"Jasper," said his dad, holding his granddaughter's hand. "Come see your niece. You too, Vee. Let me introduce you."

"Can I hold her?" asked Gillian.

"Of course," said Royce, handing her Greta.

"I'm still expecting an answer," said Jasper quietly, still holding Vee's hand and leading her toward the others. Vee didn't know how to react. Jasper had just started a serious conversation, but now she had to put a smile on her face.

"She's getting big," said Jasper, reaching out to grasp Greta's fingers. "You were brave to bring her, Sarna."

"I know you would have disagreed," said Sarna. "But I couldn't leave her behind."

"You couldn't stay with Wiles? I told you he would keep you safe."

"I know," said Sarna. "And he did. But when I learned what happened to you because of me, and what your dad was planning, I took the chance and trusted my instincts."

"It was still a huge risk."

Her brow rose. "Don't start with me, Jasper."

Carson chuckled. "You two sound like Royce and his sisters."

Eve took Greta from Gillian. "That was a long time ago, Dad."

"Maybe, but I still remember."

"How long are you staying?" asked Grayson. "Are you going back to Eudora?"

The siblings went quiet as they waited to hear their father's answer. Greta babbled and pulled on Eve's hair.

Carson sighed as he watched Greta. "I've thought about that ever since I realized what was happening with Royce. I knew then that if I ever had the opportunity to see my children and my beautiful Lilly again, then I would seize that chance and never let go." He looked at Jasper. "I hope you understand. I care for your mother, son, but she and I were not meant to be. You and Roma were the only good things to come from our union."

Jasper nodded. "You don't have to explain anything to me. I know you're ready to follow the path you've wanted for a long time."

"Thank you." He regarded Eve and Gillian. "I hope you don't mind if I stick around for a while."

Gillian squealed, and Eve grinned. "I can't wait to tell Mom," said Gillian.

"I hope she'll still have me," said Carson.

"She's loved you every day. That hasn't changed," said Eve.

"You better bring her a ton of flowers," said Royce.

"She deserves more than I can ever give her," said Carson.

"She does," said Royce.

Vee listened with a bit of envy. Did Jasper love her like that? Or did he only think he did? All her insecurities fired at once. Jasper still held her hand, and he squeezed her fingers.

"Tell Mom I love her," said Royce.

"Why don't you tell her yourself?" asked Eve.

Royce's gaze met Sarna's. "Because I'm going to Eudora."

· · · · · · · · · ·

Eve's jaw dropped. "You're what?"

Sarna faced him, her face stoic. "You're sure?" she asked.

"We don't have a choice," said Royce. "If I don't take my rightful place, they'll keep coming. Anso is already headed back there. Roma will send others and endanger all of us. I have the chance to change that. I have to protect my family."

Jasper stepped forward. "Anso can't get away with anything. I have the ship's logs. I downloaded them. Or I should say Vee downloaded them."

Vee perked up. "I did?"

"You did. That task I asked you to do? You accessed the larger ship's data banks and transferred the logs to my ship." He spoke to Vee. "Was the light blinking on the console when you left?"

"Yes," said Vee.

"Then I have everything, including what happened here."

"What's on the logs?" asked Ramsey.

"All of our ships automatically record and transcribe all activities that happen on and around the craft during a mission, plus all of Andolina's mission notes, unless that function is turned off, but Andolina was not a pilot and was overconfident. Anso may have piloted the craft, but I suspect he was unaware of the feature. I took a risk it was still accessible, and it was." He looked at Carson. "The download required Vee to enable certain functions on my ship, which emitted the signal you used to find us."

"We can take this information to Eudora and show it to the Council?" asked Sarna.

"We can," said Jasper. "They'll know of Roma's deceit and lies, and what Andolina and Desde did at her direction. They'll have no choice but to remove her and put Royce in her place."

"It's still dangerous," said Gillian. "You have no idea what you'll face. She'll fight back."

"I'll be with him," said Sarna. "With Greta too. They won't be able to deny the rightful High Child and his offspring."

Royce frowned. "Maybe you and Greta should stay here until things settle down and I've claimed my place on the Council."

Sarna's eyes widened. "Absolutely not. Our place is with you. We said we would not be separated again. Greta is the next High Child. She needs to claim her title as well." She held his arm. "The safest place for us is by your side."

"I'll be with you too," said Jasper. "I can testify to what occurred and produce the data from Andolina's ship. They won't be able to ignore it."

"You're leaving?" asked Vee.

"Royce," said Eve, handing Greta to Adam. "You're sure? You have to leave now?"

Royce nodded. "I do. It's not safe to wait. The sooner we can confront Anso and Roma's lies, the better."

"He's right, Eve," said his father. "If he intends to do this, then now is the time." His father faced him. "But you don't have to go. If you choose to stay, none of us will think less of you."

"I have my family to think of, and I can't keep them safe if I run from this," said Royce.

"But when will we see you again?" asked Gillian.

"*Will* we see you again?" asked Eve.

"Of course, you will," said Royce. "Once I get assimilated and secure my role on the Council, then open travel will be reinstated, and my first visit will be here."

"But you have no idea how long that will take, or even what will happen when you get there," said Eve. "If this goes bad, and you're not reinstated, we may never see you again."

Royce nodded. "I know, Eve. There are a lot of unknowns, but I have to take that risk."

"That's not going to happen," said Sarna. "This is going to work." She took his hand and squeezed it.

Carson put his arms around Eve and Gillian. "Eve and Gilli, you have to let your brother follow his calling, regardless of where it may lead. This is his path."

"He's right. Trust destiny," said Ramsey. "It sucks sometimes, but in my experience, it usually works out."

"But right now?" asked Gillian. "Can't you stay a day or two?"

"I wish I could," said Royce, "But the longer we stay, the harder it will be to leave."

Everyone stood quietly until Sarah stepped forward and gave Royce a hug. "You be careful. Take care of yourself and Sarna and Greta."

Royce hugged her back. "Thank you, Sarah. What you and your family have done for me and my family can never be repaid."

"Just come back. That's all the repayment I ask," she answered.

He nodded as she stepped away, and he shook hands with Ramsey and Declan, who wished him well, and Gray and Adam. "You take care of Gilli and Eve. Make sure they're safe," he said to them.

They agreed, and Royce faced his sisters. Gillian wiped her eyes, and Eve sniffed. "Come here, you two."

He embraced them both in a bear hug. His own emotions rose, and he tried not to consider the possibility that he may never see them again. The pain of that was too great. "I love you. Watch out for Mom. Tell her I love her and I'm sorry I couldn't be there to tell her goodbye."

Gillian squeezed him back. "Please be careful."

"Try not to piss anybody off, okay?" said Eve. "Try a little diplomacy if you can."

He smiled. "I'll do my best."

They pulled away, and Royce's eyes welled. He felt a hand on his back and turned to see his dad.

"I finally get here and now you up and leave," Carson said. He squeezed Royce's shoulder. "I'm proud of you. I hope you know that."

Royce bit his lip as a tear escaped. He saw Sarna wipe her cheek as well.

He pulled his dad in for a hug. "Thanks, Dad."

"You're a good son. Go be a great High Leader," Carson said into his ear.

Royce held his dad, wishing he could have more time. He pulled back and brushed away fresh tears. "I will."

Carson sniffed too. "And don't be a stranger."

Royce nodded. "I won't."

"I love you."

"I love you too."

Royce breathed deeply, trying to clear the emotional haze in his head. If they were going to do this, they had to do it now, or he'd never make it.

He faced Sarna with watery eyes. "You ready?"

Sarna hugged Gillian and Eve and took Greta from Adam. "I'm ready."

"You know how to drive this thing?"

She smiled. "I know enough to get us back. Most of it is automatic."

"Good. Otherwise, we just said a lot of goodbyes for nothing."

He looked for Jasper, who was talking to Vee. "Jasper, you ready?"

Jasper turned back. "Take the ship up to max rush. I'll be right behind you."

"I hope you know what that means," said Royce to Sarna.

"I do," said Sarna.

Royce watched as Jasper walked away with Vee. "Hey Officer Chappell."

Vee stopped and looked back.

"Thank you," he said.

She nodded, and Royce understood how she was feeling. "I promise. I'll do my best to keep him safe."

She stilled. "You better."

Royce walked up the ramp with Sarna. Reaching the top, he turned and waved a hand as his family looked back. Nodding at Sarna, she touched a button. The ramp retracted, and the door closed on the only world he knew.

Chapter Thirty-Seven

JASPER WALKED WITH VEE back to his ship. Vee said little as they stepped through the woods. He'd tried to engage her in conversation, but she only gave one-word answers. Reaching the clearing where he'd landed, they stopped. The area was quiet, save for the occasional squawk of a passing bird. Vee handed him the silver pen she'd used to decloak his craft. He hit the button, and the ship reappeared in the waning sunlight.

"Come with me," he said.

"Excuse me?"

"Come with me, to Eudora."

She laughed. "I can't go with you."

"Why not?"

She sputtered. "Because–because I can't."

"What's keeping you here?" he asked.

Her jaw dropped. "I have a life here. This is my home. It's Earth, for God's sake. Why would I want to live on another planet?"

"Because we love each other."

Vee held her head. "Listen, Jasper. I don't know what I think. My brain is in shambles right now. I'm confused and uncertain about everything. Royce is going to claim his rightful place on a throne? You've got secret data on your ship? We barely know each other, and you want me to move with you to another planet? This is like some crazy movie."

Jasper nodded. "I know, it's crazy, but all that really matters is how we feel about each other."

She snorted. "I think leaving Earth matters, too. This is all I know."

"You're not going alone."

She wrung her hands and paced. "What about my job? My home? I have people here. A life. I can't just up and disappear."

He walked over and took her hand. "Look at me."

She did as he asked.

"Take my other hand."

She did, and they gazed at each other.

"Now just be still. Let all other thoughts fall away."

She squinted her eyes. "Jasper ..."

"Shh. Be quiet. You're thinking too much." He closed his eyes. "Just listen."

She stopped fidgeting and went quiet, and he allowed himself to relax, allowing the events of the last few days to disperse. Her energy warmed, and it traveled up his arms. "Good," he said. "Now think of our first meeting in the hospital." He recalled in his mind's eye the moment he'd cracked an eyelid and saw her sitting beside his bed. Something within him had stirred and had never left. Standing there, his own heat combined with hers and sparked in his chest. The memory shifted to the kiss they'd shared on the patio and where it would have led if they'd had the opportunity. His heart raced as he knew hers did.

He opened his eyes and saw her watching him. "Feel better?"

Her cheeks were pink, but her eyes were wary. "I'm scared," she whispered. "I'm in love with a man I can't have."

He pulled her closer. "But you can have me. I'm right here."

"But you can't stay, and I can't ask you to stay."

"So come with me."

She let go of his hand and touched his cheek. Sliding her fingers behind his neck, she raised on her tiptoes and brought her lips to his. He slanted his mouth over hers and kissed her deeply. Her mouth was like warm honey and he was a hungry bear. All he wanted to do was scoop her up and run onto the ship and have his way with her. She wrapped her arms around him, and he pulled her against him, savoring the feel of her. Her hot breath caressed his cheek, and he almost started to walk away with her when she pulled back.

They stared for a moment, breathless, and she touched her forehead to his, then peppered his mouth with small kisses. He tried to deepen the kiss when she put her hand on his chest and pushed away.

He noticed the tears in her eyes, and he loosened his hold on her.

"I can't go with you," she said.

"Vee, what we have—"

"Is unique to say the least, but it can't work. It never could. You're Eudoran. I'm from Earth. You must save your planet. I must save the latest kid whose bike was stolen. We are two totally different people with two completely different backgrounds. I can't go just like you can't stay. There are too many barriers. It's sad, but it's true."

"We could make this work. Look at my father and Lillian."

She stepped back, and he let her go. "You want to tell me that their love story was easy? How many years have they been apart?"

He paused.

"Exactly. That's not fair to either of us. Go live your life, Jasper. Go save the world, meet a pretty Eudoran lady, get married and have Eudoran kids. Don't worry about me. I'll do the same here, and fifty years from now, we'll look fondly back at this time and be thankful we dodged a bullet."

It felt like that bullet had just hit him in the chest. "I don't believe any of that, and I don't believe you do either."

"You should. Right now, you think you're in love. You're full of emotion, but that will fade. It always does."

He stood there, hoping to say something to change her mind. "I believe we are fated for each other."

"You believe in fairy tales. Which is fine, but I don't."

He tried to take her hand, but she pulled it away. "You said so yourself. You're scared. But that's not a good reason to end anything. It's the worse reason imaginable. I don't think you'll look back, thinking you dodged a bullet. I think you'll look back with regret, knowing you had the chance for true love but were unable to take the risk."

She wiped at her eyes. "Maybe. Maybe not. But all I can do right now is tell you how I feel. And I can't give you what you want."

His chest felt like he had rocks in his lungs, and it was hard to breathe. "Vee. Be sure about this. Don't just react. Think this through."

"I have. Please don't make this any harder than it already is."

The rocks in his chest doubled their weight. He desperately wished he could change her mind. "Okay. I can't force you to come with me."

She crossed her arms and bit her lip.

"But don't think this is it, Vee. Once I have the chance, I'll come back for you. I promise."

She shook her head. "Don't. Because I can't do this."

"I don't believe that."

"You should. Do us both a favor. Get on that ship and don't look back. Let's just enjoy this moment of respite for what it was. Just a passing fancy."

Her words stung. In his heart, he knew she was protecting herself, but it was still hard to hear. He nodded. "Is that what you want?"

She uncrossed her arms and looked down. "Yes. It's for the best."

He paused, wishing he knew what to say. "As much as I hate it, I'll honor your request, because I love you ... and I know you love me."

Her face scrunched, and she held her stomach. "Please go."

He reached out, but stopped himself. He wanted so much to comfort her. Feeling his own emotions surface, he swallowed. "Okay."

He turned and walked toward the ship. Reaching the ramp, he stepped up and ascended. At the top, he turned. "I wish you every happiness, Vee. If we never see each other again ..." he struggled to continue, "Just know I will never forget you."

She watched him, eyes red, but didn't answer. Sighing deeply and memorizing her face, he hit a switch, and the ramp came up, the door slid shut, and she was gone.

Chapter Thirty-Eight

RAMSEY PLACED THE SIDE dish on the table.

"That looks delicious. Is that your famous potato salad, Sarah?" asked Adam.

Sarah placed two glasses of water next to the brisket. "It is."

"I hope you made two batches, cause that's not going to last," said Grayson.

"There's more in the fridge," said Gillian, sitting next to Grayson. A napkin covered her large belly bump. "I helped her make it." She held her stomach and cringed.

"You okay?" asked Eve, who put a bowl of salad on the table.

Gillian nodded. "Yes. Just another contraction."

"What?" asked Declan, who sat with Hannah across from Gillian. "You're having contractions?"

"Braxton-Hicks," said Gray. "She's been having them on and off for the last two weeks."

"It's completely normal," said Hannah. "I've been reading about them."

"You're reading that book I gave you?" asked Gillian. "There's a lot of good information in there."

"I am," said Hannah, rubbing her own belly.

"When are you due, Hannah?" asked Eve.

"Not for another five months. Gillian's helping to prepare me."

"You're going to have to help me too," said Declan. "Braxton-Hicks?"

Ramsey smiled. "You've got so much to learn. Braxton-Hicks aren't actual labor contractions. But they can happen frequently. Sarah had them too."

"I had them for the last two months," said Sarah. She rubbed her own stomach as she remembered. "Drove me nuts."

"When is your due date?" Declan asked Gillian.

"Not for another two weeks, but being my first baby, it will likely be longer," said Gillian, taking a deep breath and exhaling.

"You okay?" asked Grayson.

Gillian nodded. "Yes. It will pass in a second."

Declan glanced at Hannah. "I think I need to read this book, too."

"Books? Is someone reading a good book?" Morgana stepped outside. "I'm always eager to hear recommendations."

"I don't think this book is going to make your book club list," said Ramsey. "Unless you have more secrets you care to share."

"You can't handle my secrets, Ramsey, which is why they're secrets," said Morgana.

"Have a seat, Morgana," said Sarah, pulling out a chair.

Ramsey studied the group in his backyard. It had been six months since Royce and Jasper had left and there had been no word from them. Glancing at the house, he noted the tarp over the back room. They were still in the remodeling stage. After careful consideration, he and Sarah had decided to stay and rebuild. Despite the pain of what had occurred, the house still held too many good memories, and they chose to focus on those instead. It had taken Ramsey some time, though. After Royce's departure, the grief had hit hard, as well as the guilt. But time healed. He'd questioned his decision many times to stay in the home, until one day, after a sleepless, grief-filled night, he'd come to the damaged house to think. Despite the construction going on around him, the evidence of the explosion still replayed in his mind. Finding Sarah injured, his terror as he searched for his children, Leroy and Olivia's bodies on his lawn. As the memories surfaced, his stomach had churned, and he'd struggled to hold it together when he saw the plant.

Leroy had given it to him on his birthday ages ago, during a difficult time when he'd felt almost as bad as he did now. Ramsey had questioned Leroy's decision-making since Ramsey had never boasted about having a green thumb, but despite that, the plant had survived, and even thrived.

Ramsey had always wondered if Leroy was secretly fertilizing it, but he didn't question it. After the explosion, Ramsey hadn't thought twice about the plant, believing it had been destroyed along with everything else. Until that day on the porch, amidst the sounds of hammering, sawing, and the smells of sawdust, he saw it. It was in a new pot, and it was bigger than before. Fresh growth was sprouting from the stems, and it looked taller. Ramsey had walked over, touching its leaves, wondering what had happened, when the construction foreman had come over to him. He told him how he'd found the plant in the living room. Its pot was broken, and other than a few tattered leaves and exposed roots, the plant was intact. He'd taken the initiative and repotted it and placed it in the backyard. He'd admitted he hadn't done much with it since and was surprised it hadn't died.

Ramsey stared open-mouthed at the green leaves. A breeze ruffled his hair, and an intense wave of energy fluttered through him, and he heard a chuckle. It was so clear he turned, expecting to see Leroy behind him, but there was only a construction worker measuring a piece of wood. He shook his head, but the energy remained. He realized then that Leroy was there. Touching the leaves, he closed his eyes, took a breath, and listened. His friend's voice spoke clearly in his head. *It's time to move on, Sherlock. Death is not the end. I'm still your best friend. Don't let me be your last.* Ramsey had shuddered and opened his eyes, feeling grief but thankful that his friend was still near. He'd known then that keeping the house had been the right call. Seeing the plant now on his porch, along with his family and friends, he smiled.

"Where's Charlotte, Ramsey? Isn't she joining us?" asked Morgana.

"She's on a well-deserved girl's trip, probably enjoying a nice glass of wine right now," said Ramsey.

"Good for her," said Morgana. "Spending time with friends is always well advised. I think I might help myself to some wine as well." She reached for a glass and picked up an open bottle of Cabernet on the table. Her phone buzzed, and she set the bottle down and pulled her cell from her purse. Ramsey clearly saw the name 'Sonia' on the display. Morgana frowned. "Excuse me a moment." She stood, stepped away, and answered.

Ethan and Rosie ran out of the house and toward the swing set. "Come push us, Uncle Declan," said Rosie.

"You too, Uncle Adam," said Ethan.

Both men chuckled and stood.

"You better get used to it," said Ramsey to Declan. "Your time's coming. You too Adam."

"Not if I can help it," said Eve.

"Give it time. You'll want one soon enough," said Gillian.

"Don't hold your breath," said Eve. "Nieces and nephews will do for now."

Declan and Adam headed toward the swing set when the doorbell sounded.

"I'll get it," said Ramsey. He ran inside, bypassed Morgana, who was speaking on the phone, and opened the front door. "Carson. Lilly. Nice to see you. Come on in." Gillian and Eve's parents entered the house.

"Thank you for inviting us," said Lilly. "I've been looking forward to it." She looked around. "The house is looking great."

"Thanks," said Ramsey. "They're still working on the back rooms, but the main areas are livable."

She handed him a covered platter. "Here," she said. "I brought some brownies."

"I've heard about your famous brownies," said Ramsey.

"I've gained ten pounds since I've been home," said Carson, smiling. "Her cooking is doing me in." He put his arm around her.

"Mom. Dad." Ramsey turned as Eve popped her head in from the porch. "Did you bring the brownies?"

Ramsey held them up. "She sure did."

Ramsey started to close the door when Carson pulled him aside. "You might want to look out on the street."

Ramsey paused. "Why?"

"You have a guest who appears hesitant to enter. She's sitting in her car."

Ramsey glanced outside to see a white car parked in front of the house. A woman sat in the front seat.

"I believe it's Officer Chappell, if I'm not mistaken," said Carson.

"Lilly. Carson," said Sarah, entering the front foyer. "I'm so glad you could make it. Come in. Can I get you a drink?"

Carson greeted Sarah as Ramsey handed him the brownies. He saw Morgana hang up, lower her phone and stare off.

"Everything okay?" he asked her.

She shook her head as if to rouse herself. "It's always something, Ramsey."

Concern rippled through him. "Not bad, I hope."

She studied him, and he wondered what she was thinking. "A few things have come to my attention I had not anticipated. I'll handle it, but your assistance may come in handy at some point."

"Is my family safe?"

She relaxed. "Of course."

"Then just let me know what you need."

"Excellent." She smiled. "Now, where is that wine I was about to pour?" She returned to the back porch.

Figuring Morgana would tell him more when she was ready, Ramsey stepped outside. Seeing the white car, he headed toward it and knocked on the passenger window. Vee jumped in the seat.

He spoke through the glass. "It's a lot easier to visit when you actually enter the house."

She stared for a second and then opened her door. Ramsey detected a quick wipe of her eyes when she stepped out.

"You okay?" he asked, straightening.

She took a deep breath. "Sorry. I guess driving up, it all sort of hit me."

Ramsey nodded. "I get it." He looked back toward his home. "A lot has happened since that day."

"I know."

He rested his hand on the roof of the car. "Glad you could come. I wasn't sure you would."

She closed the door. "I had my doubts."

"I don't blame you. We haven't seen much of you since everything happened."

She nodded. "I wasn't sure if you really wanted me around ... being a human and all."

He chuckled. "We have a high tolerance for them. Especially for the ones that save our lives."

She kicked at the ground. "I can't take credit for that."

"But you can. Your actions turned the tide. You should take credit."

She blushed. "Maybe."

Ramsey watched her as she studied her toes. "You hungry?"

She looked up. "I am."

"I could bring the food out here."

The side of her mouth turned up. "That's not necessary. I'll come inside."

"Good. Otherwise, I think Sarah will eat your brownie."

She stepped around the car and, as they walked, she muttered. "I miss him."

"I know," he answered.

· · • • • • • • · ·

Vee greeted Sarah and the rest, still debating whether she should have come. It had been a long six months. After Jasper had left, she'd taken a few days off work, feigning illness, although she might as well have been ill. She'd had no idea how difficult it would be without him. How could she miss someone she'd just met? She'd been attracted to men before, had even loved one or two, but when it was over, she'd moved on. But this was different. No matter how much she told herself it was for the best, that it was not meant to be, and how she had to move on, she couldn't seem to do it. She'd gone back to work, requesting overtime, expecting the long hours to dull her mind and her desire, but it didn't help. It seemed the harder she tried to forget him, the more she wanted him. Her sleepless nights became foggy days, to the point where she'd accused a bar owner of robbing his own store. He'd matched the description of a local thief and Vee had almost arrested him. After that, her sergeant had told her to take some time off and figure out what was wrong. She'd taken a leave of absence two months ago and had yet to return. If she didn't go back soon, she wouldn't have a job to go back to. But Vee couldn't summon the energy to care. She didn't watch the skies at night anymore either. All it did was make her think of him.

When she'd received the invitation to dinner at the Ramsey's, she'd declined, but Sarah had called and insisted she come. She didn't want Vee to disappear from their lives. They'd been through too much together. Vee had agreed to join them, but when she'd pulled up to the Ramsey house, it had taken everything she had not to drive away. And she might have if Ramsey hadn't stopped her.

"Vee," Sarah came up and hugged her. "You made it."

Vee nodded. "Apparently, you were going to eat my brownie if I didn't attend."

Sarah nodded. "Absolutely."

"You don't want to miss out on Mom's brownies," said Eve, who welcomed Vee with a hug as well.

Vee said hello to the rest of the group and noted Gillian's large belly. "Wow. When are you due?"

"I know. I'm huge. But it's close," she said. "Not much longer."

"Actually, you look amazing. Pregnancy becomes you," said Vee.

Gillian smiled and Vee greeted Carson and met his wife Lilly and noticed how the couple never stopped touching each other. Jasper sprang to mind again, but she pushed him back, as she seemed to do so often now.

"Have a seat," said Ramsey. "We're about to dig in."

"Officer Chappell, pleasure to see you," said Morgana, whom she sat across from. "I take it there've been no more excursions through the woods?"

"I chased a meth head into Lambert Park. Does that count?" she asked.

"I'd say so," said Morgana, "assuming you caught him."

"He's doing six months at county."

"Good for you," replied the stately woman.

Ramsey tapped the side of his glass with his fork and stood at the head of the table. Declan and Adam brought the kids over and set them in their chairs as Ramsey spoke.

"First of all," said Ramsey. "I'd like to thank everyone for coming. I know that the last time we did this, it didn't end well." Sarah came over and stood beside him, putting her arm around him. "I had my doubts, considering. But my lovely wife here insisted that we add fresh memories to replace the old. And I remembered what my Grandma Rose used to tell me—that we can't live in fear. Life goes on."

Sarah squeezed his waist and put her head on his shoulder.

"We've lost loved ones, some forever and some hopefully for just a short time, but because of that, we can't forget. So, since we're all here, alive and well, and we have much to be thankful for, we'll continue to move forward, ready for whatever comes next, and ready for new ones to arrive."

"Here, here," said Declan, then kissed Hannah's cheek.

"The sooner, the better," said Gillian, rubbing her stomach.

Ramsey raised his glass. "Here's to us, both here and beyond. May we all find what we're looking for and enjoy the time we have with the ones we love."

"And to destiny," said Morgana. "May it always be our guide."

Everyone lifted their drinks and clinked their cups. "Cheers!" said Rosie.

"Cheers," said Ethan, smacking his cup against Rosie's.

Ramsey kissed his wife. "Dig in everyone."

"Hand me some potato salad," said Adam.

"Not before I get some," said Declan, reaching for the bowl.

Vee watched as the group helped themselves to the food. The same sadness she'd felt over the previous six months enveloped her again, but she made a concentrated effort to ignore it. She was tired of feeling bad. She was not the kind of woman to let a man's presence in her life dictate her happiness. Seeing the people in front of her choosing to move on and find the joy in what was left despite all they'd lost encouraged her. She reached for the salad.

"I wonder where they are right now," asked Eve, taking some brisket off a dish.

"Royce and Sarna?" asked Adam.

"Yes."

"I hope they're okay," said Gillian.

"Knowing Royce, he's barking orders," said Adam, "setting everyone straight."

"I sure miss him," said Lilly.

"Don't worry, sweetheart," said Carson. "Our son can take care of himself."

"I can't believe I didn't get to meet Sarna and Greta," said Lilly. She pointed a finger at Carson. "You better hope they come back soon. I want to meet my grandbaby."

"I'm sure you're missing Jasper," said Grayson to Vee. "You two were hitting it off."

Vee swallowed and pasted a smile on her face.

"I'm sure he's fine too," said Gillian. "He's probably hanging out with Royce right now, having a Eudoran beer."

"Eudorans don't drink alcohol," said Carson, taking a bite of food.

Everyone looked up.

"Well, if Royce had known that, he probably wouldn't have left," said Ramsey.

"If he's in charge," said Eve, "then they're drinking it now."

"Why do you think I came back to Earth?" asked Carson. He smiled and grunted as Lilly nudged him in the ribs.

Vee took a bite of her food and smiled, appreciating the ability to talk about Jasper without wanting to cry. It was a first.

They ate and laughed, talking about Royce and Jasper and recalling the past. Before long, they talked about their own stories. How Eve and Adam met, and Gillian and Gray, and then Sarah and Ramsey told their story. Vee marveled at their shared history and wished she could be a part of it.

Ethan and Rosie finished and jumped from the table, eager to play. They ran off to the yard, chasing a ball.

"Stay close to us, kids. The fence isn't finished yet," said Ramsey.

"Anyone care for one of Lilly's famous brownies?" asked Sarah, rising.

"I'm so full, I could roll out of here, but I'll take one," said Declan.

"I'll make some coffee," said Ramsey. "Everybody want a cup?"

"Decaffeinated, please," said Morgana.

"I'll help you clear the plates," said Eve, as she stood.

"Me too," said Adam.

"Ugh," said Gillian, grimacing, "Here comes another."

"Just breathe through it," said Gray, holding her hand.

"Come on, little Anderson Thomas Steele," said Gillian. "Time to vacate the property."

"Is that what his name is?" asked Eve. "I didn't know that."

"He's named after our grandfathers," said Grayson.

"That's so sweet," said Hannah. She touched her own baby bump. "If ours is a boy, we'd like to name him Henry Leroy."

Ramsey stopped mid stride.

"You don't mind, do you?" asked Declan. "I thought it would be fitting."

Ramsey paused, but smiled. "I think he would love that."

Vee smiled too at the kind gesture. The children squealed in the yard behind her. "Higher," said Ethan. "Go higher."

Rosie squealed too. "Higher, Uncle Royce. Push me higher!"

Vee froze, as did everyone else. Gillian and Sarah turned and dropped their jaws. Eve dropped the plate she was holding, and it broke into shards, but no one noticed.

Ramsey widened his eyes. "Holy ..."

Declan and Hannah stood from the table as Vee looked behind her. To her astonishment, Royce was pushing the kids on the swing.

"Oh my God," said Lilly, before jumping up and running toward her son.

Gillian swiveled on her chair, and Gray helped her up. Everyone moved at once. All Vee could do was stare.

"Royce," said Eve.

Royce stopped swinging the kids and smiled. "I was wondering when you'd notice me."

Eve jumped into his arms as Lilly embraced him as well. Tears coursed down the older woman's cheeks.

"I'm okay, Mom," said Royce. "I promise. Gillian, you should be at the hospital."

Gillian gave him a hug and pulled him as close as she could. "How long have you been here?"

Royce hugged his dad and Sarah, too. "I'll admit. I may have snuck up on you."

"You cloaked yourself, didn't you?" asked Eve. She smacked him. "Stop doing that."

"Where're Sarna and the baby?" asked Lilly. "Are they here?"

"What's happening on Eudora?" asked Adam. "Are you High Leader?"

"Did you oust Roma?" asked Declan.

"Where's Jasper?" asked Ramsey.

Vee froze at that question. Her heart thudded.

Royce laughed. "So many questions. I'd think you guys missed me."

"When did you get back?" asked Ramsey.

"Don't be mad, but we arrived yesterday," said Royce.

"Yesterday?" asked Gillian.

"And you didn't come see us?" asked Lilly.

"It's a long trip for a toddler and an expectant wife. I thought I'd give them some time to adjust."

"Expectant wife?" asked Carson.

"Is she pregnant? Is Sarna pregnant?" asked Eve.

"You got married?" asked Gillian.

"I am, and we did," said Sarna as she stepped out from the side yard with Greta in her arms.

The group left Royce alone as they all gathered around Sarna and Greta.

Her heart racing, Vee had finally stood but could only watch.

"Hello, Officer Chappell," said Royce as he walked up to her. "Good to see you."

Vee nodded and swallowed. "Hi. How are you?"

"Pretty good. It's good to be home."

"I'm sure it is." The question was on the tip of her tongue, but she was afraid to ask it.

"He didn't come with me," said Royce.

Vee's heart deflated and everything in her wanted to curl up in the fetal position.

"He came separately. Said he might want to stay awhile."

Vee peered up as Royce smiled down at her. "I suspect he's at your place, wondering where you are."

It took her a moment to react, but when she did, she couldn't help but grin. "He's here?"

Royce nodded. "Of course he's here. The man's been in misery since we left. About drove me crazy and would have if I hadn't known what he was going through."

Vee ran her hands through her hair as her heart pounded. Jasper was here. He'd come back.

"It looks like you've been a little out of it yourself. You've lost weight," said Royce. "Of course, if you'd rather he go home, I could give him the bad news ..."

Vee didn't wait to hear the rest. She ran past the group and into the house, passing the living area and throwing the door open, intent on jumping into her car and breaking the speed limit to get back to her house.

She'd made it halfway across the yard when she heard a "Hey."

Recognizing the voice, she swiveled in mid run to see Jasper standing on the front porch. He looked just as good as she remembered, but he'd lost a bit of weight as well.

He took a few steps toward her. "I didn't find you at your place, so I just about broke every speed law getting over here. So please don't tell me you're leaving."

Vee broke from her shock and ran toward him. He met her midway, and she threw herself into his arms. Holding her tightly, he spoke into her ear. "All I did was think about you."

Vee kept touching him to ensure he was real. "You're back. I didn't think ..."

His breath raced against her skin. "I couldn't leave you, Vee. You're mine and I'm yours, and that will never change, no matter what separates us."

She pulled back enough to see his face. She cupped his cheeks and rested her forehead against his. "The last time we did this, I thought I'd never see you again." A tear escaped and ran down her cheek.

He smiled at her. "Those times are over. No more hemming and hawing. I love you and I want you. And if you'll have me, I'll be yours forever."

She smiled and brushed her lips against his. "I'll have you, over and over again."

His lips captured hers, and she kissed him hungrily. All her doubt and worry vanished as her body moved against his and his tongue roved over hers. She'd never felt so much want and need in her life. Their lips briefly parted before they met again, each caress more desperate than the last. His hands gripped her waist as hers moved down his back and up again.

He pulled back, breathing hard. "What do you say we go back to your place?"

Barely coherent, she nodded, but the sound of voices interrupted them.

"Hurry. We have to get you to the car."

The voice penetrated Vee's fog, and she looked to see Gray exiting the house with Gillian beside him, holding her belly. "I'm fine honey. It's just my water," said Gillian.

Gray ran toward the car. "How can you be so calm? Your water just broke."

The rest of the group came out of the house.

"We're right behind you, honey," said Lilly.

"Get her to the hospital, Gray," said Royce. "There's one about a few miles—"

"I know where the hospital is," said Gray. "Come on, honey." He opened the car door.

"I'm coming," said Gillian. "I can't believe this is happening now. I thought I had two weeks."

"I'm going to be an aunt," said Eve. "This is so exciting."

"Ohhh!" Gillian grabbed her stomach and leaned over.

"Honey," yelled Gray as he ran over to her and took her arm.

"It's a contraction," said Gillian. "A big one." She breathed fast. "Ohhh." She went down on her hands and knees.

Vee broke from Jasper's hold and ran over.

"Take it easy. Breathe. That's it. Can you walk?" asked Gray.

Royce leaned over and picked his sister up with ease. "Get in the car, Steele." He carried Gillian over to the passenger side and placed her in the seat as Gray slid behind the wheel. Gillian gripped the dash. "Hurry," she said. "This is moving fast." She breathed in short, clipped bursts. "Aaahh. It's another one."

"That's way too soon," said Gray. "They shouldn't be that close together."

"Stop talking and drive," said Royce.

Vee ran over to the car. "I have my police light," said Vee. "I could give you an escort. Make sure you get there safely."

"Please," said Gray, looking ashen.

"I'll ride with you," said Jasper.

"We'll follow," said Royce.

Gillian moaned again. "Hurry." She leaned against the door frame, her hands braced against the roof. "This is happening so fast. Oohhh!"

Vee ran to her car, pulled out the light, and stuck it on her dash. Jasper jumped in, and she started up the car. Grayson drove up behind her, and she pulled away and sped off toward the hospital.

· · • • • · • · · ·

Ramsey watched from the porch as Royce, Sarna, and Greta got in one car with Lilly and Carson and Eve and Adam sped off in another, following Vee.

Sarah put her arm around him, and Declan and Hannah joined them.

"Guess that will be us one day soon," said Hannah.

"I hope a little less dramatic," said Declan.

"Well, I think that's it for the dinner parties though," said Ramsey. "We can't seem to get through one without some serious drama playing out."

"I'll take new arrivals any day," said Sarah. "Drama or no drama."

"It definitely makes it interesting though," said Declan. "Can't wait to see what happens at your next party."

Ramsey turned into Sarah's arms. "No, the next party is on you, Declan. You've always wanted to outdo me. Now's your chance."

"I think I'll tip my hat to you on this one. No need to ask for more than I can handle."

Ramsey smiled and held his wife. "You may be surprised at what you can handle, Declan."

Morgana stepped out onto the porch. She wrapped her scarf around her neck and carried her small handbag. "I agree. Sometimes the greatest tragedies can bring us the greatest joy. It's just hard to see it sometimes."

"I agree too," said Sarah. She gave Ramsey a squeeze. "I'm going to check on the kids. It was good to see you, Morgana."

"You too, dear."

Sarah went inside, and after saying goodbye to Morgana, Declan and Hannah followed.

"You sure you want to go home, Morgana?" asked Ramsey. "No brownies?"

Morgana patted her hair, which was perfectly placed in its usual smooth chignon. "I'm sure they're delicious, but they're all yours." She came up close to him. "You and your family have been through a lot. Go enjoy them. Sweets are always better when you haven't had them in a while." She patted him on the shoulder. "Thank you for dinner."

Ramsey tipped his head. "No sarcastic remark for me? You feeling okay?"

"Better than ever," she answered. "I'm just ..." She stared off.

"Just what?" asked Ramsey.

Her eyes found his. "I'm proud of you."

Ramsey narrowed his eyes. "You're what?"

"You've pulled this little group together despite great adversity. I didn't know you had it in you."

Ramsey didn't know how to answer.

"You're a good man, husband, and father. You should know that."

Ramsey felt a lump swell in his throat. He thought of his grandmother. "Thank you."

She turned toward her car. "Don't thank me," she said. "Thank destiny." She laughed as she walked away, her scarf blowing in the breeze. "It's going to be a beautiful night. Full moon, too. Perfect for skinny dipping." She got into her car and spoke out the open window. "Don't let those brownies go to waste. You never know when you'll get another."

Starting up the car, she waved, and Ramsey smiled as she drove away.

What Happens Next?

The saga may be over, but the mystery continues. Who is the secretive Sonia that Morgana was talking to? If you're caught up with the Red-Line books, then get ready for Bishop's enthralling paranormal thriller series, *The Family or Foe Saga*, which introduces the bantering and affable detective duo, Daniels and Remalla, and the enigmatic Sonia. This set of four books will follow the trail of a murderer determined to exact revenge on the family he believes wronged him. But there's more to the story when his secrets reveal unexpected connections, and shocking revelations come to light.

In book one, *First Cut*, former detective Jill Jacobs must face the Makeup Artist, an elusive serial killer who took everything from her and is eager to do it again. When the Artist strikes in a new city, Detectives Daniels and Remalla seek her help, but her only hope to catch him is to return to the mindset that connects her to him; the mindset he craves from her. But falling for one of the detectives is an unexpected complication. One which leads her to a terrifying confrontation with a killer that could give him exactly what he wants...her life.

Enjoy an excerpt below.

How did it all begin with John and Sarah Ramsey?

Read *The Red-Line Trilogy,* which includes *Red-Line: The Shift, Red-Line: Mirrors,* and *Red-Line: Trust Destiny.* A boxed set is available, too!

Sarah Randolph holds the key to the survival of a secret community. But first she must survive her "Shift." Her protector, John Ramsey, is assigned to keep her alive, but falling for her was never in his plans. When a powerful adversary reveals himself and his intentions for Sarah, her unique destiny may be their only hope.

Want more from J. T. Bishop?

Sign up for her newsletter at jtbishopauthor.com to get the short story, *Red-Line: Prelude to The Shift,* and future books, plus a Daniels and Remalla prequel novella, missing scenes, excerpts, and fun promos for **free**.

Follow J.T. on her Amazon author page to be notified of new releases.

Get to Know Detectives Daniels and Remalla.

After *The Family or Foe Saga,* the two charismatic detectives battle psychopaths, unexplained evil and unsolved cases. In *Haunted River,* book one in the series, the ghost of a woman haunts a small town where she lived and died. When a second woman's body turns up twenty-five years later, Daniels and Remalla become suspects, and the next targets.

Or pick up the omnibus *Shadows and Secrets*, which contains *Haunted River*, *Of Breath and Blood*, and *Of Body and Bone* (books one through three) of the paranormal mystery thriller series.

A Note From J.T.

I love to hear from my readers about their experiences with my books, and I'd love to know what you thought about *Forged Lines*. It was difficult to wrap up the stories of the Ramsey and Fletcher families. I've grown attached to all of them during the course of creating and writing about them. I hope I brought it to a satisfying conclusion and that you're happy with where I left them. Will they show up again in future books? Maybe. Sonia might have some involvement with that, but you'll just have to keep reading to find out. Considering how much I enjoy surprising my readers and the thrill of the unknown, you never know where the next book will lead.

My next series introduces two bantering detectives who are going to be thrown into cases that will challenge their view of the world and those around them. Their exploits and discoveries involve some interesting new characters, plus some paranormal encounters, and are going to make this next saga a bunch of fun and one I'm excited to share with you. I hope you enjoy it, too.

Reviews are a huge plus and big help for a writer and potential readers. I would love it if you could please take a couple of minutes to leave a review for *Forged Lines*. And if you'd like, please leave a few comments, too.

As always, thank you for your time and readership. It is deeply valued and appreciated.

Now, onto the next book!

Books in Chronological Order

ALTHOUGH RECOMMENDED BUT NOT required, in case you prefer to read in order...

Red-Line: Prelude to The Shift, a short story (subscribers only)
Red-Line: The Shift
Red-Line: Mirrors
Red-Line: Trust Destiny
Curse Breaker
High Child
Spark
Forged Lines

· · · · ● · ● · · · ·

The Girl and the Gunshot, a novella (subscribers only)
A Hamburger Christmas, a novella
The Magic of Murder, a novella (subscribers only)
First Cut
Second Slice
Third Blow
Fourth Strike
Murder Unveiled
Haunted River
Of Breath and Blood

Lost Souls
Of Body and Bone
Lost Dreams
Of Mind and Madness
Lost Chances
Of Power and Pain
Lost Hope
Of Love and Loss
Lost Lives
Dominion
Lost Time
Illusions
Lost Love
Vendetta
Black Bird

Acknowledgements

ANOTHER SUCCESSFUL BOOK ON the shelf does not happen without help. Thank you again to my amazing family and friends. Your rock-solid support never waivers, and I am so grateful to have all of you in my life.

I also want to thank my editor and book cover designer, Amie McCracken, for helping me get this book into solid shape.

And to those beloved ones who've crossed over, don't think I don't recognize you looking over my shoulder. Your help is just as valuable as any other. I miss you and I love you.

About the Author

AWARD-WINNING AUTHOR, J.T. BISHOP, is a writer of mystery thrillers with a paranormal edge. Growing up, she read Stephen King, Mary Higgins Clark, and Dean Koontz, devoured every episode of the X-files and watched plenty of TV shows with great partnerships that leave you wanting more. She loves tangled relationships, unexpected twists and turns, heart-stopping love stories and the complications that come with all the above. Throw in a little supernatural fun and she's hooked. Her evil plan is to hook you, too.

She's the author of The Red-Line Trilogy and its sister series, The Fletcher Family Saga, which features touches of urban fantasy, light sci-fi, and paranormal romance. She's also happily writing mystery thrillers featuring two charismatic detectives who may occasionally encounter a supernatural villain or two, and a crossover series which follows the exploits of a gifted, but troubled, paranormal P.I. and his spunky sister.

All the above keeps her busy, but in her spare time, she loves good movies, tasty food, an unfortunate sugar addiction, and traveling.

Enjoy an excerpt of First Cut, Book One in the Family or Foe Saga

SEEING THE GUN, DANIELS pulled his weapon, aiming at the woman. He stood at a diagonal to Remalla, so his partner was not in the line of fire. His heart rate tripled, and he watched Rem hold up his arms.

"Drop the gun!" he yelled.

The woman glanced at him, but she held the gun on Rem. "Who are you? What do you want?"

Rem kept his hands visible. "Take it easy. We're cops," he said. "I'm going to take my badge out." He slowly moved his hand toward his back pocket, making it obvious so the woman could see he wasn't going for his weapon.

The woman, eyes wide with uncertainty, kept looking between Rem and Daniels. "You, too," she said to Daniels.

Daniels didn't move. "Take that gun off my partner."

Rem pulled out his badge and opened it. "I'm Detective Remalla and this is my partner, Detective Daniels. Are you Jill Jacobs? Sergeant Merchant told us where to find you. All we want to do is talk." He kept his hands up and spoke in a soothing voice.

The woman hesitated. "Talk about what?"

"Drop the gun first," yelled Daniels.

Remalla took a small step forward, and Daniels held his breath. "We didn't mean to scare you. We want to talk about the Makeup Artist."

Even from a distance, Daniels could see her face pale. She stared for a second, her forehead furrowed, and then she relaxed her stance, lowered her weapon, and tucked it into the waistband of her shorts.

Rem dropped his hands and glanced back at Daniels, who let go of a lungful of held breath and holstered his gun. He debated arresting her, but realized she wasn't a threat, and they would need her cooperation. He walked over to his partner, but stayed on alert.

"You okay?" asked Daniels to Rem.

Rem took a shaky breath. "That'll wake you up."

"Still scared of zombies?"

Rem didn't answer as the woman approached with wariness.

"Jill Jacobs?" asked Rem.

She walked past them and toward her beach chair. Reaching it, she grabbed another bottle from the bucket. "That's me."

They followed. "You want to tell us why you pull guns on strangers?" asked Daniels.

She twisted the cap off. "You came up behind me," she said, taking a healthy swig.

"It's a public beach," said Rem.

She waved. "Does it look public?"

"You go around waving guns, you're going to get arrested," said Daniels.

"I'll take my chances," she said, and sat in the chair. She removed her weapon and put it beside her, careful to do it slowly to not alarm Rem or Daniels.

"Well, we don't mean to interrupt your 'me' time, but we'd like to ask you a few questions," said Rem.

"Can't promise I'll answer." She took another swig.

Rem raised a brow at Daniels. "You were a cop in Seattle, right? Worked on the Makeup Artist case?"

"That was a long time ago. In another life," she said, resting her head back.

Daniels nodded. "Been in the RV park long?"

She watched the waves. "A while."

"It's a charming place, but a little crazy." Rem paused. "It matches your personality." She gave him a quick appraisal, but didn't respond. "Your sergeant thought you'd be helpful to us. We're working on a case you might have some insight on."

She took another pull, and Daniels wondered how often Jill Jacobs drank. It was a lot based on how fast she was draining her beer.

"He wasted your time. I can't help you," she answered.

"You worked on the Makeup Artist case in Seattle, didn't you?" asked Daniels.

She hesitated, picking on the bottle's label. "I did."

"Then I'm pretty sure you can help us," said Rem. "We've—"

"You don't get it," said Jill. "I don't want to help you."

Rem crossed his arms and set his jaw, and Daniels knew his partner was getting agitated. He could be cool and calm with a gun pointed at him, but could lose his temper with an uncooperative stranger in a heartbeat.

"Fine," Daniels interjected, before Rem could say something less fruitful. "We'll go back and let our captain know that the two victims who were slaughtered in the last six weeks and their families are no closer to finding justice and the madman who did it. Even though he's already stalking his next victim and will continue to enjoy the same freedoms as you and me. We'll be sure to let your Sergeant Merchant know that his suggestion was a waste of our time."

Her face pinched, and she picked off a chunk of the label. Daniels saw her swallow.

"Merchant gave us your name for a reason," said Rem.

"He did," she said. Daniels could barely hear her over the waves.

"Listen," said Rem. "We don't know your story. I don't know why you're sitting on a beach, drinking alone, and living in an RV in Horrorville, but you were a cop. You worked on a grisly case and you must have been good, or your sergeant wouldn't have sent us."

"I know why he sent you," she said, before taking another swig.

"So why not help us?" asked Daniels. "Look over—"

"No," she said, standing and wobbling slightly. "I'm going to pick up my gun. Don't shoot me." She leaned over and picked up her weapon and tucked it back in her shorts. "Good luck with your case." Turning, she walked back toward the waves, never looking back, and assumed her former position with the waves crashing over her feet.

"Son-of-a..." said Rem, turning toward Daniels. "What the hell's the matter with her?"

"A lot," said Daniels. "I think a lot is the matter with her. She's done. Like we thought. Burned out."

"It's more than that," said Rem. "Did you see her when she pulled her weapon?"

"Quite vividly," said Daniels.

"Did you see her eyes?"

"I was more focused on preventing her from shooting you."

Rem paused. "I could see it. I think she's terrified."

Daniels watched Jill standing in the surf and drinking her beer.

"Whatever happened, it wasn't good," said Rem.

"That's probably why she threatens to shoot strangers."

Rem put his badge back in his pocket. "I don't think she was expecting us. She was expecting someone else."

Daniels shook his head. Rem patted Daniels on the arm. "Let's go."

· · • • · • • • · ·

Lozano stared at his apple for the hundredth time that day. He'd had his roasted chicken, cauliflower potatoes and grilled veggies for lunch, but his stomach rumbled. This low-salt, low-sugar diet his doctor had recommended was going to kill him before this job ever would. But his high cholesterol and higher blood pressure were saying otherwise. He needed to lose about twenty pounds. So far, he'd lost seven. Rem had invited him to the gym to spar, and Daniels had offered to take him to lift weights, but he'd declined both offers. He saw his detectives enough as it was. He didn't need to work out with them. Lozano opened his drawer and saw the loose change. The vending machine beckoned down the hall.

A knock on his open door made him close the drawer. Remalla stood there, grinning. "What you doin', Cap?" He pulled a candy bar out of his pocket and started to open it.

Lozano's stomach rumbled again. "Mind your business, Remalla."

Daniels walked up behind Remalla. "You got a sec, Cap?" He saw the chocolate in Rem's hands and rolled his eyes.

"I do. Have a seat. How'd it go with Jacobs?"

The detectives sat, and Daniels pointed at the apple. "You gonna eat that?"

Lozano eyed the fruit and his detective. He sighed, picked up the apple, and tossed it. "It's all yours."

"Thanks," said Daniels, and he took a bite.

"Jacobs was a total bust," said Rem as he licked the chocolate off his thumb. "She has no interest in helping us."

"She's a recluse," said Daniels. "She lives in a run-down RV park, drinks a lot and waves guns at people. I'm not sure why Merchant recommended her."

Lozano sighed and sat back in his seat. "I know why. I talked to Merchant and got her file."

Rem paused before taking the next bite of his candy. "Really? Now I'm curious."

Lozano tapped on his keyboard and the monitor came to life. "I'm going to send you the info, but in a nutshell, she's the youngest female promoted to a detective on the Seattle force. She rose quickly in the ranks. Scored high in every area. She was book smart and street smart. Her father is a Federal judge. Did you know that?"

Daniels leaned forward. "That didn't come up in the conversation."

"The honorable Thomas Jack Jacobs. Known as—"

Daniels raised a brow. "Jailtime Jacobs?"

"The one and the same," said Lozano.

"I've heard of him," said Daniels.

Rem shot Daniels a puzzled look. "Since when are you familiar with the Seattle judicial branch?"

"You remember when I took that course on criminal law? They mentioned him. His harsh sentences are legendary. He's famous in Seattle law enforcement." He studied his apple. "Jill's his daughter?"

"She is," said Lozano. "Probably why she was so impressive on the force."

"Like father, like daughter," said Rem, as he took another bite of his candy bar.

"Anyway, when the killings started in Seattle, the city was in an uproar. Merchant had a slew of detectives on it. But he was dealing with the same issues as us. No prints, no DNA, nothing. The guy was a ghost."

"Wonderful," said Rem.

"Jacobs was a policewoman, but her ideas and observations about the killer caught Merchant's attention. Said she was like a profiler. She could almost predict the killer's next steps. By then, they had three victims and Merchant needed a plan, so he promoted her to detective and put her on the case. At that point, they were keeping the press at bay, but Jacobs had her own ideas. She wanted to use the press to draw him out. Merchant wasn't convinced. Not long after her promotion, Jacobs took it upon herself to hold a mini press conference outside one of the victim's homes. Called the killer..." he studied the screen, "...frightened, disturbed, with a slew of sexual issues." He sat back. "You get the gist."

Daniels chewed and swallowed another bite of his apple. "I don't know if that makes her brilliant or incredibly stupid."

"It certainly makes her fearless," said Rem. He popped the last bit of candy in his mouth. "How'd that go over with Merchant?"

"Not well," said Lozano. He laced his fingers together and put his hands behind his head. "It pissed off the higher-ups, and Merchant took the heat. But that's when the writing on the walls started."

Daniels' eyes widened. "Really?"

"Really," said Lozano. "After the next victim, the first message appeared, written on the bathroom wall in the victim's blood. It said, 'I see you.' There was also a rose."

"A rose?" asked Rem. He licked chocolate off the rest of his fingers. "What rose?"

"At the crime scene. The killer left a rose in the tub, and on the wall above it, written in blood, were the words 'For you.'"

"You got to be kidding me," said Daniels. "I didn't hear that."

"Seattle PD never released it to the press, for obvious reasons," said Lozano. "They kept it under wraps. Once we get the files from Seattle, you'll read all about it."

"And they think the killer was referring to Jacobs?" asked Rem. "Those messages were for her?"

"I guess her portrayal of him got his attention," said Daniels. "What exactly was she hoping to accomplish by pushing his buttons?"

"Probably exactly that," said Rem. "Get the guy to do something stupid. Something different from his routine and pray he makes a mistake."

"It worked," said Lozano. He opened his top drawer and pulled out a granola bar. His planned foray to the vending machine would have to wait. "Problem is, it worked too well."

Rem wiped his fingers on his jeans. "It got him to change his routine, but he didn't make a mistake. Only now, Jill's in his crosshairs."

"Right," said Lozano as he opened the granola bar. "According to the file, not long after, Jill started receiving mail, flowers, phone calls, all from the killer."

Rem leaned forward and put his elbows on his knees. "Wow. He started contacting her?"

"And following her. He sent photos, too," said Lozano.

"Shit," said Daniels.

"And with all of that, they still couldn't catch this guy?" asked Rem. "It seems she gave Merchant exactly what he needed. Between the contact and photos, they couldn't nail him down? If nothing else, they could follow Jacobs."

"They did it all," said Lozano. "The phone calls were too short to trace, and if they weren't, the killer was long gone before they got there. No prints or DNA on the letters. Following Jill led nowhere. It was like he found a new way to taunt them, and he was having fun with it."

"And torturing Jacobs at the same time," said Daniels. He took a last bite of his apple and tossed it in the trash.

"Merchant said she handled it pretty well at first. She thought like most of them that it would lead to his capture. If she could just keep up the game, he would screw up. She played her part, talking to him, and trying to get him riled enough to slip up. Merchant put a detail on her to keep watch even though Jacobs argued with him about it. Said it would be hard to lure the murderer out if she was being followed all the time. Merchant argued back that he didn't need a dead cop on his hands."

Daniels let out a sigh. "Brave lady."

"I'm sensing this didn't end well," said Rem.

"You should be a detective," said Daniels.

Rem smirked.

"You're right, it didn't," said Lozano. He held his granola bar. "The murders continued, as did the messages. More notes to Jill at the crime scene. More photos and phone calls. Crazy thing is, Jill had an uncanny sense about the guy. Merchant said she knew when he would strike again and could almost sense the killer's and victim's pain. She lost weight, spent sleepless nights working, and yelled at other cops when they didn't keep the same regimen. The respect she'd garnered through all of this began to wane. Merchant said after a while, the stress on the department caused fractures. There were grumblings that maybe Jill knew the killer all along. Maybe she was in on it, which is why she could predict his actions. Maybe she liked the attention, so she strung everyone along, not telling them everything she knew."

Rem rubbed his face and stood. A strand of hair fell in his face, and he pushed it back. "That's great. She's killing herself to find this guy and her department's turning on her." He leaned against the wall and crossed his arms.

"What did Merchant do?" asked Daniels.

"He defended her. Did his best to protect her. Most knew none of the rumors were true, but the squad was just tired and fed up. They wanted a scapegoat."

"They couldn't get the killer, so they had to blame somebody," said Daniels.

"It seems so. But according to Merchant, the more he told Jacobs to slow down and take a break, the harder she worked. She ignored the rumors, but at some point, the cracks showed. Arguments broke out on the job. She became less and less tolerant of her fellow officers and more belligerent with him. She even lost it with the killer. He'd called her, and she'd let loose, daring him to come for her, saying he didn't have the balls to kill her. Merchant took her off the case after that."

Rem cursed under his breath. "This story just keeps getting better and better. How'd she handle being taken off the case?"

"About as well as you can imagine," said Lozano.

"Merchant was right. She was in too deep," said Daniels.

"Is that when she left?" asked Rem.

"No," said Lozano. He paused and stared at his granola bar. He'd yet to take a bite. "Three days later, a policeman was killed." He studied his monitor. "Officer Rick Henderson. They found him in a bathtub, stabbed, his face painted. There were notes written on the walls to Jacobs, telling her it was all for her."

Rem stared at the floor, and Daniels leaned back, rubbing his eyes. "Holy shit," he said.

"That's when Jacobs left the force, and hasn't been back," said Lozano. "That was the last murder. The killer went silent afterwards. It was as if he'd had his fun with her and when she left, he did too. Until six weeks ago."

Neither detective spoke.

"So, if you're wondering why she's not too social, drinks a lot, and pulls guns on people," said Lozano, "now you know."

Daniels nodded and sighed. "And now the killer's back and he's picked our little corner of the world to prey upon," said Daniels. "Lucky us."

Rem raised his head. "But now we know why."

Daniels shared a look with Rem, and his brow furrowed. "He's come back for her."